A HEALER'S HEART

MOLLY PARKER

Dear Reader,

Within these pages, I have tried to weave a thread of light and magic through the darker shadows that play out in this story.

This story contains **violence, blood, gore, sexually explicit scenes, grief** and **death** including **deaths of loved ones**. These moments were written with care and serve the emotional journey of the characters, but they may be difficult for some readers.

Please take care of yourself as you read. Take a break if your heart feels too heavy. Akureyrian will be here when you return.

With love & gratitude,

Molly Parker

To anyone who spent their childhood running barefoot in the woods, while dreaming of an imperfect faerie tale, this is for you.

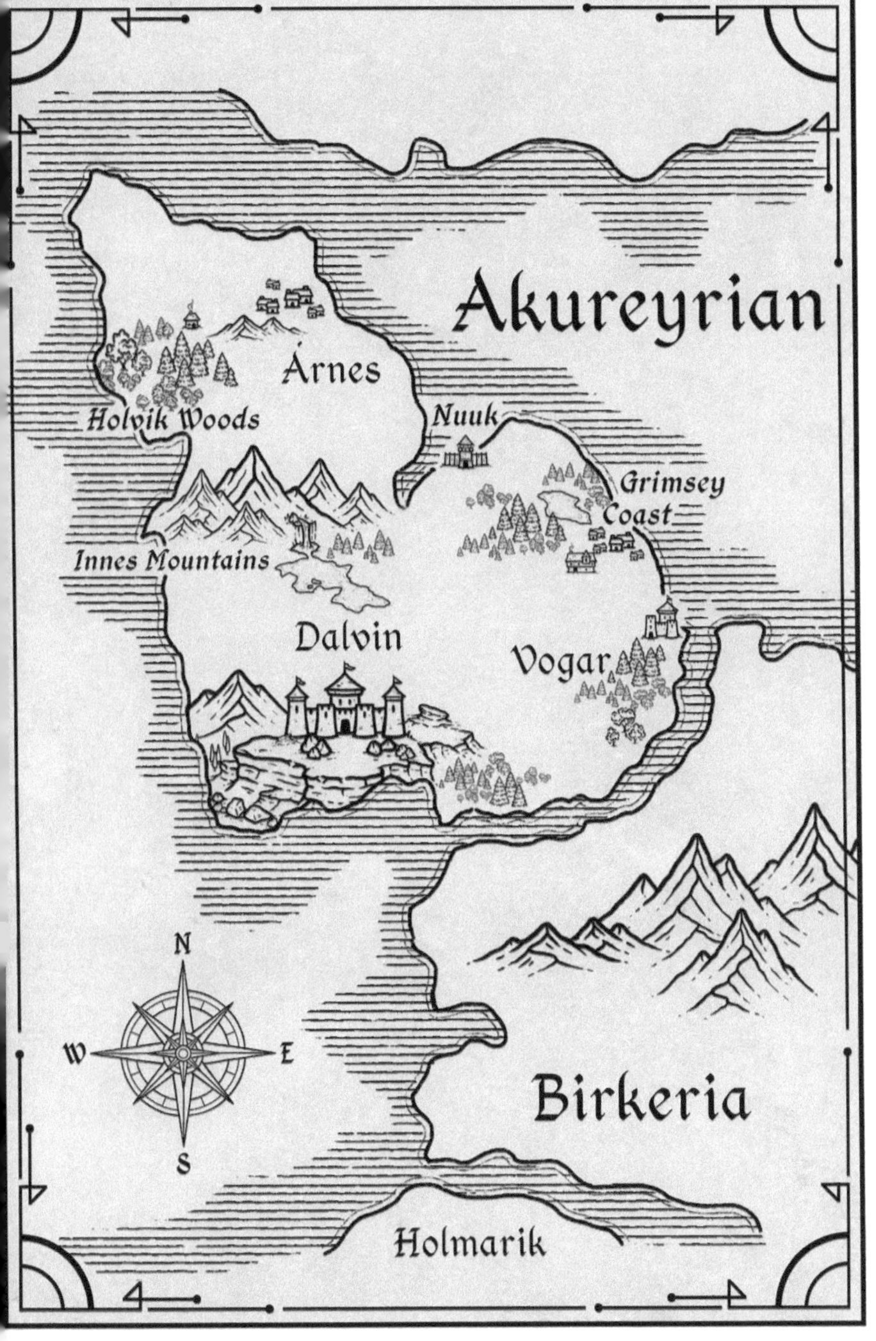

Akureyrian
Árnes
Holvik Woods
Nuuk
Grimsey Coast
Innes Mountains
Dalvin
Vogar
N
W
E
S
Birkeria
Holmarik

I twisted on my heel, creating space between my flesh and the mindless beast that was lunging for my throat. The deep gash my blade dug into its side was leaking a constant stream of black blood. It lunged again, and when the scythe-like claw tore across my tunic, I should have been terrified. My fear, however, would have been misplaced. I'd fought against dozens of drekavac in my long life and none of them had killed me. But every one of the foul creatures had left me covered with odious stains.

Washing away drekavac blood is an arduous task. The inky black stains cling to every possible surface. After this encounter, my clothes, hair, skin, and fingernails would undoubtedly require endless scrubbing—and I was not in the mood.

I slashed my sword again, twisting my wrist like a wave, and as I plunged the blade into the creature's sunken belly all I could think about was the splattering of black blood that suddenly adorned my favorite tunic.

It would take *weeks* to get clean. A quick mental inventory told me I only had two tunics left in my drawer.

I hadn't expected to see a drekavac on this outing—I rarely came across the undercreatures in this part of the Holvik Woods. Although to be fair, I had noticed an increase in encounters over the past several months.

Recently, more locals had come to me to tend to injuries after being attacked in the Woods, and the local gossip thrummed with word of the ghastly creatures of the Underworld.

"*Bölva*," I cursed in the Old Language when another spray of blood splattered my neck, jolting my attention to the predicament in front of me.

Goddess, I *hated* drekavac.

I spat out a mix of dirt and blood and steadied my feet. My hands were sticky from the mugwort plants I had been harvesting before the creature attacked, making it difficult to switch the grip on my blade. I swung low, aiming for the creature's bony legs, knowing any injury there would throw it off balance. Their bulbous heads made them awkward when they stood on two legs—giving me an advantage I gladly accepted.

The sound of metal on bone sent a shiver up my spine but the resounding shriek from the drekavac was equally as terrifying as it was a relief. I watched the creature stumble and aimlessly thrash its clawed arms towards my tender stomach. My foot followed my sword in a sweeping motion and as the blood sprayed from the jagged slice, I kicked hard against its knee.

The creature stumbled as its legs gave out and it crumbled into a broken pile of leathery skin and black blood. I squeezed my eyes shut as I pierced the blade through drekavac's head, pushing and twisting until the beast went limp. My sword was a blessing that stole the creature's misery, sending it to a morbid grave.

I shook out my arms, sending sprinkles of blood across the mossy ground. I kicked its head, ensuring it was truly dead, and released the breath I was holding.

The drekavac had come out of nowhere, typical for an undercreature. The beasts were designed for killing and terrorizing the Underworld and excelled at stealthy approaches and merciless attacks. Despite my heightened senses, I hadn't realized the creature was close until it was in front of me, shrieking like a hawk and throwing its dagger-like claws at my face. I had rolled on the ground to grant myself the space to pull my blade, leaving just enough time to lunge towards the assault.

My foraging basket had been thrown behind a nearby hedge and the herbs and plants I had gathered lay strewn across the ground as if stirred by a windstorm. Thankfully, nothing had been trampled or sprayed with blood, so I neatly tucked the feathery stalks back into place.

I returned my sword to its sheath and looked down at my tunic. Even if it hadn't been coated in blood I realized now that it was shredded beyond repair. Reaching under the torn fabric, I ran my hand along my stomach to feel for any damage—a couple of small scratches on the right side of my ribs but nothing serious.

I needed to wash the cuts and change my clothes. But the moons seemed to pulse with their snowy glow, reminding me I still had lavender to harvest before the sun set.

I knew of a small stream nearby where I could wash before returning home. I didn't love the idea of staying in the Woods to bathe, but I also wasn't keen on the idea of dying from an infection.

After so many years walking through the Holvik Woods, I could sense where the twigs and branches were hiding under the fallen leaves, allowing my silent passage through the worn trails. I lifted my chin slightly to smell the change in the breeze as wisps of my chestnut-colored hair brushed against the side of my cheek. It was easy to notice the subtle changes in the scents of the surrounding flora and I instinctively made a mental inventory of the nearby plants.

As I approached the stream, the soft rush of water purred like a worn drum. The stream rolled over the moss-covered tholeiite—the clay color of the rock turning the water a rusty brown. I started stripping my tattered clothes before I was at the water's edge, eager to rid myself of the morbid stench. I kicked my boots off, letting the spongy ground cushion my tired feet.

When I dipped my toes, the water was frigid—just the way I liked it. I washed myself as best I could without any soap, using sprigs of mint from my basket to freshen my skin. Before I had finished scrubbing the black stains from my arms, my feet were numb, and my teeth chattered from the cold.

I stumbled slightly as I stepped out of the stream. My deposited clothes lay in a heap on the mossy ground.

Thankfully, my pants were still intact, and the blood had not seeped through to my undergarments. I cursed as I balled up my tunic and tied it to a nearby tree. There was no point in trying to mend it and I knew some creature would enjoy sniffing the mix of scents that saturated the fabric.

As I finished tying the knot, an eery silence fell around me. The Woods should never be quiet. My heart raced as I adjusted the band that secured my chest and grabbed my blade. The breeze that normally rustled through the leaves had stopped. Breathing a silent curse, I closed my eyes, allowing my Fae ears to work their magic—well, it wasn't quite *magic*, but it was a powerful ability in times like these. I easily detected the sound of soft steps padding across the moist leaves as they slowly moved in my direction. Switching my hold on my small but heavy sword, I crouched deeper into the mugwort. The stillness of the Woods was somehow palpable as I let my senses reach out like tendrils into my surroundings. A shiver ran down my spine as the unmistakable muskiness of damp fur coated the mist that glistened in scattered moonbeams.

I was *not* in the mood to fight another undercreature.

I had just started to sift through the list of furred undercreatures that might be attracted to this area when I noticed a tinge of lavender mixed with the scent—and I breathed a sigh of relief.

"The next time you sneak up on me, Lyyli, I won't be so inclined to share my meals with you," I huffed, sliding my sword back into its sheath. The auburn-colored enfield crept out from behind a large oak tree, her black eyes locking onto mine with sly amusement. Her nose twitched, undoubtedly smelling the foul drekavac blood. Despite my annoyance, I felt a smile pull at my lips as she approached, the creature purring savagely as I patted the soft fur of her hind legs.

"Rolling in my lavender field again?" I cooed.

The enfields, while unmistakably magical, were not one of the banished creatures that had escaped the Underworld centuries ago. Lyyli was able to roam free anywhere inside or outside the Holvik Woods.

Several months ago, I had found her ensnared in a poacher's trap. The iron barbs had pierced one of her delicate legs like a needle through a twine of thread. It had taken several weeks to tend to the wound while feeding and housing her as if she had been a domesticated pet.

At first, the strange creature's presence unsettled me, her constant shadow a reminder of how out of place she seemed. But over time, I came to appreciate her more than I ever expected. Her foxlike coat allowed her to melt into the underbrush effortlessly, a predator disguised as something almost ethereal. The talons on her forelegs were no mere decoration—they were savage, sharp, and lethal when needed. Her delicate wings, shimmering in certain light, spoke of an ancient world long forgotten, a kingdom once teeming with winged beings like her. Time and again, she had proven herself, fiercely loyal and protective.

I watched her sniff at the basket, her nose twitching slightly as she brushed against a bundle of thyme leaves. Even if my stubbornness told me I didn't need anyone else, it was nice to know I wasn't alone.

In reality, I had been alone for so, so long. It had been one hundred years since I left my home in Vogar. One hundred years of foraging, healing, and hunting—and trying to forget why I had been forced to leave.

"I hope you're hungry Lyyli, I left a rabbit stew on the fire."

Lyyli didn't voice a response, but her tail perked up and wagged enough that I easily deduced the creature's excitement.

The thought of stew made my empty stomach groan with hunger. I had barely eaten anything all day—only snacking on a measly tasting of edible plants and herbs I had found while foraging. The Nilsen family had given me a hearty stash of root vegetables and a rabbit in thanks for the salves that I had brought them after their old woman's fall. I had left the stock to simmer before leaving, the smell of fat and grease tantalizing as I walked the path into the woods behind my home.

The path out of the woods was not marked or cleared, yet I knew the way with my eyes open or closed. Quietly and carefully, I made my way through the dense trees and overgrown shrubs. The enfield, always close behind, matched the rhythm of my steps even with her faint limp.

After an hour, we came to the marked path that would eventually lead to one of the small villages in Árnes. Stepping over the edge of the woods, I slowly released the grip on my sword—my white knuckles aching as the tension released. There was always a sense of relief when leaving the magical boundary of the Holvik Woods to return to the relative safety of the rest of Árnes.

This far north, safety was measured by how close you were to the Holvik Woods. Once you stepped beyond the wards and into the Woods, any relative guarantee of security blew away with the breeze. The dangers were ever present. The shadows cast by the dense trees were a warning and promise of the darkness that roamed freely within the forest. Leaving the Woods was like the first breath after you've been underwater for too long—a reminder that you might get to live another day.

Stretching my fingers, I glanced down at my outstretched palm. The muscles were sore from holding my sword so tightly. I noticed the familiar fine lines that mapped my hands and the way the bulges of veins crept across the otherwise smooth surface like rolling mountains through a sandy desert. My skin was kissed with a golden hue from countless hours in the sun tending my garden and walking the fields. My gaze stopped on the outside of my right wrist where the smooth skin ended abruptly, obscured by the long scar that snaked across the top of my wrist like a rope-shaped pearl gleaming in the sun. Although I possessed Fae healing abilities, this wound had still managed to leave a permanent scar. I often wondered how the scar would have looked if I were mortal, or whether the injury and ensuing infection would have been fatal. I rubbed my wrist, as if the movement could banish the memories associated with the scar and continued walking ahead.

The smell of stew greeted us as we approached the small cabin, Lyyli's bushy tail wagging with increasing ferocity with each step. I had found the cabin a few months after I arrived in Árnes. Initially abandoned, I gradually transformed it from bare beams and cracked floorboards to a cozy and secure space. The beams of the ceiling were now lined with hundreds of hanging herbs in various stages of drying. A chimney was tucked across the far wall with an open cook space where a large kettle hung on a centuries-old iron pole, filled with simmering stew. There was a long wooden table that served as a workspace for crushing herbs, mixing salves, and jarring tinctures on the other side of the room. The shelves on the wall behind the table were packed with tiny jars and glass containers, all labeled and organized.

Some days, I would catch myself looking at my bed and I would wish that I had someone to share it with. But the mattress was small and worn and I couldn't imagine anyone would want to spend more than one night crammed beside me.

Lyyli confidently strode through the front door as I pushed it open and jumped into the bed, immediately curling into a tight ball. I sat beside her for a moment, petting her soft snout and iridescent wings, and smiled as she began to purr. Leaving the enfield to rest, I went to the chest of drawers and pulled out a fresh tunic. Lifting it to my nose I breathed in the clean scent of lavender, reminding me that I needed to make more of the soap I used to wash my clothes. I pulled the shirt over my head and tucked it into my pants.

"Hurry up and eat. I still need to go up to the lavender field," I said, scooping a large spoonful of the steaming broth into a shallow bowl before placing it on the floor. Lyyli huffed with displeasure at having to leave the comfort of the bed, but immediately raced over and began lapping up the meaty broth.

Spooning a second portion, I went through my mental inventory of herbs that would need to be harvested over the coming days. Certainly, lavender for soaps and oils, but also yarrow to make tinctures to help heal wounds, mugwort for making teas to aide digestion, and nettle for aching muscles. The lavender had flowered earlier in the week, and I wanted to make sure the fragrant flowers were harvested in time to dry them. Harvesting lavender was a time-sensitive matter, and I firmly believed that the best time to harvest the herb was at dusk, before the moons were full.

Glancing out the window towards the two moons, I spooned one last mouthful. The broth was hot and greasy, and the carrots were perfectly saturated with onion and garlic. I only wished I had a loaf of crusty bread to soak up the broth that lined the bottom of the bowl. But still, the stew had managed to fill my empty stomach which was all I needed.

After switching cloaks and baskets, I was ready to head to the lavender fields. As if sensing I was leaving, Lyyli nuzzled against my leg in appreciation and then left to return to her den for the night. Just as I reached up to grab the sides of my cloak to pull the hood close to my ears, I heard the rapid pace of footsteps approaching down the path outside my home.

Cursing, I turned to peer out the window. A man was coming towards me with a quickness that set me on edge. When he got close, he pulled his dark hood down to reveal his face. I relaxed slightly. I knew this man—Lars Søren. He lived in the nearest village, and I would often go to him to have my sword sharpened in exchange for a bushel of the rosemary I grew.

Lars was alone, and as he stepped into the light, I could see the unmistakable look of fear that stretched across his face. Cursing under my breath, I opened the door and started walking down the path.

"Ms. Trygg!" he called, clearly grateful to see I was home. "I am so sorry to bother you. Please... it's my son... he was attacked by a draugr while crossing through the Woods." Lars' voice trailed off as he tried to catch his breath, clearly winded from running the distance to my remote house.

Shit, I thought.

The draugr was one of the undercreatures encountered frequently within the Holvik Woods. They were most likely to be seen in the area at sunset and would linger deep into the night, their lifeless bodies moving mindlessly in search of warm flesh. It was not uncommon for a lone mortal traveler to die in the vast area, and later rise in the gruesome draugr form themselves.

Villagers surrounding the Holvik Woods were dependent on the hunting and foraging that could be found within the lush forest. So, despite the danger, they ventured there often. Unfortunately, mortals were particularly vulnerable to attack by the undercreatures who had been banished there. The mortals had come to me many times over the decades to seek help for their loved ones who had been attacked.

Cursing again, I realized I would inevitably miss my lavender harvest. I grabbed my small bag of medical supplies and reached for my sword. "Show me where," I demanded, already moving toward the door.

The light from the setting sun turned the fields a golden brown as we ran along the edge of the Woods. Shadows dancing across the tall grass seemed to chase us as we went. Next to me, the man was sweating and panting, his mortal body reaching the limit of his endurance. My breathing, however, had slowed to an eerie stillness despite the pace we had set, and my steps were almost silent as I raced through the field.

The anticipation of seeing Lars' son sparked a gentle buzz of nerves that felt heavy in my belly.

Healing common injuries was simple, in a way. Bone breaks, burns and lacerations were an expected part of life in these parts. The injuries sustained from the undercreatures, however, seemed like a curse. They were gruesome and mindless and impossible to explain.

Still, I was glad that the mortals in the area came to me. There was no hiding that I was different from them—not feared like the undercreatures, but not entirely trusted either.

My Fae heritage gave me sharper features than my mortal neighbors. I had overheard people say I had a 'sharp jaw'—whatever that means—and despite my best efforts, my eyes tended to look hardened even when I was pleased. They were a brilliant blue, like my mother's had been, and were shadowed by the long lashes of my father. My lips were fuller than either of my parents and my hair was a long chestnut brown with a lustrous sheen—normally pulled into a tight braid.

I glanced to the mortal man running next to me. He was not a small man, and yet I was slightly taller with a muscular frame and curved hips that stayed curvy no matter how toned my arms and shoulders got each harvest season.

I liked it that way. I liked being a mix of sharp lines and soft curves on the outside.

As we approached the Søren family's house, the lingering scent of the draugr made my nose twitch—a rancid mixture of rotten earth and sour meat.

The cries coming from inside the house sent chills up my spine—the sound of tremendous pain and imminent death. I realized then that I had been to this house before. It was several decades ago, but the memory was clear. I had come to this house to help a woman deliver a child. My stomach rolled as I realized that the injured man was likely that woman's son, now grown and on the brink of death.

Bursting through the door, I quickly spotted Lars' son lying by the fire as an older woman sat close to his side. She was desperately pressing a cloth, drenched in bright blood, to the man's side. Her face was almost as ashen as her son's.

I took a breath, trying to calm my mind so I could step into a state of necessary detachment that made healing grave injuries more manageable, a space where emotion yielded to precision and the weight of urgency sharpened my focus instead of clouding it.

"I need to see where the blood is coming from," I said gently as I knelt by the man's side. The woman reluctantly stepped away. Her shirt matted with dried blood—more blood than a mortal should lose. I felt the shrouded thrum of my magic under my skin as if begging to be put to use, but I willed it away—for now.

It would be easier to use magic. But easy was not always the safest way. After so many years as a healer,

I trusted my skills with a needle and herbs more than I trusted myself to control and reveal my magic. I lifted the man's shirt to expose a gruesome flap of skin that had been stripped away enough that the smooth rib muscles was visible beneath. A slow trickle of blood dripped relentlessly onto the cloth as I quickly packed the area with clean bandages from my bag of supplies.

"What is his name?" I asked.

"Eilif," the woman whispered. "His name is Eilif. Will he live?"

"I need to clean Eilif's wound. Would you bring me a pot of boiled water," I said as gently as possible, quickly readying my supplies.

Eilif's mother was staring at the saturated cloth and her blood-stained hands as if she couldn't understand when they had become soiled. I knew that the only reason Eilif was still alive was because she had held that cloth to her son's side with the full force of a mother's embrace. The devastation in her eyes was a reminder of her fear of losing someone she loved.

I needed these reminders. I had seen so many bloodied bodies and ashen faces that it was easy for me to dissociate when healing someone. I let her despair fill my heart for a moment before steading my breath and putting all my emotions aside.

The woman brought a steaming pot of water and set it beside me. After washing my hands, I watched the rise and fall of Eilif's chest and was slightly relieved to see that at some point he had passed out from the pain—or blood loss. *Good*, I thought. His breathing was steady as I reached my fingers under the flap of skin to make sure the draugr's brutal nails had not pierced his lungs. Once satisfied that the wound did not extend into the deeper layers, I began meticulously cleaning the area of debris, replacing the bloody gauze so I could inspect the skin flap.

It took two rolls of woven gauze to fill the space between the skin and muscle. Thankfully, these strips of fabric had been boiled and soaked in a willow bark tincture to help ward off pain and infection.

The flap of skin that had been stripped away like a ribbon was pink and viable. For a moment, the torn skin reminded me of the pink ribbons my family would weave around the harvest pole every Regn—vibrant waves of color signaling the start of the blooming season.

I shook my head, desperately needing to clear the thought so I could focus. Having erased the utterly morbid vision, I thoroughly draped the area with more of the willow bark-infused gauze, allowing the tincture to work as an anesthetic. Once I was satisfied that the tissue had been doused, I removed the gauze and began the painstaking process of stitching the flap of skin back together.

The room had gone silent, the only sounds from my needle piercing skin and the man's mother's occasional sniffling as Lars whispered hopeful reassurances. It was a relief when she finally stopped crying as the bleeding slowed to a trickle.

It had been easy enough to approximate the flap of skin back to its original position. The only benefit of the draugr's razor-sharp claws was that they made clean and even cuts. My callused fingers moved effortlessly as I pulled the needle through the motions of the running suture that would close the torn skin. After decades of perfecting this technique, I knew the sutures would hold tight.

Once the skin was reattached, and the bleeding controlled, I used another cloth to wipe the man's chest clean before finally turning to look at his family.

"He will need a lot of water. Feed him slowly, starting with bone and vegetable broths. And make sure he rests until the sutured skin has regrown. The thread from the stitches will need to be removed in two weeks."

Eilif's family nodded slowly as I spoke. I knew he would eventually recover, as long as they could make him rest and keep the wound free of infection. Thinking of this, I pulled a jar of my best honey from my bag to use when they changed the bandages.

As I washed my hands in a bucket of cool water, Eilif's mother approached. Her voice was still laced with fear as she said, "I know you didn't have to come, but I am grateful you did. We are indebted to you. I will pray to the gods to bless you for all you have done."

I forced a smile. As much as I wanted to appreciate the woman's words, I doubted the gods would be inclined to shower me with any of their blessings.

The goddess must have a sick sense of humor, because I desperately needed to wash—again. I could only imagine how the cumulative stench of drekavac, draugr, and mortal blood would smell to a passerby.

It was something of a miracle that I had any clothes at all. My life was a constant battle of stains. Some of which I didn't mind. The muted greens and swatches of yellow were like brush strokes from the herbs and pollen in my garden. Other stains were more morbid in nature, reminding me of the threat that loomed just beyond the edge of the Woods.

This time, I stopped at the stream I had passed earlier after killing the drekavac. It was one of my favorites. Fed by one of the higher waterfalls in the area, the water was always exceptionally clean, and bitterly cold. I had bathed here so many times that I knew which rocks would be slippery and which were stable enough to stand on.

Stepping into the freezing water made my toes go numb and I held my breath as I plunged under the dark water. I briefly thought about how strange I would seem to the High Fae of my homeland. I doubted many of the women in the Akureyrian courts preferred to bathe in a freezing stream under the light of the moons. I could picture them easy enough, soaking in stone tubs filled with steaming water that swirled with the scent of sweet perfumes.

Call me feral, but I much preferred water as cold as a glacier and the scented oils I made from the herbs in my garden.

Plunging my clothes into the stream, I washed away the grime from the day's work and the blood from Eilif's wound. Washing blood stains was almost cathartic, as if I could wash away reality. It was almost easy to forget about the threat that lurked just beyond the tree line.

After so many years of healing wounds, injuries, and illnesses it had become easy to separate my task from the reason behind their need for me. It was only when I failed that I began to ask questions. Why did this happen? What could I have done differently? Should I have used my magic? It was the failure that made me feel the weight of the goddess' glare. And when you have lived as long as I have, you are bound to have ample opportunities for failure.

The frigid water did wonders to settle my mind, and I splashed my face several times before I felt calm enough to wrap myself in my cloak and walk home.

The path from the village to my house twisted across an expansive field that the locals used for harvesting grain. Tall stalks of grass waved in the moonlight, the flowing shapes as delicate as lace against the dark sky. My home was closer to the border of the Holvik Woods than most mortals dared to live, and since I was the only Fae for miles, it granted a solemn sense of privacy.

Being alone suited me, I supposed. Being alone meant I didn't have to worry when my magic slipped in a moment of frustration. Being alone meant no one was around to suspect that I was more than a *typical* Fae.

The warmth of the small house was a welcome contrast to the chill outside. I threw my cloak on the hook by the door and changed into my remaining tunic before flopping myself on the bed. My mind felt foggy as it often did after fighting undercreatures or healing a complicated injury—and tonight I had done both. I stared at the beams overhead, counting bundles of herbs like some might count sheep. I rolled over and tucked myself into the warmth of my quilt, the blankets engulfing me like an old friend. It would be nearly impossible to sleep and still wake in time to get out to the lavender before the sun was up.

Sleep, it seemed, proved elusive and after tossing and turning to no avail I finally rolled out of the warmth of the blankets. I pulled on a clean pair of pants, before making a cup of acorn coffee—hoping the warmth would help settle my mind. The coffee was rich and nutty, and the bitter flavor helped banish any lingering thoughts of sleep. Something about today had felt different, and it left me feeling unsettled. A drekavac and draugr in the same day was not normal. I needed to clear my mind, and there was nothing quite like a long run to help regain my focus. The rhythmic pounding of my feet against the path, the wind rushing past my ears, and the steady thump of my heartbeat were all I needed to quiet the noise in my mind and find my center once again.

I drank the last of the coffee and pulled on my worn shoes before heading outside.

Moon beams marked my path as I sprinted through the open fields. With each footfall, thoughts of the undercreatures faded from my mind. The midnight mist against my cheeks forced my focus on the pure bliss of my legs moving across the land. I pushed myself faster, my muscles burning with exertion. There was no need to slow my pace as I crossed the mossy fields.

I kept running until the moons were high in the sky and my skin was slick with perspiration. By the time I was ready to stop, the ground had become more uneven, covered with jagged volcanic rock covered with mossy patches and pale lichen. Not wanting to twist an ankle, I decided I would walk back—even if it would take a few hours.

The rows of lavender were a short walk from my cabin to the Southern side of the field where the sun was hottest during the day. At this hour, the morning light danced across dew-drenched grass, and the ancient trees seemed to stretch in the breeze as if trying to conceal the secrets of the Woods. Within the border of grass were several rows of thickly planted lavender. The tips were a brilliant shade of purple and the calming scent billowed around me with each gust of wind. It didn't matter how many times I had seen this landscape, its beauty still managed to take my breath away.

I settled onto the ground and started snipping the stalks with my foraging blade. I had cut through the first few plants when a sound beyond the edge of the forest made me pause. I glanced to the left and slowly reached for the sword strapped across my back. The unmistakable huffing of a frustrated horse sounded abrasive and out of place coming from within the Woods. Slowly creeping to the tree-lined border, I scanned the area until I glimpsed a blond horse with a mane that was as black as a raven's wing. A muffled voice carried on the breeze like the seeds of a thistle, sounding exasperated and exhausted.

My eyebrow peaked as I heard the string of whispered curses the traveler unleashed. *Goddess, his mouth is worse than mine,* I thought. I was close enough to notice his scent and was surprised at how refreshing it was—cedar perhaps, with a hint of vanilla. The Fae possessed vibrant scents like this—

although I rarely saw other Fae in this area, especially not within the Holvik Woods. It was the other lingering scent that gave me pause—the faint smell of ether. The smell of magic.

Carefully, I worked my way deeper into the brush until I could see through to the small clearing where the horse and its companion appeared to be resting.

I snorted in surprise as I watched the way his long muscular body moved as he worked to tie up his pack. He certainly *looked* like Fae. His movements exuded a potent grace, yet it was difficult to overlook his limp as he tried to secure his pack onto his mare. When he turned his head I caught a glimpse of his ears, which tapered into delicate points.

Definitely Fae.

Alarm bells sounded somewhere in the back of my mind. Why was this Fae in my Woods? He didn't appear to be a forager—his clothes were too fine, and I didn't see any baskets or bundles of plants. He seemed to be alone, and while the short sword strapped to his back was enough to give me pause, he clearly looked unwell. The Fae were naturally gifted with rapid healing abilities. If a Fae looked unwell it meant that whatever injury they had sustained was potent enough to tax them.

Securing the grip on my sword, I moved closer to the clearing where he had set up camp. Based on his limp and the sheen of sweat on his brow, I knew I could escape if he made me feel threatened. I stepped on a small twig to create a sound and watched as he turned towards me. He was taller than me. I figured the top of my head would *just* reach below his chin. He was dressed in a blue tunic with gold ribbing, white pants scuffed with dirt and blood, and well-worn boots. His tan skin was a tribute to the considerable amount of time he spent outside, but the elegance of his movement suggested he was not spending his time outside on laborious work. His face was brutally handsome—although I hated to admit that the thought even crossed my mind.

Upon spotting me, his head stilled, and his chin lifted slightly. His jawline created a shadow on the side of his neck, and I found my gaze following the line down to his broad chest before returning to meet his stare. His eyes appeared to be a golden brown, but it was hard to tell from this distance. His dark brown hair was long and had been tied back into a knot on the top of his head and the sides were shaved down to a rugged stubble—a common style among Akureyrian warriors.

He seemed surprised to see me, shifting his stance and squaring his shoulders. "Hello? I'm sorry if I startled you. I will be out of your way as soon as I finish this pack," he said. His voice sounded stronger than his limping suggested.

I took a moment to consider if checking on him was worth the risk before cautiously asking if he was alright.

He dropped the pack he was holding and adjusted his stance, my eyes darting to the deep red stain seeping through his right pant leg. There was a rudimentary bandage tied around his thigh and I couldn't help but roll my eyes at his meager attempt at bandaging.

"You're bleeding," I huffed. I gripped the hilt of my sword and carefully crossed the distance that separated us. I couldn't help but marvel at the golden specks that seemed to dance within the chestnut hue of his eyes. "Sit down and let me look at that."

"It's nothing," he snapped. "I'm sure the bleeding has stopped by now."

Ah yes, I thought, *the unrelating arrogance of Fae men.*

"If all that blood came from you, you should rest and allow yourself to heal before mounting a mare that will have you bouncing about." I made sure to let my annoyance ripple through my words.

Wisps of hair pulled free of my long braid as I pulled my hood back and planted one hand on my hip while the other gripped my sword. My skin was so damp from the mist that I had to blink away the small droplets that had collected on the tips of my long lashes.

"I am a healer," I said with conviction and years of practice. "Let me look at it."

"I don't think that's necessary. I am riding with a small camp. We got separated but they should return any minute."

"You obviously don't have any healing supplies, and I don't feel like watching you bleed out while you wait for them. Now, would you like to roll your pants *up* or pull them down?" The shock on his face was enough to tell me he was not accustomed to being told what to do. "I am the only one who will be willing to help you for many miles. You won't find comfort in the mortal homes nearby."

The bandage had started to slip down his muscular thigh, revealing the wound that lay beneath his torn pants. It was large, an irregular tear that resembled a peaked mountain.

He looked defeated—as if he knew I would not relent. *Good.* I had been told that my dark blue eyes made it clear I did not take kindly to stubbornness. "What did you do?" I demanded.

"If you must know, I was thrown from my horse. She was spooked by something, and I landed on a fallen branch that pierced my leg."

Before stepping closer, my voice lowered as I added, "I will ask that you put your sword down before I come any closer." His eyes never left mine as he slowly reached behind his back to take hold of his sword. He carefully released the blade to the ground, not saying a word. I couldn't tell if it was out of disdain or shock that he kept quiet, but he never once took his gaze off me.

"If you didn't get all the pieces of wood out of the wound, your body will not let it close. What type of branch was it? Was it like this one here?" I asked as I picked up a smaller branch that lay by my feet.

Looking at the trees around him, he pointed to a fallen rosewood several yards away. The bloody branch he had fallen on pointed towards the sky waving its crimson stain like a war banner.

I released a drawn-out breath and pinched the headache that had started to form between my eyes. "You are coming with me. We need to get any splinters of wood out of the wound. That's a *rosewood* branch and the splinters can be incredibly irritating, even for Fae. I have a workspace just beyond the clearing." And because he still looked at me like I was a beast from the Woods, I used my best, most comforting, healer voice, "Can you walk?"

"I still think this is unnecessary, and my—uh—friends, will be here soon," he said as he looked to the tree line, his long lashes fluttering like a hummingbird's wings.

"They haven't come yet, and I am here now. Do you think you can walk, or do we need to get you on your horse?" I reached out to hand him a stick to use as a crutch. With a guttural grunt, he accepted the walking stick, adjusting it under his arm before moving to follow me out of the Woods. I scoffed, muttering under my breath, "I forgot how stubborn men can be." His eyebrow raised at the commentary, but he kept quiet as I crossed over to grab his pack and secured the reins on his mare. I checked to see that he didn't have any other weapons, only finding the sword, a bow, and a quiver of arrows clinging to the pack. Thankfully, his horse was more agreeable and nickered gleefully as I patted her withers.

Once we made it to the edge of the clearing, I nodded towards the smoke from the chimney of my cabin.

"It's right up here."

"Really. I'm *fine.*"

I tried not to smirk as he stubbornly grunted and cursed his way to the cabin. I had forgotten how satisfying it could be to prove a man wrong. Shaking my head, I swore at myself for being so insensitive. He seemed kind enough—arrogant maybe—but he hadn't acted like a complete asshole when I had questioned him.

I glanced at his face as we approached my home, curious how he would react to the space. I imagined any Fae would be surprised to see that I lived here— willingly.

The redolence of lavender oils, freshly cut herbs, simmering stew, and the smoldering fire was like a warm embrace as I opened the heavy oak door.

His brow furrowed and his jaw clenched as he glanced at the bundles of drying herbs and jars of various concoctions. "Are you a witch?" he asked, his eyes wide. "You are obviously Fae, which doesn't make sense either. Why are you this far north in Árnes? Do you *live* here?"

I shook my head, ignoring the influx of questions. I didn't need this Fae digging into my reasons for living in Árnes. I had spent a lifetime surviving with secrets—I didn't have any plans to start sharing now. Instead of answering, I got to work gathering bandages and cleaning solutions. I washed my hands with the rosemary and clove soap I had made earlier in the week as I scanned the shelves to see what else I might need.

"This really would be easier if you pulled the pant leg down," I said. His broad shoulders slumped as he seemed to surrender to the notion that he had little say in the matter. "You can use this cloth... to cover yourself."

He mumbled something foul under his breath as he took the cloth from my outstretched hand. Golden eyes assessed me like a threat as he pulled the waist of his pants down to his knees while simultaneously covering his more intimate parts with the cloth. Once covered, he took a seat on the bench.

My jaw ticked as I crouched down in front of him. It had been a *long* time since I had been this close to a Fae man. I cleared my throat as I glanced at the length of his thigh. He was powerfully built, and I could sense the vibrations of his muscles as they spasmed from what must have been significant pain. Centered on the inside of this thigh, the large gash was a mix of dried blood and torn flesh with a peppering of dirt. I cursed, noting the small area where fresh blood was pooling before trickling down the curve of his knee.

"I need to clean this... and you need to stay still. The pain will likely be considerable." I moved my sword belt into reach on my waist. A healer always wants to convey a gentle sort of kindness, but I also wanted to make it clear that if he made me feel threatened, I would not hesitate to plunge the sword into his groin. He nodded, gritting his teeth so hard that the muscles in his neck began to twitch.

I startled when he let out a low hissing sound as I wiped the area clean. He shut his eyes, slowing his breathing to a deeper rhythm as he tried to conceal the pain. From where I crouched, I could observe his features with greater scrutiny. His thick eyebrows furrowed with tension. His sculpted, sturdy jawline casting shadows over his neck. Handsome. He was really quite handsome.

"It looks like there are two or three larger splinters at the base of the wound, which would explain why it hasn't closed yet," I said mostly to myself. "I'm going to need you to hold *really* still."

With a brief nod, he bared down and clenched his fist while I used a small hook to dig into the wound—turning the splinter just enough that I was able to grasp it. Fresh blood pooled as the shard jostled against his flesh and pulled free. Finally, I grasped the first splinter. I couldn't help but marvel at how quickly the upper section of the wound started to close—I had forgotten how easy it was to treat Fae.

The other two splinters came out easily and I poured a tincture of willow bark onto the skin before wiping the area clean, making sure to remove any last pieces of dirt and debris. Once the skin was washed, I covered the wound with a damp cloth and tied a bandage around his leg to keep a gentle compression on the area. I patted his knee as I stood and then balked as I realized how awkward the gesture had been.

Looking quite pale, he ran his hand over the fresh bandage before meeting my gaze. "Thank you," he said. "I'm sorry, I don't even know your name." My stomach flipped at the way his golden eyes sparkled in the early light.

I cleared my throat. "You'll need to rest that leg for a while until you finish healing the area," I instructed with as much authority as I could muster. And seeing the way his eyes watched me with appreciation, and a hint of wonder, I quietly added, "My name is Kaari."

espite his eagerness to get back on his horse, my patient had agreed to wait until the wound had closed before attempting to leave. I hadn't asked for his name, and I had not given him time to offer it. The sooner he was on his way the better. He had put on a good show of resisting, but once I had convinced him to lay on the bed he had finally surrendered to his exhaustion and fallen asleep. I watched him for a few moments, partly to see that he was actually asleep, and also because the sight of a huge Fae warrior in my bed was an unexpected shock.

I moved to the other side of my home, quietly pulling the bundles of lavender out of the basket and laying them on the table. Time passed quietly as I chopped the stems and tied sections so I could hang the flowers to dry. The rhythmic chopping of my blade seemed to match the slow breaths from the warrior in my bed. *Who was this man?* I wondered for the hundredth time.

My stomach was rumbling by the time he stirred. He looked thoroughly confused as his golden eyes flickered open and assessed his surroundings.

"Hi," I offered. "Feeling better?"

He rubbed his face and scratched the side of his head, smiling earnestly. His lips looked soft. I liked the way the side of his mouth tilted when he smiled. It was charming—and I wasn't used to being charmed.

"I have a stew on the stove if you would like some," I said, turning my back to him as I stirred the large cook pot that hung over the fire.

"Thank you for the offer, but I should be on my way."

"You still reek of blood. And while we are outside the border of the Woods, other animals could be drawn to you." I turned to face him, sure that my ice-blue eyes were like daggers as I assessed him.

"That is an incredibly generous offer. I'm Torben," he said.

"*Torben*? Like the prince?" The Prince of Akureyrian's name was Torben. It was a popular name throughout the kingdom, but it still came as a surprise to hear this stranger shared him namesake. He certainly didn't look like a prince. He looked like a warrior who had worked long enough to afford rather fine garments.

"Yes, like the prince." He swallowed and cleared his throat as my gaze intensified.

I opened my mouth to question him, but I simply clenched my jaw and feigned a smile. "Well, welcome to my home, Torben."

The clouds outside had stolen any glimmer of sunlight, leaving the small cabin dimly lit, the only light coming from the glow of several candles. Torben's presence had engulfed the room and created a heaviness that filled the air. It felt strange to have someone in my home. I felt exposed—like a freshly sheered sheep. Instinctively, I planted my feet in a defensive stance as his assessing eyes trailed back to mine.

"You never answered my question, are you a witch?"

"I do not have the power of the Wise if that's what you're asking. I have simply made a point to familiarize myself with the plants and herbs that can be used as medicines. When you live this far from anyone, you learn to use what you have."

"And do you have the occasion to use these skills with any frequency?"

"You could say so. If you are unfamiliar with Árnes, most villages are home to mortals who tend to die from injuries you or I would consider minor. Some of them trust me enough to let me help... but others are more weary."

Torben rubbed his hand where the bulky bandage stretched beneath his pants.

"I should check the bandage... just to make sure the bleeding has stopped." I gathered my supplies and tipped my head, silently instructing him to sit on the bench.

Torben grabbed his trusty cloth to cover himself as he pulled his pants down to his knees, exposing the bandage and his defined thigh. The muscles were tense and quivered slightly. I wondered if the spasms were a result of pain or because I had to settle myself between his spread legs since the gash stretched along the inside of his thigh.

"Have you had to heal many injuries before?" I asked pointedly as I carefully unwrapped the bandage, my face pinched in concentration until I could see that the jagged wound had closed into a tight scar.

"Aye," he winced, "but never because I was attacked by a tree branch."

I huffed in response, not entirely amused at his attempt at humor. He opened his mouth to say something but stopped and sucked in a breath as I started rubbing a thick salve over the scarred tissue, the sweet tang of honey wafting from my hands. "You healed this nicely," I said. "The salve should help with scaring." I brushed my hands on my apron.

"Thank you." Torben stood and pulled up his pants. His eyes never left mine as he pulled his buckle closed. It suddenly felt very warm in my small home. Clearing my throat, I opened the nearest window, desperate to let the breeze wash over my flushed cheeks.

I was grateful he had a decent amount of healing power at his disposal. The sooner he was healed the sooner he could be on his way, and I could go back to my life of solitude. It had been a long time since any man—Fae or human for that matter—had spent this much time in my home and I was becoming increasingly aware of how cramped the space was.

He watched closely from the table as I put supplies away and stirred the stew that simmered over the fire. I could tell he wasn't being entirely forthcoming— there was no reason a warrior should be alone in the Holvik Woods, but I also didn't sense that he would harm me. Everyone had secrets, I supposed. I sure as all hells did.

The scent of the stew had started to fill the small room and I bit the inside of my cheek at the thought of a hot meal. I had just started to dish out two hearty servings when shouts ricocheted through the open window.

"Torben!" a range of deep and panicked voices bellowed through the wind.

I froze and snapped my head to the window, grabbing my sword with a quickness that startled Torben.

I heard him curse under his breath as he tried to stand, bracing himself on the back of the chair as he tested his leg.

"Are they looking for *you*?" I felt my temper flare, I was not happy about yelling voices near my home. Yelling voices drew attention and the goddess knew I had spent a lifetime trying to be as mundane as possible.

"Aye, I would imagine. Those would be my travel companions."

The figures stalked closer to the house, all reaching for their swords and daggers as they approached.

"Are you going to call them off, or let them wake the entire Holvik Woods with their shouting?" I was nearly shouting myself.

"Here!" he called. "Put your damn swords away, I'm in the cabin."

The door burst open moments later as three massive Fae stormed inside. They were dressed in finely made white tunics with golden ribbing and their emerald green cloaks were like waves crashing through the open door. I felt an inexplicable rush of power that made my palms warm with the surge of my magic. Their eyes darted savagely around the space and landed on Torben.

"Your Highness, are you hurt?"

Acid hit the back of my throat. Even as they said the words I fought back disbelief. I should have known the minute he said his name.

"Your *Highness*? When you said your name was Torben 'like the prince', you didn't say you *were* the prince," I growled, not caring about my murderous tone, my hands squeezing into fists at my side.

Prince Torben, the sole heir of King Havard, had made a name for himself as a fierce warrior who had fought in all the major battles over the past several decades. He was credited with planning the most brutal battle of The War that ultimately led to victory for the Akureyrian army. People across the land, mortal and Fae, spoke of the prince in whispers as if his name was a prayer on their lips. I had heard that he spent very little time in the capital and was often seen traveling with other warriors across the land. It always surprised me that even as far north as Árnes, people talked about the beloved prince, wondering where he was traveling and when he would find a bride. And while his reputation as a warrior was intriguing, people spent the most time talking about his immense magic.

As I scanned the men who stood by my hearth, I couldn't find any physical signs that would have given away his identity. His clothes were finely made, but he did not wear a royal seal or even the royal colors. And he certainly hadn't been wearing a crown. By contrast, his companions—or guards I supposed—were the epitome of royal power. The one in the center seemed to hold the highest rank, but the taller one in the back captured my attention with his powerful presence. His blue eyes were the color of the deepest ocean, so alluring I feared I could get swallowed by his gaze. The intensity of his stare was different from the others—he didn't seem fearful for his prince, he seemed utterly shocked.

I was sure my eyes were burning blue flames as I scanned the group that now stood in my house. I had just opened my mouth to demand an explanation when Torben finally spoke.

"Aye, I guess I was rather vague with my introduction, and for that I am sorry." His soft lips lifted into a half smile as he turned to his guards. "I'm fine. I got tossed around a bit. But I'm *fine*. This is Kaari, she is a healer. She, uh, helped me recover from a minor injury," he added, his voice painfully nonchalant.

Stubborn fool. "The prince sustained an injury to his leg when he was thrown from his horse," I interjected, feeling rather annoyed that the Prince of Akureyrian would downplay his injury to the ones who were sworn to protect him.

The once cramped room was now suffocating as they looked to their prince. The dark-haired one in the center stepped forward, "I don't know how we lost you. One minute you were right in front of us and then that wild gust of wind stirred the leaves and when they settled you were… *gone*."

Torben shrugged his shoulders, but I interrupted before he had the chance to speak. "A gust of wind strong enough to throw him from his horse? While you were in the Holvik Woods? Was there a sudden darkness as well? *Please* tell me you covered your swords and valuables as you passed through." The barrage of questions seemed to hit them unexpectedly.

The guards and the prince looked at each other and then at their swords in question.

"*Fools,*" I said under my breath. "You walked into the Holvik Woods with gleaming swords decorated with gems and didn't even *think* about the risk of attracting a braviken." I was close to shouting at this point, beyond frustrated with their ignorance.

"What exactly is a *braviken*?" Torben asked, cautiously glancing at his guard.

The large one with the piercing blue eyes looked inclined to speak, but I answered first. "A braviken is a demon of wind. They are attracted to shiny objects and use gems and stones to store their powers. It must have thought you died when you fell from your horse," I added, running my hands through my hair in an exasperated gesture. "They prefer to chase their prey and grow bored with stationary targets. But still, you may want to check the hilt of your sword... Your Highness," I added, nodding towards the sword that was leaning against the hearth.

Torben walked to his sword, the tightness in his leg already receding, and grasped the hilt so he could rest the blade on his upturned palm. There, in the center of the pommel where I suspected a large gemstone once sat, was an empty hole. Torben's gaze bore into me like the sun. "Well, that would explain why my unshakable horse got spooked. It seems we might have a lot to learn about these lands," Torben offered as he looked at his guards, "but then again, that's why we're here."

"The Holvik Woods are ancient and are mostly untouched. Many forgotten creatures roam here." I finally lowered my gaze and my voice, realizing my tone was dangerously close to sounding insolent.

The guards exchanged another round of glances. It was clear that these men spent a fair amount of time together as they seemed to communicate without the need for spoken words.

Finally, the dark-haired one said, "Your Highness, we should start the journey back, we need to set up camp."

"Yes, we have burdened Ms.… ?"

"Trygg," I supplied, rolling my eyes. They were really planning to leave. I should let them go, let them figure out that traveling through the Holvik Woods at night is an easy way to die. But something tingled at the base of my skull, the same nagging sensation that had made me pause while crossing a frozen lake, only to have the ice break moments later or double check a berry that looked edible to discover it was in fact wildly poisonous.

"We have burdened Ms. Trygg long enough." Torben bowed and made to leave with his men.

"You can't travel here at night!" I barked, slamming my hand on the rough table. The panic in my voice was enough to make the prince pause and he turned to face me again. "You would have to travel back *through* the Woods to get to the road to Dalvin." I paused and looked around my small but warm home. "You are welcome to camp here for the night. Outside. You'll be fine now that the bleeding has stopped. You can leave at first light."

The Prince of Akureyrian met my gaze as he bowed his head again, "And for that, I am grateful, Kaari Trygg."

An hour later, I peeked through the window at the front of my home, watching the four companions as they set up their camp.

The prince.

The Prince of Akureyrian was in my home.

I replayed the things I had said and the way I had acted before his identity had been revealed, then rolled my eyes at my foolishness. It was a miracle he hadn't ordered me shackled the moment his guards appeared. They likely assumed I was a lesser Fae. Even as a healer I doubted they would appreciate my demands for the Prince of Akureyrian to undress. A healer who was High Fae might have been allowed to behave that way. But the healers who were High Fae used magic—and I had been sure to keep mine tucked deep inside.

He was every bit the powerful warrior I had imagined him to be. His body was built for battle, the scattered scars across his bronze skin were proof that the stories of him were true. And yet, he had also been kind and appreciative.

My stomach groaned, reminding me that I had only eaten a small bowl of stew and a handful of herbs all day. Looking at the pot on the fire, I let out a sigh and started to gather enough bowls and spoons for the prince and his guards. It had been a long time, but I still remembered the basics of being hospitable.

Opening the front door, I peered around to catch the eye of one of the guards. "I have stew on the fire if you're hungry, it's not much, but it's hot."

The four men looked at me with predatory hunger.

"It does smell wonderful," Torben said as he stood from his crouched position by his pack. He brushed the dirt from his knees and smiled as he met my gaze, stretching his powerful leg from side to side. "My leg is as good as new, thanks to you."

"It was nothing, really," I replied, surprised at the compliment.

The prince and his guards packed themselves around my old table, their broad shoulders pressed together.

Goddess above, if my mother could see me now.

I had to admit, I was pleasantly surprised to see bliss stretch across their faces as they began sipping the steaming broth. I imagined their palettes were accustomed to more refined flavors than the earthy soup in front of them—but they seemed happy, nonetheless.

After spooning myself a small bowl, I moved to sit in the corner of the hearth.

Torben stood. "Please," he said, "take my seat." The guards watched closely and shuffled in their seats.

"That's very kind, Your Highness. But you should sit and elevate that leg."

Torben shrugged his shoulders. "In our short time together, I have learned not to argue with you," he said as he smiled broadly before nodding to each of his men as he called them by name. "General Emil Helvig, Captain Leif Sörensson, and Captain Theo Axtell. They are the top-ranking officials in the royal guard—my *Treyst*." They were imposing figures, their forms solid and chiseled from years of training.

Emil was taller than Torben, his dark braided hair tucked behind his pointed ears. His left arm was covered with intricate tattoos that were mostly hidden under his white shirt. Leif had a charmingly handsome face with a warm smile accentuated by deep dimples that adorned his cheeks. As much as Leif's appearance was youthful and warm, Captain Axtell looked rugged, and battle tested. My palms tingled with the hint of magic as his sapphire eyes pierced through me, the large scar that stretched across his right cheek gleaming in the light from the candle. His skin was smooth and free of any wrinkles that might reveal his age—but there was an aura about him that made him seem more ancient than the others. He watched me with penetrating intensity that made my knees feel unsteady. I tapped my fingers against the bowl I held, pushing a swell of magic under the surface.

His *Treyst*—his most trusted.

I acknowledged each of them with a simple nod before returning to my meal.

"This soup is incredible. It reminds me of one my mother made when I was a child. Is it rabbit?" Leif said cheerfully as he slurped another spoonful.

"Rabbit, yes. It was gifted to me by one of the mortal families in the area. They tend to need my help... their old lady is rather prone to accidents."

Their spoons stilled as they watched me with calculated focus, clearly waiting for more of the story.

They listened intently as I told them about Old Lady Nilsen, a near-death mortal who still insisted on working her family farm and had recently fallen... again. Fortunately, the woman's injuries had been superficial this time, but it had still taken most of my reserve of mugwort salve to cover all the bruises and scratches the poor woman had sustained two days ago. Despite the trek to get to their small farm, I was glad that the woman's grandson had come to me for help.

I briefly mentioned other mortal families in the area that I had helped over the years—although I intentionally omitted details about the recent injuries caused by undercreatures. I wasn't sure why, but it seemed too private—like that was a secret that should be held in Árnes. I couldn't imagine they would understand.

Torben, Emil, and Leif took turns asking questions as I spoke, wanting to know more about my way of life. Theo, for the most part, remained silent. His silence was such a contrast to the chatter of his comrades that it was slightly unsettling. I wondered what he was thinking. It was as if he was trying to peel back the layers of my life—like I was an onion on his chopping block.

After several silent minutes, Torben placed his spoon on the table and then moved his hands to rest on his knees. "I have to tell you, Ms. Trygg, I don't know that I have ever encountered someone willing to give so much without asking for anything in return."

The compliment—I *thought* it was a compliment—seemed genuine.

I brushed a stray curl behind my ear as I met his eyes. "It's nothing. It comes with the territory when you live this far north. I do hope you will be able to rest tonight." I bit my lip, cursing myself. I sounded like a fool. It had been a long time since I had participated in casual conversation. When I was called upon as a healer, conversation was limited to assessments and instructions. Dealing with blood and gore was simpler than making conversation with strangers.

I felt *flustered*.

I couldn't remember the last time I felt flustered. It was an unsettling thought, and I immediately began cleaning up the bowls and spoons in the wash bin.

Thankfully, my guests took the hint that they were excused and stood to leave. The three guards nodded their thanks, but the prince held back. I could feel his eyes burning into my back as I stood in front of the small wash bin.

"You have the most interesting accent," he said. "If I had to guess, I would say Vogarian."

I gritted my teeth as I turned to face him, cursing myself for not muting my accent—it had been so long since I had talked to anyone who would have noticed. "You are skilled with the dialects of your kingdom, Your Highness," I said. "Yes, I once lived in Vogar, although it has been many years since I have been back." I kept my voice quiet, but I knew it was laced with a hint of sadness and longing.

"Vogar is beautiful," the prince said gently, stepping beside me.

Not wanting to speak of the place I once called home, I cleared my throat and straightened my stance. "If I may ask, what brought you this far into Árnes?"

"Every year, for my birthday, I take a trip to a different part of the kingdom. I am always surprised that after so many of these trips, there are still places I have never been." He paused, and then his lips turned into a handsome smile. "I assure you. I don't usually need to be rescued." His smile was as warm as sunbeams after a rainstorm. "But I have taken enough of your time, I am indebted to you, Ms. Trygg... for the meal and the leg."

"Keep it elevated," I instructed, meeting his intense gaze, "and please, call me Kaari."

Torben smiled deeply, his dark brown eyes like swirls of night as he opened the heavy door to go outside.

I let out a long breath, releasing the awkwardness I had felt during the encounter. The whole evening felt like a blur. And the realization that the Prince of Akureyrian and his royal guards were staying outside my home was enough to make my stomach roll. I didn't do houseguests. Even on the occasion that I found someone to share my bed, I never let them stay for the night.

I returned to the task of cleaning up the table, pausing to let my fingers brush along the worn surface. The wood held memories of crushing and mixing herbs and concocting tinctures and salves that had helped through the years in this strange land. There was something about the rough surface that was comforting and reassuring. I could only imagine how different my home was from the palace in Dalvin. And yet, he hadn't balked at the way I lived.

The brown jar of healing salve was still on the table, and I paused before putting it back on the shelf. Once the splinters had been removed, the prince's healing powers had done a remarkable job of closing the wound on his leg, but even Fae powers sometimes left scars. I knew the salve would help reduce any lingering marks—although I rather enjoyed the jagged shape the cut had made. Sighing, and cursing for the hundredth time that day, I grabbed the jar and turned towards the door and the prince I would find on the other side.

5

Torben sat with his Treyst around the fire. I was impressed that they managed to spark a flame despite the breeze. Here, on the edge of the Holvik Woods, the dense trees created a barrier from the frigid, unrelenting wind, but the air was still crisp enough that they would need a fire to keep the chill from their bones. Árnes could be brutally cold and the weather, carried from the northern seas, was unpredictable.

I approached cautiously and they all lifted their heads to watch my approach.

"I brought you the salve from earlier," I said as I bowed my head. "It will help reduce any scaring... if you want it."

Standing to meet me, Torben accepted the small jar.

"Come to Dalvin with us," he blurted, his voice huskier than it had been before.

The Treyst was staring at me now, their eyes as shocked as I felt.

"The palace is currently short a healer... and the gods know we could use one." He smirked as he looked to his companions.

When I didn't immediately respond, the prince relaxed his stance and added, "And we would also be grateful to learn more about the creatures you have encountered in these parts. Your knowledge is invaluable."

I hoped he knew that he was shamelessly flattering me at this point. He had fallen down the well of his impulsive request and now felt obligated to back it up with something tangible.

"Of course, I am honored, Your Highness—"

"Please, call me Torben."

"Oh, alright... Torben. It is an honor to be considered for any position within the palace. Could I perhaps consider the offer and give you a decision in the morning?" I paused, watching the way his eyes danced with the reflections of the stars. "Unless this is a command, in which case I will certainly honor your wish." My tone held a hint of a challenge—testing to see what kind of prince I would be working for if I agreed to this surprising offer.

"Of course, it is your decision. Take your time to consider. We would certainly provide you with generous pay and housing... if that makes a difference," he added, his voice level and impartial. "Thank you again for the salve, I'll be sure to use it on the scar."

Once inside, I leaned into the back of the door after closing it with a hurried kick of my foot. I ran a hand through my now disheveled hair, fidgeting with my braid as my mind raced. My long fingers delicately unwrapped the long braid and brushed out the tangles I was horrified to encounter. I wondered what the prince had seen in me that caused him to make such a bold request. Surely there wasn't a shortage of healers in Dalvin—and I imagined those healers used magic.

I hadn't considered that my efforts to heal a stranger's leg would earn me an offer of employment, much less as a royal healer.

Thoughts swarmed through my head like bees in spring around a bustling hive. The idea of returning to the capital filled me with an array of emotions ranging from pure undiluted fear to staggering excitement.

It had been so long since I had been to the southern region. If I closed my eyes, I could still remember how the warmth of the southern wind kissed my cheeks when I traveled to the capital as a child, smelling of sea salt and blooming flowers.

Maybe, this strange prince had stumbled into my woods for this reason. Maybe, this was the gods' way of telling me it was time for something new.

Through the window, I watched the group as they sat around the small fire. I noted the ease with which they spoke to each other, finished each other's sentences, and laughed and taunted as if they were brothers. If I hadn't known, I never would have guessed it was the Prince of Akureyrian and his royal guards—his *Treyst*—sitting around that fire. Part of me envied their closeness. I had not known that kind of bond since long before I had been forced to leave my home to come to this strange and ancient land.

I moved from the window to sit in the chair by the hearth. I sipped another steaming cup of acorn coffee, mindlessly brushing my thumbs on the warm cup, and watched the flames burn. My mind was circling faster than a pinwheel in the breeze as I watched the sparks jump in fleeting bursts of white and orange across the blackened brick. I would have to give the prince—*Torben*—a response in the morning. Even though my muscles begged me to crawl into my bed and pull the worn quilt over my head, it seemed as if it would take all the minutes of the night to make a decision.

The last time I had been to Dalvin, I had been a child, innocent and naive to the wicked ways of the world. As I closed my eyes, I could vividly remember the tall stone buildings and storefronts embellished with crawling ivy and bright window boxes. The streets had been crowded with Fae and mortals, all dressed in gowns of silk and flowing muslin and tunics made of fine leather. My mother had brought me to a vendor down a windy cobbled street that sold various fruits dipped in the darkest chocolate I had ever seen. I remembered how the sweetness of the sugar made my eyes squint with delight. My mother laughed and hugged me close.

I cursed, shaking my head. These were exactly the types of memories that would come crashing to the surface if I were to go back. Memories from long ago that seemed to be painted with joy and love but were actually stained with ripping heartbreak and pain.

Was the fear of the memories of my past so strong that it was worth staying isolated and alone for my immortal existence? The scar on my hand stung with burning realization and I rubbed my wrist to quell the sensation.

The only thing keeping me here was fear. Fear was my anchor. If I didn't have fear, what was the purpose of my solitude? Fear was the reason I had left my home. The reason I kept to myself even after all these years. And the reason I hid my magic.

Fear had kept me safe.

Of course, I had the occasional opportunity to help locals with an ailment or injury but none of those people would care if I suddenly disappeared. My aching muscles groaned at the thought of not having to spend my days foraging and hunting to provide all my essentials. I had been self-sufficient for so long, and yet I began salivating at the thought of the simplicity of going to a market in Dalvin for fresh bread... and real coffee.

It was my freedom I worried I would lose by moving back to the capital—or any of the areas of the kingdom where the Fae tended to live en masse. Would I lose the freedom to bathe in the freezing water of a waterfall or run through a field as the moons danced across the sky—my bare feet cushioned by the moss that covered the paths?

The mug of acorn coffee had gone cold while I considered the prince's proposal, and I pursed my lips as I tasted the bitterness of the cold liquid. *Yes, I thought, real coffee would be nice.* Breathing deeply as I stood, I paused to stoke the fire before walking over to the wash bin to clean out my mug. Setting it to dry with the other dishes on the table, I thought of how nice it had been to be surrounded by others, even if they had been brutish men I didn't know.

The choices were clear: return to civilization and face the memories of my past or stay and live an eternal life of freedom and solitude.

Hours later, the fire had dimmed leaving the coals to flicker and glow, the embers filling the small space with muggy warmth. I pulled the blankets down to expose my bare shoulders as I breathed in the humid air. The moons had dipped low in the sky as the first hints of morning light started to creep over the tree tops outside.

A decision.

I had to make a decision.

I rolled onto my back and placed my hands on my belly, feeling comfort in the persistent rise and fall of each breath. Sleep had been elusive as images of my life flashed through my mind. I rubbed my hands together under the heavy blanket, pausing to feel the scar on my hand—a nervous habit for as long as I could remember. The scar was a reminder of what happens when secrets get out. I had been too young at the time to heal it properly, leaving the pearly skin that ached when rain was coming.

What would it be like to work as a healer in Dalvin? What ailments would I have to heal? Would I be bored without the ever-present threat of undercreatures once I no longer needed to venture into the Woods?

Tracing the curved line of skin from my hand to my wrist, my mind wandered to the image of the jagged scar that had been left on Torben's leg.

Rubbing my hands over my face, I took another breath and pulled the blankets down so I could crawl out of bed. The floorboards were refreshingly cool on my feet. *At least the weather will be warmer in Dalvin*, I thought as I pulled a heavy cloak over my shoulders. And with that, I realized I was surrendering to the idea of leaving my home in Árnes.

Torben had said it was my choice. I wondered if that meant I was free to leave Dalvin if I wanted. My eyes narrowed as I peered through the window towards the tent. I was surprised to see him sitting on an overturned bucket cleaning his sword, his gaze settled somewhere off on the dim horizon. His face was calm and pensive, but his jaw was set as if he was grinding his teeth. He *was* strikingly handsome—his features highlighted by the early morning light. He had removed his cloak, despite the chilled air, and I could see the definition of the muscles in his arms as he ran the wool cloth down the blade. *A strange prince indeed*, I thought.

I crossed to the other side of my home to see what was in my small pantry. I assumed the guards would have food but felt a sense of obligation to offer *something*.

Acorn coffee would have to do.

I scooped a handful of peeled acorns from a large glass jar and poured them into a mortar before settling into the rhythm of grinding the nut into a chalky powder.

A soft knock on the door sent a ripple of goosebumps across my skin. Quickly smoothing the wild pieces of hair that had once again escaped my braid, I pulled my cloak closer around my shoulders before opening the door. Torben's smile was as soft as the morning light that kissed his bronze cheeks.

"I'm sorry to intrude but I saw you were awake," he said as he glanced at my unruly hair. "We have strips of jerky and moderately fresh cheese if you would like some."

"Thank you, that sounds wonderful," I said honestly. "I can brew some coffee... it's acorn but it does the trick to warm the belly on a cold morning."

He glanced at the mortar on the table that was filled with the crushed powder. "Acorn coffee?" he asked. "Now that is something I *must* try."

I stepped back into the warm house and poured the powder into the pot on the hearth. "Did you sleep well?" I asked as I slowly stirred the coffee mixture.

"Aye. I enjoy sleeping under the stars," he replied as he arched his back and stretched his neck.

I hummed in amusement as I watched him try to stifle the movement.

"I would like to come to Dalvin with you... and your guards," I blurted. The thrum of anticipation had boiled over in my belly before I had time to decide if I agreed with myself.

Torben's eyes widened in surprise and the right side of his mouth tilted into a smile. "I'm glad to hear it. I—*we*—will be glad to have you with us," he said, his voice filled with forced neutrality. "Please take your time getting anything you might need," he said as he glanced around my small home. "One of our horses has an empty pack."

I nodded and adjusted my cloak. "It won't take me long," I said, acknowledging the unspoken but obvious fact that I did not have much worth packing. I reached for the cloth I used to strain out the powder and poured steaming cups of coffee, setting three of the mugs around the table before handing the last to the prince.

"A local delicacy," I quipped, as a soft brown curl dropped across my face.

Torben's brow lifted in surprise as he took a sip. "It's so... earthy."

I looked into my mug and a faint smile formed on my face, "I'm sure the coffee in Dalvin tastes better than this."

After breakfast had been cleared away, I took a moment to bask in the blissful feeling of my full stomach. The guards had left me alone so I could go through my things as they worked on packing up their tent and readying the horses. I grabbed the leather travel bag I used during longer foraging treks and my smaller canvas herb bag with the mugwort from the day before. I would have to fit all my things in these two bags. I only had two dresses, one made of muslin for the warmer months in Värme, and the heavier cotton dress I wore now. My two remaining tunics were stained with traces of calendula and sage and my favorite pair of pants had holes in the knees, but they were good quality and fit me snugly.

Slipping out of my dress, while keeping an eye on the window to make sure the men couldn't see me, I changed into a lavender tunic, form-fitting pants, and my sturdier leather boots. I crammed my lightweight cloak into the remaining space and closed the flap, then went through my most recent tinctures and salves, packing several of the most potent jars into the canvas herb bag.

I figured I wouldn't need to bring any bedding since Torben had said the palace would provide my housing, but a part of me ached at the thought of leaving behind the worn quilt that was delightfully soft from so many years of use. I ran my hand down the multicolored pattern and offered a silent nod of thanks to the blanket for keeping me warm for so many years.

All my possessions had served a purpose for my survival in solitude. Most of my things would be useless in the capital and wouldn't be worth enough to anyone else to try to sell. I knew that someday one of the mortals in the area would stumble across this cabin and claim it as their own, as I had done long ago. I only hoped they would find use for the things I left behind.

Standing in the small space for the last time, I looked around, trying to memorize all the details. After a final breath to fill my lungs with the familiar smell of dried herbs, old wood, and the smothered fire, I stepped outside into the sunlight that shone on me like a beacon of new beginnings.

Before walking to the horses, I placed a small bowl of stew on the front step. I knew Lyyli would come back at some point today, and my heart ached as I thought of her realizing I left. I knew the creature wouldn't understand—but I still wished I could have said goodbye.

I didn't want to talk with my new companions about leaving. As I walked over to Torben's horse to start securing my packs, I could feel a lump in my throat the size of a goose egg. I imagined the feeling was likely to linger for a while. Torben and the guards seemed to read my body language well enough, because they quietly followed my lead and finished the final preparations for the long trip to Dalvin.

"Frigg is gentle and stubborn, and she seems quite infatuated by you," Torben said as he reached for the mare's rein. "You are welcome to ride with me... unless you would prefer to ride alone." Knowing the alternative meant someone was walking, I was inclined to accept his offer and nodded my head.

"I packed the *shinier* weapons under a blanket after your suggestion last night. Is there anything else we should know about traveling through these parts?" Emil asked before mounting his horse.

"The time of day will work in our favor, but we should still leave the Woods with plenty of time make camp before nightfall. The further we get from the Holvik Woods the better." The men glanced towards the forest in unison. "As long as we aren't carrying any raw meat the wargs should leave us alone."

"Aye, we've heard about wargs." Torben gave Theo a pointed glare before returning his attention to me. "Are you ready, Ms. Trygg?" he asked, his voice softening.

My eyes swept over the small cabin and surrounding woods a final time. Árnes had been a strange sort of sanctuary for me. I had come to this rugged land when I was desperate and scared, and had spent years—decades—learning how to survive on my own. The crisp breeze swirled with hints of juniper, the woody scent invigorating and reminding me of home—my true home, in Vogar.

I approached the mare and swiftly swung my leg over the saddle. It had been a long time since I had ridden a horse. I was grateful the movement was mostly graceful, and I didn't make a complete fool of myself. As Torben pulled himself up and settled behind me, I was keenly aware of the way his arms wrapped around me as he reached for the rein. His broad chest seemed to envelop me like a heavy cloak and his muscular thighs pressed against mine in firm reassurance. As his chin settled next to my head and I felt his breath on my neck, I said a silent prayer to any god who might help my heart stop racing.

Torben tensed as his chest settled against my back. I imagine he was surprised to feel the unmistakable shape of the sword I had strapped there, concealed beneath my cloak. *Probably a little different than the ladies in his court*, I thought, *good, let him know that I carry my own weapons.*

The path through the Holvik Woods leading to Dalvin was overgrown with vines and shadowed by the spruce that grew in abundance. The horses stepped carefully as we passed, avoiding the loose stone that had been turned up during the last heavy rain. Torben would whisper sweetly to Frigg, and she would nicker with delight, trotting more confidently with each ounce of praise. The cool morning mist was refreshing despite the nervousness I felt. Torben and his Treyst seemed adequately alert and curious as we ventured further into the dense forest.

"How often do you see undercreatures when you come into the Wood?" Leif asked quietly.

"It depends," I answered honestly. "The entrance to the Underworld is further north, and the closer you get to the Gate, the more densely populated the area is with undercreatures. Unfortunately, the soil is richer there, yielding the most vibrant plant-life, so it can be tempting—and necessary—to venture into those areas. The further south you travel, the lower the chance you will see one of the creatures.

"I never traveled into the Woods without a blade and always wore colors that would blend into my surroundings—light green to match the spruce and lavender like the muted flowers that grow low to the ground. Most of the undercreatures have poor vision—since they come from darkness—and rely on their ability to detect scent and motion." I paused, feeling a shudder run up my spine. "The Fae—even lesser Fae—are better matched against the undercreatures. But the mortals don't have the benefit of heightened senses and speed."

Leif's mouth was practically agape. "I have fought in wars where I have feared for my life with every breath. But I have always known my enemy. The undercreatures seem so wildly unpredictable. I think that's what makes them so terrifying."

I laughed under my breath, but I felt my shoulders straighten with a hint of pride. I didn't fear the Holvik Woods, and I didn't fear the undercreatures. My father had told me stories of war. War terrified me—but I was not a warrior.

After several hours, the path hardened with packed dirt and scattered stones replacing the lush moss that had stretched like a carpet through the Woods. There was always something cathartic about leaving the Woods. Whether it was relief of not being torn to shreds by an undercreature or the reminder that the barrier at the edge of the Woods allowed the kingdom to survive, passing through the wards always made my heart race and skin tingle. The others didn't seem to notice—except Theo. As his horse stepped over the threshold, Theo's broad shoulders tensed, and he shivered.

"It feels good to see open fields again," Torben said, his breath warm against my ear.

Now I was shivering. It did feel good. "Oh, yes. It's always a relief to cross the wards."

The Holvik Woods was the only place in Akureyrian that was wrapped in wards—even the palace didn't have magical boundaries. The magic that had been used to keep the undercreatures within the Woods hadn't been seen in a thousand years.

"Mhmm," he hummed. "Are you doing alright? You've been rather quiet since we spoke of the beasts."

"Yes, well." My voice trailed off. What was there to say? Leaving the Woods felt too final—like I was leaving a piece of myself behind, and I feared I would be lost without that piece of me. "I just have a lot on my mind."

Every so often, as we rode through the seemingly endless hills of long billowy grass, Torben would ask about certain landmarks and I would tell him what I knew of the history of the land. The Innnes Mountains that separated Árnes from Dalvin came into view in the distance, their sheer size obliterated the horizon where the rock reached for the sky. The four massive peaks were as sharp as the tip of a serrated blade—a drastic contrast to the lushness of the surrounding area. The mountains were notoriously unforgiving and even from a distance, seemed to tower over the entire kingdom. From here, it would take a day to reach the range and another two to cross the pass... if the weather held.

As midday approached, we stopped to water the horses. The stream we found gently meandered through the rich land and I eagerly grabbed my herb bag and went to gather blueberries from the bushes that were scattered near the flowing water.

Emil was passing around small chunks of cheese and crusty bread when I suddenly stopped picking and reached for my sword. The others noticed the movement and looked towards the brush where my gaze fell.

With the sword in my right hand, I signaled to them to get low. I imagined they were all reaching out to their surroundings with their heightened senses like I was, but they remained veiled in an eerie silence. As the breeze shifted, the unmistakable scent of blood and earth wafted along the stream.

The guards moved slowly to arm themselves with shields and swords as they aligned themselves next to Torben. I was closer to the stream, several yards away from the others, my gaze unwavering, still directed towards the woods on the other side.

An instant later, a blur of black fur and muscled limbs was upon me. Before the others had time to charge towards me, I had lifted my blade and twisted it around my head with impressive speed. I landed a powerful blow to the beast's head and the resounding *crack* of metal against ancient bone was deafening. Jumping to the left, I slashed my golden sword across the creature's ribs. Blood sprayed and the creature released a bone-crushing screech of pain, its red eyes glimmering with hate and fury. Twisting again, I knocked the beast with the hilt of my sword. The movement earned enough time to adjust my grip, and with a final graceful strike, I brought the sword down just below the beast's large black ear.

The creature dropped to the ground as I stood facing the heap of fur. Slowly, I turned to face the stunned men behind me. Torben and his guards exchanged mystified looks. "Are you alright?" Torben asked cautiously.

Heart racing, I slowly lifted my chin. My sword hung from my right hand, dripping with the dark liquid. My face and tunic were covered with a splatter of black blood. Torben handed me his cloak and I quickly used it to wipe my face.

"What in all hells is *that*?" Leif bellowed.

The heaving of my chest slowed, and I met the prince's eyes. I felt like I couldn't breathe—like I had been pulled under a great waterfall and the current was slowly ripping me to shreds. "*That* should not be here," I whispered.

They gave me as much privacy as they could while I went to the stream to wash the stains from my face and tunic. We had barely said a word since the beast had burst from the edge of the stream and the air was heavy with unanswered questions.

"Garmr," I said blankly, squeezing water from my freshly braided hair when I returned.

"What the hell is a *garmr*?" Emil asked, his face pinched with concern.

"A creature of the Underworld," Theo answered, and I stared at him blankly.

"It should not be *here*. Garmr rarely leave the Underworld, and they certainly should not be able to cross the wards of the Holvik Woods," I responded impatiently.

"How in all hells did you learn to fight like that?" Theo's voice was brusque.

I looked down at my hand as if surprised to see I still held my sword. "I have lived near the Woods for a hundred years. I wouldn't be standing here if I didn't know how to protect myself."

Leif whistled under his breath, glancing from me to Theo.

"I may not be a warrior," I snapped, "but I am not helpless." I didn't like being underestimated. I had survived well enough on my own.

My tone and the fierceness on my face were enough to tell them the discussion was over until we were far away from this place. We packed in silence, and I walked over to Torben's horse, whispering reassuringly to the mare before swinging myself into the saddle.

We rode until the sun was low on the horizon, a constant reminder of the approaching darkness. *Did more undercreatures lurk in the shadows?* I wondered. I had never thought to fear them outside the edge of the Woods. It was unsettling to say the least.

Despite my unease, the weight of my blade was a familiar comfort. And yet, bringing my attention to my back made it hard to ignore the hard body pressed against mine. Torben felt tense behind me. Was he regretting his decision to invite me to Dalvin? Or was he as concerned about the garmr as I was?

We needed to find a place to set up camp and make a fire. A rock formation in the distance caught our attention. It would provide enough protection from the elements for the night.

The fire burned brightly as we all worked to set up camp. We had positioned ourselves in the curve of the rock and the flicker of the flames created shadows that danced along the stone's rough surface. I sat silently next to the fire cleaning my blade for a third time since the encounter with the garmr.

Never in my long life had I encountered a creature of the Underworld *outside* the border of the Holvik Woods. It seemed that I had completely underestimated how much my life was about to change.

# 7

The night sky was bright even though the sun had set hours ago. The stars beamed like fireflies in a dark forest. Though the warmth of the fire made my eyes heavy with the promise of sleep, my mind was thundering like a band of wild horses. The canvas sheet behind me moved and I saw Torben step outside. He didn't look like he had slept either.

"Mind if I join you?" he asked.

"Oh, of course… Your Highness."

"Please, call me Torben. Anyone who fights a beast from the Underworld to save my ass has earned the right to call me by my name."

I felt quite pleased that he knew I had saved him. I appreciated his attempt to ease the heaviness that had filled the air since the attack. Bowing my head slightly, I looked at the fire, the flames reflecting in the center of my eyes as I spoke. "I hardly ever see garmr roaming in the Woods."

The prince lowered his voice to a gentle whisper. "You said you have spent a hundred years near the

Holvik Woods." It was a statement as much as it was a question.

"Give or take a few years, at some point I think I stopped counting. But yes, I was only twelve when I arrived in Árnes."

"Well, you're in the company of another centenarian. A hundred years ago I would have been twenty."

I wasn't sure about his motivations for probing into my past. Instinct, and my parents' insistence, had taught me to be on guard anytime someone asked about my life. The threads of my life were like a tightly bound tapestry—the colors muted and obscured so that they did not give away the whole story.

My mother's voice whispered in my memory— something about common curtesy and manners. I scoffed, but figured I was obligated to offer him some details about myself. "My father would let me travel with him when I was young. The first time I went to Árnes was with him. After my parents died, I had nothing left in Vogar, so I traveled to Árnes. The memories I had of Árnes were happier than the memories I had of Vogar. I have seen my share of creatures over the years, and this wasn't the first time I have had to fight for my life... but I have *never* seen a creature from the Underworld outside the border of the Holvik Woods." I cleared my throat, pain, and sadness radiating through my voice.

"Was your father knowledgeable about the creatures of the Woods?"

"Yes."

"I see." His sharp features shifted, softening. "I wonder if there is any record of the undercreatures roaming outside of the Woods. Perhaps when we get to Dalvin, you would like to help me check the archives?"

"I would," I said. I could only imagine the resources he had access to in the royal library.

"I hope your father knows that I am grateful for your service today," he said quietly.

"Thank you, Torben." I ran my fingers over the scar on my hand, feeling the press of Torben's gaze on my haggard face. "I'm sorry I ruined your cloak," I added.

Over the next several hours, Torben told me about the state of Dalvin. The capital city had been erected several thousand years ago, the location intentionally selected due to its proximity to the sea and the natural barrier created by the Innnes Mountains to the north. For centuries, the city had been a bleak pit of crime and crumbling buildings, an unfortunate result of rampant corruption and magic amongst those with the most power. An ancient queen had been the first to emphasize the aesthetic of the city and had used her powerful magic to fertilize the ground, so trees and flowers replaced the crumbling bricks that littered the streets. The investment had paid off, and as the capital flourished so did those who lived there.

A lot had changed in the capital since I was a child, and I was surprised to hear about the museums and galleries that Torben said lined the cobbled streets. He seemed especially proud as he talked about the public garden that had recently been constructed in the center of the city to honor his mother. For the first time, I felt a look of genuine delight cross my face, my eyes lighting with excitement as I asked for specifics on all the plants that could be found in the garden. Torben laughed from deep in his throat, apologizing that he couldn't answer my questions. "When we arrive, I would love to show you. Maybe you could teach me about the plants we have growing."

As time passed and the moons slowly made their way across the dark sky, it seemed as though the wall I had built up around myself was crumbling like a stone fraught with age. I couldn't quite place the feeling that was brewing in my chest. It felt like a storm. Like the vibrations that rattle your insides when thunder is near. Torben's voice was deep and warm, almost hypnotic as he described life in Dalvin. It made me want to see it—to feel it. It had been a long time since I felt excited about something new. We were both surprised when the sun started to come up over the horizon, realizing we had been talking most of the night.

Leaving the curve of the boulder I stretched my arms over my head while I looked towards the mountain range. I stood for a moment, breathing in the silence as I ran my fingers along the fine embroidery along the hood of my cloak. It seemed like a lifetime ago that I had stitched the floral pattern.

"How mad are they going to be that you took watch all night?" I asked, smiling at the prince. Torben had missed his watch rotation with Theo by several hours. There would undoubtedly be hell to pay when the others woke and realized Torben had been awake all night, and we both knew we would be brutally tired for our long ride.

"Furious," he said with a smirk.

The wind stung my skin like a swarm of bees the closer we got to the mountains. By late afternoon the range was so close that I had to lift my head to see the massive peaks towering over us as we rode closer. The Innnes Mountains were the setting for many ancient stories I had grown up listening to and I remembered the awe I had felt the first time I had seen them with my own eyes—that same awe was not lost on me now.

The prince's broad chest was blocking the worst of the chill from my back, and I was grateful for the steady warmth that radiated from his massive form. I pulled my cloak up closer around my neck, pinching my elbows together to block the breeze that assaulted my exposed skin.

I was mortified to realize the prince had been within earshot when I'd sung an ancient song to his horse while we were preparing to leave—I wasn't sure how much he'd heard. It had been reckless to sing *that* song. But the words were a comfort as they flowed through me and despite the darkness of the song, I felt warmer and lighter after. *Fjallia-dýr* was a song of Akureyrian history—of a time when beasts roamed the land and people lived under a shroud of fear. I closed my eyes as I translated the words.

> *The river runs red as it was before.*
> *But I go on to battle the beasts inside.*
> *For my blood is the gate*
> *and my soul shall be the sacrifice.*

The ancient dialect of the Old Language was beautiful, and I had always preferred to sing in that tongue. Knowing the language, however, marked me as High Fae. The High Fae of Akureyrian were granted their status because their bloodlines were saturated with ancient magic. For centuries, the High Fae had wielded their magic to their benefit, creating wealth they were able to pass down in the chance they had children.

It was customary to teach the Old Language to High Fae children—the descendants of the most ancient bloodlines desperate to keep the language from being lost. Of course, those who worked the estates of the High Fae occasionally learned the language as the children had their lessons.

Whether he believed me to be High Fae or not, speaking the language fluently would undoubtedly mark me as having connections to a High Fae family.

I looked down at my hands and quickly clasped them into fists as a faint blue light simmered in my palms. *Bölva,* I cursed silently. My magic always simmered when I was stressed. I glanced to the side to see if Torben had noticed anything, but his gaze was firmly set on the mountains ahead.

"Did you cross through the Innnes Mountains when you first went to Árnes?" Torben asked cautiously.

"Eh, no." I rubbed my hands on my thighs. "When I traveled from Vogar to Árnes, I went through the Grimsey Coast."

"Ah, you are in for a treat then, the view from the pass is spectacular. The fjord seems to stretch for miles when you're up in the mountain pass," Torben said, brimming with pride.

To get to Árnes from Dalvin, or Vogar, the only options were to cross the Innnes Mountains or travel up the eastern coast to get to the stretch of jagged cliff walls known as the Grimsey Coast. Both paths had obstacles and challenges and once in Árnes, many of the Fae didn't find there was much to their liking. A thousand years ago, Queen Maiken had gifted most of Árnes to the mortals who lived in Akureyrian and to this day, many of them preferred living in this remote region of the kingdom. The mortals and Fae tolerated each other—to an extent. The mortals were uncertain of the Fae because of their magical abilities, and the Fae were frustrated with the mortal's reliance on Fae magic. The polarity was not as strong as oil and water, but tensions diminished when they each had a place to call home.

We spent the remainder of the ride to the base of the mountain in relative silence. When we stopped, I was relieved to see a fresh stream adjacent to our campsite. I desperately wanted to wash my body and clothes after so much riding and hoped a bath would give me a few moments of privacy.

The men got to work setting up a shelter for the night. The dropping temperature would likely force me to sleep in the tent with them and while I had certainly developed some level of trust, I still bristled at the thought of sleeping so closely to any man, let alone three.

With the tent raised, Leif started building a fire and resumed his normal chattery—excelling at drawn-out stories of travel and battle and women. Torben laughed and punched him affectionately in the shoulder. Once again, I was struck by how comfortable they seemed together, and how casual their interactions were with the prince. They were nothing like what I remembered of the stiff and silent royal guards I had seen as a child.

Leif raced by, slapping Theo on the shoulder. "The first one to catch a fish gets the last watch!" They quickly grabbed their makeshift rods and rushed after Leif towards the stream.

Goddess, they were like children.

I was growing accustomed to their personalities and presence. I almost felt like I had inserted myself into their band. Emil was strict and careful—always the voice of reason. Leif managed to bring humor to any moment—even the most mundane. Theo was an enigma who's shell I desperately wanted to crack. And Torben—goddess above—Torben was making me rethink everything. He was powerful and strong, living up to his reputation as a decorated warrior, and also gentle and kind. I had never met a man like him—or any of them, to be fair.

Gathering a bag of rice and a small bunch of rosemary, I inhaled the familiar scent, my mouth salivating at the thought of fresh fish and herbs. I found a cook pot and followed them to the stream to collect enough water to boil the rice.

They returned an hour later, dripping with water and exertion, a string of six fish slung between them. A mix of thyme and rosemary scented the air as they approached, and when they saw the rice I had made, they beamed at me. We charred the fish over the open fire and then added the smoking pieces to the herbed rice, it was the most complete meal any of us had had in weeks.

After dinner, our bellies full and cheeks sore from laughing, Emil and Leif moved to a patch of grass near the clearing. With swords in hand, they started to strike and parry in a beautiful dance of swordplay. Theo stood on the side and bellowed insults at his friends while Torben sat down next to me, extending his arms behind him to support his weight. His face lightened as he watched his Treyst and chuckled as Leif unleashed a particularly crude insult at Emil.

I watched them intently, noticing their militant technique. Even though this was play, I could tell they took the exercises seriously.

Leif parried as Emil struck on his left, spinning to gain distance as he stepped closer and switched his grip, landing a brutal strike on Leif's sword. Twisting again, Emil swung his sword around and used his shield to knock Leif's sword away, he lunged until his blade was inches from Leif's throat. Leif scoffed, "One day, general. One day it will be my sword at your throat." Emil smiled as he pushed his friend away.

"Not if you keep dropping your left hand when you step back as you parry," I said under my breath.

Leif's dark eyes shot to meet mine. "I do not!" he said, out of breath.

"You do. And Emil is lucky you haven't caught on to how much he favors his left leg when he spins like that," I added, shrugging my shoulders. Emil made a choked sound deep in his throat as Torben burst out laughing. "Tuck that arm in captain, it will help keep you balanced."

"Alright, healer, let's see what you've got!" Leif's white teeth glistened as he smiled. Torben shot a threatening glance at Leif, but I reached for my sword and threw off my cloak, the brisk air so cold it stung my bare shoulders.

I stood across from Leif and casually extended my sword. Since I lacked a shield, I tucked my left arm tightly behind my back. Out of the corner of my eye, I saw Torben sit up straighter, and Theo crossed his powerful arms. It had been a *long* time since I'd sparred with anyone who had been born outside the Underworld. It was exciting to think of facing someone with a brain that functioned on more than bloodlust. I wondered, though, if my particular skillset would translate into fighting against a brutish warrior.

Without warning, I lunged at Leif, filled with a fierceness that was matched by the glow in my icy blue eyes. I felt the eerie sense of calm that always took over when I practiced my swordplay. My breathing slowed despite the strain of my movements. My sword felt like an extension of my arm and my feet felt weightless as I danced away from a jab of Leif's sword. He lunged at me and moved his shield to parry, likely expecting me to swing. But before he could adjust his feet, I ducked and rolled on the ground, popping up behind him, then I froze with my sword an inch from the left side of his throat.

"Just like I said, you leave that left side *completely* open when you step to parry," I cooed into his ear, patting his shoulder like he was an old friend.

"Holy gods," Leif blurted, shocked and panting.

The others were staring at me, their jaws dropped and eyes wide. I knew that despite his facetious nature, Leif was a hardened warrior—his skills would have earned him his spot as one of the prince's top guards.

I started to walk back to the fire, but Torben stood and grabbed his blade. He had taken off his cloak and wore only a light undershirt that had come untucked from his trousers. The look in his eyes was primal as if he were a hunter assessing his prey. My heart was pounding as I took in the scene in front of me—I was about to spar with the Prince of Akureyrian. As I stroked the hilt of my sword, I willed away my thoughts until that eerie calm set in and I felt as light as the breeze.

My breathing slowed, and I looked him in the eyes—marveling at the glint of gold that highlighted his dark gaze. Torben tipped his head in a quick bow.

Torben lunged first, aiming for my chest. I effortlessly dodged and swung at him with my blade, but Torben lifted his powerful arm and blocked me. Leif hooted a cheer and the prince grunted as he dodged to avoid another brutal swing of my sword. As we fought, our steps were like a dance that had been perfectly choreographed and practiced a thousand times. My movements were nimble and controlled—the perfect complement to Torben's brutal power and strength.

The sound of metal against metal echoed off the mountain that loomed above the camp. I was vaguely aware that the guards had stopped cheering. Torben was one of the most famous warriors in Akureyrian, a prince who was rumored to never shy away from a battlefield and always walk away mostly unscathed, and yet he had still not gained the advantage. A smug smile spread across my face.

I moved with a quickness that was purely Fae. Although Torben's sword came down with incredible force, each time he struck I was able to move fast enough to gain a position of advantage.

There, I thought. When he stepped his foot out, he dropped his shoulder slightly—the movement was small, but it created distance between his shield and sword and offset his balance. I tucked my arms and swung around, landing on his left, and then swiftly jabbed my blade towards his neck while using the elbow of my unshielded arm to crash into his wrist, knocking his shield to the ground.

Silence.

Absolute silence surrounded us.

Torben looked from his shield to the sword pointed at his throat, his chest rising with each heavy breath before he lifted his head to meet my gaze. His brown eyes glittered with gold and as vibrant as a phoenix's wing. It felt like an eternity before he finally spoke.

"Holy gods," he breathed, "how in all the layers of hell did you learn to fight like that?"

"You dropped your shoulder, Your Highness." I smirked. "I can tell you and the general practice together."

Emil choked out a laugh and Leif looked on with his hands still planted on the top of his head, completely dumbfounded at what he'd just witnessed.

"Are we sure we want to send her to the infirmary, Your Highness?" Emil said as he rubbed his callused hand over his chin.

"I am happy to be your healer, Torb—Your Highness," I said, surprised at how easily I had almost called him by name. "If you'll excuse me, I'm going to go wash off the dust." And with that I turned towards the stream, leaving the prince and his Treyst to watch me go in stunned silence.

orben's shoulders must be aching. He had been rubbing his hand over one particular spot for the better part of the past hour. I couldn't fault him for being sore. Our fight had been incredibly physical—beautiful really. We'd matched each other's movements as if they had been the most natural thing in the world.

Flickers of light from the nearby fire illuminated the contours of his arms as he used a thumb to dig into the front of his shoulder. I found myself marveling at how large he was—all hard muscles shaped from decades of rough training. My cheeks flushed against my will as I remembered how it had felt to push against his strength. It was a wonder I had managed to hold my own. But as the Prince of Akureyrian had learned, speed and smarts would always be a valiant match for brutal strength.

I hadn't answered his question about how I had learned how to fight—and thankfully, he hadn't pressed me.

The sun had set, and the stars were bright and clear by the time we finally shuffled into the tent to sleep. Theo, who hadn't caught any of the fish, was stuck with the first watch. They had all decided that I was the only one who deserved to sleep all night.

Torben was lying next to me on his back with his hands tucked behind his head, his uneven breaths a contrast to the steady sounds coming from Emil and Leif. I wasn't convinced he was asleep, and it left me feeling bare and exposed. I had to remind myself to breathe, being pressed between powerful men in a small tent was not something I was used to.

"I wasn't embarrassed that you beat me," he whispered suddenly.

Interesting, I thought. But I somehow knew he was telling the truth.

"I know," I whispered back without opening my eyes.

I didn't need to open my eyes to know that Torben was smirking as he stared at the roof of the tent. His emotions seemed to permeate through the warmth that seeped from his body.

The sound of the breeze brushing against the side of the canvas tent was like a rhythmic purr that eventually lulled me towards sleep. My last thought before my eyes closed was of the sweet scent of cedar and vanilla that seemed to swirl around me in a familiar embrace.

The sun rose over the fjord in the distance, beams of light glittering on the surface of the water like gold. I had been up and out of the tent an hour before the sun peeked over the horizon. Leif was on watch, and I waited until I heard him walk to the far side of camp before I slithered outside and made my way to the stream. Even though I had washed last night, I craved the feeling of the bitterly cold water against my bare skin.

My feet turned to frozen weights as I waded into the water, carefully stepping along the larger rocks at the bottom of the stream to avoid slipping. Finally, I came across a flat rock in the center of the stream, and I crouched to submerge my chest and shoulders. The cold pierced my body as I worked to control my breathing—overriding the instinct to hyperventilate with each measured breath. My lungs burned and my skin froze. And the longer I sat, the more my mind became devoid of worry and fear and uncertainty.

My thoughts turned to my mother and father, wondering what they would think if they knew what I had gotten myself into. Most likely, my father, Steinar, would have held his breath as he forced a nervous smile. He would have been paralyzed with worry that I would do something unmannerly—like not yielding to the prince as we sparred. My mother, Liva, would have simply beamed with pride, her pale skin glowing from the vibrant hint of her magic.

If I focused, I could still picture their faces, although the clarity had started to fade over the decades. My parents had been warm and loving. Unlike most of the families in our class, they had been keenly involved in their daughter's life. Despite having tutors and nursemaids, my father would come to my room each night to tell me stories of adventure and about the magical creatures that roamed the lands and flew across the skies. My mother would walk with me through the forest near our home, taking care to call out the names of the flora that we passed.

My parents had been ancient in their own right. They had lived in Vogar for centuries and were incredibly proud of the region they called home. My mother would often say that my father knew more about the history of Vogar than any scholar or Keeper. She had always had a wild heart and even though her status dictated how she *should* act, she had rarely followed those rules. She was known to wear pants and enjoyed walking barefoot through the woods. While the women of the area scoffed at her behavior, it only made my father love her more.

It had taken decades for them to conceive a child and they made sure I felt cherished—until their final breaths.

Their deaths had been merciless. And no matter how many happy memories I revisited, thoughts of my parents always ended with the memory of how they had died—and how I hadn't been able to stop it. I doubted there would ever be a time in my immortal life that I would forget them. But if I did, I wondered if I would cease to feel the guilt and emptiness that burdened my every step.

The shock of the crisp air radiated across my skin as I stepped out of the stream—sending goosebumps from my toes to my bare neck. Glancing around to see if anyone was watching, I closed my eyes and welcomed a drop of my magic to the surface—willing the power to dry the beads of water that dripped down my body.

It was over in an instant, the magic receding as quickly as it had been summoned. But a hint of warmth remained, and I ran my cold hands over my face to quell the glow that lingered on my cheeks.

Thoughts of my mother often convinced me to touch my magic, the power was like a warm embrace that connected me to my bloodline. But as much as the magic was a comfort, it was also a reminder of how easily my world had come crashing down.

After tugging my shoes onto my freezing feet, I wrapped my cloak around myself and headed back towards camp. I was surprised to find Torben walking towards me down the short trail. His hair was wild as he worked to pull the longer section into a tight knot, exposing the shaved sides of his head. "It's freezing," I offered in greeting. "But I stayed in for five minutes… in case you would like to try to stay in longer."

"Well, I guess I'll see you in *six* minutes." The prince winked as he stepped past me and removed his cloak.

I laughed—typical Fae. But as he reached to pull his shirt off, I found my eyes lingering on his broad shoulders and muscular back. I was surprised to see a long scar that started at his shoulder and snaked down his rib cage. Not wanting him to catch me staring, I quickly averted my gaze. I wondered if healers had ever tried to help with the scaring—or if he had preferred to keep it as a reminder of whatever injury had caused it.

Back at camp, the three guards were busily packing their things and feeding the horses a final meal of dried grass and raw vegetables. Emil glanced up at me, his soft brown hair ruffled by the breeze, "There's bacon and bread over by the fire if you're hungry." I nodded in thanks, my stomach grumbling with anticipation of a hearty meal. "You know," Emil added, causing me to turn towards him, "the prince is one of the most skilled swordsmen I have ever known... and you could have killed him without breaking a sweat."

"It must have been beginner's luck," I said, shrugging.

"Aye? I doubt that." Emil smirked. "When we get back to Dalvin, you are welcome to come train with us anytime... just as long as you wait more than two minutes before walloping me in front of my soldiers."

"I can't make any promises. But I would like that, General. Thank you."

Torben arrived back at camp with his shirt still off, his chest beaming red from the sting of the cold water. It was impossible not to watch the drops of water trickle down his toned muscles. He had trimmed the shaved sides of his head and tied the longer section into a tight knot, making the strength in his jaw even more prominent. I dropped my eyes to my bread as the prince sat down next to me and leaned back on his arms, his bare chest now a foot away from me.

"I win," he said as he reached for a piece of bread then dipped it in the grease from the bacon.

I couldn't help but laugh. "Are you always this competitive?" I asked as I took another bite. "Because if you are, I worry that my new job as one of your healers may be busier than I expected."

Torben smirked. "Oh, you will see me *a lot*. The four of us are on a first-name basis with all the healers at this point. Leif was there four times in a single day once." His smile was brutally handsome as he bellowed a laugh.

"Well, I'm not on duty yet and you are going to catch hypothermia if you don't get dressed soon. And I doubt Emil wants to carry you through the mountain pass," I nagged, my voice rippling with playful annoyance.

Holy gods, I thought, *was I flirting with the Prince of Akureyrian?*

Torben laughed and reached for his cloak, using it to wipe beads of water from his chest before slipping back into his shirt. I looked up to see Emil watching us closely with an unreadable expression on his face.

"Well, my lady, if I die now your job will be *much* easier." He winked and then walked over to the tent to finish packing.

Yes, definitely flirting.

As I watched the prince, my hands swelled with a familiar feeling of warmth and power. Cursing under my breath, I rubbed them on my knees, willing the power to stay hidden below the surface. Since leaving Árnes, I had felt a stronger pull from my magic. I could deal with the prince discovering my heritage, I would find a way to explain that part of my history. But I fumbled at the thought of having to explain my magic. That, I knew, would change everything.

10

The mountain pass that stretched within the Innnes Mountains was truly breathtaking. Forged centuries ago with powerful magic to facilitate travel and trade between the northern and southern regions of the kingdom, the soft, meandering trail was a stark contrast to the rugged mountain surrounding it. My breath caught in my throat as I looked up at the rocky walls towering high above. It felt as if I had been swallowed by the gods and sent back to the core of some ancient world.

I looked in wonder at the view of the fjord as we climbed higher into the range. The blue-green water reflected the sunbeams that passed through an endless sky of white clouds as if the gods themselves were scattering the light across the water.

In the distance a panorama of rugged peaks and valleys stretched as far as I could see. The wind was bitterly cold, and the air had turned thin, but the ancient landscape seemed to whisper to me the further we rode, enticing me to continue into this vast unknown.

Torben whispered words of encouragement to Frigg as she navigated the steep switchbacks. *A strange prince indeed*, I thought, not for the first time.

"It looks like rock has fallen recently up ahead. We will go check it out before we pass." Emil's voice echoed off the wall of rock beside us. Torben held our horse back as the three guards went ahead. Torben stretched his arms overhead and then pulled his cloak up around his neck as the breeze whipped past us. His warm breath brushed the back of my neck, sending an electric shiver down my spine.

"After so many years with them, I have learned not to argue when they boss me around," Torben whispered as we watched the Treyst ride away. "They are like brothers to me. I've been telling them for decades that I see them as equals, and I've never paused to run into battle beside them… but they have never forgotten their duty as royal guards. And on the occasion that they boss me around, I've learned to listen. Come to think of it, it's kind of like the way *you* boss me around." His smirk was sinfully warm.

"They are not like other guards I have seen. All of them were insufferably pompous."

Torben's eyebrow peaked. "And exactly how many guards have you—"

A sudden rumbling reverberated through the narrow mountain pass, interrupting Torben's next thought as his ears twitched against the sound. The ground below trembled with such force that our teeth rattled. Panic flooded my bloodstream. Torben tightened his grip around my waist, clicked his tongue, and pulled the reins, willing the mare to turn and run. Frigg reared up in fury as a massive wall of rocks came crashing down towards us. My eyes shot up as the enormous piece of jagged earth tumbled down the side of the mountain.

"*Run!*" Emil screamed, his distant voice raw and desperate.

A thunderous roar filled my sensitive ears as we attempted to flee, the relentless sound of Frigg's hooves pounding against the rocky ground almost deafening. Cursing, I looked up as another massive boulder came crashing towards us. We would never outrun it. Closing my eyes to pray to whatever gods might be listening, I grabbed the reins, pulling Frigg to a stop as I jumped from the saddle and desperately willed my magic to the surface.

Time, sound, and space seemed to stop as I lifted my chest to the sky and reached my hands over my head, blasting my magic out towards the falling rock. I felt shaky and out of practice, but the blue dome of light stretched over us stronger than any man-made shield, glowing with each impact from the rock that fell overhead. The glimmer of light surrounded us like searing embers, the endless well of my power singing as I reached deeper inside myself. I had forgotten what it felt like to let my magic flow freely. My blood warmed and my head spun as the power spilled out of my hands.

When the walls stopped trembling, I pulled back on the endless flow of magic. I was panting with exhaustion by the time I dropped my hands—a faint blue light a lingering glow in my palm.

Once the magical veil had fallen, the dust from the rockfall swarmed around us. I grabbed my cloak to cover my mouth and nose with the fabric—the last thing I needed after surviving a rockslide was to choke to death on dust.

Torben was staring at me as he slowly dismounted. I dropped my hands to my side, forcing the weight of the magic to disappear.

It didn't matter, I knew I was still glowing.

"Holy gods, you *are* High Fae," he said quietly, "and your magic… your magic is *raw*?"

"We need to find the others," I said, brushing the dust from my pants. I couldn't meet his eyes. The smell of ether was still heavy in the air.

Torben walked over to me cautiously. "Kaari, do you have raw magic?" His voice was deep and firm and the cut of his jaw quivered as he worked to control his voice. When I didn't answer, he slowly reached for my hand, unafraid of the power I had just spilled. His hand tensed as he touched my skin, still warm with lingering magic. I cursed. My head was spinning. I did not have a choice—when faced with getting crushed under the rocks and dying as a very young immortal or using my magic and living, I decided to risk ruining a hundred years of hiding my secret.

"Yes," I huffed. "I have raw magic… and I promise I will explain later, but right now we need to keep moving."

The prince's eyes were wild, the brown in his iris was almost black as worry etched into his face. He shook his head as he looked at me. "There hasn't been a Fae with raw magic since Queen Maiken… and that was a thousand years ago."

A towering wall of rubble now stood where the path used to be. Torben and I had scrambled up the rock as much as we dared before turning back, not wanting to cause more rock to fall—especially if the others were already trapped. We had desperately listened for any sound from the Treyst, but each time we called for them my throat filled with bile as silence filled the space around us.

Torben was pacing and running his hands over the sides of his head. I couldn't imagine what he was feeling. His entire Treyst—likely gone. He looked as though he couldn't breathe. The fear and panic on his face was palpable.

"They were far enough ahead before the rock fell…." His voice trailed off, laced with desperation.

"They could still make it to the other side of the pass. We need to find another way around to get to them," I said, wanting to believe they were alright.

Torben was watching me intently as his eyes suddenly turned blank and unreadable. Within seconds, the dazed look was replaced with the bright eyes I had grown accustomed to. "They are alive. We need to go back to the camp and take the road around the fjord," he said. "Once we get around, we can head to the other end of the pass. That's where we will find them."

The conviction in his voice was heartbreaking.

"How do you know they'll be there?" I asked gently.

"Because Kaari Trygg, you aren't the only one with useful magic. Leif has the power of telepathy."

My eyes widened. I had never known anyone with the power to speak mind to mind. "He just *spoke* to you?"

"The message was faint, but I could hear him. We need to go."

"Are they *all* alive?"

"'All I could hear was, '*Alive, almost made it out, trapped now. Hurt.*' After that, I couldn't hear him anymore."

"Is that normal? To lose touch with him?" I was afraid to hear the answer.

"He may be trying to reserve his power, especially if he is hurt."

As he reached out to help lift me onto the horse, he slowly ran his fingers over the back of my hand. His eyes lingered on the faint blue light that glowed across my palm. "That's three times you have saved my life. If you keep up this pace, I'm going to lose count before we get back to Dalvin."

I rubbed my other hand through the loose strands of hair that were blowing around my face and gently squeezed his hand. "This time doesn't count," I said, forcing a smile. "Using magic is cheating."

11

The road around the fjord hugged the water's edge leaving only a narrow path for traveling. The rough water was deep green, and white caps sparkled across the surface like fireflies. The rugged terrain of the mountain range extended out into the peninsula making it impossible to cross any other way.

We stopped at our old camp to check our supplies and let Frigg settle—and quickly realized that the others had carried most of the provisions. Torben found several strips of jerky and a loaf of stale bread tucked into his pack in addition to his extra cloak and flint for starting a fire. All my belongings were accounted for since they had been strapped to Frigg.

Torben had not mentioned my magic again. The air felt thick with the questions he wasn't asking, and his shoulders seemed to ripple with tension. I would eventually have to give him answers. My reality had been locked in a vice for so long that I wasn't quite sure how to let anyone in—especially someone as powerful as the Prince of Akureyrian.

My parents had tried desperately to hide my magic, always fearful of what would happen if someone bent on power discovered my abilities. A power like mine had the potential to shape worlds and rewrite the course of history. In the end, that fear had come to fruition and cost my parents everything. In the last moments of their immortal lives, they had fought hard enough that I had escaped, their love shielding me like unbreakable armor.

"We will have enough to eat. Hopefully, the weather holds until we make it around the fjord." Torben looked towards the path around the peninsula as he stroked the side of his horse.

We had decided to start on foot to give Frigg a chance to rest. Whether we said it out loud or not, the effort of walking would be a good way to distract us from worrying about the others. The dirt road was wide, and patches of grass were scattered along the way. It appeared trade between the northern and southern parts of Akureyrian was not producing much traffic this way.

The silence was becoming unbearable. I took a breath, blinking my eyes towards the horizon. "I was just a child when I started to show signs of having raw magic," I said. Torben's head snapped towards me. "My father had typical Fae magic—swift and brutally strong. But my mother... my mother's power was more *wild*. She rarely let me see her magic but there were times when I would catch her glowing with her power.

"One day when I was outside playing in the garden a bee stung my arm. The pain was unbearable and before I knew what was happening, I felt the magic boiling over as it shot out from me. When I opened my eyes, the field I was standing in had been singed to dust. It wasn't *fire* exactly, just pure power." I paused as the memory washed over me. Torben kept silent.

"After that, my parents worked with me every day to try to teach me how to control it. My father had been a warrior, so he taught me how to control my body and mind. My mother understood the intensity of the magic and taught me how to keep it locked away. But the fear of being discovered was always there." My voice dripped with sadness even as I tried to tuck it aside. "When my parents died," I added, "I had no one left who understood my magic... so I ran away. Árnes was the safest place for someone like me. When you offered me the chance to live a normal life, I couldn't say no... but I'm starting to think I never should have left."

My eyes were damp, and my shoulders felt heavy as if my confession had released an immense burden. I hadn't told him everything, but it had been enough... for now.

The fine muscles of his face rippled as he clenched and unclenched his jaw. "You didn't have to tell me, but I'm glad you did... and Kaari, your magic might scare the shit out of me, but I would never force you to use it for my advantage." The golden specks in his eyes danced in the sun and somehow, I knew he was telling the truth.

By the time the sun started to set beyond the horizon, the temperature had dropped enough that I could see my breath in the air. We stopped near a small stream and tied Frigg up for the night. The ground was lush, and I found a flat, moss-covered, area to lie on—the spongy surface wonderfully soft under my aching joints.

I watched as Torben pulled off his heavier shirt, exposing a thin undershirt and the chiseled shape of his chest that rolled underneath. He folded the shirt into a tight square and handed it to me. "In case you need a pillow," he offered. It was a kind gesture. The type of unprompted kindness I wouldn't expect from a warrior prince. Then again, I hadn't met many warrior princes in my life.

"Thank you, but won't you be cold?"

"My cloak will keep the sting of cold off just fine. I'll sleep better knowing you're comfortable." I snorted at his blatant chivalry but accepted it all the same.

I kept my eyes on him as he finished laying out his extra cloak for us to sleep on. He certainly took care of himself. *You have seen plenty of attractive men in your life*, I told myself. The thought still stirred as I removed my boots and settled onto my side.

The crisp breeze coming down the mountain was bitter enough to force our bodies closer together for warmth, and we lay facing each other as if trying to read the thoughts and emotions that undoubtedly danced in our eyes. My eyes felt heavy with exhaustion, but I studied the prince as the last of the evening light caressed his face. My heart flipped when I realized he was studying me as well, and I held my breath when his hand gently touched my face.

A shiver went down my spine and I closed my eyes as the tips of his callused fingers traced the lines of my jaw, surprised at how easily I was surrendering to his touch.

"Have I told you that you're the strangest woman I have ever met?" His voice was barely a whisper. "I'm starting to think I would like to know everything about you, Kaari Trygg."

"Ha," I huffed though my voice was breathless. "I promise you, my life is not actually that exciting."

The prince grunted and lifted an eyebrow as he pulled his hand away, leaving a void where the warmth of his hand had been.

"You're the *prince.* I'm sure your life is much more interesting. Tell me about the Treyst. Do Emil and Theo have magic as well?"

"Ah, that is an interesting question." Torben adjusted himself so that his arm was supporting his head. "Emil has the power of tongues—meaning he can speak and understand *any* spoken language. And Theo's magic… is a little more complicated."

"That sounds ominous. I didn't know magic could be *complicated.*"

"Well, when you are as old as Theo, the normal rules don't always apply."

I got the sense that Torben didn't want to talk about Theo's magic. I made a mental note to ask once I knew if they were all safe.

"And what about *your* magic? The legends say you are quite powerful as well."

Torben laughed, "Oh aye? The legends. Well as with all legends, some are true, and others are fabricated."

"Alright, so no talk of magic. Tell me something the legends don't know about the Prince of Akureyrian."

"I'm betrothed to someone I can't stand to be around," he said blankly.

"You're *engaged*?" I blurted, pulling myself up to lean on my elbow. This bit of information had certainly not reached the far corners of Akureyrian.

He adjusted himself as well so that he still met my gaze. "My father has been trying to ensure an alliance with Birkeria. Last month, after returning from a trip across the border, he informed me that he had struck a deal and my engagement to the princess was the price he had paid." He paused as if collecting his thoughts. "Princess Merja is beautiful and powerful and absolutely *vile*. So, I'm sure it will be a wonderful marriage."

Despite his obvious sarcasm, I caught a glimpse of sadness in his eye that made my heart roar. I reached out and gently stroked the back of his hand with my thumb. "I'm sorry," I whispered, "she sounds like a bitch."

Torben choked out a deep laugh as he rolled onto his back. "You are an excellent judge of character, Kaari Trygg."

"What would she think if she could see you sleeping under the stars with a healer from Árnes?" I teased. I couldn't help it.

Torben grunted again but the corner of his mouth pinched into a smile. "I'm sure she would be furious."

"Good." I adjusted my hips to move away from a pebble that pressed into my side, but the movement pressed me closer against his solid form. He was warm and his cedar and vanilla scent were nearly intoxicating. I bit the inside of my cheek as my heart skipped.

"Well, I will be sure to tell her you said that."

I watched as his eyes darted across my face. It had been a long time since anyone had looked at me with such intensity. The feeling was slightly unsettling, but I found myself sinking into the closeness.

"We should sleep," I forced myself to say. "We will want to leave by first light to head for the other side of the pass."

Torben chuckled under his breath and shifted his hips to create distance I despised. It was like he knew that I was slowly coming undone.

I woke several hours later. The sky was painted with the first strokes of sunlight that danced across the water in the fjord. Despite the crispness in the air, I found that I was delightfully warm. I had pressed myself closer to Torben at some point during the night and his broad chest was like a wall of heat behind me. His hand resting atop the curve of my hip had me jolting awake. The sensation sending a shiver down my spine, all the way to my toes. After so many years of solitude, the feel of Torben's body next to mine was as blissful as a warm day in Värme after a cold Kall— and utterly improper.

I bit my lip as I tried to decide whether I should try to move out of his grasp or close my eyes and pretend to be asleep. I turned slightly, noting how his face was set in a quiet scowl. The sides of his cheeks tensed, and his mouth twitched.

Goddess above.

He was dreaming.

How many women in the kingdom had dreamed of the chance to lay next to the Crown Prince?

I felt a rush of anger that he was being forced to marry against his will. Arranged marriages were common among nobility, especially when there was a chance to gain political advantage. Rarely did the nobility in Akureyrian marry for love, unless of course, they found their mate. This type of bond was more intense than any other. The mating bond of the Fae was set by the gods.

This was the type of love my parents had shared, a bond so strong that once they had both acknowledged it, their fate had been sealed. This connection was considered a sacred thing—something not even a king could break. Could Torben ever find love with the Princess of Birkeria? Or would he be subjected to an immortal life with someone he detested?

The Princess of Birkeria. I choked down bile at the thought of that awful country. Growing up in Vogar, I had heard about the horrors of neighboring Birkeria and had met many mortals, and Fae, who had escaped the brutal rule. The choppy waters of the Krossá canal that separated Akureyrian from Birkeria had claimed many lives as desperate refugees attempted to reach the peace of Vogar. My family had employed several Birkerian refugees in our estate, all of them would have rather died than ever return to their homeland.

Torben shifted in his sleep, and as his hand slid down the curve of my hip to my waist. His mouth curved into a dreamy smile. Perhaps, through this marriage, Torben would be able to influence change for Birkeria. In our short time together, I had only known him to be kind and fair, which made the travesty of his engagement even more heartbreaking.

Crawling out from his embrace, I breathed in the crisp air and willed the chill to calm my nerves. The early morning was still cloaked in darkness which made it easy to sneak away. Frigg was quietly munching on tall reeds of grass and neighed lazily as I approached. I patted the mare on the rump as I walked by and promised to bring back any herbs I found near the stream.

The stream turned out to be more of a brook—the water babbling over the rocks with relentless force. It was delightfully cold, and I knelt next to the bank so I could drink from my cupped hands.

As I watched the water roll over the smooth moss-covered stones, I was reminded of the stream that had passed through my family's estate in Vogar. As a child, my mother had been known to reject any attempts by the maids to fill her washtub, preferring to do all her bathing in the glacier-fed stream. I supposed that was where I developed my preference for bathing in cold water—although the thought of having running water in Dalvin was quite appealing. After splashing my face one last time and grabbing a handful of nettles and dandelions for Frigg, I dried myself off and headed back to the camp.

When I returned to the small cave, Torben was awake and kneeling on the mossy ground as he pulled on a clean shirt. I watched as he reached behind his head to pull his hair back, his smooth skin seeming to glow as the first beams of light stretched across the nearby hill.

Without pausing to think, I walked up behind him, gathered his hair between my hands, running my fingers through the length of it. His shoulders tensed as I twisted a section into a tight braid along the side of his head. Once the braid was set, I pulled the longer section into a tight knot.

The gesture had been surprisingly intimate, and I found my heart racing by the time I finished tying the string. The side of Torben's mouth pulled into a surprised smile as he ran his hand over the braid. "Let me get this straight," he said as he lifted a finger. "You are a master healer, an expert with a sword, you wield raw magic, *and* you can tie a warrior's plait? What else can you do?"

I cursed, feeling my cheeks blush. Every compliment felt like a blooming rose that threatened to fill my heart with life.

The air rippled with a sense of anticipation as we packed our things and readied Frigg for the day's travel. The mare had settled after the scare on the mountain and was now happily snacking on the apple Torben had given her. We would finish making our way around the edge of the fjord by late afternoon and would have until dusk to try to find the others. My chest tightened at the thought of what would happen if we couldn't find the guards, but I shook my head and swallowed down that fear.

Torben came up behind me as I was packing the last of my things on Frigg's back. As he reached around me to tighten the straps, he gently placed his other hand on the small of my back to support himself. The contact made my stomach flip. He must have sensed my tension because he quickly pulled his hand away as he reached for the other strap.

I pulled myself into the saddle, my cheeks now flush with color, and Torben lifted himself to sit behind me. At a click of his tongue, Frigg burst into a gallop. The path around the narrow inlet of the sea was tucked against the lush cliffs that formed the peninsula. Despite the constant breeze, the air felt ancient, as if it was constantly supplied by the breath of the gods.

"Believe it or not, the air in Dalvin is even saltier than it is here," Torben said breaking the heavy veil of silence. "And when the wind is right, the ocean breeze fills the halls of the palace."

"I have missed the smell of salty air."

"I really hope… I hope that you'll be happy in Dalvin."

I turned my body to meet his gaze and could have sworn his grip tightened slightly around my waist.

"I'm glad I came with you. And I think I will be happy once I find my purpose."

Hundreds of small waterfalls were scattered along the cliffs around the fjord. As the sun rose higher, it kissed the sprays of water and thousands of prisms seemed to dance across the falls. I felt myself getting sucked into the thrum of the wild around me, and my magic danced under my skin.

By late morning, we had made it around the curve of the peninsula. Torben had pushed Frigg faster down the road, knowing that once we reached the other side of the pass, we would be close enough to search for the others. Small bridges had been constructed to connect the land between the passages of water and I could see several of them along the road ahead.

I whispered sweetly to Frigg in the Old Language, gently coaxing the mare to cross the rickety bridges, while Torben listened intently, trying to follow along.

"Did you grow up speaking the Old Language?" Torben finally asked.

"I suppose," I answered briskly. I did not want to have *that* conversation. "Tell me how Leif's magic works. What does it sound like when he *speaks* to you?"

Torben responded with a low grunt in his throat, clearly annoyed that I had changed the subject. "Leif's magic allows him to reach into the mind of another. Once he's there, he is capable of sending messages... or stealing information. The gift can be incredibly powerful and can make a difference on the battlefield, even though most warriors are trained to block such a blind intrusion. I have heard Leif speak through his channels for decades... but yesterday was the first time I ever heard panic in his tone." Torben ran his hands over his head. "I'm going to find them." His voice was a low growl, his eyes burning with resolve.

Approaching the end of the bluff, we stopped so we could walk, finding it easier to look for any signs on the ground that his friends had been here. The mountains loomed overhead, and I smelled the rock dust that coated the ground. I willed my breath to stillness, my empty lungs forcing the fluttering in my stomach to subside.

I gasped when the opening to the pass came into view. The entire entrance was blocked by the massive rocks. Torben looked back at me, his eyes wild with fear and desperation. I followed him as he ran to the rocks and began scrambling up the jagged pile. We had to reach the top to see how far down the pass the rocks had fallen—only then would we know if his Treyst was still alive.

The Fae were immortal but there were certainly ways for them to die. And getting crushed by a landslide was certainly a way to end an immortal life.

Once he reached the top, Torben quickly started searching below. The sun was starting to set but he would still be able to make out the details of the rock. "There," he shouted. Beyond the next section of rubble, a white tunic hung like a flag on a ragged piece of rock.

I had already started following the path up the rock when I saw his shoulders suddenly sag—in relief, or grief, I wasn't sure.

"I can make it over there," I panted.

"Wait here, I'll go see what I can find." Torben looked at me with forceful eyes.

"To all hells with that," I barked. "I'm coming in case they are injured."

We had reached another massive pile of debris when a shout in the distance made us freeze in our tracks. Torben called out, his voice booming off the walls of the surrounding cliff and mountain wall. A familiar voice returned his call and sent us scrambling faster until we reached the top of another pile. Torben swore under his breath as we looked down and saw Leif, shirtless and covered with rock dust.

The guard looked terrible, but he was alive. Torben called down to him and Leif whooped with weary excitement. As we made it down the last of the rocks, we realized why Leif hadn't attempted to climb out. Emil and Theo were sitting against a large rock, both covered in blood. But when they looked up and saw us, exhausted smiles erupted on their faces.

Leif let out a strangled sigh of relief as Torben hugged him before racing to check on Theo and Emil.

"Are you hurt?" I asked Leif.

"No. I'm fine. Help them," he pleaded as he looked back to his friends. I turned and ran to the others.

Emil was covered in the most blood, so I started with him. Torben was holding a piece of a torn cloak against his left side. I reached down and lifted his tunic, cursing as I scanned the jagged rip across his ribs.

"Gods in hell," I cursed as the trickle of blood pooled on the waist of his pants. I quickly stripped off the cloak I had wrapped around myself and pressed it to his ribs. Emil looked at me with a dimpled smile.

"It's almost closed… you should have seen it when Leif pulled me from the pile." I rolled my eyes and pressed the cloak harder against his chest.

I turned to Theo, needing to assess his injuries to determine who would require the most immediate healing. Theo's leg was bent at an impossible angle—clearly broken. Fae magic could heal broken bones but not when the bone was twisted like a vine.

My mind was racing, there was no way to carry Theo out unless we came back with a stretcher. Emil would be fine once I stitched his chest. But all of that hinged on us getting Theo out of the mangled mountain pass and back to my supplies.

Unless I used magic.

I could use healing magic. That wouldn't be too suspicious.

But I also needed to do *something* to move the rock out of the way. My power roared under my skin as I imagined blasting the rock out of the way so we could pass through. It would be a dangerous show of power—there would be no doubt that raw magic flowed through my veins if I blasted the rock *and* used healing powers. But my healer instincts were pushing me to act, even if it was foolish.

"I can get them out of here," I whispered to Torben, already starting to tug on my magic.

He reached out and grabbed my wrist, his broad hand easily wrapping me in a firm hold. "You don't need to do that," he said. "Let me be the one to save the day—this one time."

My eyes glossed with confusion as the earth around us began to vibrate. Torben's bronze skin had started to glow. The smell of ether permeated from him as he closed his eyes and extended his hands, releasing streams of light that shot towards the piles of rocks.

I stood in shock as a glowing orb of white light grew between the prince's palms. With a thrust, Torben's magic slammed into the massive stones, pushing them out of the way. The sound of boulders scraping across the jagged path was like thick rolls of thunder. Rock and dust swirled through the air, and I could only imagine how powerful the prince must be. With a breath, Torben dropped his hands as the last pile of rock shifted enough for us to pass.

I whipped my head around to look at him, the message in my eyes was clear, *the legends about your power were* not *fabricated.*

"Later," was all he said as he passed by me on his way to help Theo stand, his lips twitching into a sly smile.

It seemed the prince and I both had secrets worth protecting.

Once we made it back to camp, I stitched the wound on Emil's chest. The general was dangerously pale, and I had silently prayed that he would pass out before I started threading the needle under his skin. To my dismay, he just gritted his teeth as I cleaned the skin and approximated the edges. Thankfully, the bleeding stopped soon after the wound was closed. Emil had nodded his head to show his satisfaction with my needlework, still gritting his teeth through the residual pain.

While not life-threatening, Theo's damaged leg still proved to be more complicated than Emil's torn skin. I needed Torben's help to pull his leg back into place while Leif held him down. The snapping sound reverberated off the stone cliffs as we worked to set the bone. Theo was exhausted and would have to replete his magic before he was able to start healing everything that was broken, but at least the leg was straight again.

Leif had several minor scratches that had mostly healed thanks to the Fae blood flowing through his veins, but I still gave him a salve to prevent infection and help reduce any scarring. Once they were all resting, I went over to where Torben was gathering firewood. I hadn't decided if I was mad that he hadn't told me how powerful he was when he learned about my raw magic. "Well, I guess now I know why you understand magic like mine," I growled.

Torben squared his chest, standing close enough that I could feel his breath on my cheek. "First of all, I don't think of my magic as being anything special... not like yours. My magic is not *raw* it's just strong. And second of all, I wasn't *hiding* my magic, I just don't use it unless I need to. I have felt what your magic is capable of, and my magic is barely a drop of what flows through you."

"I saw you blast through an entire mountain pass! How can you say you don't have raw magic?"

"Powerful magic is not the same as raw magic, Kaari. Magic like yours can be wielded into *any* type of power. For me, my magic is very powerful, but it is only the power of force. I can't access any of the other Fae magics beyond the basics."

I cursed under my breath, shaking my head, and closing my eyes. This was why I had smelled ether on him when we first met. The aromatic scent was only released when the most powerful magics were used.

"Kaari." His voice was deep as he looked at me, slowly reaching out to pull me towards him. "Thank you for saving my friends." He gently touched his forehead to mine and let out an exhausted breath, releasing all the fear he had been holding. The contact sparked goosebumps that spread down my legs like wildfire. The incendiary warmth seemed to flow through him. It was no wonder he had kept me warm last night.

Another realization hit me suddenly and my eyes shot to his. "You knew that I was going to use my magic to get them out, and you knew that if I did, they would all discover my secret... so you used yours instead?"

"Something like that," he said with a quiet laugh as he slowly pulled away. "It's your secret to share. You can tell them when you're ready."

I watched as he walked back to his Treyst and clapped Emil on the shoulder before sitting down next to Theo. A chill in the breeze sent goosebumps over my skin and I wrapped my arms around myself. He couldn't know how much it meant to me that he was giving me the choice. Deep in my core, my ancient power rumbled as if it had been invited to wake after a long slumber.

Sitting around the fire, the guards told us what had happened in the mountain when the rocks began to fall and how they had found a fallen boulder to hide under as the chaos unfolded around them. They had not been able to save the horses and had set them free to make the run on their own. My heart pulled at the thought and hoped that somehow, they had escaped.

Torben explained the trek we had taken around the fjord road and grumbled that he would be allocating resources to fix several of the dilapidated bridges we had crossed. As the evening went on, despite the lingering injuries, they eased into their familiar banter, and everyone seemed to breathe a collective sigh of relief that we were back together.

Torben and I found a soft patch of grass on the far side of the fire and used my cloak to cover the mossy ground. I had sloshed it around at the water's edge, trying my best to get the blood stains out. It was still slightly damp, but it would have to do.

"Shall we leave you two alone?" Leif smirked, nodding his head to where Torben and I had set up our shared sleep mat. I felt my cheeks flush, realizing I hadn't thought twice about sleeping next to him.

"Oh aye, I certainly prefer her company to yours." Torben was using the bottom of his shirt to wipe rock dust from his face. "If you haven't noticed, she is the only one here who doesn't smell like two days of sweat and blood."

"I can't argue with that logic." Leif chuckled, stretching his arms overhead, smelling his armpit in the process. "Definitely a good choice. Are we going to draw straws to see who is going to help Theo take a piss?"

"I do not need help," Theo grumbled, rolling his eyes, but I could see the way his jaw tensed as he tried to shuffle around our small camp. It must be incredible painful to walk around on his still broken leg.

"Can I check your leg again?" Theo tensed as I approached. "I might be able to help."

"I'll be able to heal it soon enough. I've had to mend plenty of broken bones in my life." And then seeming to remember basic manners, he added, "Thank you for the offer."

I stared at him for a few moments, hoping I could break his resolve with my gaze. Instead, I felt myself being swept into the intense pools of his ocean blue eyes. There was something so enchanting about them, as if they held all the secrets from history and a prophecy of tomorrow. I broke the stare first, not trusting where I would end up if I kept meeting his gaze. He grumbled softly and turned to walk— hobble—down the path towards privacy.

The ground was soft and cool and did wonders to cushion my aching muscles. I hadn't realized how sore I was from the days of riding and hours of scrambling up the fallen rocks. The glow from the fire warmed my cheeks and I pulled my cloak up to my chin as the quiet around me seemed to swallow me whole. My eyes were heavy with exhaustion. But just as my breathing began to slow with the steadiness of sleep, Torben crawled into the spot next to me, sighing heavily.

I wondered if this was the first time the prince had come so close to losing any of his Treyst. I figured they had all fought in The War fifty years ago—the ribbon-like scar that snaked across the prince's back was a tell-tale mark of the brutality of war. I shuddered as I imagined Torben and his men fighting against the Birkerian invasion that had nearly crushed the capital of Dalvin. Although the invasion was over after three brutal weeks of bloodshed and magic, it had taken a decade for the city to be rebuilt to its former glory.

Torben's breathing had slowed, and I watched the steady rise and fall of his chest. The prince's magic had been an unwavering blast of power, capable of moving the scrambled rock that had fallen onto the trail. The power of force, while not raw magic, could certainly be shaped into various forms with devastating effects.

Was he the type of prince, I wondered, who would use that power for good?

By first light, everyone was awake and starting to shuffle around the small camp. Emil's wound had closed neatly—although he was still slightly pale from the blood loss. Theo's leg was straight again thanks to the splint we had made from two large sticks, but he would certainly be the one on horseback for the journey to Dalvin.

When it was time to move, Emil and Torben lifted Theo's muscular body onto Frigg. The mare huffed as he settled into place—his weight alone was likely comparable to mine and Torben's combined. He begrudgingly let me rewrap the splint so the bone stayed straight and accepted a piece of willow bark to chew on to help with the pain.

It was still two days to Dalvin on horseback... and we only had one horse. Luckily, there were several villages on the way where we would hopefully be able to buy more, but the closest village was half a day's walk from our camp.

We settled into a rhythm as we walked the winding road that would lead us to Dalvin. And the closer we got, the more the anticipation of my new life started to weigh on me.

"I keep thinking about that garmr." Emil was cleaning his sword as he walked, his gaze on the horizon. "How many times have you seen them?" The question surprised me, Emil, like Theo, had not said much to me since we first met in my cabin.

"In the Holvik Woods? A fair amount. Especially when I had to go into the denser part of the forest." A shudder crept up my spine. I had encountered undercreatures for most of my life, but there had always been a comfort in knowing that I could escape them if I crossed the border of the Woods. It seemed that was no longer the case.

"Can you imagine what it was like when those things roamed free?" Leif's eyes were wide. "I'll take my chances with the dragons in Birkeria."

Theo scoffed and shook his head.

"You disagree?" Leif asked.

"The undercreatures were bred to destroy us. At least the dragons could be tamed."

"But the dragons disappeared from Akureyrian around the time the undercreatures were locked within the Woods." I had always been relieved that the dragons were gone long before I was born. I couldn't imagine constantly worrying about being scorched from above.

"Aye, but they still rule the skies in Birkeria." Theo glanced to the sky as if he expected one of the beasts to fly overhead.

"My mother always said the dragons left Akureyrian in their grief," Leif said.

"Because the undercreatures were banished?" I hadn't heard that before. I only knew they disappeared around the time the wards were erected to keep the undercreatures within the Holvik Woods.

"No," Theo said firmly. "They grieved the loss of Queen Maiken."

A chill went up my spine. Something had shifted in Theo's tone. I didn't know him well enough to read him, but his sapphire eyes dug into me like a pitchfork to firm ground. I had a thousand questions—but he didn't look like he was in the mood for any of them.

The smell of manure wafted towards us as we approached the first village. *At least we know they have livestock,* I thought.

Emil and Leif had volunteered to go ahead to see about securing horses and supplies. They returned smiling an hour later, saying they found a farmer who had gladly offered three of his horses to the crown. They would be saddled and ready within the hour.

We took the back road to the farm, not wanting to draw too much attention to our battered crew. The homestead was quaint with a sprawling field where horses and cows grazed in long grass. The farmer, a lesser Fae who was starting to show signs of age, had a sun-kissed face that was warm and welcoming. His wife, a full-figured mortal, was stirring a strong-smelling stew over the fire as we walked inside.

It was impossible not to salivate at the smell of onions and garlic that filled the small space. The couple bowed deeply as Torben entered their home and the woman scurried around to present bowls of steaming soup, insisting that we sit and eat while her husband finished readying the horses.

The stew was delectable. The thick broth tasted of carrots, potatoes, and herbs. I had to pace myself as I inhaled it and then used a crusty piece of bread to soak up the grease at the bottom of my empty bowl.

The woman had been thoroughly concerned about Emil and insisted he eat three heaping servings and a thick piece of jerky before we left. She finally nodded her head in approval as the color started to show again on his cheeks. When the farmer came back to tell us the horses were ready Torben gave them a small bag of coins that likely amounted to a small fortune. They tried to protest, saying it was double what the horses were worth, but Torben simply smiled at them, telling them that their kindness was worth more than he could pay in coin. The farmers bowed deeply, clasping their hands together in thanks.

Once again, I marveled at the way Torben interacted with the people in his kingdom. He was gracious and kind. There was no air of superiority or authority when he spoke to them.

He was not at all what I imagined a prince would be like.

With four new horses, a pack full of food, and full stomachs, we started down the dirt road towards Dalvin. Frigg had bristled when Torben tried to ride her without me, so I mounted her while Torben rode one of the new steeds. Leif joked that Torben might be Prince of Akureyrian, but I had become the queen of Frigg's heart.

"Ekki geraa haenn afbrýðisamanna," I whispered to Frigg—*don't make him jealous.* Frigg shook her head and jumped into a quick gallop. I laughed under my breath as I passed Torben, my hair blowing wildly in the wind.

The scenery changed as we headed south. Rolling hills covered with lush moss and grasses seemed to spread for miles, and we passed countless shimmering lakes and rivers. The landscape was wild, and I breathed in the scents of life that were brimming around me.

After several hours of riding, Torben came up alongside me. The knot in his hair had come loose and the brown strands blew across his tan face. I didn't miss the look on his face as he passed Theo—concern and something like pity darting across his gaze. My eyebrows pinched together as I said, "I could heal his leg. I am a healer after all, and for all they know I have a healer's magic—they don't need to know about the rest... for now."

"An average healer would not be able to mend a break like that." Torben's eyes rested on Theo—a deep grimace spread across his otherwise handsome features. It was clear he was in pain from riding horseback with a broken leg. "Are you sure? They will know you are High Fae. Even if you only use a little magic," Torben said blankly.

"Yes… besides, I'll go crazy if I have to listen to him whine for another two days." Perhaps it was the recent brush with death, or the fact that I had spent more time with Torben and his Treyst than I had spent with anyone in a long time, either way I felt like I could trust them. Perhaps knowing I was High Fae would help them to understand me better.

Torben whistled to the group and told them we would stop at the next stream to water the horses and eat a meal. In the distance, jagged peaks glittered with flowing waterfalls that fed the endless supply of streams that scattered the land. Everything felt ancient and raw. The misty air that blew off the waterfalls seemed to whisper the secrets of the past and warnings for the future.

When we stopped, I quickly went to check Theo's leg. He groaned deeply as Leif helped him off his horse.

"*Djöfulmi*," I cursed under my breath.

Theo's eyes went wide. "*Talarðun gamlai tungoumálið?*" he whispered with shock.

"Yes," I huffed, "I speak the Old Language. But right now, we need to talk about your leg." A purple hue now tinted his toes. The swelling was significant.

The harrowing twist of the bone was increasing pressure as time passed without being set properly. "It's not healing properly, and I worry the pain is just going to get worse. You could be unconscious by the time we reach a healer in Dalvin."

Theo's eyes glossed over as he gulped down a breath. Despite his brutal strength and experience with battle wounds, his magic had not been able to mend this type of break.

"Lucky for you, I don't just make tinctures and salves." I paused, glancing at Torben to find reassurance in his eyes. "I would like to heal your leg, Theo."

Theo's eyes were wide, protest brimming as he scanned my face. For a moment I thought he would refuse, but he nodded and gritted his teeth.

I knelt next to his mangled leg and closed my eyes. It felt as if the air was slowly sucked from the expansive field. The grasses that had flowed rhythmically with the endless breeze suddenly drooped as the wind faded. I reached deep into my well of magic—the place that very few had ever seen me access. Warmth crept into my chest as I pulled on my power and, as if instructing a living thing, told it exactly what I needed it to do.

The orb that grew in my hands was crystal blue and it pulsed as I held my hands out over his leg. Leif and Emil cursed under their breath and Theo's eyes widen impossibly further as I started to drag the orb across the broken bones. He bit down and his face contorted into a feral grimace, as if he could feel the bones and ligaments resetting as I pulled on the string of my magic. The smell of ether filled the air as the orb receded and I opened my eyes, gasping slightly as I caught my breath.

I felt them stare at me with bewilderment.

It was Leif who broke the silence. "A healer indeed," he said before releasing a low whistle.

"Now can you please stop whining?" I said, looking at Theo with an affectionate smile and clapping him on the shoulder.

Theo shook out his foot and ran his callused hands down the straight shape of his leg. Color had already started to flush to his toes as the blood flow returned. To everyone's amazement, he was able to stand without assistance, a slight limp the only sign that his leg had been broken moments before.

Theo's blue eyes seemed to pierce into mine. He was strikingly handsome. His sandy brown hair was just long enough to brush across his thick eyebrows, highlighting the scar on his right cheek and shading his cobalt eyes that watched me so intently. "Thank you," he said as he exhaled, his voice low and sincere, a hint of vulnerability breaking through his otherwise composed demeanor.

Emil shuffled his feet behind us, his protective gaze set on Torben. I imagined he was wondering if the prince had realized what this meant about my heritage. Torben simply nodded at his general. "I knew there was a reason I asked her to come with us."

They knew I was High Fae. They knew I possessed healer magic. How long would it take before I was forced to show them the extent of the power that flowed through my veins? And what would happen when I did?

15

Ttraveling was much easier with Theo's leg mended and we started to make up lost time by the next day. The anticipation of reaching Dalvin in the morning weighed like a heavy stone in my stomach.

The night before, I had asked Emil to spar, desperately needing to release some energy. He had lasted longer than our first match, but after several minutes, I knocked him onto his ass and pointed my sword at his throat. He had been quick to blame his recent blood loss, but I knew I would have won either way.

The guards mostly rode together as they started planning our approach to the capital. They had debated using one of the secret tunnels to avoid onlookers, not wanting the crowds to see the prince and his royal guard in such a state of disarray. I had enthusiastically voiced my approval of this plan as discussions unfolded—I too did not feel ready to meet a crowd.

By nightfall, the city could be seen in the distance—still far enough away that the torchlights surrounding the towers of the royal palace looked like the sparkle of fireflies. *This* was going to be my home. The sprawling city seemed to glow as the twinkling lights from thousands of windows dazzled in the night. I could remember brief images of times I had visited the city with my parents. But that had been before the Birkerian invasion and before the city had been destroyed and rebuilt.

My mind wandered like a leaf in the wind. What would my days be like once we arrived? What type of ailments and injuries would I have to treat as a palace healer? Would I still see Torben and the Treyst?

My stomach flipped and I was surprised to find myself with a genuine sense of hope that I would still see them after we returned.

The farmer had given us a large tarp that we used to create a makeshift tent for the night. We had all taken trips to the stream to wash ourselves and our clothes, hoping to look somewhat presentable when we arrived at the palace. When it was my turn to see to my needs, I walked down to the stream carrying my muslin dress to change into after I washed. I figured I shouldn't arrive at the palace feigning to be a healer while dressed in a tunic, tight pants, and worn leather boots—with a sword strapped to my back.

The water in the stream was surprisingly comfortable and deep enough that I could easily waded in enough to cover my chest. I untied the strings that held my braids and let long waves of my hair dip in the clear water.

The snap of a branch had me spinning around in an instant as a tall figure approached through the surrounding brush.

"Are you lost, Your Highness?" I barked as I covered my chest with my hands.

His eyes darted to my chest before slapping a hand over his eyes and turning around. I rolled my eyes and huffed out a laugh—*typical man*, I thought. "Can I help you?" I hissed.

Torben still had his back to me, the contours of his broad shoulders gleaming under his damp shirt. "Kaari, I don't know what it will be like when we get back... but I was hoping it would be alright if I came to visit you... and not just when I have an injury that needs mending." His voice was surprisingly breathless.

"I would like that very much, Torben. Is there a reason you couldn't wait until I was dressed to tell me that?"

He turned his head slightly, still playfully covering his eyes, and I could see his mouth pinch into a crooked smile. "You have a strange affinity for freezing water, Kaari Trygg."

"I always have. And do you normally have an affinity for sneaking up on people while they are bathing?"

"Not usually. I guess I just wanted to see if you actually *enjoy* the freezing water. I can see now that you do."

"Indeed. Now if you don't mind."

"Of course. Sorry for the intrusion."

It didn't feel like an intrusion. It felt welcoming and familiar, like being wrapped in the worn quilt I had left in Árnes—and left me feeling breathless.

"I'll see you back at camp," I whispered. I was already looking forward to the next time he might come to visit.

16

The entrance to the tunnel was hidden deep in a wooded area outside the city walls. My palms tingled and I had the sense that the ancient iron door blocking the way was protected by some kind of magical veil that allowed selective access. It was decorated with swirling patterns that looked like the night sky, and the hinges groaned with age as Emil opened it to reveal a dark tunnel. The smell of damp earth surrounded us as we started down the path, Emil leading the way with a single torch. Leif had gone ahead to bring the horses to the stable and Theo had ominously grumbled about *needing to take care of something*. Even without them, the space felt cramped—I couldn't imagine passing through the tunnel with all four warriors. Still, I tucked myself close to Emil and Torben. They didn't seem bothered by the eeriness of the cramped space, I guessed this was not the first time they had used it to sneak back into the city.

The passage twisted and turned the further we went, the ancient stone walls seemed to whisper with the secrets of those who had passed through over the centuries. My mind wandered as I thought of the Fae who had built this tunnel. By the looks of the door and the ancient iron support beams, I guessed it was hundreds—if not thousands—of years old. If these walls could tell stories, I could only imagine what they might reveal. I wondered what landmarks were above us as we ventured deeper under the city. Torben had told me that it would take about half an hour to walk the length of the tunnel until we would finally reach the door into the palace.

Once we made it to the palace, Torben would be expected to greet King Havard in the great hall and provide an overview of his trip to the northern region. It was at this encounter, that Torben would also introduce me to the king.

I had never met a king.

Would he question me about my past? Would I have to demonstrate my skills as a healer? Or would he trust his son's judgement? Goddess above, I didn't know if *I* trusted the prince's judgement.

The lump in my throat was almost unbearable and for a moment I felt like I couldn't breathe. A warm hand settled onto the small of my back and I looked up to see Torben walking next to me. "We're almost there. There is a stairwell around the next bend that will bring us in through the library," he said gently. He had pulled his hair back into a high knot which made the tension in his jaw more pronounced as the shadows from the torch danced across his face. Though I had to fight through decades of instinct, I did not pull away from his touch.

A few moments later, our footsteps echoed as we scaled the steps, and it seemed as if we all held our breath as we reached the door at the top. Emil looked through a small pinhole to check that no one was on the other side, then pushed his shoulder into the door until it slowly opened.

I gasped as I stepped inside, overwhelmed by the sight of so many books, manuscripts, and scrolls. The library was bigger than anything I had ever seen. Countless aisles of shelves seemed to stretch endlessly through the cavernous room. How many lifetimes would it take to read them all?

We skirted around the edge of the room, heading for the door that would lead to the rest of the palace. I felt myself dragging my feet, not wanting to leave without devouring the pages all around me. I breathed in the smell of leather bindings and worn pages, wishing I could bottle the scent and carry it with me. I owned exactly five books in Árnes. One was a farmer's manual that one of the mortals had gifted me after I healed an ulcer on his foot. It was outdated by at least a century, but the floral drawings were meticulous, and it had taught me how to dry herbs without them going brittle. Three of them were mediocre novels that I had read a dozen times each. The last was a collection of faerie tales—written in the Old

Language—the only one I had managed to fit in my travel bag.

"This is your home now, Kaari. You are welcome to come here whenever you like." Torben's whispered words were as warm as his shoulder as it brushed against mine.

I wanted to thank him, but my voice caught in my throat. Realization crashed through me like a thunderstorm—this was my home. I managed to nod and hoped he couldn't see the mist coating my eyes.

Rounding a corner, we entered the hallway that led to the throne room. We found Leif and Theo waiting for us and they fell into line as we walked the hallway that was feeling more like a gauntlet. Emil walked behind Torben, and Leif and Theo walked with me several paces behind. "I look like a godsdamn prisoner being escorted to my sentencing," I mumbled.

Leif winked. "I promise that your room will be *much* nicer than the dungeons." I rolled my eyes.

The door to the throne room was constructed from a massive piece of glittering gold, decorated with an elaborate scene that had been etched into the soft metal. I could have studied the remarkable detail for hours. The image of a doe drinking from a babbling stream danced with life, but Torben squared his shoulders and pushed the door open.

The massive hall was filled with light pouring in from expansive windows that lined the back wall. Flowing banners adorned the walls with the alternating green and gold of the Akureyrian seal. I sucked in a breath as I looked up and saw the ornate throne that was perched on top of the gleaming marble dais.

Wearing a green silk shirt with a golden cloak edged with white ribbing, the king was massive with a broad chest and a strikingly handsome face. I quickly realized where Torben's captivating features had come from. They shared the same straight nose and strong jawline. The king's eyes, though. were a mystic blue, a contrast to Torben's rich brown.

"I see you finally decided to grace us with your presence, my son," the king said with a hint of annoyance. Torben bowed his head deeply to his father and we followed his lead.

"It is good to be home, Your Majesty, it has been an eventful trip," Torben said, his deep voice booming through the hall.

The king glanced behind Torben to where I stood with the Treyst. My stomach clenched and I thought I might vomit as his eyes bore into me. "Eventful, indeed," said the king, "and who is this unfamiliar woman?"

"This, Your Majesty, is Kaari Trygg."

Torben's voice was as strong as the steel that was strapped to his back. He was a remarkably good storyteller, weaving his words into a vivid description of his travels. When he spoke of Árnes, I closed my eyes as he described the lush forests and jagged cliff walls he had seen adorned with glittering waterfalls. Each description was like a splattering of paint on a well-stretched canvas and when he was done the image of my old home was so vivid I thought I might cry. He had seen all the wonders of Árnes—and had appreciated its raw, unrelenting beauty.

I startled, realizing he had started to recount the attack by the braviken, his voice deepening as he recalled how the creature had taken him by surprise. He glanced at me and explained how I had healed his injuries after he was separated from his Treyst.

The king scratched at his chin as he listened, his piercing blue eyes drilling into his son as he spoke. My throat clenched as Torben narrated the attack by the garmr and described the way I had slain the creature.

The king's intense gaze shifted to me as he learned about our escape from the mountain pass. By the time Torben had finished recounting the ordeal, my head was spinning at the thought of all that had happened since I first came across the prince in the Wood. The air in the room was suddenly stifling. I pulled at the front of my dress to force fresh air across my chest. Torben hadn't revealed that I had raw magic and it left me feeling a welcomed sense of camaraderie.

"It seems I am indebted to you, Kaari Trygg," the king said, his tone unreadable. "But it also seems that we would be remiss if we did not learn from your many skills. Has my son made you any offers of employment?" he asked transactionally.

I paled, realizing the King of Akureyrian was addressing me directly. "He has, Your Majesty. Prince Torben has graciously offered me the opportunity to work in your infirmary as a healer." I was impressed with how confident my voice sounded, especially since my knees trembled beneath my dress.

The king continued scratching at his chin. "It has been many years since there has been a sighting of the garmr outside the Holvik Woods." The king paused and his voice became somber. "If you are knowledgeable of such creatures, I fear we may come to rely on you for more than your skills as a healer." The king redirected his attention to Emil. "General, I want you to help Ms. Trygg prepare a full report on the creatures she has encountered during her time in the Holvik Woods and bring it to me by the end of the week. I would like to compare her list against our archives. Thankfully, there have been no other reports of undercreatures outside the wards. We must use this time to learn all we can. In the meantime, Ms. Trygg, we are grateful to have you as a healer. Prince Torben will find you adequate accommodations." And with that, we were dismissed. The king stood, pausing before he turned to leave. "Ms. Trygg, have we met before? You have the most familiar eyes."

Shit. I needed a half-truth. Enough to get by without blatantly lying to the king. "Perhaps, Your Majesty. My mother was also a healer and I traveled with her many times when I was a child… but that was many years ago… and I'm afraid to say there are many things I don't remember about my childhood." Not a lie—but certainly not the whole truth. I had never met the king, of that I was sure, but I couldn't say the same for my mother.

The king nodded, looking at me as if he was trying to match my face against the hundreds—thousands— of Fae he had encountered during his long life.

Torben bowed his head and the others followed before leaving the massive room. Standing outside the golden door, Emil, Theo, and Leif told Torben they would head to the barracks to clean up before checking in on the training yard. Torben assured them he would meet them after he showed me around my new home.

"Well, that went pretty well," Torben said, his words reverberating off the tall walls as we walked. "My father remembers the days when the continent was infested with the undercreatures." His tone was more relaxed now that our meeting with the king was behind us. He seemed almost jovial as he pointed out features of the palace—the best view of the coast on the third floor in the southern tower, a painting near the library that had a hidden image of a deer wearing britches, and the easiest way to sneak past the guards stationed outside the kitchen.

I felt like I was in a daze as I was led to a staircase at the southern end of the palace. The palace had four massive towers—two facing the north, and two facing the Southern Ocean. The walls of the southern hall were lined with large windows that made it seem as if you could reach out and touch the ocean that lay beyond a jagged beach. Rough waves with swirling white caps crashed along the shoreline, and I imagined the thunderous sound they must make as they crashed on the rocks. But inside the massive walls, all I heard were the familiar sounds of a bustling palace.

Torben stopped in front of a large wooden door carved with the image of a forest of gnarled trees. It looked like the Holvik Woods, except for the intricate dragon that had been carved into the sky.

Like the door to the great hall, the details were stunning, and I reached out to touch a carved leaf that appeared to be falling from one of the drooping branches. All the doors down this hall had been carved with a scene from the natural world; a swan in a lake, a field of wildflowers, and another that resembled the peaks of the Innnes Mountains.

"This room has been vacant for a while… I hope it will be ok." Torben's voice trailed off as he opened the door with a golden key I hadn't noticed he held.

As the door opened, beams of delightful sunlight greeted me through the tall window in the back of the room. The view of the sparkling waves in the distance took my breath away as I scanned the sizable space. To my delight, a large bed was centered on the back wall, strategically positioned to allow for gazing out at the ocean while lying in bed. A large armoire was tucked in the corner and next to it was a door that led to a private washroom. Beside the bed was a small desk that appeared to be equipped with plenty of ink and paper. The room was more than double the size of my home in Árnes.

I turned slowly to face Torben, my mouth slightly agape. "This is—I don't—thank you so much." I felt warm and flustered, like I was living in the twisted reality of a fever dream.

He smiled and stepped closer, taking my hands in his. "I am indebted to you, Kaari… for everything." Without taking his eyes off mine, he lifted my hand to his mouth. His lips were soft and warm, and he closed his eyes as if savoring my skin. The feel of his lips sent shockwaves down my spine.

"Will you dine with me tonight?" he asked suddenly as he released my hand. "I was thinking we could share something other than stale bread and jerky." He smirked and I couldn't help but laugh.

"That sounds wonderful. This is all so wonderful."

17

The washroom in my apartment was stunning. White marble floors that gleamed with the reflection of the afternoon sun led to an enormous tub in the center of the room. I turned the tap and squealed as steaming hot water poured out.

It had been *so* long since I had running water—let alone *hot* running water.

I let the tub fill as I continued exploring the new space. I wondered if all the healers stayed in rooms like this, or if Torben had chosen this immaculate space with me in mind. I shook the thought away, of course, the other healers would be treated this well.

Opening the door to the armoire, I found several beautifully crafted dresses made from fine silk, muslin, and cotton. I ran my hands over the fabrics savoring the smooth feel on my callused fingers. I wondered where they had come from. Was the room always stocked with dresses my size? Or had Torben somehow ensured I would have what I needed.

My mother's dresses had always been made of the finest muslin and I could remember how she had glowed in the pastel blues and purples she favored. The climate in Vogar had always been warm enough that the flowing fabric could be worn most of the year. I clenched my teeth as I ran my hand along the array of dresses, the memory of my mother hanging like a veil of sorrow on my shoulders.

Returning to the tub, I slipped off my dress and gasped as I stepped into the steaming water. I let myself sink in and then reached for one of the jars of scented oil and started scrubbing my body. The herbal scents of rosemary and lavender filled my lungs and refreshed my soul, the steam enveloping me in a cloud of bliss.

I sat in the tub until the water was lukewarm and my fingers had turned soft with wrinkles. A gentle tap on the door made my eyes fly open. "Yes?" I whispered.

"It's your maid, Ms. Trygg." The voice from beyond the door was quiet and gentle, with a hint of an accent I didn't recognize.

"Oh, come in," I said, trying to reach for a towel. A petite Fae with hair the color of sunshine entered the room and closed the door, a stack of folded linens piled atop her bronze hands.

"Let me get that for you, my lady." She crossed the room to get a soft towel and held it out—inviting me to stand so she could wrap me in it.

"Thank you. I'm Kaari," I said as the warm embrace of the towel wrapped around my dripping body.

"Of course you are, dear. Call me Milla. I will manage your room and help you with all your dressings. Gods you are beautiful… my lady."

"Please, call me Kaari."

"Very well my… Kaari. Shall I help you dress for your dinner with Prince Torben?"

"Oh, ah, thank you… I haven't had to wear a dress to dinner in a *long* time, Milla… and never with a prince. I'll take all the help I can get." I smiled sincerely. Milla's face was bright and pretty with round green eyes, a pointed nose, and lips that were as plump as a budding rose. Her smile was warm, and kind and I found my shoulders relaxing in her presence.

The dress Milla picked out was exquisite. I ran my hands down my sides and over the curves of my hips as I looked at myself in the mirror. The emerald silk had hints of golden flecks that sparkled in the light from the windows. The sleeves were long, and the golden flecks gathered into glittering cuffs that wrapped around my wrists. The slender fit and plunging neckline left little to the imagination.

I had never worn a finer garment.

Milla had insisted on putting my hair into a complicated style she swore was popular with the other ladies of court, but I adamantly protested and pulled it back into a loose bun. Milla rolled her eyes, but her lips pulled into a kind smile. "Let's go then, we don't want to keep His Highness waiting."

"Milla," I whispered, "do all of the healers live in the palace and have their own maids?" The question had been burning my mind since I first entered the exquisite room and saw the luxury the prince had granted me.

"Of course, dear," Milla said, looking confused. "The healers are treasured in Dalvin. Although Prince Torben seemed especially excited that you were here. He and his Treyst do find themselves needing healer magic with some frequency. Now come, we should go to meet the prince."

Milla led me further down the hall until we reached the base of the tower, then she pulled open a door to a winding stairwell. "Where are we going?" I asked.

"To the prince's room, of course. He always prefers to dine in his room," Milla said cheerfully before steering me towards Torben's chambers. The windows lining the hallway had been left open, allowing the evening air to fill the space. The breeze smelled of salt and pine as if the ocean itself had carried the essence of the forest to greet me.

My nerves twisted and tightened with each step. The palace seemed larger in the evening shadows, its vastness amplifying the sound of our footsteps, echoing back to me like a heartbeat. I was keenly aware of every flicker of torchlight, every whisper of fabric against my skin, as if the palace itself were watching, waiting. I tried to steel myself, but the idea of being alone with him—in his bedroom—seemed impossible to prepare for. My mind raced, skimming through a thousand possible outcomes, each one more disconcerting than the last. I felt both exhilarated and vulnerable, a strange warmth stirring beneath the coolness of my exterior.

Milla pressed on, chatting sweetly as we walked. Goddess bless her for keeping my mind occupied with pleasantries.

On the right, was a hall that was even more impressive than the one that had led to my room. The intricate doors continued here, the craftsmanship becoming more ornate the further we went. A lush emerald carpet spanned the length of the hallway, its golden thread glimmering in the evening light. It was as if the royal halls had been covered with thick moss and sprinkled with moonlight. When Milla finally stopped, the arched door that stood in front of us took my breath away.

It was made of gold that had been carved into a map of Akureyrian. Tiny roads and trees had been etched into the gold that filled the space between the towns and villages scattered across the kingdom. In the top left corner, I spotted the cluster of trees that marked the Holvik Woods, and my heart clenched to see how far I had come.

"I expect you will be able to find your way back to your room?" There was a slight hint of playfulness in Milla's voice and even though my confidence waivered I nodded as the maid knocked on the door.

Torben opened it after the second knock. His eyes widened and his mouth opened as if to inhale a breath. "You look incredible," he whispered. "Thank you, Milla, for showing her the way." It should have been surprising to hear the prince address a servant by name, but not with Torben. He had proven he was not like other royals. Milla bowed her head and quickly departed as Torben brought his gaze back to me—and my dress. His eyes caressed every dip and curve as slow as dripping honey.

"Please, come in." Torben stepped back, allowing me to enter his room—rooms.

Light poured into the main space through windows that stretched from the mahogany floors to the peaked ceilings. Torben's bed was tucked against the far wall and looked like a cloud with billowing white linens. There was a couch against another wall where an expansive bookshelf spanned the length of the space. There must have been hundreds of volumes pressed into the shelves.

I could feel the weight of Torben's gaze as his golden-brown eyes scanned the details of my face. He watched me with an intensity I had only seen in the eyes of a warrior before a battle. I wondered, for a moment, why such a powerful Fae would waste his time treating me to dinner. Was it simply because I possessed a magic that was somehow more powerful than his? Or had something else drawn us to this moment?

"Is this a social call, or are we actually eating? Because I am starving." My voice quivered with undigested nervousness.

The prince laughed. "I once saw you eat three bowls of stew in a single setting, I know how seriously you take mealtime." He winked at me, and I gently punched his arm. Terror gripped my throat. I unclenched my fist and began running my fingers across my loose bun. I had just *struck* the Crown Prince. Torben must have recognized the look on my face because he smiled warmly and laughed as he said, "Don't worry, Aulis will bring dinner up shortly."

"Aulis?"

"My cook."

"Do you know all of your servant's names?"

Torben dipped his head slightly. "Yes, although I confess that sometimes I mix up the scullery maids—they all wear the same color dress."

My eyes narrowed. "I don't think many royals make a priority of learning the names of those who keep their palaces up and running."

Torben smiled and then took my hand, leading me over to the enormous window that wrapped around the tower wall. The view from this high up was breathtaking and I gasped as I looked out into the endless ocean. The feel of Torben's grasp was like an anchor holding me in place.

"So, first impressions?"

"Well, you *certainly* clean up nicely," I joked. Holy gods, was I flirting with the prince again?

"I meant about the palace," he quipped, "but we can start with me if you insist."

I laughed, but there was a faint tremor in it. Beneath the easy banter, an intensity lingered in his eyes, a warmth that sent my heart racing all over again. I was acutely aware of how close we were, of how his every word seemed to draw me in, making the grand palace and all its formalities feel like they were worlds away. "It is... wonderful, Torben. Everything has been wonderful. I hope I did alright with your father."

"You did beautifully. He may be king, but I swear he has a soft heart." Torben paused, "You would know if he didn't like you." The way he said *beautifully* seemed to carry more weight than it should.

"Thank you for the clothes as well. I'm glad no one will have to see me wear my tattered clothes from Árnes." I ran my hands along the soft fabric of my dress. "Did you choose them for me?" I don't know why I asked but I had to know.

"I wish I could take credit. But no, it was actually Theo."

"Theo? But he seems so..." my voice trailed off. I wasn't exactly sure how to describe Theo Axtell.

"Gruff? Cranky? Stern?"

"Precisely," I said, matching the prince's smile. "I didn't get the sense that he was overly pleased that I was here."

"Theo Axtell is one of the most surprising characters I have ever known. He may come across as cantankerous most of the time, but I promise he has a big heart. And the fact that he volunteered to help Milla select your wardrobe tells me he has accepted you being here."

This was all overwhelming. If I had stayed in Árnes I would be working to gather my lavender into tight bunches to hang dry. Lyyli would probably be sleeping on my bed, her amber fur glowing in the light from the hearth. But instead, I found myself in an exquisite dress that had been hand selected by a captain of the royal guard while talking to the Prince of Akureyrian—in his bedroom.

I swallowed, forcing my nervousness away. A soft knock at the door interrupted my next thought as Torben called Aulis into the room. The cook carried two large platters and got to work setting the small table that was situated in front of the windows. Aulis was tall, and slightly plump around the middle, with golden hair and a warm smile. The smell wafting from whatever was under the platter made my mouth water. Torben clapped the cook on the back in a surprisingly friendly show of gratitude.

I had been around plenty of High Fae and nobles when I was a child and *never* remembered seeing any of them display such genuine gratitude and kindness. Even my parents had not been overly warm to their staff.

Aulis pulled the covers from the platters, releasing an intoxicating plume of savory steam. He bowed deeply, tucking the lids behind his back, and left me and the prince to enjoy our meal. The platters were overflowing with steamed vegetables that had been mixed in garlic and butter, and crisp potatoes surrounded a generous portion of white ocean fish. I slowly reached out my hand and laid it on top of

Torben's. "Thank you, this is a wonderful welcome. You didn't have to do this."

"You saved my life three times and then saved my three closest friends. Believe me, this is the least I can do." Torben turned his palm so that my hand rested in his, he squeezed slightly, and my stomach flipped. "And you did all that after leaving your home because *I* invited you here." It was a simple touch, innocent enough, but it felt like he'd unlocked something I'd hidden deep inside me—a quiet longing, a yearning I hadn't dared to acknowledge. I could feel the calluses on his fingertips, rough from years of training, and somehow that small detail made him more real, more trustworthy.

With everything that had happened since I first met the prince, I hadn't had a moment to grasp the reality that I had actually left my home in Árnes—that I would likely never go back. The thought had been hovering at the edges of my mind, a heavy presence I'd avoided acknowledging, and yet here it was, undeniable. As much as I wanted to shrug off Torben's words, I couldn't ignore how deeply they resonated. Somehow, hearing him say it—that all of this had happened to me, to us—felt like someone had reached through the chaos and steadied me, grounding me in this strange, unfamiliar life I'd stepped into.

We talked while we ate, easily transitioning from discussing our favorite books to where I could find the best cup of *real* coffee. The conversation pressed on until the candles were burning low in the crystal holders that adorned the walls, their flickering light casting a warm, golden glow across the room. Shadows danced along the walls, softening the edges of everything and creating an almost dreamlike atmosphere. Each word we shared felt intimate, as though it belonged to a world where time slowed. I caught myself lingering on his every word, the easy cadence of his voice and the way his eyes sparkled with each story he told. In that dim light, with the palace beyond us quiet, it felt like a fragile, precious secret neither of us wanted to break.

Torben promised to bring me to the infirmary so I could get acclimated to my new workspace. "After seeing the number of little jars and bottles in your house, I think you will be happy with the space. There are at least three times as many."

"It will be nice to have access to supplies without having to barter with the mortals."

"Now that is a story I am dying to hear," Torben said as he leaned back in his chair and put his hands behind his head, causing the muscles in his arms to pulse from the movement.

The sun had dipped below the horizon by the time a servant came to clear the platters, and yet we continued talking until the moons were reflecting off the water beyond the window. I couldn't remember the last time I had smiled or laughed so much, or if I had ever had a conversation that was so effortless.

"I train early in the morning if you would like to join me before going to the infirmary," he said.

Training with the prince was certainly not something I ever expected to do, but I had to admit that having a physical outlet to work off my nervous energy would probably be a good idea. "I would like that, just as long as the ladies of the court won't be too shocked to see me in the training field... wearing pants."

"Oh, they certainly will be," he said with a sultry smirk, his gaze drifting over me with a hint of mischief. "But I'm sure they'll survive. They're used to gossiping about me—I imagine they'll relish the chance to talk about us both."

I felt a rush of heat on my cheeks. *Us both.* He said it so casually, as though the very idea of us together was nothing unusual, as if he didn't care that he was *engaged.* For a moment, I could almost picture it: the two of us sparring in the early dawn light, our movements sharp and precise, a language spoken in feints and parries. The idea made my pulse quicken, though whether from nerves or something else, I couldn't quite tell.

"I should probably see about finding my way back to my room," I said, looking down at my hands. "I really have had a wonderful time, Torben." Saying his name should have felt so strange—he was the Crown Prince of Akureyrian. And yet, I found that calling him by his name felt completely natural.

"Let me walk you."

"Worried I'll run away?"

"No... it just gives me a little extra time with you."

My heart was racing as he stepped closer and looked down at me, gently cupping my cheek with his strong hand, studying my face with his piercing eyes.

"Promise me... promise me you won't kick my ass in front of my soldiers tomorrow."

I choked out a nervous laugh. "Perhaps I'll take you down with my bare hands—I won't even need a sword." My skin tingled with the challenge, my heart racing faster at his touch.

"I don't doubt that for a minute, Kaari of Vogar."

18

Sleep had stolen my consciousness and filled my dreams with tangled visions of my dinner with the prince. Even in my dream, the feel of his touch sent a shiver down my spine—warmth lingering where he had touched my cheek.

By the time Milla came into my room my whole body felt warm and dizzy.

"Good morning, Kaari. I trust you slept well?" She opened the curtains before shuffling around to pick up the items of clothing that I had left in small piles on the floor around the bed.

"Mhmm, yes, very well," I said as I rubbed my eyes. "Goddess what's the hour?" It was as if the events of the past week had finally caught up with me—I felt like I could sleep for a week straight and still be tired.

"Very early. Prince Torben mentioned he invited you to join him in the training yard this morning. I take it you will not need a dress for this... meeting?" Beyond the windows the misty pre-dawn light stretched across the waves, barely illuminating them as they crashed against the rock wall.

"Goddess help me, the sun isn't even awake yet. A tunic and pants will do. Thank you, Milla." My magic flushed under my skin in anticipation of seeing him in the training yard.

Milla looked at me with a queer look of surprise. I wondered if she had ever had a lady in her care request to wear pants before. She smiled and walked into the washroom while I started to roll myself out of the massive bed. I tried not to think about the training yard or about the prince who would greet me—but I failed miserably at both.

Milla picked out a simple blue tunic with lavender ribbing that dipped below my collarbones and brown pants that were snug and comfortable. As I finished tying the laces, I wondered again how Theo had guessed my size so precisely.

I was grateful that Milla had walked me through the twisting hallways of the palace until we reached a door that led outside. Leif was waiting, and I straightened as I saw his assessing eyes. To my relief, he smiled and bowed to Milla. "The prince started early. I will take Ms. Trygg to meet him."

"Thank you, captain," Milla said, her gaze dipping to her folded hands.

Leif watched Milla as she walked back to the palace, his eyes glimmering.

I knew that look.

"So, you and Milla?" I questioned once she was out of view. The captain looked at me with wide-eyed innocence. "Yes Leif, it is that obvious," I said, crossing my arms.

"It's nothing. Or at least it hasn't been anything for a long time." A sadness crossed his face and his eyes darkened. It was devastating to see his charming mood dissipate. Minutes passed as we walked down the pebble-paved path away from the palace. The silence heavy on the morning air before he spoke again. "I have known Milla for a lifetime... but I have never deserved her."

I placed a hand on his arm as we walked. It wasn't my place to pry into the love life of a captain of the Akureyrian army. Leif's deep dimples darkened as he smiled sadly and dipped his head, his flowing hair brushing against his eyelashes.

Changing the subject, I said "This certainly isn't the way to the training yard." We seemed to be walking *away* from the palace grounds.

"No, Torb—the prince—starts his mornings outside of the palace walls."

I narrowed my eyes, "Does he let everyone call him by his name?"

"No. Only those he trusts the most." He ran his hand through his dark hair, his mood lightening. "Torben is like a brother to me. He treats his Treyst as if we were his blood. For him, there is no difference in rank amongst us."

I considered this, remembering the way I had seen them interact. "So, when you use his title in front of me it's just for show?"

Leif chuckled. "He is the prince after all. We at least *try* to have a sense of formality when we are around others who will notice."

The trail he led us up passed through a jagged rock path that ran along one of the sea walls. Leif had said that Torben would meet us at the top of the overlook. This high up, the ocean breeze was crisp and salty, and the cool mist kissed my face as we stepped higher up the path. The salty air was a reminder of a life I had spent an eternity trying to forget.

As we approached the top of the overlook, a new scent carried on the breeze. This scent had become quite familiar over the past week, and I felt a faint flip in my stomach as the mix of cedar and vanilla swirled around me. Torben came up and over the other side of the overlook. He was shirtless, his broad chest heaving with the exertion of climbing the wall, and small beads of perspiration and sea mist coated his bronze skin. His hair had been pulled into a tight braid making it easy to see the filth that covered his face. Dust, dirt, and sand seemed to stick to every inch of him. I snorted a small laugh as I scanned his haggard form. "Is this because I said you clean up nicely?"

Torben reached down, brushing the dirt from his knees. As he leaned over, the long scar that ran down his side highlighted by the morning light, a stark contrast to his bronze skin. He tipped his face to look up at me, still brushing his legs, and met my stare. "Ah, Kaari. Haven't you realized by now that I prefer dirt and grime over being drenched in robes and silk?" His deep voice had a rough edge to it, like rocks shifting beneath the surface, giving everything he said a raw intensity.

"I will take my leave, Your Highness," Leif said. "We will have the recruits ready for you when you return."

Torben clapped Leif on his shoulder and then walked over to stand in front of me. Despite the filth and sweat, the smell of cedar was still strong on his skin. I had noted a hint of the woodsy scent in the king as well, although it was not as strong and had not been mixed with the hints of vanilla that made me want to breathe Torben in when he was close.

"What exactly did you have in mind when you invited me to train with you at this ungodly hour? I don't see any weapons."

"You already know how to wield a sword. This morning, we run."

By the time we finally came to a stop, the sun was just lifting over the horizon, the shining light leading in the promises of a new day. My lungs felt like they were on fire and my legs were shaking as the muscles protested the immense distance we had covered. Torben was watching me intently—he barely seemed winded.

We'd run for *miles*. The path had been steep and rocky, only smoothing out once we had reached another massive overlook. I spent a fair amount of time running in Árnes, but it had been some time since I had crossed this type of distance.

"How do you feel?" he asked casually.

"Well, my lungs are on fire, my head is spinning, and I'm not sure my legs will work at all tomorrow. But thanks for asking." My words were choppy as I gasped for air. He scanned me from head to toe as if assessing a fascinating attraction.

"The gods be damned," he said as he shook his head slightly. "You didn't touch your magic."

"You thought I would *cheat* by using my magic?" I hissed, annoyance rippling through my words.

Torben chuckled softly. "Using your magic to boost your endurance and ease your discomforts is not *cheating*. You are High Fae, and the first Fae in a millennium to possess raw magic. For you, it would take less than a drop from your well of power and you could double that distance without breaking a sweat." Torben's eyes held steady, unyielding as he continued, "But instead, you choose to hold it back. Why? Are you afraid of your own power, or is there something else?" His voice softened, but the question lingered, pressing against the walls I'd built around myself.

I glanced away, tension prickling at my skin. "I *do* dip into my magic when I need to. The fact that you didn't get flattened by a landslide should be proof enough," I huffed and crossed my arms.

Torben reached out, his hand brushing my arm, a touch that both anchored and unraveled me. "It's part of you, Kaari. Just as much as your heart or mind."

I clenched my jaw, swallowing hard. He didn't understand. To give in to that power was to walk a line I wasn't sure I could pull back from. But the way he looked at me now, as if he saw potential where I saw danger, left me questioning everything.

For a century, I had survived on my own without relying on my magic. I had healed countless Fae and mortals with traditional herbal medicines and techniques when I likely could have had the same outcome with an effortless wave of my hand.

The truth was, I had always been fearful of my magic. My parents had tried to keep it hidden and even sought help from other magic wielders to teach me how to keep it locked deep inside. Once I left Vogar, my magic marked me as High Fae. And once you were known as High Fae, it wasn't hard to start digging into lineage—where the secrets from the past would quickly come to find me.

"I don't know what your power feels like, Torben, but mine feels like... it's hard to explain," I began, searching for the right words. "It's like... fire and starlight, flowing through my veins. It's hot, cold, everything at once, and it feels alive. When I tap into it, the world just... sharpens. Colors get brighter, sounds clearer—almost like I can feel every single thing around me. It's exhilarating but terrifying, too, because it's so vast and raw. I feel like I could reshape the world if I wanted, but there's always this whisper in the back of my mind, reminding me how easily it could all go wrong. This power—it's ancient.

Untamable. It *is* a part of me, I just don't want it to be all of me," I replied.

"You are remarkable, Kaari."

"I—thank you," I said, flustered. I didn't want to talk about my magic anymore. "Show me how remarkable you are, Prince. Let me see you run back without using *your* powers."

Torben gave me a wicked grin as he reached his hand to his sculpted chest. "You know, having a death wish for the Crown Prince could be considered treasonous." He winked as he started running back down the path leading to the palace—back to this strange new life that I was starting to live.

In my room, I finished rubbing my skin with rosemary oil and then blotted myself with the soft towel Milla had left for me. The cold bath I took when I returned to my room had felt marvelous on my throbbing legs. I cursed at my stubbornness for not taking the prince's bait to use my magic on the run back. I would be sore for a week. But the thought of letting my magic roar through my blood to fuel my lungs and legs felt like plummeting off a cliff into an unforgiving sea. That same magic had cost me everything I had ever loved. Gritting my teeth as I stretched my legs, my thoughts wandered to the undercreatures I had been tasked with cataloging.

I sank into the chair at my desk, still wrapped in my towel with the lingering sting of cold water clinging to my skin. The fire crackled softly in the hearth, its glow casting a golden hue over the scattered papers and pens. I tucked a damp strand of hair behind my ear and wrote a few names across the page. Each name felt like a spark, little shadows of things lurking at the edges of memory and nightmares.

A soft knock at the door jolted my attention and I scrambled to get dressed before opening the door. Leif was standing in the hall, his shaggy black hair wild and windblown, and his playful smile stretched across his face. "Ms. Trygg, the prince has asked that you join him in the training yard before he shows you the infirmary."

"He just made me run for *miles* and now he wants to spar. Does he train like this every day?" Based on his muscular shape, I wouldn't be surprised if he did.

"Oh aye, he has always been like this." Leif looked over his shoulder as if checking to see if anyone was in earshot. "Don't tell him I told you, but I think you got the best of him this morning. He was panting like a panther when he left you."

"Panting like a panther? Well, that is an image I will treasure." I smiled. This felt almost like friendship.

As we walked, Leif explained how they trained their recruits. Theo, unsurprisingly, taught most of the combat skills and Leif and Emil coordinated the challenges that would help them advance through their training. Torben, I learned, took an active role and had left the field with bloody lips and swollen knuckles on more than one occasion.

The training yard stretched out in a broad, expansive field, its surface worn from countless drills and sparring sessions. Scattered training dummies, sandbags, and wooden weapon racks lined one side, while wooden targets were set up at varying distances, each bearing the scars of recent training sessions. The space hummed with a lingering energy, the air thick with the scent of sweat, leather, and dirt. The grounds were teaming with warriors—men *and* women. My jaw dropped slightly as I saw a group of women practicing their sword skills. They were powerfully built, and their toned bodies had been carved into graceful weapons that danced in gowns of glittering violence. Around them, the men watched with darting eyes—clearly unsure if they should be aroused or intimidated.

As I continued to search across the field, I paused at the large wooden dais that overlooked the yard. There, in the center of the platform stood Torben, arms crossed in deep concentration as he watched the novices perform their exercises. He had put on a clean shirt that he left untucked, and his knees were still scuffed with dirt.

Leif and I walked to the platform and Torben turned to look at us before yelling to the large group of recruits to hold. "Your timing is impeccable," he said to Leif, before quickly turning back to the crowd of soldiers. His voice boomed like thunder across the yard, commanding attention and respect.

"This," he said, gesturing to me, "is our newest healer and Master of Undercreatures. She outranks all of you, and you will *definitely* want to be on her good side the next time you end up bruised and bloodied, so act accordingly."

I froze and my eyes must have doubled in size because Leif gently placed his hand on my back as he guided me towards the front of the dais.

Master of Undercreatures. The title ripped through me as memories flashed to the wicked beasts I had encountered throughout my life—was there no one else in Akureyrian who was more qualified for such a title? To my amazement, the soldiers faced me and bowed their heads. I noted that the women dipped their heads a little lower, their faces bright with admiration.

"You will return to your stations and finish the morning with General Helvig, Captain Sörensson, and Captain Axtell. Tomorrow, we will assess your progress." The recruits all bowed their heads again before resuming their exercises.

He walked towards me and smiled. "You look wonderful."

"Thanks for the heads up," I said rolling my eyes. "Master of Undercreatures? It's so… *morbid.*"

"Really? I thought it had a nice ring to it?"

Torben's grin faded, and he met my eyes intently, the golden specks seeming to pulse as he spoke, "Kaari, after seeing the braviken and the garmr and hearing your stories from the Woods, my father and I agreed that we have been foolish to ignore the possibility of this threat." He swallowed before continuing, "I travel my land looking for potential threats to my people. And if there are now creatures like the garmr lingering in my kingdom, I intend to be prepared. I'm hoping you will help me."

The clanking of swords rang behind us as I studied the prince's face. His eyes were a warm, earthy brown, grounding and inviting like rich soil after rain, and his jaw was clenched with resolve, but he looked at me with a sense of hope that made my heart swell. "That's what you were doing on your birthday trip? Scouting Árnes for threats?"

"Yes. And even though I found creatures that have only been seen in Akureyrian nightmares... I think the gods also led me to you."

The infirmary was located on the north side of the gardens. The oblong stone building was covered with climbing vines and fragrant honeysuckle, making it look like something out of a faerie tale. A large garden had been planted to the left of the main door and my excitement peaked as I saw the array of herbs and medicinal plants that were growing in the rich soil.

"This is wonderful," I said breathlessly as I brushed my hand through the rows of greenery. I was still slightly shaken from Torben's surprise announcement, but the wariness had started to fade as we walked to the infirmary.

Torben had wiped most of the grime off his tan face and his eyes danced with gold as he watched me. "My mother designed this space," he said, clearing his throat. "She insisted that the palace grounds have an infirmary so anyone living here would have access to a healer."

The sweet smell of honeysuckle that surrounded us staled as the prince mentioned his mother. My heart pulled as I imagined the late queen and the immense loss the kingdom had experienced after her death.

Torben opened the large oak door and familiar scents of willow bark, rosemary, and calendula enveloped us as we stepped into the bright space. Sunlight poured in through the large windows that lined the back wall where several cots were arranged. In the back corner, a petite Fae brushed her hands on her apron as she turned to see the prince. "Your Highness! What a surprise." The healer instinctively looked over his powerful form assessing for injuries. "Are you injured?" she asked assertively.

"No, no Laila. I'm fine. I have exciting news. We have found a new healer. This is Kaari Trygg."

Laila looked at me with the same assessing intensity and smiled, her ice-blue eyes pausing at the scar on my hand.

"Oh, that is wonderful, we will certainly need you now that the recruits have started. They are worse than children the way they manage to get injured. Come, I'll show you around." She seemed to float as she led me through the space, her voice like an ethereal song.

To my surprise, Torben waited while Laila showed me around. He seemed genuinely interested to hear about how the infirmary was set up and how the healers worked their herbs and potions. There were two other healers, Laila explained, and they all possessed healing magic. Most of the ailments they treated were common household injuries such as burns, sprains, lacerations, and other minor illnesses. For the soldiers, however, the injuries could be more severe. Recently, they had treated several soldiers with major broken bones and dislocations that had been sustained during training. "In times of peace, we are blessed to have a relative predictability to the types of ailments we see." The insinuation was clear that during wartime work in the infirmary was anything but predictable.

The door opened as we spoke and one of the royal guards entered holding his arm. I had seen this guard around the palace, usually stationed at the large doors near the courtyard.

"Niklas, what happened?" Torben asked with genuine concern. *Goddess, did he know* everyone?

"Your Highness. I was patrolling around the southern rim when the rock on the path shifted, and I fell. I think my wrist may be broken."

Torben smiled as he clapped Niklas on the shoulder. "Well, you came to the right place. I'll leave you to it then." He winked at me as he turned to leave. "Oh, Master Trygg, will you meet me after? I would like to review your upcoming report."

I nodded at the prince before remembering to bow. I hadn't expected Torben to use my new title and it still felt surreal.

My stomach was twisting with nerves as the warmth of my magic gathered in my palms. In this space, I was allowed—*expected*—to use my magic to help others. My palms warmed in anticipation, as if my magic was alive and giddy.

Laila was watching me closely. "Would you like to help Niklas? Or take some more time to settle in?" Her brow lifted as if she could sense my reservation.

"I'm happy to help. Come, Niklas," I motioned to the guard, "let's get that bone set for you."

Once he was seated on one of the exam chairs, I ran my hand across his forearm. It was certainly broken, and the swollen area had already started to turn a bright shade of purple. I couldn't help but smile as I summoned my magic to the surface and sent a small orb across his arm, the blue light seeping into his skin to pull the shattered bones back together. It was a simple break, the type most Fae could heal on their own. He must be young if he had not yet mastered using his magic for this type of injury. Even after the bone was set there could be lingering pain for hours to days, depending on how strong his magic was.

Laila nodded her head approvingly as she watched me work. "I will prepare a tonic for the pain. You are in good hands, Niklas."

I wasn't sure if I had ever really felt like I had a purpose. But at this moment, as my magic flowed through the guard in front of me, I was filled with an immense sense of freedom and resolve.

By midday, I was covered with sweat, and wisps of hair that had escaped my tight braid blew across my flush and sticky face. After ensuring Niklas' pain was controlled and the function in his arm had returned, Laila and I worked together to create a batch of tonic that could be used to put patients to sleep if need be. The healer had chatted as we worked, telling me about the infirmary and the other healers who worked with her. Laila, I learned, had been a healer during The War and after the fighting had stopped, she had come to work at the palace.

She was blunt and thorough. It was obvious she was a master of her craft.

I liked her instantly.

When I finally left to meet Torben, the lingering glow I felt from using my magic clung to me like a heavy blanket. Although the release had been liberating, I felt like I was still brimming with residual power. It was as if each nerve was tuned to a higher pitch, humming with a fullness that wasn't fading. My fingers tingled, my heart thrummed with a strange vitality, and my skin seemed to be both warmer and more sensitive to every shift of air. Is this what it felt like when Fae used magic regularly? The sensation was intoxicating, almost overwhelming. It made me feel both lighter and more substantial, as though my physical form couldn't quite contain the power coursing through it. I wondered if using my magic in the infirmary would help me adjust to this feeling.

I walked through one of the gardens on the south side of the palace and was surprised to find a table had been set for lunch. The smell of wildflowers and roses had replaced the dusty air of the yard, and I looked in wonder at the expansive rows of colorful flowers and lush hedges.

Torben was standing by the table as I approached. He had not changed out of his filthy clothes and a new smudge of dirt lingered on the side of his neck. His massive form towered over the table, and I couldn't help but laugh at the contrast of this hardened prince standing in a garden bursting with delicate flowers.

"You smell like honey and calendula," Torben said in greeting, his lips pulling into a crooked smile. "I trust you had success with Niklas?"

"Yes, he will be fine. We also mixed up a batch of honey for wounds and cuts and a calendula tonic for one of the chefs who suffers from stomach ulcers."

"Did you use your power?"

"I did. The fracture was *much* simpler than Theo's leg. It felt good... to use my magic."

Torben grinned as Aulis arrived pushing a cart of food. My stomach growled as I breathed in the smell of hearty soup and fresh bread. The chef's eyes glanced at my filthy tunic and pants—a drastic contrast from the emerald gown I had worn the night before.

Torben pulled a chair out for me before taking his seat. "I didn't know the Akureyrian army had so many warriors who are women," I said, sipping a steaming spoonful of broth.

Torben was buttering a piece of bread and lifted his eyes to meet my gaze. "It hasn't always been that way," he admitted. "Probably for the past fifty years or so. It took time to adjust. Many of the men didn't like having their asses kicked by women who were half their size." He paused as he smirked. "But they soon learned that the women were more patient and observant, and they were usually stealthier than their larger male counterparts. Now more and more women are volunteering to join, and our army has never been stronger."

The pride in his voice was palpable. Once again, I was struck with the sense that he truly loved his people. For a moment, my mind wandered, imagining what my life would have been like if I had never left Vogar—if I had been able to stay and live the life of the other High Fae. Would I have followed in my father's footsteps and become a warrior? Or would I have spent my days dressed in fine gowns while meeting with diplomats and entertaining traders?

"Will you have dinner with me again tonight?" Torben asked bringing me out of my thoughts.

"As long as I can take a *long* bath first. I think I have an inch of dust on my skin," I said, before taking another spoonful of soup.

"I'm sure that can be arranged, although I have to admit, I think you are just as stunning in a dusty tunic as you are in a silk gown."

I swallowed.

This felt like flirting.

A flush filled my cheeks as I took a bite of bread and wondered if Torben was this charming with all the healers.

"Have you and Emil had the chance to start your report?" Torben asked casually.

"I have started to make some notes. It has been years since I encountered some of the creatures—I wish I had known at the time that I should be keeping notes." I tried to keep my voice light, but I had grown increasingly anxious about how to formulate a usable report of the undercreatures.

"Emil is an expert at organizing reports. Don't worry, Master of Undercreatures, I have no doubt the two of you will come up with something that will satisfy my father's request."

I appreciated his confidence. The last thing I wanted to do was disappoint the King of Akureyrian.

20

I woke in my bed the next morning to find bright beams of sunlight creeping across the room. I couldn't remember the last time I slept so late. I pulled the blankets up over my head, needing to feel the warm embrace of the linens. I had slept like the dead and my hair was wild around my face.

Dinner the evening before had stretched late into the night. Torben and I had returned to the garden for our meal and Aulis had brought us hearty portions of fish with garlic and wild mushrooms mixed with exotic vegetables that had been bursting with flavor. Once again, we talked in the garden until the moons were high in the sky.

As much as I hated to admit it, opening up about my life was not so terrifying... at least not with Torben. He seemed to be fascinated by my life in Árnes and wanted to know all the details of my daily life.

"How did you manage to find enough food? What was it like during the colder seasons? Is it true that mortals smell like licorice when they are afraid?" he had asked with dogged attention.

I told him how I managed to forage for herbs and grew a range of vegetables in my gardens and how I was frequently gifted meats and jerky as payment for healing mortal illnesses and injuries. That the colder months in Kall gave me a chance to hunker down in my cabin and process the herbs and medicinal plants I had collected during the warmer seasons. And that no, I had never noticed a mortal to smell like licorice—and I had sniffed *plenty* of terrified mortals.

Torben had worn a striking blue shirt and had rolled his sleeves up, revealing his muscular forearms. He must have bathed after his day in the training yard because his cedar and vanilla scent had been intoxicating as it mingled with the sweet roses that surrounded us. It was growing increasingly difficult to ignore the way his eyes swept across my neck or how his voice seemed to lower to a sultry vibrato when we were alone. He was unlike anyone I had ever met and the more time I spent with him, the more I wanted to banish the distance between us.

I knew that my new title gave me a reason to spend so much time with him, but I also knew that the guards and servants likely still whispered about what business we might be discussing so late at night.

A tap on my door made my head poke out from under the blankets. "It's just me," Milla said softly.

"Come in, Milla." I rolled over and crawled out of bed. Milla looked at me with wide eyes as she entered the room.

"Did you wrestle a bear in your sleep?" Her voice was kind and playful as she nodded towards a mirror.

I sighed. "I think I am making up for a hundred years of sleeping on a wooden pallet." I stretched, releasing an audible *crack* from my stiff back.

Milla's eyes were full of questions, but she simply nodded again. "Well, I hope you are feeling rested, you have been asked to attend the welcome ceremony for lunch."

"A welcome ceremony?"

"Oh yes. Princess Merja of Birkeria has arrived."

My stomach turned to stone. Torben's betrothed was here. Had he known she was coming? "Well, what an honor *that* will be." I couldn't keep the bite from my tone.

Milla's eyes glinted knowingly. "I will pick out your dress."

When I emerged from the washroom, Milla was holding a stunning sage-colored dress, and I could have sworn there was a wickedness to the maid's smile.

As I slipped into the dress, I gasped at my reflection. This would certainly make a statement. The neckline plunged low on my chest and the fabric hugged every dip and curve along my waist. The bottom was light and airy and flowed delicately as I spun like a flower in the breeze.

Milla helped style my hair into a loose updo that made my chestnut-colored waves flow down the nape of my neck. The contrast of the light sage of the dress and my dark brown hair made my bronze skin glow with life. Milla looked me over and nodded her head, satisfied with her work. "You look lovely, Kaari. I'm sure the princess will be simply delighted to meet you."

I doubted the feeling would be reciprocated. Then again, I was pretty sure that picking out this dress was Milla's way of stabbing the princess where it would hurt the most.

Since I didn't need to be anywhere until the ceremony, I decided to continue working on the report the king had requested. Yesterday, Emil said we would work on it a little each day until I had recounted all the creatures I knew. It had felt like a daunting task but talking to Torben last night had helped to organize my thoughts.

Sitting in the bright bedroom as the morning light seeped through the windows, I started recalling all the creatures I had encountered over the last century. I figured I would start with a rough list and then Emil could help me add any additional details the king would want. A knock at my door made me pause. "Come in Milla," I said absently.

There was a moment of silence and then a deep voice said, "It's me." I jumped at the sound of the prince's voice, and I had to clear my throat before telling him to come in.

He looked exhausted as he closed the door and crossed the room. As he approached, his usual confidence softened into something almost reverent, his eyes tracing the lines of my dress with a slow, appreciative intensity. A shiver ran through me as his gaze traced along my neckline, lingering just long enough to make my pulse quicken. His attention felt like a warm current against my skin, both thrilling and unnervingly intimate, leaving me hyper-aware of every inch he looked upon. It was as though his eyes alone could ignite something beneath my skin, and I fought to keep my breath steady, even as the space between us seemed to thrum with an electric charge. I stood to meet him and bowed my head slightly—he was, after all, the prince.

"She's here," was all he said. His eyes were glazed with a mix of sadness and anger that made my magic flare beneath my skin.

"So, I hear. Was this an expected visit?" I tried to keep the jealousy from dripping off my words. There was no reason I should feel jealous—possessive—but I did.

Torben caressed me with his golden eyes. "No. Apparently, she decided there was still more she wanted to see in Dalvin before the wedding. Which I find hard to believe." His voice was dark and laced with anger. I could feel that his magic was brewing within him. I stepped forward, close enough that I had to tip my head to meet his gaze. Without pausing to consider what I was doing, I reached out and placed my hand on his forearm. I could be killed for touching a prince without invitation, but I didn't care. Something about this closeness was intoxicating. And something about this prince told me the touch was welcome. Torben's jaw clenched as his eyes traveled to my hand and then over my body, resting for a moment too long on the deep V of my neckline.

"I can't wait to meet her," I said, my voice soft with lingering sleepiness. Torben's jaw clenched, and he huffed out a breathy laugh. "Do you like the dress Milla picked out?"

"Ah, Milla chose the dress. You are a wonder to behold, Kaari Trygg. Milla must like you."

My body flushed and I pulled my hand away and stepped to the window to look outside, needing to put space between us. Torben walked up behind me, stopping just close enough that I could feel the warmth that radiated off his glowing skin.

"Kaari," he breathed, "will you go for a run with me?" I turned to look at him, surprised at how breathless he sounded. "I don't plan to do anything differently now that she is here. And I could use some fresh air."

There was no reason I should be out galivanting with the prince now that his future wife was in the palace, but I couldn't bring myself to turn down his offer. "I'll go change. But I will blame *you* when Milla finds out that I need my hair redone."

"Aye. I'm sure she will have words for me." Warmth had returned to his eyes, sending a rush of color to my cheeks.

It broke my heart to see the turmoil that shadowed his face. I had spent a fair amount of time studying him since we first met, and it was only when he spoke of his engagement that his face darkened with disdain. There was no reason he should be forced to marry the princess of Birkeria. No alliance was worth an eternal life of misery.

Life, after all, should be *lived*. And living is more than passing days while your heart sullenly beats. Living happens when your soul is fueled by the desire to do *more*.

nodd

Living makes you want to plan and dream and experience. Because the more you live the more you *feel*.

After a century of solitude, I had stumbled on something new. Something that made me feel countless emotions at once. With every breath of salty air, I felt fear and relief, joy and sorrow, and heartbreak and love. Over the last several days, I had found a place where I felt like I could make a difference. I had found others who pushed me to be the best version of myself—and saw the best in others.

And in that moment, as I watched the way his golden eyes danced, I realized I might be falling for the Prince of Akureyrian.

21

We ran along the coast. I allowed traces of my magic to roar through my muscles, sending us further down the coast than I had ever been before. The breeze carried the ocean mist, and I felt the scratch of salt as it coated my skin.

Torben's magic was like a dense cloud that followed us as we ran.

He was seething.

But the further we ran, the more his shoulders seemed to settle. By the time we reached the trailhead, we were both slightly aglow with simmering power, and Torben almost looked happy.

"I have one more stop to make." He took a long gulp of water from his water skin and then offered it to me with a sly grin.

I wiped the sweat from my brow and looked at him quizzically. "Where exactly might that be?"

Torben grunted but his lips turned into a devious smile. "I owe you a real cup of coffee."

"Coffee? *Now*?" Without answering Torben reached behind a nearby tree where he had stashed a simple black cloak. After wrapping it around himself, he started walking towards the center of Dalvin. "You think *now* is the best time for a cup of coffee?"

"I promised you that I would treat you to a cup of *real* coffee when we got to Dalvin. I have yet to deliver on that promise. Today seems like a good day." I watched as he casually shrugged.

"I see," I said, accepting the smaller cloak he handed me. "I can't imagine this extra distraction has anything to do with your upcoming lunch."

Torben stopped walking and turned to look at me, his broad shoulders trembling with power. His eyes were suddenly swirling with black shadows that concealed the familiar browns and golds. It reminded me of the darkness of night as it swallows the evening light.

"You are *not* a distraction, Kaari. You are my reprieve. You surprise me at every turn, and I would fill my days with you if I could. The world is a distraction. You are my reminder."

Heat flushed across my cheeks as his gaze intensified. "A reminder of what?" My heart was racing too fast. I wasn't sure I was ready for his answer.

"A reminder that there is wonder still left in this world. That an immortal life is not an excuse to pass up truly living."

There *was* still wonder and mystery in this goddess-damned world. For so long I had lived my days to survive but never to actually feel alive. Torben's voice was filled with a promise. That he was willing, that perhaps he *wanted* me by his side.

"Alright. In that case, coffee sounds wonderful." It felt like I was accepting more than a cup of coffee.

Torben's eyes brightened with devious resolve. "There is a shop on the outside of the city that I think you'll like… and it tends to be quiet this time of day."

"And quiet is important because I imagine Emil will be furious if he hears you went into the city without a guard." I tried to keep my voice light, teasing.

"I have something better. I have the Master of Undercreatures." He turned and pulled the cloak over his head.

I rolled my eyes, but it was hard to quell the excitement. This felt like something new. And I was ready to dive in.

The small shop was delightfully quaint with stone siding and window boxes that were filled with fragrant flowers. The woman working behind the counter smiled warmly when we entered and directed us to sit at a table in the corner. Torben kept his cloak up to keep his face shadowed beyond recognition. The smell of sweet cakes, teas, and coffee permeated through the small space as the shopkeeper approached. She wore a worn apron and wiped her hands mindlessly on the fabric as she glanced towards Torben. Her silver hair was tied into a long plait that waved to the side as she turned her head. As if anticipating his silence, she turned to me and asked what we would like.

"Everything smells amazing," I blurted as my senses went into overdrive. "I've heard you make an incredible cup of coffee."

"Aye, I do. I'll get you one." She paused again to look at Torben's shadowed face. "And I'll bring a lemon cake for your *friend*… on the house."

"Oh, that's incredibly kind," I said, a little confused.

The woman smirked and nodded before turning towards the counter in the back of the shop.

I looked at Torben, the firm set of his jaw peeking out beneath the cloak. I leaned closer, "It really smells incredible in here." I still couldn't believe I was sitting in a coffee shop in Dalvin.

"Well, I would expect nothing else from Ailse."

"Is that her name? You really do make a point to know everyone."

Torben's laugh was a low rumble. "Aye, I do. Especially Ailse. She taught Aulis how to cook."

I looked back towards the woman and noticed the delicate features of her face and the way she carried herself as she poured the coffee and cut a piece of cake. "Is she Aulis' *mother*?" I asked, stunned.

"She is. And we can trust her not to tell anyone that she saw us here."

Ailse approached carrying a tray with a large piece of lemon cake and two steaming mugs of coffee. She placed the items in front of me as if Torben wasn't even there.

"If your friend would like anything else, let me know," she said. "I'll start a tab for you Master Trygg."

"But I…."

"Drink that coffee, dear. You look like you have already had quite the day."

I did as I was told as Ailse walked away. The ceramic mug was almost too hot to touch but I pressed it against my lips and drank deeply. The coffee was rich and bold and delightfully sweet thanks to a generous drizzle of chocolate. I moaned softly, closing my eyes as I sipped.

"Alight then?" Torben asked, the shadows highlighting his severe features.

"I don't know that I'll ever be able to drink acorn coffee again," I purred, closing my eyes as bliss washed over me.

Torben snorted in amusement as he leaned back in his chair. Though his eyes were shadowed by the dark cloak, I could feel his gaze on me, and it sent a rush of warmth to my cheeks.

We talked quietly as I finished my coffee and devoured every crumb of the lemon cake. We would need to get back to the palace soon for lunch and my stomach rolled at the thought of eating another meal—especially since there would undoubtedly be more treats.

"As much as I am enjoying this, I do need to change before going to the welcome lunch."

"I suppose you're right. Although I would much rather stay here all day."

"Do you do this often? Sneak into the city to have cake and coffee?"

"Only when I'm sure Emil isn't looking. Theo likes to come here in the evening for a pint and Ailse's famous dumplings."

I choked out a laugh as I pictured Torben and Theo sitting in a dark corner, under the cover of dark cloaks, getting drunk while gorging on dumplings.

"Well, I hope next time the two of you sneak out you'll invite me."

"I wouldn't dream of coming without you."

We had returned to the palace covered in sweat and sea mist and full to the brim with lemon cake. I had bathed quickly before calling for Milla to help me fix my matted hair. She had tipped her eyebrow in annoyance until I told her that I had been with Torben. As she brushed my hair and twisted it into flowing waves, she placed a hand on my shoulder. "He is as good as he seems."

The great hall was brimming with activity as servants worked to prepare the tables. To my surprise, Emil had come to escort me. He looked dapper in a white shirt and green vest that made his dark skin glow—the sleeves rolled just enough to reveal his forearms. My gaze caught on the fine lines of the tattoo that stretched up his arm. I hadn't noticed before, but the tattoo was comprised of delicate strokes of text in a language I had never seen.

He was quiet as we walked, his hands firmly clasped behind his back. I startled when he finally spoke. "I trust you enjoyed your time in the city," he said darkly. My head snapped to face him, my mouth agape as I tried to think of something to say.

Emil looked at me knowingly as he said "I am sworn to protect him. I always know where he is, especially when he sneaks into the city." I opened my mouth to speak but Emil raised his hand to silence me. "I also know that the prince has been happier these past few weeks than he has been in *decades*."

My heart flipped as I considered what the general was suggesting.

"My job is to ensure his safety… and happiness."

"I like you, Emil," I said, and the general gave me a glimpse of a smile.

He held out his hand to lead me back to the hall. "It's time," he said, and I squared my shoulders before walking inside.

The hall was alive with the smells and sounds of a royal party. Dishes clanked as final arrangements were set and drinks were poured. The smell of warm bread and sweet tarts wafted through the space. I figured that Aulis and the other cooks must have been up *very* early to prepare such a spread.

As Emil and I entered the expansive room, I glanced at the dais where the king sat on his throne with Torben at his side. The prince was striking in a fitted maroon shirt with gold ribbing and jet-black pants. I didn't miss the somberness of the colors he had selected, but I marveled at the way the dark colors made his brown eyes glow. He wore a warrior's braid, a subtle reminder that this engagement was a battle he would have to face. He somehow managed to look polished and rugged at the same time.

Seated next to Torben, the Princess of Birkeria was looking blankly across the hall and out the large windows. She wore a stunning crimson gown with black lace sleeves, the fabric hugging every contour of her curves leaving absolutely nothing to the imagination. Her skin looked like velvet, impossibly soft and sun kissed. While her face was undeniably beautiful, her jaw was set with a tightness that made her eyes look hollow. I doubted she ever smiled.

After scanning her face, looking for flaws I couldn't find, my gaze paused on the necklace that hung around her long neck. The small glass charm sparkled as the light from the sconces danced across her chest. It was a peculiar little charm. As we stepped closer, I could see that it was filled with a liquid as red as her gown.

"No doubt the blood of her enemies," I mumbled under my breath. Emil cleared his throat in warning, and I straightened my shoulders.

Once we reached the front of the dais we bowed deeply in unison and the king rose. "Princess Merja, may I introduce General Helvig and our Master of Undercreatures, Kaari Trygg." The princess' eyes widened as the king announced my title and I heard a general stir from the onlookers of the court who whispered amongst themselves. I bowed my head again and smiled sweetly at the king before Emil and I moved to take our seats.

King Havard walked down the stairs and took his seat at the head of the long table. Torben and the princess followed behind, neither one acknowledging the other. Torben was seated next to me, and the princess sat next to Emil so she was across from Torben. I held my breath as Torben's leg brushed against mine, his cedar scent filling the space as he sat down.

"Master Trygg, thank you for coming." Torben's voice was as smooth as silk. "It's about time the court got to meet our Master of Undercreatures."

"Oh, thank you... Your Highness."

"Your accent, Ms. Trygg... it's quite *unique*." The princess' words were as sharp as knives and laced with what I could only imagine was disgust. I felt a fire spark in my belly as I returned the sharp gaze.

"My family was from Vogar. But I spent many years living in the north. I have only recently arrived in the capital."

The tension between us made the air feel thick. "Vogar? Our neighbor to the north," she cooed. "Have you ever been to Birkeria?"

"I can't say I have. But I'm sure the land is beautiful." It was an effort to keep the bite out of my words, but I could sense the king's dark eyes watching me, so I forced my face into something neutral.

The king clapped his hands and Aulis and the others from the kitchen entered with trays of food. As they started passing out the first course, the king turned to Torben. "Will you be taking the princess with you to the training field today?"

Torben nearly choked on his first bite of food. After taking a long sip from his wine, he cleared his throat. "Of course, she is welcome to come. We have a final challenge for our newest recruits before they are assigned to their new units." Princess Merja looked at him with a bored expression as Torben added, "Hopefully we won't have to send too many injured recruits to Master Trygg before the day is over." Torben glanced at the princess and then nodded towards me. "We are quite fortunate. Not only is Master Trygg an expert in undercreatures, but a skilled healer as well."

I felt my cheeks blush at the sound of my new title on Torben's lips. I had a feeling he had used it intentionally since Merja had made a point to address me as '*Miss*'.

"I see." Merja's lip curled as she looked at me. "Master of Undercreatures, that sounds *terribly* interesting. What, exactly, makes someone qualified to be named the Master of Undercreatures?"

I opened my mouth to speak, ready to defend the fact that I was awarded a title I never expected, but Torben beat me to it. "Master Trygg has expert, first-hand, knowledge of the undercreatures that makes her uniquely suited for the title." His thigh brushed against mine with intention, sending a delicious warmth across my skin.

"In Birkeria, knowledge of the undercreatures would not grant someone access to a master's title, or our royal palace. In Birkeria, that type of trust is a sacred thing. It has to be earned." I could feel her distaste as much as I could see it written on her perfectly formed face. She tilted her nose upward, her eyes sweeping over us with thinly veiled contempt. "

I seethed. Gods, she *was* vile. How could Torben marry someone like her, even if it strengthened his kingdom—it would mean spending his eternal life with someone who radiated misery.

"Kaari," Merja suddenly continued, "you must feel terribly out of place at a meal like this. I would imagine healers do not normally sup with kings."

I bit into a piece of bread to keep from replying, but Torben's hand tensed on the table beside mine. "Here in Akureyrian, healers are *treasured*. Kaari has been invaluable to me—to us," he said sharply, his voice cutting through the subtle undercurrent of her barbs.

Merja's gaze flicked to him, her smile faltering for just a moment before she smoothed it back into place. She leaned forward, as if to reclaim her ground, placing a perfectly manicured hand on Torben's arm. "Of course she has," she purred, her eyes glinting with false sincerity.

The king, oblivious to the tension, chuckled over his wine. I sat straighter, refusing to let her words land, though my grip on the silverware tightened. Torben shifted in his seat, his gaze fixed firmly on his plate, but I could feel the barely contained irritation radiating from him. Merja, satisfied she had the king's attention again, began recounting some story about court life in Birkeria. I tuned her out, focusing instead on the quiet strength I drew from Torben's presence beside me.

The room had cooled as tensions blistered. My magic hummed under my skin, and I swore I could feel a strange sense of molten power radiating off the princess. My skin prickled with heat as I met her blazing green eyes.

Evil. The only way I could describe the feeling of Merja's power was pure, undiluted, evil. As I broke her gaze, I couldn't help but think that this power would inevitably be the root of an insurmountable amount of pain and suffering.

After lunch, Theo had escorted me back to my room so I could change. I was surprised when he offered—and even more surprised that Torben had requested I join them in the training yard. "What's wrong with my dress?" I had asked, planting a hand on the curve of my hip. Theo's jaw feathered as he scanned the length of my dress, an inarticulate sound escaping through the corner of his mouth.

"Milla would personally make my life a living hell if I let you ruin that dress." I laughed outwardly at the thought of the petite maid scolding a giant like Theo.

"What exactly is going to happen with the recruits?" I asked. Theo sighed and then told me what to expect.

An hour later, I stood next to Theo at the front of the dais, and I swore I could feel a glow of energy emanating from his massive form.

"Your eyes are churning like a storm," Theo said under his breath.

I cleared my throat, slightly embarrassed that my face was giving away what I felt.

The recruits had already started to form a circle around the ring as Torben and Merja approached the yard. The sense of anticipation was heavy in the air and seemed to vibrate with pent-up energy.

A hush fell over the crowd of soldiers as Torben led the princess to a seat on the dais. Once seated, Merja draped her hand over Torben's arm—the gesture more possessive than affectionate. Torben seemed to wince from the contact, shifting in his seat before nodding to Theo in a silent command.

The captain's voice boomed across the yard, "Alfarr, you proved that you possess the makings of a skilled warrior, ranking at the top of your class. We now offer you a final challenge." Theo shuffled his feet and the muscles in his neck tensed. "Your final opponent will be our very own, Master of Undercreatures. The rules are simple; no magic and the first one to secure the kill shot wins."

Torben shot to his feet, nearly tossing Merja's hand with the abrupt movement. His glare could have leveled an entire city. I made a point not to meet his eyes.

"If you win Alfarr," Theo continued, "you may choose your next assignment. But if you lose, you and the others will spend tomorrow running to the eastern edge of the Innnes Mountains... and back." A low groan rippled through the recruits, but Alfarr stepped forward and nodded. He stood a full head taller than me and was twice as broad, his forearms alone were the size of my thigh.

I watched as Torben stood and grabbed Theo's shoulder as he walked by. "What is going on? I thought *you* were supposed to fight the winner," he growled through gritted teeth.

Theo simply shrugged his shoulders. "She insisted."

Torben stared at me as I entered the ring. I set my feet, standing in perfect stillness as my breathing slowed enough that one might wonder if I was breathing at all. My crystal blue eyes darted across my opponent, assessing him for any signs of weakness. My lips curled into a mischievous smile, and I made sure that not a glimmer of doubt danced in my eyes.

Theo handed me a heavy sword that I flipped from one hand to the other. Finally, after handing me a shield, he nodded, his gaze lingering for an extra breath in silent encouragement.

The sun was still high in the sky and the air was muggy. Princess Merja was fanning herself and looking at me with cruel assessment as I walked to face Alfarr. I did not return her gaze. I knew Torben would have words for me when this was over, regardless of the outcome. But right now, it felt good to have a sword in my hand. It was longer than the sword I normally practiced with, but it was perfectly balanced, and the metal was ancient and strong.

I had asked Theo if I could be the one to challenge the winner of the contest after he had told me that he would be fighting. As much as I hated to admit it,

Merja's suggestion that I was not qualified to be the Master of Undercreatures had burrowed under my skin, festering until I felt rabid with the need to prove myself. I needed this challenge. I needed to remember my strength and by the gods, I needed to burn off some of the energy that had been building since lunch.

I watched Alfarr as he stood across from me, and for a moment I questioned my decision. He was *enormous*. I had to tilt my head to meet his predatory gaze. He was smiling as if he had already won. I wanted nothing more than to wipe that look of confidence from his face.

I had fought undercreatures that were bigger than me and they had not lived to see another day.

I felt my muscles tense, my body ready to respond to my every command. I smiled sweetly at Alfarr before finally glancing at the prince.

Torben was scowling.

Theo was grinning.

Suddenly, Alfarr lunged swinging his sword over his head before crashing it down with brutal force. The clank of metal rang through the field as I lifted my sword to block the blow, bending my knees to absorb the power of his strike. Goddess, he was strong. Swinging my shield around, I sent it crashing into his ribs as he worked to return his sword to a starting position. Alfarr let out a low growl as I spun again and jabbed my sword at his core. He lifted his blade with just enough time to block my lunge and pushed away with ruthless strength.

But I was faster.

I jumped forward in pursuit, my sword swinging with expert precision. The movement was as familiar as a song I had been singing for over a century.

We circled each other, attacking and blocking, spinning and dodging, until we both glistened with sweat. After a particularly brutal blow to Alfarr's sword, I spoke between breaths, "Not once have you anticipated my move before it was upon you." I lunged again as he grunted. "You are *reacting*." I felt as light as a feather as I swung my body around and lifted my sword and shield. Alfarr's footing stumbled as if surprised at my words and the unrelenting quickness of my feet. Before anyone could breathe, I rolled onto the ground and erupted behind him—slashing my sword into the back of his knees and knocking his massive form to the ground with a thud that echoed across the field. I jumped to my feet and pointed my sword at his neck while stepping a foot onto his chest.

Kill shot.

Silence stretched across the field, heavy and tense, as if the very air held its breath. A single leaf drifted down, caught in the quiet, and even the distant hum of the palace seemed muted, as if the world itself paused to witness what would happen next.

Emil walked up behind us and clapped Alfarr on the back. "I hope you brought good shoes. It's a long run." He turned to face the other recruits. "If Master Trygg ever gives you guidance, you would do well to listen to her words." He looked at Alfarr with a grin as he added, "Don't worry, Alfarr, she kicked my ass too."

I shook Alfarr's hand before walking to the front of the dais. Torben's eyes narrowed as I approached, his jaw tensing as if he was holding back a litany of words. I swallowed quickly and cleared my throat before bowing my head deeply. As I lifted my head, I felt the look of alarm that lined Merja's face. I smiled at her sweetly. "If you'll excuse me, I have work to do in the infirmary."

Torben nodded with approval, but I could feel the way his eyes burned into me as I walked away.

I was almost to the infirmary when I heard footsteps on the path behind me. I braced myself for the familiar scent of cedar and vanilla, but it never came. Instead, I felt a pulse of power that seeped into my marrow.

"Kaari," Theo's voice rumbled like a storm.

"Theo," I said, turning to face him. Goddess, how powerful was he? "I should have thanked you for letting me participate in the challenge." I was grateful that he had given me the outlet I needed—for believing in me.

"There was never a doubt in my mind that you would win," he said, casually shrugging his broad shoulders. There was a strange pull whenever I stood in his presence. I gathered that he had lived a long time and I wondered if his ancient blood was somehow more potent than more modern Fae.

"Well, I appreciate the confidence. How mad is Torben?"

"Aye," he said. "He will get over it. Torben has a big heart… he worries."

When he didn't say anything else, I asked, "Did you need something, Theo? I'm heading to the infirmary."

Something like sadness crossed his face. "I just wanted to tell you that your match was impressive. I have never seen anyone wield a blade like you. You have a wild type of technique—but it works."

I couldn't help but laugh. "Thank you… I think." I turned to leave but Theo grabbed my arm, pulling me back to face him. His brow had creased to a deep look of concern that made his eyes shadow.

"Be careful, Kaari. Now that the princess is here… just be careful. I don't trust her."

The look on his face was so earnest—so intense— that it took my breath away. What was he so worried about? Was he worried she would see how much time Torben and I spent together? Or would she see something else? When I finally managed to speak, my thanks was barely more than a whisper.

The infirmary was surprisingly busy when I arrived. Two workers lay on cots, one clutching his arm, the other with an obviously broken leg. Laila was spooning a tincture into one of their mouths as I went to the sink to wash my hands.

"Right," the healer said by way of greeting, "do you want the arm or the leg?"

I quickly settled in next to the one who was clutching his arm and Laila continued spooning the other a dark liquid that I hoped would send the writhing man into a deep sleep.

As I summoned my magic, the worker told me how a stone had fallen on them as they repaired the southern wall, crushing them both. Luckily, the break was simple, and I had the bone mended within several minutes. My magic had seamlessly wrapped around the broken pieces until they were firmly set.

Laila nodded her approval as she watched me give him a small jar of willow bark tincture to help with the lingering pain.

I needed this. The contest in the training yard—and Theo's comments after—had left me feeling like a bee in a hive as the vibrations of nerves took hold. I needed something to ground me, and touching my magic felt liberating, and terrifying.

I still marveled at how easy it was to heal someone when I actually used my magic. Having become so accustomed to the power of herbs and salves, I had forgotten how much I enjoyed the feel of my magic spreading through injuries to heal and mend.

When I was a child, my mother would let me use my magic to heal those around the estate who encountered minor illnesses and injuries. But she had always stayed close by, not trusting that my immense power would stay controlled whenever I touched it.

My patient thanked me adamantly and assured me he would return in a week to have the bones checked.

The one with the broken leg had proved to have the more complex injury. I joined Laila by his side.

"I feel three separate breaks. And what appears to be a crush injury further down." Laila's voice was methodical and direct, but her gaze was an invitation for me to check the leg for myself.

Reaching my hands out, I sent waves of magic into his leg. The warm blue light seemed to peer inside, whispering the extent of the injuries.

One, two, and a third further down. I simply nodded in confirmation. I had felt it all just as Laila had described.

"Together then," Laila said, as she placed her hand on the lower leg. I followed her lead and placed my hands next to hers. As we sent our healing magic into the mangled bone, I swore I could feel my blue light dancing with Laila's magic, swirling like fireflies at dusk.

Back in my room, I found that Milla had already filled the tub and added my favorite drops of oil so that the steam in the room smelled of rosemary and lavender. After several hours in the infirmary, I was covered in fragrant dust from grinding herbs and a sweaty sheen highlighted my brow. I stripped off my clothes and stepped into the tub as Milla peered around the door. "You are amazing," I said to the maid, my eyes closing as I melted into the blissful heat.

Milla approached tentatively with her hands clasped in front of her waist. "Was the princess at the training yard?" she asked quietly.

I blinked my eyes open, surprised to see the look of fear that had darkened Milla's face. I sat up slightly in the tub, not caring that the top of my breasts were exposed. "Yes, she was there. Why do you ask, Milla?"

The maid dropped her head slightly and closed her eyes. "I fear the day she marries the prince." Her eyes were heavy with concern when they opened. "The last time she was here, she spent her days criticizing everything about the palace and those of us who work here. She is so unlike Prince Torben, it breaks my heart to think of him with her. Please forgive me, I know I am out of line to speak ill of her."

"Not in this room, Milla. You are free to speak as you like." My mouth turned into a sinister grin as I added, "Especially if it involves the princess."

In the yard, Merja had watched me the way a hawk watches a mouse, her green eyes turning black with deadly focus. By the time I had defeated Alfarr her face had paled to a lovely shade of alabaster. It was sublimely satisfying to know she had underestimated me.

She didn't deserve to sit on that dais. She didn't deserve Torben.

Milla laughed softly and walked over to the armoire. "Shall I pick out your dress, Master Kaari?"

As much as I had tried to convince Milla that she didn't need to address me formally, I had a feeling she was using my title as a jab against the princess. "I would be honored, Milla."

After my bath, I twirled my hair into a tight knot and slipped into the dress Milla had picked. The deep blue silk was delightfully soft as I ran my callused hands over the curve of my hips. The front of the dress was surprisingly modest, following a straight line across my collarbones. The back, however, plunged so low it exposed most of my back.

Milla stilled as she noticed the scattered scars that were etched into my skin. "Shall I pick another dress?"

"No, Milla. I am not ashamed of the scars. They remind me where I come from. The one on my shoulder is from falling out of a tree when I was a child. That zigzag on my spine is from a *Klenar* I encountered in the Holvik Woods—I barely got away that time."

"How about these?" Milla gently traced her fingers over a cluster of scars on the side of my ribs.

"Those are from the night my life changed forever." I rubbed the scar on my hand—also from that night— and hoped Milla understood that I didn't want to discuss those scars in detail.

"Very well. I'm glad you don't hide them, Kaari. I will see you in the hall for dinner."

I grumbled, realizing that we would be dining with the princess, but I found that the warm bath and captivating dress had helped to boost my morale. I sat at the small desk, tapping my finger as I chewed on the end of the pen. Emil had sent word that he wished to work with me before dinner, anxious to see my compiled list of creatures, so my ears perked as I heard steps in the hall before a soft knock rapped at my door. "Come in," I said as I added two more creatures to the list.

Onista.

Agrabuamelu.

"Well, that dress will certainly make a statement at dinner." Torben's deep voice rippled through me as I spun around to find him standing in the door.

"What are you doing here?" I said, rolling my eyes—hoping the gesture would hide the fact that my stomach flipped at the sight of him.

"I'm the prince." He shrugged, closing the door behind him. "I tend to go where I want." His voice was a low rumble as he added, "You really are incredible. Alfarr didn't stand a chance."

"No. He didn't." I kept my voice level, trying to hide the shock that he was here. Torben leaned against the door, watching me like I was something worth worshiping. Warmth spread through my core as I cleared my throat. His presence felt too strong, even as he stood across the room. I wanted him to close the distance between us.

"It's not like Theo to be swayed. How did you convince him to let you fight in his place?" Torben was clearly torn between sincere curiosity and being genuinely pissed.

"Theo already told you. I asked nicely." It came out like a challenge.

Torben opened his mouth, ready to offer a retort just as Emil announced himself on the other side of the door.

I cursed at the interruption. Before I could move, Torben reached back and opened the door.

Emil's eyes seemed to double in size as he stared at Torben standing in my room.

"General." Torben smirked. "I see you have come to help our Master of Undercreatures with her report."

Emil let out a sigh and rolled his eyes. "And I see you are going to make it impossible to keep *this* a secret." Emil was gesturing at the two of us as he spoke. I thought about defending myself against his subtle accusation but decided against it. In all honestly, I *wanted* Merja to see him enter my room without a chaperone.

Torben clapped a hand on Emil's shoulder and smiled. My cheeks flushed and I found it hard to meet Emil's stare. I wasn't doing a very good job feigning innocence.

Another knock at the door made the three of us freeze. "Master Kaari, you are needed in the throne room," Theo said urgently, his powerful voice reaching us through the door. Emil opened it and Theo's eyes widened as he saw us all standing in my room. "Oh good. The king wants to see you two as well."

"What's this about, Theo?" Torben asked.

"A report just came back from the Grimsey Coast. The king has called a council meeting… and he wants Kaari to be there."

My pulse quickened as alarm bells rang in my mind. I stood, closing the notebook I had been writing in. "Well, we don't want to keep the king waiting." I headed out the door, leaving the three of them standing together in utter silence as they watched me pass.

24

The throne room was eerily quiet as we walked in. A small table had been set with enough seats for Torben and his Treyst, me, and two other High Fae that I didn't recognize. The king sat at the head of the table with a dark scowl on his face.

"Hersteinn, report," the king bellowed once everyone had taken their seats.

One of the High Fae stood slowly and looked around the table before speaking, his voice trembling as the words poured out. "Your Majesty, we have gathered several reports of brutal attacks from the locals on the north side of the Grimsey Coast that our scouts have since confirmed." Hersteinn paused as if needing to catch his breath. "Several farms lost livestock and three Fae were attacked. Scouts were sent to one of the farms to see what was left of the livestock. The poor beasts had been completely shredded. Their insides had been removed with a viciousness that is not consistent with the known predators in the area, and the empty carcases were left behind in a pile to rot. The Fae, fortunately, were able to escape but were left with grievous injuries."

Hersteinn's face had paled. I imagined that under normal circumstances he might be handsome. But his eyes were gaunt, and his jaw was set in a nervous frown.

"Did the locals report any other oddities or changes in the area around the time of the attacks?" All eyes were suddenly on me, and I realized it was probably not acceptable to speak without being asked.

Hersteinn looked to the king as if needing approval to answer me. When the king nodded, Hersteinn squared his shoulders and said, "I'm not sure what you mean by 'oddities'. We don't have a lot of information. The Fae in the area will not go out at night for fear of attack so they likely have not seen much."

My eyebrows pinched together as my mind raced. I knew the Grimsey Coast. I knew that the normal animals that roamed the area would not be capable of *shredding* livestock. "So, all of the attacks have happened at night?" I asked.

"Er, yes. So far as we can tell." Hersteinn had finally stopped trembling, but his color remained pale. "One of the farmers said they heard a horrendous scream before his mate was attacked." My pointed ears twitched at the words and my blood started to swirl like a raging storm.

Torben must have sensed the change and sat taller in his chair. I glanced at him before looking at the king and bowing my head. "Your Majesty, I would like to go to the Grimsey Coast."

Torben's eyes narrowed into slits, making them seem like weapons on the verge of striking—that was *not* what he expected.

The king raised his eyebrows and he gestured with a flick of his hand for me to explain myself. I could feel Torben's eyes burning into me. How could I explain something that was impossible? "If we are sure this isn't some territorial Fae bullshit... then I am thoroughly concerned that *somehow* there could be a drekavac wandering the Grimsey Coast."

The king didn't seem to mind my cursing although the High Fae looked at me in horror—I imagined most nobles were not accustomed to someone speaking freely in front of the king. I remembered how Torben had looked when I had demanded he let me examine his leg.

I smiled, making royal men speechless was surprisingly satisfying.

"And tell me, Master of Undercreatures, how exactly would a drekavac end up in the Grimsey Coast? The beasts have been banished for a thousand years." The king's voice was calm and direct, but I could hear the touch of concern that laced his words.

"The drekavac are known to terrorize anyone who wanders close enough to the Holvik Woods, even from behind the wards. When they scream, the mortals in the area are too afraid to leave their homes—even when they know the creature can't leave the wards of the Woods. They scream with enough force that the blood-piercing sound can be heard for *miles*. Their claws grow quite long and certainly leave their prey looking *shredded.*" The directness of my voice was enough to hold their attention. "I have only ever seen drekavac *within* the Holvik Woods. I don't know how they would break through the wards, but I would be quite concerned if they are suddenly finding ways to expand their territory. It was concerning to see garmr outside the Holvik Woods, but if drekavac are also breaking through we have a *serious* problem."

The king looked around the table. "Very well. Dinner is cancelled. Head to the Grimsey Coast at first light and see what you can find about these attacks. Captain Axtell and Prince Torben will be your escorts to ensure you have the access you need. General Helvig and Captain Sorensson, you will manage the palace in their absence." And with that, we were dismissed. After the king left, the two High Fae bowed to Torben and left through the side door, leaving me with Torben and his Treyst.

"Great," Theo said, his voice dripping with annoyance. "Be dressed before the sun is up. There is a boat leaving for the Coast in the morning. And bring the materials for your report. I don't want to listen to Emil complain about it being incomplete." Theo's gaze lingered on me for a moment before he turned to leave with Leif and Emil following behind.

Torben was pacing. His broad shoulders were tense as he held his hands behind his head, the muscles in his arms seemed to pulse as he walked. "Torben." My voice was barely a whisper, but he still turned to look at me. "When we saw the garmr I knew there was something wrong... but if there are drekavac as far east as the Grimsey Coast," I whispered, "who's to say that other creatures won't follow." While Árnes and the Grimsey Coast were both located in northern Akureyrian, it still took days of traveling to cross from one region to the other. I couldn't imagine the type of terror that could be unleashed if the undercreatures were covering that type of distance.

"I have heard stories about what it was like in Akureyrian before the undercreatures were banished to the Holvik Woods. I never thought I would see it with my own eyes." Torben stopped pacing and rubbed his hands over his face. He looked tired and the tension in his jaw pulsed with a mix of concern and determination.

"We will figure this out, Torben." I stepped closer, my hand reaching out to rest on his forearm. I tilted my chin to meet his gaze while tracing my fingers along the contours of his arm. His skin was warm and smooth like velvet, but it prickled with goosebumps in response to my touch.

"I'm glad you're here, Kaari," he whispered earnestly.

The walk back to my room had been quiet. I was sure Torben could hear my heart racing as I tried to think of an excuse to invite him inside. Even though I knew we would be traveling together for the next several days, I still wasn't ready to let him go. His presence felt like being wrapped a warm cloak after being outside in snowfall. His warmth was all encompassing and I longed to be wrapped inside.

By the time we arrived at my door, I felt lightheaded, a brutal effect of the fear and excitement rippling through my body.

Torben leaned against the outside of the door as he turned the knob. He looked down at me as I stepped forward, his breath gliding across my neck as I passed him. "Kaari," he whispered, "I didn't want you to have to put yourself in danger. When I asked you to come, I never imagined that you would be crossing the kingdom to find some creature from the Underworld."

I could feel the anguish in his words. He really felt guilty for putting me in this position. "Torben," I said, emphasizing his name, "you may not have known it when we first met, but by now I would hope you have learned that if there is someone I can help, I will go to them." My voice was strained as I tried to make him understand.

For the past one hundred years, I had spent my days looking for others to help—an eternal lifetime to make up for not saving the lives of the ones who had meant the most to me. But this was different. How would I make a difference when the threat was something as sinister as the creatures from the Underworld? This was not the same as mending broken bones or suturing torn skin. A sense of panic started to turn my stomach like sour milk. I knew these creatures. I had a duty to try to find answers if it meant saving lives.

The smell of ether wafted through the air, and I looked down to see that my palms were glowing. Torben quickly grabbed my hands to try to block the light that they emitted. I slammed my eyes shut and slowed my breathing until the warmth in my hands started to cool. Torben's hands remained locked over mine as he glanced down the hallway to make sure no one had seen, and then shifted into my room and shut the door. He was clearly still concerned about the magic I had let slip.

This was not the way I had envisioned coaxing Torben into my room, but I felt myself relaxing as his hands squeezed mine.

"Does that happen often?" Torben's jaw clenched with concern as he studied the way my hands glowed.

"I'm sorry," I said, my voice cracking. "It happens when I'm overwhelmed… and when I think about my parents. I made a promise after my parents died, that I would always defend those who could not defend themselves. But sometimes it feels like I could spend every minute of every day and there would still be someone who needs help."

"Your heart is too big for this world, Kaari." Torben ran his thumb over the top of my hand, tenderly tracing each of my knuckles until I started to feel the magic pull back under. I studied his face. There was a tension I hadn't noticed before. Something was bothering him, and it wasn't his worry about my magic.

"What's happened? There's something you're not telling me."

His breathing was heavy, and I could hear his heart racing just as fast as mine. "Kaari," he breathed. "I have to go see her tonight." His words were like stones thrown against my chest. My gaze filled with questions I couldn't say out loud. "I have to explain to her why I am leaving the day after she arrived."

"Because she is a vile woman who doesn't deserve you?" The words came out with a bitter harshness as I pulled my hands away. Goddess, what was I admitting? I didn't have time to regret the words as Torben reached up and gently brushed his thumb along my cheek.

He chuckled softly, his lips parting as he looked at me. "Well, you are an expert in monsters. Get some rest, Kaari. I will see you in the morning."

Torben winked as he snuck out the door, leaving me breathless as I tried to keep my magic at bay. The lingering sensation of his touch radiated on my skin like a burn from the sun. The thought of him going to see Merja felt like daggers in my belly. There was that feeling again. *Jealousy.* I was jealous that she would be spending time with him.

The room suddenly felt cold and empty without his muscular form filling the space. I wished Milla was here, I needed reassurance from someone who despised the princess as much as I did.

After another minute of staring at the closed door, I surrendered. "I guess it's back to my homework," I mumbled under my breath as I walked over to the small desk and began to write.

After an hour of working on the report, I stretched my arms and arched my back, moving through what felt like a year's worth of tension. My mind was still racing and despite the distraction from writing, the thought of Torben with Merja still filled my stomach with acid. Aulis had sent a plate of dinner and enough lemon cakes to feed a small army. I licked frosting off my fingers before pushing away from the desk.

The air outside was crisp, and the saltiness of the ocean mixed with the sweetness of the roses, the aroma whirling around me as I walked the paths in the garden.

Torben had told me that his mother, Queen Gunilla, had designed the gardens and that as a child he had spent hours playing in the hidden paths while she tended to the flowers. I admired the queen for doing the work herself rather than relying on servants. I imagined that many of the High Fae of the court were perplexed to see the queen with dirt under her royal fingernails. I thought she sounded like my kind of queen.

A chill went up my spine the more I thought about Torben's mother. The queen had been renowned for her powerful magic. It was undisputed that she had been more powerful than the king. Despite that power, she had been brutally murdered, and the king had never discovered who was responsible.

Soon.

I would have to talk to Torben about his mother soon… before the guilt ate away at me until there was nothing left.

Voices in the distance caught my attention and I instinctively crouched behind a large rose bush. The deep voice was unmistakable.

My heart flipped at the sound, and I peaked my ears to try to hear what he was saying—and who he was with. Torben's voice was low and firm—so different than the voice he used when he spoke to me.

"—it is my *duty*. These are my people, and *they* are my priority."

My blood curdled at the voice that responded.

"My father sent me here so we could figure out how to make this work—so we can get to know each other before spending a lifetime together—and now you're leaving," Merja snapped.

"As I have told you, princess, my duty is to *my* kingdom and *my* people." Torben's words were like knives slicing through stone. I tried to decide if I should make my presence known or turn around and hope he told me about his encounter later.

As I adjusted my stance, a thorn from the rose bush sliced against my arm, just sharp enough to draw a drop of blood. I bit my lip to contain the yelp of surprise and cursed softly. Maybe it was a sign to step out into the path. Perhaps the gods, or the queen herself, had had enough of my hesitancy.

Standing tall and squaring my shoulders, I began walking through the path as if I were oblivious to the world around me. I heard Torben stop talking and hold his breath, there was no doubt that he heard footsteps approaching. As I rounded another large rosebush, I walked right into view of Torben and Merja.

Torben blinked as if he thought he might be hallucinating.

I smiled cheerfully. "Oh Your Highness, I am so sorry for interrupting. I see that I am not the only one who wanted some fresh air on this beautiful night." The princess just stared at me and then looked to Torben. Her green eyes like poison.

"Aye, I—uh—was just telling the princess about our upcoming trip to the Grimsey Coast."

I wondered if I should duck for cover as the princess snapped her head to look at Torben. "*She* is going with you?" The air had lost its refreshing appeal as Merja growled into the night.

"Kaari's expertise is needed for this mission. I apologize if your father gave you the impression that I would sit by idly if there was a threat to my kingdom." Torben's frustration was palpable—I swore I could feel a slight tremble in the earth that radiated from where he stood. How hard he was working to keep his magic at bay?

"Well, I do hope you enjoy your evening. I should get some sleep before it's time to leave." I turned, revealing the length of my back that the dress exposed. I heard a muffled cough from Torben and smiled. I had never felt particularly possessive—or jealous—but ever since I met the prince, I couldn't shake the nagging feeling that his eyes were meant for me alone.

As I walked away, I heard Torben as he bid the princess goodnight. I held my breath as he followed me and I quickened my pace—not because I wanted to outrun him, but because I didn't want the princess anywhere near us when he caught up.

"*Kaari*," he whispered down the path. I froze and tucked myself behind a large bush as I waited for him to find me in the dense hedges. Torben's face was a mix of relief and resolving anger, the sharp lines of his clenched jaw shadowed by night.

"I didn't mean to interrupt, I *had* to get out of my room and away from that report."

"Thank the gods you did. I couldn't stand another minute with her." There was a sadness in his eyes that made me reach my hand up to his chest—and my breath caught in my throat as I felt the hard muscle beneath his shirt. I flinched, realizing what I had done, and started to pull my hand back. But the lines in his face softened at my touch and his hand reached to cover mine. "What would I do without you Kaari Trygg?"

True to his word, Theo knocked on my door before the sun was up. I rolled out of bed and threw on a sage-colored tunic and black pants and quickly braided my hair and tied it into a crown around my head before opening the door. The captain's eyes were alert despite the early hour, and he glanced behind me assessing the space.

"He's not in here." I rolled my eyes as I turned to reach for the bag I had packed.

Theo grunted. "I heard you had a pleasant encounter with Princess Merja last night."

I snapped my head up. "How did you hear about that?"

Theo matched my eye roll. "I am a captain of the royal guard. It is my job to know *everything* that goes on within the palace... especially if it concerns the prince."

The prince.

I had touched his chest last night and he had grasped my hand to hold me in place. I didn't know what had come over me in that moment, I just needed to feel him. And he had not pulled away.

"Do you honestly think he should marry her?" I asked as I gathered my bag.

Theo grumbled predictably. "It doesn't matter what I think." I turned to face him, clutching my bag against my chest.

"Well, it should." There was something devastating about Theo surrendering to the idea of Torben marrying Merja. If Theo wasn't allowed to have an opinion about Torben's betrothal, then I certainly wasn't either.

The walk to the dock from the palace led us down a winding cobblestone road in the center of Dalvin. The smell of fresh baked goods wafted through the streets as we walked and my stomach grumbled, reminding me that I had not eaten breakfast. Thank the gods I remembered to pack my ginger tincture to help with the inevitable seasickness I would experience on an empty stomach.

"I will be sharing a room with you and Torben until we arrive," he mumbled.

I smirked, glad that he was talking. "Just like old times then?"

Theo murmured something under his breath but to my relief, he didn't press about the unspoken dynamic between me and Torben. If I was honest, I wasn't sure

I knew what—if anything—was happening between us.

The streets were bustling with activity. High Fae and lesser Fae mingled at the shops and open-aired vendors. I breathed in the scents of so many Fae in one place. It had been so long since I had been among so many of my kind. I marveled at the way the Fae in the city moved with a graceful steadiness, never seeming to be in a rush—likely since they had their immortal lives to get where they were going. Despite the breeze, the air seemed frozen in place, as if time passed slower here.

As we walked, most of the Fae dipped their heads as they saw Theo approaching, not wanting to invite any chance of inquiry from a royal guard—especially one who scowled as much as Theo. I felt a pang of guilt that I didn't know more about his life outside of his duties as a captain of the guard—that is, I wondered if he *had* a life outside the guard.

I was well aware that Theo had been slightly suspicious of me since we first met. His gaze seemed ever present. I had the constant feeling that he was assessing me—trying to put the pieces together that would solve the puzzle of my life and my identity.

Our ship could be seen on the far side of the dock, the two large masts seemed to reach to the clouds, inviting the winds that would pull us along.

Once on the ship, Theo led me down several rickety wooden stairs and into a back room on the lower level. The door opened after Theo knocked and

Torben greeted us, his broad shoulders filling the width of the door frame. "Ah, wonderful, I hope you're hungry," Torben said as the smell of fresh bread and seafood stew wafted from inside the room. My mouth watered and I thanked the gods that maybe I wouldn't spend the trip with my head in a bucket after all.

Torben led us to a small table in the center of the room where he had spread out a map of Akureyrian. The candle on the table had melted leaving drips of wax along the upper corner of the map—leading me to wonder if he had spent the night here. As if in answer to my silent question, Torben shrugged as he said, "I got a head start on preparing our space and planning the trip… I didn't sleep well." The corner of his mouth turned up slightly as he looked at me. Was he suggesting that our interaction had been the reason for his insomnia?

Goddess help me.

Theo tensed and rolled his eyes. "I will make my rounds. I like to know where all the exits are when I'm confined inside a floating deathtrap."

I snickered at his incessant dryness and saluted him as he left. "Theo seems *thrilled* to be here," I said, raising a suspicious eyebrow.

Torben chuckled. "The captain *hates* ships. He is also convinced something is going on between us… and he is not looking forward to overhearing something indecent coming from our corner of the room."

My stomach flipped. "And why would he think something is going on between us, Torben?"

"I thought for sure you would be more interested in my suggestion that we share a corner." Torben stepped closer and his eyes glittered as he watched my reaction.

"I guess I have grown accustomed to sleeping next to you when we travel. I will be sure to keep quiet, so Theo isn't bothered." My cheeks flushed despite my fruitless efforts. What was I suggesting?

Torben growled softly in his throat as he looked up to the ceiling of the wooden room. "You are going to make this a living nightmare for Theo if you keep saying things like that."

I laughed as I walked to the table, needing to create space between us before the tension became too strong to ignore.

I grabbed a chunk of crusty bread, slathering it with creamy butter, before sitting down to look at the map.

Dalvin was easy to spot. I placed my finger on the small icon where the palace stood before following along the Krossá canal that would take us to the Grimsey Coast. My finger paused as I passed Vogar. The canal had been like a lifeline for my home region, bringing prosperity to the landowners and nobility. My family had lived in a marvelous estate that overlooked the canal, and I felt my heart sink when I realized we would pass by my former home.

Torben was watching me as I looked at the map, I could feel his eyes on my back as if they were sparks from a fire. He approached slowly until he was standing on the other side of the table. I was still running a finger along the map as he leaned over, placing his hands on the table to support himself, the muscles in his forearms dancing as he moved. "Kaari," he said softly, "would you like to go home... to Vogar?"

He couldn't have known what that question meant to me and why I hadn't allowed myself to think about going home for the past hundred years.

"I can't," I breathed, "not yet."

Torben's eyes were gentle, his lips twitched as he clenched his jaw and nodded his head. "Well, whenever you're ready, I'll make sure you can get there."

I choked out a sob I didn't know I had been holding and reached out for his hand. He was warm and solid, like a spruce that has endured a thousand storms. "Thank you... perhaps you could come with me." I sniffled and cleared my throat before rubbing my damp eyes with my free hand. A strangled laugh escaped my throat as I looked at where my hand rested on his. "I'm sorry I still don't really remember how to act around royalty... I'm sure it's not supposed to be like this." My words were a garbled mix of a sob and laughter.

He walked around the table as I spoke until he was so close I could feel his breath on my cheek. The room felt so small, the waves under the ship lulling us into a trancelike rhythm, but the man in front of me was suddenly the surest thing I had known in a long time.

"Kaari. You don't ever have to be ashamed because your heart feels the weight of the world. And I appreciate that you do not act like the others in court. I think you are the first woman who has ever seen *me*... really seen me. Not because of my power or my crown," he said, the deepness of his voice making my legs weak. "Unless you have been playing me for a complete fool."

I shivered, realizing he had done the same for me. He had seen past my power to my soul at the center that yearned for something more.

 26

The water in the canal was relatively calm, the rolling waves a deep cobalt that sparkled with the light of the setting sun. The gentle rocking of the ship gave way to a persistent sleepiness that made me want to stay in bed until we reached port.

We spent the first day on the water looking at the map and reviewing the reports from the locals. By dinner, we had a plan for where we would go once we reached port so we could secure horses and provisions. Fortunately, being a royal envoy would entitle us to the resources of the base that was stationed just outside the harbor.

By the time the moons lifted high above the water, I was so exhausted that I fell asleep in my clothes. Theo and Torben's whispers as they surveyed the map had been like a warrior's lullaby that lulled me into a dreamless sleep. Eventually, I felt Torben crawl into the small bed with me, his warm body pressed so closely against mine that I could feel the rise and fall of his chest.

It should have felt strange to sleep next to him… but it didn't. Sleep that night had been heavy and deep, as if we had all tucked into our beds ready to hibernate for a long Kall.

The ship was approaching the end of the canal by the time the sun crested over the horizon. I was silently grateful that we had passed most of the coast of Vogar during the night, but I knew that as midmorning approached, we would pass by my family's estate. My childhood home was nestled high on the cliffs overlooking the estuary at the end of the canal. As a child, my bedroom had overlooked the water and I had spent countless hours watching the waves as they crashed along the rocks, always hoping to catch a glimpse of the Kraken that my mother swore swam nearby.

For all I knew, the estate might have been destroyed at some point in the past century. After I escaped, I had run for my life and never looked back.

I woke to find Torben and Theo scouring over the map again, whispering as they strategized. They both smiled at me when I woke. I grunted and waved my hand in the air. I wanted to know what they were discussing, but not until I had returned from taking care of my personal needs and changing my shirt behind the curtain that hung in the corner of the small room.

"Permission to speak?" Theo asked slyly once I approached the table. I tried to smack his shoulder, but he was surprisingly quick for such a large man.

"Granted," I mumbled, rubbing my eyes to chase away the last memory of sleep.

"We should make it to port by late afternoon. There is an inn where we can stay for the night before setting out tomorrow morning," Theo said.

I glanced towards the door that led to the main deck. "Well, that's a relief," I said, my voice distant. "It will be good to get on solid ground."

"I have sent word that we would like to speak to those who were attacked. They are gathering in Nuuk. While we travel, we will be able to search the area for any signs of the Undercreatures." Theo traced his finger along the map, marking the path we would take. I knew I should be more interested in our plan, but our proximity to Vogar was making it hard to think clearly.

I nodded absently and then walked out the door, desperately needing fresh air—and to see where we were along the canal.

The sun was warm and the breeze off the water was cool and refreshing. My eyes glanced at the port side of the ship and the cliffs beyond. We were closer than I thought, and the realization made my breath catch in my throat. I leaned my arms along the taffrail and looked down to the water below. The cliffs that surrounded the canal were steep and jagged but lush trees and shrubs lined the land. So much of my early years had been spent exploring those woods. As I closed my eyes, I could almost feel the soft ground beneath my bare feet and smell the pine sap that leaked from the ancient trees.

The wind had picked up, helping the ship cruise through the canal at a decent speed. Wisps of hair had escaped my braid while I slept and brushed gently against my cheeks as the surroundings washed over me. Torben appeared by my side without warning. He didn't say a word as he looked out at the coast in front of us, letting me decide if I wanted to speak.

I knew that if I pointed out my family home, there was a chance Torben would recognize the estate that had once belonged to my parents. Torben knew enough from seeing my powers that I was High Fae, but I had not yet told him that I was of *noble* birth. And even more specifically, that I was the daughter of the late Lord Steinar and Lady Liva of Vogar.

Not here—I couldn't tell him here.

"It really is beautiful," he said.

"It is. It's amazing how much the trees have grown since I last saw these cliffs." I feigned a smile.

"A hundred years will do that."

"When we get to the Grimsey Coast... I want to tell you about my past." My voice was a promise that carried on the breeze. Perhaps the Vogarian air was filling my heart as much as my lungs. The earthy mix of spruce and peat collided with the salty air so forcefully that I felt like I was being pulled under— back to a place where I couldn't hide who I was. And as Torben watched me with understanding and patience in his golden-brown eyes, I found that I didn't want to hide myself anymore.

Torben's eyes narrowed. "That night I told you I wanted to know everything about you... I meant it."

I would tell him everything—even if it broke his heart.

Torben gazed thoughtfully across the canal. "The waves grow choppy. I should go make sure Theo isn't hurling into a bucket."

"We certainly don't want that," I agreed.

The ship rounded the estuary and, in the distance, I could just make out the tower that was hidden amongst the trees. There at the top of the cliff, my family home still stood.

The glimpse of the estate was enough to set my nerves into overdrive. My palms were warm with the push of my magic as I thought of my home. *Did anyone live there now?* I wondered. Were my parent's books still packed onto the shelves in the library? Or had they been ransacked when the assassins had unleased all hells within the once inviolable walls? I desperately needed to release my pent-up energy. Unfortunately, none of my normal strategies were an option. After pacing around the deck until my skin was saturated with salt and my hair had been swept out of my braid by the relentless breeze, I went below deck to pack my things.

Back in our cabin, I was surprised to find Torben reading through the report I had been working on for Emil. He sat with his feet up on the table so that the chair leaned on the two back legs, his eyebrows pinched in concentration. I marveled at how relaxed he looked.

"Doing a little light reading, Your Highness?" I asked.

Torben brought his eyes to meet mine. "You sure managed to keep busy up there in Árnes. Here I was thinking you spent your time growing flowers and mixing salves," he teased.

"Why do you think I needed so many salves?" I countered, shifting to put my hands on my hips. "If you haven't noticed, most of the creatures I encountered in the Woods have rather sharp claws and teeth." I thought I saw Torben shudder as he shook his head and put the report down. "Where's Theo?" I added, wanting to change the subject.

"He needed some fresh air. Once we dock, he will meet up with a small group of guards who will help us move to the inn—arriving at night will help, but people still tend to get rather excited when a royal envoy arrives."

"I'm sure all the women will be out in their finery, ready to offer themselves to warm your bed."

Torben scoffed, "Well they will be thoroughly disappointed to hear the position of bed warmer has already been filled."

I laughed, although I wasn't quite sure if he was kidding. We hadn't discussed sleeping arrangements once we arrived, and I figured it would all depend on the availability at the inn—there was a solid chance I would be bunking with Torben *and* Theo again. Either way, my stomach flipped at the suggestion that I was the one warming the prince's bed.

Through the small windows of our cabin, I could see the sun beginning to set. My stomach rumbled, reminding me that I had not eaten. Torben's ears twitched as if he had heard my hunger pains. At that moment, Theo walked through the door carrying a tray of food, the smell of fresh bread and fried fish filling the small cabin.

I began salivating and rushed over to help him clear a space on the table. "Well captain, you officially take the lead as my favorite man on this ship."

For the first time in days, Theo laughed.

27

The walk through the port and into the small coastal village had been relatively uneventful. The sun had set by the time we got off the ship and lanterns lit the way down the cobbled streets. As expected, a small crowd had formed to greet us. Theo and the local guards led the way to help us pass through unscathed. Torben had taken his time shaking hands and thanking the locals for their hospitality. I marveled at how easily he interacted with his people and how well-loved he seemed. Being so disconnected from the kingdom's politics, I hadn't realized that the people genuinely cherished this royal family.

A group of children approached, waving handmade wooden swords, their chubby faces smeared with snot and sand. They seemed entranced by Torben and Theo and bowed deeply when we reached them. Torben smiled warmly and patted his fist to his chest in salute. Running alongside us, they tossed questions at Torben and Theo and eyed me warily.

"How many wars have you fought in?"

"Is that sword heavy?"

"Are your muscles real?"

I swear I heard Theo choke down a laugh at the last one.

As we walked, Torben took turns scooping each of the children onto his shoulders and twirling them in vicious circles. The giddy laughter echoed off the streets, inspiring contagious smiles among the crowd.

Once the children were content and dizzy, they left Torben to recover. I watched as he bent over to brush the dust from his knees. He planted his hands on his thighs as if catching his breath and when he lifted his head, his eyes found me through the sea of people. His smile made my stomach flip like a capsized boat— pinched on the side, showing a hint of his strong white teeth. He held my gaze until Theo cleared his throat, motioning for me to keep walking.

"This happens every time," Theo muttered as we continued down the cobbled street that led to the inn. I wasn't sure if he was referring to the crowds or to Torben roughhousing with the children.

The inn was located on the outskirts of the village in an old two-story building that looked like it had been renting rooms for several hundred years. The shingles were a worn faded grey—although I imagined they were once as black as a raven's wing. A general clatter emanated from the rickety building that seemed to lean slightly. I caught myself feeling the force of the breeze, wondering what it would take for this place to finally topple over.

Inside, the owner greeted us, her red hair streaked with silver and her charming face adorned with fine wrinkles. She had been close to bursting with excitement when she realized the Prince of Akureyrian needed a room. She gave us three without hesitation, smiling with a toothy grin as she handed Torben the keys.

Desperate to peel off my salty clothes and wash my face, I had taken my key and gone straight to my room without so much as a word to Torben and Theo. The room was small with a single bed tucked into the corner next to an open window. There was a table with a bar of soap and a wash bucket that was filled with cool water. After washing the dust and salt from my skin I changed into the short dress that Milla packed for me to sleep in. The silk was delightfully soft, and the length of the dress allowed the cool breeze from the window to kiss my legs.

Flopping down onto the stiff mattress, I closed my eyes and listened to the sounds of the village that drifted through the window. Despite the hour, the village was alive with the sounds of a coastal town. My sensitive ears could hear the cats—or rats—scurrying through the alley behind the inn, hushed voices walking down the cobbled street, and seabirds flying to find a place to sleep.

It was inconceivable that I was here. It seemed like only yesterday I was tucked into my old bed, wrapped in a worn tattered quilt. And now, I was on the Grimsey Coast with a royal envoy tasked with searching for undercreatures who had escaped the wards of the Holvik Woods.

I wondered again how they had escaped. Maybe the garmr were unique in their escape from the Wood. Perhaps as guardians of the gates of the Underworld, they had found a way to expand their border. But if a drekavac was also roaming beyond the border it seemed that something had happened to the wards. What would it take to break the magical barrier that had held the beasts for a thousand years?

I shivered as I crawled under the rough sheets. For a moment, I wished Torben was lying beside me—if only for the warmth his solid body provided. But the flip in my stomach was enough to tell me that I didn't just miss him for his body heat.

The bed was narrow and uncomfortable, its sheets coarse and scratchy against my skin. The contrast of my nightdress, soft and luxurious, seemed almost mocking against the harsh texture beneath. It clung to my body, whispering across my skin with every slight movement, but none of it could distract me from the thoughts racing in my mind.

I couldn't stop thinking about him.

A shiver tingled through me that had nothing to do with the cold. I thought of his smile, warm and kind, the way his eyes crinkled at the corners whenever he laughed—how his laughter felt like sunlight breaking through the clouds.

With him, I felt alive in a way I hadn't in years. His Treyst, too, had embraced me, welcomed me into their fold with a warmth and sincerity that made me feel as though I belonged. In their company, the heavy weight I always carried seemed to lighten, if only for a few hours. It was easy to laugh with them, to forget, even for a little while, who I was and the secrets I harbored.

I turned onto my side, pulling the thin blanket tighter around my shoulders, though it did little to fend off the chill. I didn't belong in his world, not truly. If Torben knew the secret I held, would he still look at me with those soft, trusting eyes? Or would his warmth turn cold, his kindness turn to distance?

I squeezed my eyes shut, but that only made the image of him clearer in my mind. His voice, steady and sure, calling my name; the way he had looked at me that day in the garden, as though I was the only one in the world. I felt a pang in my chest at the thought. It would be so easy to give in, to let myself fall completely, to let the secrets slip away into the shadows where they belonged.

But I couldn't.

I couldn't afford to forget who I was. Because one day soon, my secrets would come to light. And when they did, I could only hope Torben and his Treyst would still stand by me.

The scratch of the sheets felt sharper against my skin, pulling me back to the cold, uncomfortable reality of the small room. I sighed softly, my fingers brushing the delicate silk of my nightdress as if to remind myself that some things, at least, could still feel soft and comforting.

He makes me feel alive, I thought.

It was both exhilarating and terrifying. It had been so long since I had allowed myself to feel anything at all, let alone this rush of warmth and affection that threatened to overtake me. But no matter how much I tried to hold on to that feeling, the secret I kept was always there, lurking just beneath the surface, ready to pull me back down.

Pulling the covers up to my nose, I let the sounds of the village wash over me until I finally slipped into a deep sleep.

28

Theo secured three horses and enough provisions for a week of traveling across the Grimsey Coast. After settling our dues with the innkeeper, he dragged me and Torben from sleep.

The road out of the village was long and winding and passed through endless fields of lush grass and mossy rocks. The closest account of the attacks had come from a small farm village a half a day's ride from the port.

"I really hope this isn't a drekavac. They are gruesome creatures. In Árnes, their screams can be heard in the surrounding villages," I offered, stifling a yawn as we rode through a misty fog.

"What do they eat in the Holvik Woods?" Torben asked. It was one of the common misconceptions about Undercreatures. That they attacked travelers in the Holvik Woods because they were hungry. That before their banishment they had feasted on unsuspecting mortals and Fae.

"The drekavac don't need to eat to survive. They, like most of the undercreatures, do not hunt because they are hungry, but because they thrive on fear. The Undercreatures don't care about flesh or blood or bones. No, they want something far more terrifying. They attack to instill fear, to spread it like a sickness. The fear is what keeps it alive, what gives it strength. If you've ever heard a drekavac scream—" I paused, my voice quivering just for a moment, before steadying again. "—you'll know. It's not just a sound. It gets *inside* you. Imagine dragon talons scraping across your mind—that's what it feels like. It paralyzes you."

I pulled my cloak around my neck, as if it could offer some protection. "Drekavac scream before they attack because they aren't afraid that you will run away. They know that even if you do, they will catch you. It doesn't stop until it's filled you with enough fear to last a lifetime. Until your heart races so fast you think it'll burst. And even then... it doesn't kill you."

"So, the reports of the screaming sound are what peaked your suspicions that these attacks might be drekavac?" Torben asked methodically.

"Mostly, yes," I admitted. My father had told me stories of what life had been like before the drekavac and other creatures were banished. The Fae, at least, had their magics to help protect them... but the mortals were not so fortunate.

"I should have paid more attention in history," Torben muttered.

"The banishment happened long before you were born," Theo grunted. "It's been a thousand years since Queen Maiken used her magic to banish the goddess-damned undercreatures."

A shiver went down my spine at the mention of Queen Maiken.

My mother always said she was the most powerful Fae who had ever ruled—perhaps who ever lived. A queen unlike any other who had used every drop of her powerful magic—and her soul—to contain the creatures within Árnes… to keep them away from the people of Akureyrian.

"I know the story of Queen Maiken," Torben snorted. "I just didn't experience it as intimately as you, captain."

Was Torben suggesting that Theo had been *alive* when Maiken reigned? Goddess, I knew he was old, but that would make him *really* old.

A quaint village came into view as the sun started to set beyond the horizon. We were far enough inland that the breeze no longer smelled of salt and the landscape was a mix of grassy fields and rolling hills. Waterfalls in the distance fed the lake that wrapped protectively around the village.

Theo doubted there would be an inn in a village this remote, so we had packed a tent and sleeping mats. We settled for a small clearing near the edge of the lake and made camp. The Grimsey Coast was known for its jagged shorelines and cascading waterfalls and the view from our camp certainly lived up to the reputation. Waves rolled lazily across the surface and gently crested along the shore. The water here was so clear it seemed to be made from glass.

I had taken a quick walk around our camp to look for any sign of a drekavac—or any other creature—before sitting down next to the fire that Torben was tending.

Theo went further down along the water to wash and fill our canteens, leaving me and Torben alone. I had the sense that he had a thousand questions he wanted to ask me, but he was quiet as he sat with his arms crossed over his knees and stared at the flames. I needed to break the silence—I needed to tell him something about my past.

"The Grimsey Coast is where I learned how to fight," I said, still staring at the fire. Torben's ears twitched and he turned to look at me. "When I left Vogar, I traveled through the Grimsey Coast on my way to Árnes. I spent some time living in an abandoned hunting shack that overlooked the royal training base. Every day I would watch as the guards went through their exercises until one day I got the nerve to grab a stick and follow along."

"A stick?" Torben asked with a smirk on his face as he playfully nudged his shoulder into mine, the contact sending goosebumps down my arms.

"Well, I didn't exactly have a *proper* weapon," I sneered. "Three years... I spent three years in that cabin. I would wake up before dawn to go hunting so I was back before the soldiers started their training. I would follow along from a distance. I saw countless units go through their training on that field—but I stayed and watched, learning everything I could." My voice had dropped to a whisper as the memories engulfed me. "I knew I didn't stand a chance on my own if I didn't know the basics of how to protect myself."

"Kaari," the prince paused, "why did you leave Vogar?" There was no hint of judgment or suspicion in his voice, only concern... and something like sorrow.

I needed to tell him.

It was time.

Just as I opened my mouth to speak, Theo's footsteps approached down the path. I choked down the words and looked deep into his eyes, trying to convey how much I wanted to tell him.

Torben nodded softly before standing. He patted Theo's shoulders. "Did you bathe? You still smell like shit."

"You're one to talk," Theo barked.

"Fine," the prince said, "I'll go wash off."

A smile slipped onto my face as I watched them banter. "I'm going to bed. Make sure you both wipe your feet before you come inside." They looked at each other and then rolled their eyes dramatically before I turned to crawl into the tent.

Sleep found me quickly and I was only half aware when Torben lay down next to me—the smell of vanilla and cedar wrapping me in a comforting warmth. His presence softened the edges of my dreams, grounding me even as I drifted further into sleep. The weight of his arm settled gently across me, and in that moment, I felt cocooned—secure and at peace.

The scream that blasted through the tent was as shrill as a soaring hawk. I jolted awake, instinctively reaching for the sword tucked under my pillow. Panic flooded through me as I saw Torben racing to grab his weapons. Theo was already outside, having taken watch while we slept.

Outside, a shadow in the distance made my heart stop. It was instantly clear that this was not a Fae or mortal. The creature staggered awkwardly across the field as if its oversized head made it too top-heavy to be graceful. I signaled to Torben and Theo to follow me. The shadow moved towards a field where several sheep started to rouse from their sleep, and I cursed under my breath. Movement from the other side of the field caught my eye as another shadow began circling. *Holy gods*, I thought, *they are working together*.

Theo noticed the second shadow and nodded to me and Torben, a silent directive that he would approach one, while we approached the other.

I breathed slowly, trying to settle my mind. I forced my magic to stay hidden as I felt the warmth creep into my fingers as if it knew I might need it. I didn't want to use magic unless absolutely necessary. But if Torben or Theo were in danger, I would not hesitate to unleash my power on the creatures that lurked in the darkness.

Another piercing scream ripped through the night, and I released any doubt about the identity of the creatures. But seeing *two* drekavac that appeared to be working together was enough to turn my blood to ice.

We needed to stop the attack before the screams drew the farmers outside to investigate, knowing they would likely be unarmed and unprepared for what awaited them. Could they be *trying* to lure people out into the open? I picked up my pace, running towards the creature until the midnight air swallowed me in darkness. Torben followed and before I knew it, we were within range. The drekavac turned its bulbous head and looked straight at us with massive green eyes. Its body was sickly thin with ashen skin shadowed over its haggard ribcage. The creature stood on two feet—but I knew they would sometimes use their arms to run on all fours.

Cursing out loud, I lunged at the beast and swung my sword. A guttural sound filled the air as Theo pummeled the second creature on the other side of the field. Swinging my arms again, I came within inches of striking the drekavac's slender body. I jumped to the side to avoid its dagger-like claws, but the creature lurched towards me, dragging a razor-sharp finger down my side.

A blast of power threw the creature onto the ground. Torben was circling the beast as his hands pulsed with power. Hissing at the pain in my side, I used the distraction to roll so that I was behind the beast. My legs trembled but I managed to kick solidly into its bony back. The creature lunged at Torben. He didn't hesitate as he lifted his sword to jab deep into the drekavac's sunken belly. The sound of his sword as it sliced its leathery skin reverberated through the darkness until the creature fell to the ground.

Once it fell, Torben and I were immediately running towards Theo who was slicing at the other drekavac's arms, his face splattered with black blood. The beast risked a glance at the sound of our approaching feet, and it was just enough time for Theo to slam his sword into the creature's side. I raced to Theo, needing to know that the blood I saw was not his.

He waved me off. "I'm fine," he growled, his blue eyes as bright as lightning. "It's not my blood."

I breathed heavily with relief as I looked from Theo to Torben.

"*Bölva,*" Theo and I cursed in unison.

"My sentiments exactly," Torben coughed.

The sheep had cleared the field, leaving the three of us breathless and dazed.

"Fuck," I swore again.

"What do we do with the bodies?" Theo questioned, always the pragmatist of our morbid team.

"We need to *burn* them," I growled.

"We should alert the farmers, so they don't think we are trying to burn down their fields," Torben responded.

I stared at the drekavac that lay in a pile on the ground, their black blood steaming in the cool night. "Burning fields are the least of their concerns."

We would not sleep anymore tonight. Theo had gone to tell the farmers about the creatures that had attempted to attack their livestock and explained why we would be setting a fire on their land. The Fae couple had been incredibly grateful, and the captain had come back with two loaves of bread and a bag of jerky they gifted us to show their appreciation.

Needing to wash the deep cut on my side, I headed for the lake.

"Where are you going?" Torben called.

"I just need to clean myself up a little," I said, waving him off. Torben nearly growled as his gaze shifted to the blood stain on the side of my shirt.

"I promise, I will survive," I said through gritted teeth. "It's nothing I haven't dealt with before."

The sky was still dark with the shadow of night and clouds covered the light from the moons. I brought a torch to the edge of the lake, needing the glow of light to navigate the rocky path. Stepping into the water, I winced at the sting in my side as I peeled off my shirt—the fabric matted with dirt, grass, and dried blood. Thankfully my magic had helped the wound to start clotting, but it throbbed with every touch. I still needed to clean the area to prevent an infection. I had been through worse—I could handle this. My hands trembled as I tried to clean the wound, but the pain was making it hard to focus.

The snap of a stick made me jump and I spun around to see Torben standing at the edge of the water, his eyes filled with worry—enough so that he didn't even seem to notice my nearly bare chest.

I rolled my eyes as I turned around and continued washing my side. I glanced down to check that the undergarment used to secure my chest was in place, acutely aware of my lack of clothing.

My breath caught in my throat as he started walking towards me, his steps creating ripples in the water as he approached. Silently, he reached his strong arms around me as he took the damp cloth from my hand and pressed it gently against the wound. I sucked in my breath as he blotted away the crusted blood, the contrast of pain and tenderness sending goosebumps across my skin.

His touch was soft and gentle as he allowed the cool water to drip down my side. He worked in silence, his fingers brushing against my skin with the kind of compassion I wasn't used to—didn't know how to accept. His other hand rested on my shoulder, gently supporting me as I waivered from lightheadedness. Although I had slept next to him on several occasions, *this* closeness felt different. I somehow felt vulnerable and safe at the same time.

Finally, I surrendered to my exhaustion and leaned into him just enough that my back rested on his chest—as if I could simply melt into his strength.

"You said it was nothing," he spoke in a deep rumble.

"Oh, this little thing?" I hissed as he dripped fresh water on my skin, his breath warm and steady on the back of my neck. "I'll be fine, Torben… really," I said as I turned to face him. I hated this—being seen like this, being weak in front of him. But as I covered my chest with my blood-stained arms, I saw the guilt that coated his golden-brown eyes.

"I never wanted to put you in danger," he said as he ran his hands up the sides of my arms. "I know you can handle yourself and that you want to be doing this—"

"The overprotective guise is not a good look for you, Your Highness." My throat had tightened at his words, at the quiet care behind them.

"Kaari." He was holding my shoulders now, his face firm with concern. "I *care* about you. I only wish that—" His voice trailed off, but he held my gaze.

His words wrapped around me, soft and warm, and for the first time in as long as I could remember, I felt myself wanting to believe them. I felt myself *wanting* to let him in, to trust him with more than just my survival, but perhaps with my heart. I reached my hands up to his chest, needing to feel if his heart was racing as fast as mine. I shivered as my fingers traced the rugged contours.

"You're freezing," he whispered.

I was. My skin was covered in goosebumps and my teeth had started to chatter, but standing in his arms I couldn't help but feel a warmth that reached deep into my core. Torben pulled his shirt off over his head and wrapped it around my shoulders, shielding me from the crisp air.

I held his gaze as he reached down and took my blood-stained shirt out of my hands. I thought about thanking him but found that my breath had caught. Something inside me was shifting, something fragile and unfamiliar.

It felt like trust.

Torben was silent for a moment, and then his hand moved, slowly, carefully, until his fingers brushed against mine. The touch was light, almost hesitant, as if he were waiting for me to pull away. But I didn't.

My pulse quickened, the air between us suddenly charged with something electric, something that made me feel more exposed than any wound ever could. I lifted my gaze to meet his, and as the light from the moons flickered off the lake, I saw something in his eyes—something tender, something raw.

"I—" I started to speak, but the words tangled in my throat.

Torben's hand shifted, his fingers threading through mine, his grip firm but gentle. It wasn't just a touch. It was a promise.

"I care about you," he said again, his gaze never leaving mine. "More than you realize. More than I can say."

My heart skipped a beat, the weight of his confession settling over me like a warm blanket. And suddenly, all the moments between us—the quiet looks, the shared laughter, the way he always seemed to stand a little closer than necessary—came rushing back to me in a flood of understanding. He hadn't just been a companion. He had been there, by my side, not out of obligation, but because he *wanted* to be.

The realization hit me like a wave, and in that instant, everything shifted. The way I felt about him—about his steady presence, his quiet strength, the way he made me feel like I wasn't alone—became impossibly clear.

I cared about him, too.

My fingers tightened around his, and I let out a shaky breath, my chest swelling with a mixture of fear and exhilaration. "Torben… I care about you, too. More than I thought I could."

He exhaled slowly, a smile tugging at the corners of his lips, and then, without a word, he pulled my hand to his chest, holding it over his heart. I could feel the steady, comforting rhythm of it beneath my palm, grounding me in a way nothing else ever had.

"Good," he whispered, his voice barely audible above the gentle lapping of water. "Because I'm not going anywhere."

As he led me back to the fire, I could still feel the spot where his hands had rested on my arms—a reminder of how close our bodies had been. I desperately wanted to curl up against the warmth of his chest until the sun was high in the sky.

Theo was waiting for us outside the tent, his eyes lit with concern as he saw the blood stain on my discarded shirt.

"I'm fine," I huffed. "It was just a scratch."

Theo's eyes shot to Torben for confirmation and my heart warmed to see the genuine concern the captain seemed to have for my wellbeing.

"I'm going to lie down," I said.

It would be another hour before the sun came up. I gritted my teeth as I crawled into the tent, the freshly healed skin on my side pulling with each movement. Every muscle ached as I settled myself onto the ground. But after the encounter with the drekavac and the lingering feeling of Torben's words and his hands on my bare skin, I doubted I would find relief in sleep.

As predicted, sleep was futile. Laying on the mat in the dark tent, I slowly ran a cloth over my sword, desperately needing to wipe away the black blood that coated the metal.

A drekavac—make that *two* drekavac—wandering well beyond the border of the Holvik Woods where Maiken's magic had held them for over a thousand years. *What has changed to make them free to roam Akureyrian? And how far will they go?* My mind was racing, an endless string of questions without answers.

Torben and Theo were whispering outside the tent, thoughtfully keeping their voices low in case I was sleeping. I crawled to the tent flap and poked my head out. "I'm not sleeping," I grumbled, "I might as well hear what we are going to do next."

They looked surprised to see me, but Torben nodded and patted his hand on the ground—inviting me to join them by the fire. Theo watched me silently, his blue eyes bright and alert as he swallowed his words.

"We will head to Nuuk, to meet with the Fae who were attacked. We need to confirm that the drekavac is to blame." Torben's voice was firm and categorical.

I simply nodded in agreement. Nuuk was a larger seaside village, several miles from the training camp that I had observed so many years ago.

"Once we're done. Theo will bring us back to Dalvin where we will report our findings to my father."

My confusion was clear. "What do you mean Theo will *bring us back*?"

Theo was using a rock to sharpen a small dagger as if he wasn't part of the conversation, but I could see the way his jaw clicked with tension.

Torben's reply was maddeningly casual, "Theo can portal jump."

30

You mean to tell me we could have skipped days of seasickness and sore asses from riding horseback and just *portal jumped*?"

"We needed to be able to bring supplies. And the extra travel time gave us a chance to solidify our plan before roaming the coast. Besides, there isn't a portal near the village where we found the drekavac. But there is a portal in Nuuk near the training base, making it the most direct portal to get *back* to Dalvin," Theo offered.

"Why didn't you portal jump out of the Innnes Mountains?" I asked, exasperated.

"Because there isn't a portal there to jump through," Theo said simply with a slight shrug of his broad shoulders. "You have to have a portal to be able to portal jump. This is not the same type of magic as someone who can Distance Walk." He seemed thoroughly annoyed that he was having to explain how these magics worked as he stood and brushed off his knees before turning to go to the woods—whether to relieve himself or hit something, I wasn't sure.

"You know," Torben whispered, quietly enough that Theo couldn't hear, "*you* could learn to portal jump."

I shot him a look that said I would rather *swim* back to Dalvin than use my magic to portal jump.

"Just a thought," Torben quipped.

A thought that made me queasy.

Thousands of years ago, the portals had been used regularly to travel across the kingdom. The High Fae were either born with the magic that allowed them to jump or were given special medallions, called *miða*, that acted as tickets to grant their passage. I had never known anyone who could travel without *miða* and the medallions were nearly impossible to find. I had assumed the portals were useless relics of the past.

With raw magic it would be *possible* for me to portal jump—in theory. A theory I did not want to test.

There was a portal in Vogar. I remembered stumbling across it as a child while exploring the tunnels under my family's estate, and I remembered running to my father to tell him about my discovery. My father had traced the curved arch of the entrance with his hand before telling me about the history of the portals and how *his* father had used them to quickly access other parts of the realm. My father's generation had been the first that had not been born with the power to jump. Occasionally, High Fae would be born with the power, but it was exceedingly rare.

"How *old* are you?" I asked Theo when he returned, as realization thundered through me.

"Old," Torben and Theo said in unison.

We arrived in Nuuk by late afternoon. Theo tied up the horses and then walked with Torben as a small crowd gathered around him. A man named Dag had been introduced to us because his mate had been attacked. The devastation seemed to ravage his handsome face. Eyes that I imagined once shined a brilliant green looked hollow and muted like sun-stained moss—devoid of any glimpse of joy or hope. Torben had offered his sincerest sympathies before asking him to join us in the local tavern so we could hear his story. Dag accepted and told us that the others would be along shortly so they could share their experiences as well.

The tavern reeked of stale ale and stew that had been left to simmer too long, but the space was warm from the roaring fire in the hearth. Torben led our small group to a table in the back corner to allow for some privacy while Theo went to talk to some of the locals outside.

Slowly, we were joined by four other locals—three Fae and a mortal.

Once the barmaid came over with several tankards of ale and steaming bowls of stew, they all took turns sharing their stories.

Dag went first, having coordinated the meeting. He recounted how his mate, a Fae named Margret, had gone outside to check on their small flock of chickens before turning in for the night. His deep voice cracked as he described the panic that had set in when she did not return. My heart twisted as he tried to explain what it had been like to realize she was missing. The connection between mates was set by the gods, the deepest connection that Fae could have, and to lose one's mate was to lose a part of their soul. In the time Dag searched for Margret he surely felt like his soul was splitting in two.

After finding the empty basket she had brought with her to collect eggs. He had finally found her huddled behind a stack of straw, her limp body bloodied and bruised beyond recognition.

Torben was gentle in his approach as he asked Dag about anything that stood out or seemed unusual near the time of the attack. "Did you hear anything unusual?" he asked.

"No, but that's not surprising. I was at the grindstone before I realized she was gone," Dag admitted.

The man at the table interjected, "Aye, I heard a sound before the beast got my Olve." He looked to be in his seventh or eighth decade—impressive for a mortal.

Torben didn't miss a beat, "You say it was a beast that attacked your boy? What kind of beast?"

"A beast from the deepest layer of hell, Your Highness," he said stoically. "All claws and teeth, that one was. With skin as translucent as an onion. The type of beast yer mam uses to keep kids from sneaking out after dark. Never in my life—" his voice trailed off.

One by one, the others shared their stories. The mortal's son had been attacked while stacking wood— a punishment for sneaking out with a neighbor's daughter. He was expected to live but would likely never regain use of his left hand.

Next, a Fae with brilliant red hair spoke. Her arm was wrapped in a bulky bandage that she rubbed her fingers over as she spoke. "It came out of nowhere," she said. "But I grabbed my dagger after I heard the scream. If it hadn't screamed, I probably wouldn't have had time to protect myself." I felt myself straighten in my seat at the mention of the scream. The others perked up as well—nodding their heads as well, sharing the experience.

"Did you all hear a scream as well?" I asked gently.

"Aye, I still hear it when I close my eyes."

"Nothing like I have ever heard."

"It was as if the King of the Underworld came above to cast his shadow upon us," Dag added, his pitch rising and falling like the waves of an approaching storm. The image painted a vivid image of terror, challenging our group to the face the precipice of this new reality.

An hour later, Dag bowed deeply as he thanked Torben for personally making the trip to investigate the attacks.

A breeze filled the room as the tavern door opened and Theo strode in, his presence overwhelming the small space like a storm trapped in a bottle. His eyes locked onto mine as he pulled his cloak away from his face. For the first time, I noticed the fine lines that reached from the sides of his eyes, the only physical sign on his handsome face of what I suspected was his *immense* age.

"Captain," Torben exclaimed as Leif stepped into the tavern behind Theo, "to what do we owe this unexpected pleasure?"

"I should have known I would find you in the tavern. Master Trygg, it is wonderful to see you again, I hope these two haven't been too insufferable."

I smiled as Leif took a seat at our table. "How did you get here? Do *you* portal jump too?"

Leif laughed. "No, I'm nowhere near as old as this hag, but there are others in the palace who can make the jump."

"I'm not even that old," Theo grumbled.

The barmaid noticed our new arrival and brought over another large mug of ale. "Compliments of the house, Your Highness," she said with a flirtatious smile. Torben thanked her and I watched as the maid strode away with a sultry swagger that caught the attention of my companions.

"You are a bunch of pigs. Do you know that?" I snapped and Torben choked on his ale.

Leif blushed and said, "Forgive us, sometimes our manners are like a coat you bring to a friend's house—essential when you arrived but left behind in the comfort of familiarity." Leif looked intently at his friends. "You all look like shit—except you, Kaari."

"I know," I replied casually, and to my delight Torben and Theo rolled their eyes.

Leif shifted where he stood. "I had to come. You were too far for me to transmit. Word of the attacks has started to spread. Whispers have even arrived in Dalvin and the king is anxious for an update. Orders have been placed with the blacksmiths and armorers in Dalvin. But we don't yet understand our enemy. He wanted me to come to make sure your mission was yielding results."

Torben scoffed but cleared his throat and leaned in closer over the table as he began to tell Leif what had happened with the drekavac and what we had learned from the locals during our travels. Leif's eyes grew and he slowly shook his head. "So, it's true then. The undercreatures have escaped?"

"Aye, I didn't think I would see another day that the drekavac wandered freely," Theo said under his breath, as Leif let out a low whistle.

Holy gods, I thought, *he* is *that old*.

"Do you want to go back to Dalvin tonight, or stay here?" Theo asked.

I desperately wanted to take a bath and wash the stench of sour ale out of my hair and sighed with relief when Torben said we should return tonight. The stories from the locals in Nuuk had painted a harrowing picture of what life looked like when the undercreatures lurked in the shadows.

"Take me first, and then come back for Kaari. Leif will wait to make sure we aren't followed," Torben said, and Theo nodded.

"Might want to eat something first, Master Trygg. Jumping on an empty stomach is never a good idea." Leif spoke as if he had first-hand experience.

My stomach twisted at the thought, but I reached for a thick piece of bread and slathered it with butter. In my wildest dreams, I had never imagined I would be preparing to portal jump across the kingdom with the Prince of Akureyrian and his royal Treyst.

The ride to the training base brought us past a long stretch of the coast and I marveled at the stunning ocean views. I had forgotten how *big* the ocean looked from this stretch of land and the memories of my years here started to flood my mind.

The training camp hadn't changed much in the decades since I had last seen it from my perch on the cliff that overlooked the area.

Theo and Leif took the horses to the stables, leaving me and Torben in one of the small command rooms. I was nervously playing with my long braid as Torben walked up to me, his vanilla and cedar scent now mixed with a hint of dirt and stale ale.

"I'm scared shitless," I blurted, "something about going through these ancient portals is *terrifying*."

Torben laughed, the muscles in his chest dancing under his shirt. "I have seen you battle warriors twice your size and slay creatures from the Underworld without flinching, and yet a portal jump is what scares you?" The corner of his mouth pinched and the light from the nearby torch danced across his eyes, giving them a depth and warmth, like molten gold swirling in the shadows. Each movement of the candle seemed to spark a new glimmer, making his gaze both hypnotic and alive with the soft, intimate glow. "Don't worry, Kaari Trygg, the jump will be easier for you than for most Fae."

"Why? Because of my magic?"

"Aye, the magic that runs through your veins will be completely at home in the portal, whereas Leif and I always feel like we are being dragged through a pit of fire since our magic does not naturally allow us to jump. If we were to lose hold of Theo, we would be lost inside. Luckily, he has never let go of us." His expression was excruciatingly casual—a complete contrast to the shock that filled me as I imagined him plummeting through the darkness of the portal. "It'll be fine, Kaari. I will see you back at the palace." He stepped forward so his chest was nearly pressed against my own as he reached for my hand and gently ran his thumb over the scar on my wrist in a silent promise.

It was as if the ground beneath my feet had shifted—subtle at first, like a breeze stirring the air. But now, as we prepared to return to Dalvin, I could feel it in my bones—nothing would be the same. The world I once knew had reshaped itself. Like stepping into a room where the furniture had been quietly rearranged, everything felt slightly off.

The portal was located at the end of a winding passage underneath the barracks. My father had said that most of the portals in the realm were located within tunnels. The large stone arch that surrounded the portal had been crafted in the same style as the one I remembered from my home in Vogar. The dark void inside seemed to swirl with an ancient power that instinctively made me clench down on my magic.

"I'll see you back in Dalvin." Torben smiled as he took Theo's hand and the two men stepped into the void. I couldn't help but gasp as they disappeared out of view without warning.

"How long until Theo comes back?" I managed to ask Leif.

"It won't take long, but with this many consecutive jumps, he may need to rest in between. But Torben's magic is strong, so it is easier for Theo to pull him through."

After several moments that felt like a lifetime, Theo returned through the portal. His skin sparkled with a golden hue, and he had the first signs of perspiration on his forehead.

"The prince is through," he said to me, the blue of his eyes reflecting in my own. "The portal will make you feel like your body is pulling apart. It helps if you pull on your magic as if you were preparing to heal someone. Whatever happens, just keep holding my hand." Theo's voice was soft as if he were coaching a babe to take their first wobbly steps. "Ready?" he asked as he reached for my hand.

Cursing under my breath, I grabbed his hand and followed him into the abyss.

31

Everything was black. The pressure in my head was unbearable as the darkness closed in around me. I was only partially aware that I was squeezing onto Theo—even though my grip was so strong my fingers had gone numb. Images of my past surged through my mind and for a moment I wondered if I had let go of Theo's hand and was plummeting into one of the many layers of hell beneath.

I could feel my magic pulsing under my skin. It felt warm and excited as if it was returning home after a long hiatus.

A low hum seemed to buzz around me. I managed to suck in a breath and in the next instant I was stumbling onto solid ground panting for air as sweat trickled down my brow. The smell of ether filled the dank space and as I lifted my head, my heart stopped. My hands were glowing a brilliant shade of blue. But it wasn't just my hands that glowed with the faint blue light, my whole body seemed to be ablaze.

I clenched my teeth and loosed a foul string of curses as I looked up to see Theo and Torben staring at me. Theo's mouth hung wide open.

"Kaari," Theo whispered as if he was afraid I might combust. I closed my eyes as I went through my breathing exercises, desperately trying to reel in my power. "*Kaari,*" he repeated, more firmly this time.

I opened my eyes slowly, finding the two men still staring at me. Theo was looking at me with an expression I had never seen and Torben looked ready to explain that he already knew about my magic. But it was Theo who spoke first.

"Holy gods, I knew the scent of your magic was familiar. You don't just have raw magic, do you Kaari? You are an ancestor of Maiken," Theo whispered, his voice dripping with disbelief.

My world seemed to crash down around me. The secret I had fought so hard to protect—that my parents had *died* protecting—was suddenly splayed out in the open for Theo—and Torben—to see.

I had failed them.

I clenched my fists, pushing the swell of magic into its sacred vault.

"I wanted to tell you—I was going to tell you," I pled, as I desperately tried to keep a sob from escaping my throat.

Torben's jaw was clenched as he looked at me and then slowly nodded his head. "That certainly explains the raw magic. I take it '*Trygg*' is not your real surname?" His voice was laced with a deadly vibrato.

"No. It's not. I had to change it… after my parents died." I stood frozen, the weight of their stares pressing down on me like an avalanche I could no longer outrun. My breath hitched, shallow and uneven, as if the air was now too thick to inhale. The space felt smaller, every glance a spotlight burning into my skin, exposing everything I had fought so hard to conceal. I could see the shock in their eyes, the confusion, the betrayal flickering beneath the surface. My carefully crafted identity, the one I had worn like armor for so long, had crumbled in an instant, leaving me raw and exposed.

Realization flashed in Torben's eyes as he undoubtedly tracked through Queen Maiken's lineage. "Holy gods. You're Kaari *Eriksen*." My heart pounded, the rhythm chaotic, echoing the jumble of thoughts racing through my mind. I couldn't meet their gazes for long; each pair of eyes felt like a mirror, reflecting the truth I had hidden for so long. My glowing hands trembled at my sides, and I clenched them into fists, as if I could somehow hold myself together amidst the unraveling.

The silence stretched on, thick and suffocating. I could feel the shift—nothing would be the same after this. They knew. The real *me*, the parts I had buried, the past I had tried to escape, had all come rushing to the surface. And as the truth hung in the air between us, fragile and sharp as glass, all I could do was wait for the cracks to finally spread.

My family name on Torben's tongue sparked a fire in my heart. The look on my face must have been enough confirmation because Theo began pacing in front of the portal, his hands holding the back of his head. "So, it's true. You have raw magic... just like the queen did," Theo said, more of a statement than a question.

I was looking back and forth between them. "I never meant to be deceitful. You have to understand, I have spent my *entire life* not being able to trust anyone with this secret. My family died protecting me so that my powers weren't exploited," I paused, and I knew it was time to tell them everything.

Torben's face was firm, the muscles in his jaw clenching as he breathed. "Theo, go and get Leif, I'm sure he's already started to worry. We will regroup tomorrow after everyone has had a chance to sleep."

Theo's eyes were ablaze, and his jaw was set. He seemed worried about leaving Torben with me after feeling the power I held—or perhaps he was concerned for me.

"It's alright Theo," Torben said, his voice measured and firm. "I knew about her magic... I just wasn't aware of *Lady Eriksen's* lineage."

"We will have to find a time to tell Emil and Leif. They care about you too, Kaari." Theo nodded and then stepped back through the portal, leaving me with the lingering feel of his sapphire gaze.

In the empty tunnel, Torben's eyes bore through me as he scanned my face.

"I wanted to tell you," I whispered.

"I told you I would never use you for your power." His voice was.

"And I believe you, Torben. I was just scared—scared that you would see me for my failures, see me as a coward."

His voice softened then, "You, Kaari Eriksen, Master of Undercreature, could never be a coward." His warm hand reached up and cupped my chin. "Kaari, this changes nothing... and everything."

I still felt slightly unsteady after the portal jump and Torben held my hand as he led me through the tunnels. The feel of the rough calluses on his hands as they brushed against my own was stabilizing and comforting. I relied on the firmness of his grip to keep me upright.

He brought me to a set of stairs I had not seen on our last trip through the tunnels. Surprisingly, the door led directly to his private tower. Stepping into his room, Torben laced his fingers behind the back of his head as he started pacing the large space. I looked out the windows, needing something calming and constant to counter the tension. The waves roared against the jagged shoreline, each swell rising with a fury only to break apart in a violent spray, as if the sea itself couldn't contain its own anger. Watching it should've calmed me, but instead it mirrored the tension coiled inside my chest, the restless churn of thoughts I couldn't quite shake. And yet, there was something mesmerizing about the way the water surged and shattered, relentless but inevitable. It reminded me that even the strongest waves would eventually break, and maybe—just maybe—so would the storm inside me.

"I should have known that the portal would amplify your magic," Torben said under his breath, "I'm sorry."

I snapped my head to look at him and crossed the room until I was pressed against his towering form. "Don't you *dare* apologize to me. I'm the one who has not been honest with you." My voice cracked, and Torben's mouth twitched when he heard it.

"Kaari… our mothers," Torben choked, unable to finish the thought. But I knew what he wanted to say.

"Yes," I breathed.

It had been well known that Liva Eriksen and Queen Gunilla were dear friends. They had grown up as close allies in court and had fostered a deep respect for each other. They also shared a propensity to heal others. The queen was famous for the way she had used her healer's magic after the war against the Mad King and Liva had stayed by her side—mixing tonics and medicines whenever she could.

Torben breathed through his pursed lips. "I think your mother was the only Fae besides my father that she ever trusted." Heartache shadowed his features.

A soft smile had formed on my face, even though the memory of my mother made my heart twist in pain.

"Kaari… everyone thought you were dead. I remember… I remember when you died. It was around the same time that I learned my mother was dead. I will never forget hearing how your entire family had been killed." His eyes were dancing with grief. "Kaari, this means you're the rightful Lady of Vogar."

I shook my head, waving off his monumental realization. "Torben… I'm so sorry I didn't tell you sooner. I wanted to tell you… all of you."

Shadows shifted across Torben's room as the light from the candles glimmered against the darkness of our sorrow. The sea beyond the window had grown wild with rushing waves that crashed against the rock walls in the distance. I felt a similar storm building in the pit of my stomach as the past one hundred years of secrecy started to unfold in front of the Prince of Akureyrian.

He knew who I was.

He knew that I was noble by birth—and an ancestor of the most powerful queen who had ever lived. The Queen's blood that flowed through my veins would have one day made *me* queen. But Queen Maiken had died. And her husband had gone wild with rage, hungry for the power that he had lost with the loss of his wife. It was Torben's father who had overthrown the Mad King after raising an army against him. Ensuring that King Havard's line would sit on the Akureyrian throne.

King Havard had never been a wicked king. He believed that Queen Maiken's infant child should not be held responsible for the actions of her father—especially after her mother had sacrificed her life to protect the kingdom from the Underworld. And although the king had taken away the child's right to the throne, she had been appointed as heir to her mother's lands—as the Lady of Vogar.

No one had questioned King Havard's rise and when he married, the kingdom had rejoiced at their growing stability and peace. After King Havard took the throne, everyone seemed content knowing that the king was keeping them safe, and that Queen Maiken's heir was settled with a place of honor in Vogar. It was only after my parents were assassinated that some began to question whether the king himself had sent the killer. Whispers, especially in Vogar, seeped through the tavern walls like rancid smoke, where some had started to wonder if the king wanted to ensure that the queen's heir could never claim his throne.

"Torben, I still have more that I need to tell you."

The golden specks in his brown eyes reflected in the candlelight as he gave me half a smile, his features showing the exhaustion that undoubtedly filled his heart. He reached for my hand and studied the way it fit in his as he gently ran his thumb over the scar on my wrist.

"Sleep now, Kaari Eriksen. You can tell me everything tomorrow."

My shoulders slumped and I allowed myself to feel the fatigue that riddled my muscles.

"Come, I'll walk you back to your room."

32

The sound of knocking was like the steady beat of a war drum and it woke me from a dream of fire and smoke. Peering through near-closed eyes, I could see the sun peaking over the horizon like flames. The waves in the distance had settled since last night and now rolled lazily into the bay. I rubbed my hands over my face to chase away the dreams I had been lost in and wrapped a robe around myself as I paced to the door.

Torben was leaning against the door frame, his muscular shoulder supporting him when I opened the door. He looked effortlessly charming, as if discovering my lineage last night hadn't phased him at all. He was dressed in a fitted shirt the color of sea moss and casual black pants that highlighted his athletic build. I pulled my robe up around my neck.

"Do you know what time it is?" I groaned, although all my morning drowsiness had been replaced with a flutter of excitement.

"Yes. And there is no better time to go for a *long* run." He winked as he nodded towards the large window as the early rays of light spilled into the space.

"You can't be serious."

"I'll wait here," he said with easy demeanor. He tipped his head back, crossing his arms as if he had all the patience in the world.

Rolling my eyes, I closed the door in the prince's face. A run was not the way I thought I would start my day. But when I found the fresh pair of pants and a slim-fitting shirt that Milla had set out for me the night before, I wondered if the maid had known about Torben's plan. After taking care of my personal needs and tying my hair into a long braid, I opened the door to find Torben still standing against door frame, looking pleasantly bored.

"Fine," I huffed, "but you owe me breakfast after."

Torben placed his large hand on his chest. "On my honor, Lady."

The palace was quiet this early in the morning. The light illuminated the ornate carvings on the doors we passed on our way to the courtyard, the scenes reminding me of what was at stake—of the picturesque lands that were now being infested with undercreatures.

Once we reached the path that led beyond the edge of the woods, Torben started jogging. "Are we using magic today, Lady of Vogar?" He had tied his hair into a tight knot and the sides of his head were freshly shaved, leaving only a hint of stubble along his strong jaw.

My heart skipped and I felt the roar of magic that lay deep within me, it seemed to beg for permission to be released. Maybe it was time to embrace my full power—just a little bit. Closing my eyes, I willed a drop of power into my chest and felt it slip down, opening my lungs before roaring through the blood vessels and into the muscles in my legs. My power came to life like an orchestra performs for its conductor, the tendrils of magic growing until the magical symphony made my head roar with delight. I smiled wickedly at him and without a word, sprinted away.

I *was* the Lady of Vogar.

I was just as powerful as those who came before me.

The rocky fields seemed to fade into a blur as I sprinted down the dirt path. The thrum of magic roared through my body, and I felt limitless as I pushed the bounds of the speed of my legs. My hair had started to pull from its braid and wisps of chestnut strands circled my face as I ran. I was only partially aware of the man who thundered behind me, his own pace unnaturally fast.

I felt like I could run forever.

The view of a waterfall in the distance helped to shake me out of the fog of my magic. I tugged on the string of power, begging for just a little more as I pushed towards the thundering water.

By the time I reached the base of the waterfall, I was panting, and my legs trembled. Torben was several paces behind me and slowed as he approached. Placing his hands on his knees, his shirt drenched from the exertion, Torben's eyes filled with adrenaline and magic as he met my gaze. "Holy gods. You really are trying to kill me," he huffed through ragged breaths.

"Oh, come on, Your Highness, are you telling me you're tired already?" I said, wiping my face with the bottom of my shirt, revealing the lower part of my stomach. I felt Torben's eyes catch on my bare skin as much as I saw them—like searing heat sparked by his golden gaze.

"I feel like my legs might combust if I breathe too hard. You don't feel drained?"

"I will be sure to go easy on you next time." I clicked my tongue and shook my head. But a seriousness returned to my voice as I saw how intently he watched me. "I don't think I feel drained." I shrugged my shoulders. "I imagine that I am summoning my power from a fountain. It felt like I only took a couple of drops—not enough that my muscles won't be sore in the morning."

Torben whistled. "Remind me not to be around when you decide to pull a bucket worth of that power," he said as he pulled off his sweat-drenched shirt. The sun was over the horizon and the beams of light danced over the contours of his chest.

I swallowed and turned my gaze to watch the waterfall as it poured over the edge of the rock wall. There was something refreshing about how relentless the water was as it crashed into the small pool, sending thousands of ripples across the surface. The urge to jump in the freezing water was as unrelenting as the ripples that rolled across the water.

"You can head back if you want, I just want to soak for a minute," I said, reaching my hand down to touch the crisp water.

"I had a feeling you wouldn't be able to resist." He smirked, as if he had known me for a hundred years. He looked over his shoulder and nodded towards the far side of the rock cliff. "I'll wait over here."

I watched as he turned his back. Part of me had hoped he would stay and join me. But that was probably a *bad* idea.

Stripping out of my clothes, I stepped into the water and waded the short distance to the fall to allow the pouring water to wash over me. It was bitterly cold, and goosebumps spread across my skin. I inhaled deeply, letting the rushing sounds of the falls fill my soul.

As I turned around to let the water hit my back, I saw Torben walking towards me, ruffling his disheveled bun with his hand as he approached. He looked down at me and the corner of his mouth turned into a guilty smile. "Do you mind if I join you?"

Instinct had me splashing him with freezing water. "Always the competitor." My voice was huskier than I intended. My stomach flipped as I watched the way he rolled his pant legs up so he could dangle his legs into the freezing water. The end of the large scar from our first encounter was just visible under his rolled pants. His brown eyes were gleaming as he splashed the cool water against his chest.

I thought about covering myself but changed my mind as I scanned his muscular body which was now dripping with water. My head and shoulders were bobbing above the water, hiding my bare breasts that trembled just below the surface. I was keenly aware of how close I was to him. As splashes of water flew between us like the kiss of raindrops, the distance we had kept began to dissolve, replaced by a warmth that seemed to radiate even in the chill of the water.

I had studied his features hundreds of times during the past several weeks and still marveled at the strength of his jaw and the way his dark eyes seemed to dance under his prominent brow. My gaze landed on his mouth, and I bit my lip as I watched the way he winced as he splashed more cold water on his arms.

It had been so long since I felt any semblance of desire. Of course, I had found lovers over the years who had satisfied the need for physical touch and release, but I had never had someone, Fae or mortal, who had looked at me the way Torben did. But he was the prince—and then there was the fact that he was *engaged*.

Did it matter that we cared for each other?

I plunged my head underwater, desperately needing to quell the rising heat I felt in my chest.

"Well, Your Highness," I said as I came up for a breath, "I'm going to need you to turn around so I can get dressed. We still need to run back."

Torben groaned as he lifted his feet out of the water. "Fine. But this time, I'm using magic too." He splashed at me as he stood to walk out of sight, leaving his shirt behind on the mossy rocks next to the pool. "You can use this to dry off if you'd like."

I eased myself out of the water, slipping into the soft embrace of his shirt. I could have used magic to dry myself, but as his scent surrounded me, a surprising comfort clung to me like a promise—one that felt as fragile as it was undeniable.

33

The sound of tiny jars and glass bottles clinked like windchimes in the breeze as I rearranged infirmary shelves for the third time. After running back to the palace, I had awkwardly waved to Torben before racing to my room. I changed into a sage-colored dress and went straight to the infirmary, desperately needing to work with my hands—and put some distance between us.

Shaking my head again, I inhaled the pungent scent of the white sage that Laila was grinding in a small mortar. The healer was humming softly to herself, the rhythmic sound hauntingly beautiful even though the words were in a language I didn't understand—I could see where Emil's power of tongues would be a helpful asset. We worked side by side, letting her melody set the rhythm as we ground herbs and mixed tinctures, desperately working to replenish our inventory.

Hours later, I found myself still humming that rhythmic song as I sat in the vast throne room, shoulders aching and palms raw from hours of grinding the pestle. After lunch, I met with the council in the throne room where we spent the afternoon, and well into the evening, discussing what had happened in the Grimsey Coast. Torben and Theo told of the drekavac, and the king would occasionally look to me for clarification as they described the beasts. The growing sense of fear was like a heavy shroud that slowly draped over the room—until it felt as though we had all been swallowed whole.

We also spent a significant amount of time reviewing the report I had compiled. With each entry, memories surfaced—each creature more vivid than the last. And as I read my own words, part of me shivered, knowing these were just fragments of a realm more vast, more insidious than I dared imagine.

Each entry reminded me not just of the creatures, but of their intent—a creeping malice that was ancient and hungry. A reminder to wonder how many more of them lay waiting, watching from the dark?

The candles burned low by the time the council finalized a plan. Torben and Emil would stay behind with the king to start the painstaking process of mobilizing units to spread out across some of the remote areas of the kingdom, while also ensuring enough soldiers remained behind to safeguard the capital.

Meanwhile, Theo and Leif were tasked with portal jumping back to the training camp in Nuuk. Their mission was to inform the northern captains to brace for the possibility of more attacks. We had discussed sending a message instead, but Theo insisted on making the trip in person, wanting to reassure the captains that Dalvin stood steadfastly with them.

Theo had brushed off my requests to join him. As much as I wanted to help, I knew I hadn't spent nearly enough time in the infirmary with Laila. With the threat of roaming undercreatures on the horizon I knew I needed to spend time preparing for a possible influx of wounded.

I sat with Torben and his Treyst after the king and other members of his council had left. Torben opened an ancient bottle of dark whiskey and passed glasses around the table. The amber liquid stung my lips and throat as I drank, but I was grateful for the temporary warmth I felt in my belly.

"You're trying to put me in an early grave with all this portal jumping, Your Highness," Theo grumbled darkly.

Leif rolled his eyes. "You're the oldest Fae any of us know… if jumping hasn't killed you yet, I doubt it ever will."

"I think what Leif means is that he is grateful you haven't died yet," I added, batting my eyes.

"*Gyðja hjálpaðun méra að dreppa þá ekki,*" Theo mumbled in the Old Language.

"I heard that," Emil said as he poured us all another drink.

"Something about not killing us?" Torben asked.

"It really is amazing that you never mastered the Old Language."

"Not everyone has an affinity for languages like you do, Emil. Torben was more concerned with escaping the palace walls so he could climb the cliffs and sneak into the training yard than he was about learning the Old Language… or any of his lessons for that matter," Leif said while spinning a dagger on the table.

"Aye, I lost count of how many times I had to tell his tutors he was ill when he was actually in the infirmary having scrapes and broken bones mended." Despite Theo's gruff tone, the corner of his mouth lifted affectionately.

Torben looked at me and placed his arm over his chest. "We were perfectly well-behaved children, I swear it."

"I can only imagine," I said, rolling my eyes.

We talked late into the night, and I felt the walls protecting the secrets of our histories crumbling with each passing hour. Torben, I learned, had grown up with Leif, and Theo had been tasked with keeping them safe. Despite his position, it sounded like he had been more of an older brother than a guard. When Torben came of age and needed to select his royal guard, Theo and Leif were the first guards he chose. They had met Emil during The War, and he had melded into the Treyst as if he had always been there.

"What about you, Kaari?"

"Hmm? Sorry, I was imagining all of you as reckless teenagers."

"Of all the creatures you told us about, what's the most ghastly one you ever encountered in the Woods?" Leif eyed me expectantly. At some point, the conversation must have shifted to discussing the undercreatures.

"They are all ghastly, Leif," I said, soberly. "I rarely saw drekavac which was a blessing. The draugr gave me the most trouble because they tended to attack mortals who crossed into the Woods. The onista smell absolutely foul but they die quickly if you can draw blood—they don't clot as quickly as the drekavac." I closed my eyes, remembering my years navigating the Woods. They listened with growing interest. Only Theo seemed unsurprised at my descriptions. "The garmr scared me the most. When I saw them, it meant I was nearing one of the entrances to the Underworld." I shuddered, remembering the way the air would still as if the very soul of the forest had been sucked into a sinister void.

Leif whistled and Torben's eyes lit with sparks of admiration.

"Remind me to never go to the Holvik Woods again," Emil said.

"I know it sounds awful, but there is something magical about the Holvik Woods. The ancient soil seemed to breathe life into everything that took root there. Each tree stretched impossibly high, their canopies forming a vibrant, emerald ceiling that filtered the sunlight into a gentle, golden glow." I fanned my hands in an arch over my head, as if I could show them. "Ferns, wildflowers, and ivy crowded the forest floor, lush and thriving as if the very air was steeped in ancient magic. I never felt as free as I did in the Woods. It was as though the Woods saw every part of me, even the parts I tried to hide, and accepted me completely."

"Only you could make the most terrifying place in Akureyrian sound like paradise," Torben said warmly.

"She's clearly unstable, Your Highness." Leif stood and patted my shoulder affectionately. "As much as I would love more content to fuel my nightmares, I'm going to go to bed."

"Aye, I should be getting home as well," Emil agreed.

After they had retired, the room gradually fell into a heavy silence, the usual easy flow of conversation fading away as the weight of something unspoken settled around the three of us. The clink of whiskey glasses against the table was the only sound left, the amber liquid swirling lazily as each of us avoided meeting the others' eyes. What had once been lighthearted laughter now felt like a distant memory, replaced by an unyielding tension that clung to the air like smoke—the unspoken truth about my name. The silence was thick, oppressive, as if the walls themselves were closing in, waiting for someone to break the fragile peace.

"When are we going to tell Leif and Emil?" Theo asked while slowly swirling his cup.
"Soon. Right now, I just want to focus on what's happening with the undercreatures. I promise I will tell them soon, Theo." I took a long sip from my glass, the whiskey stinging like the climbing vines of a

rosebush, the prickers stabbing as much as his disappointment.

Darkness crept across the expanse of the throne room and sleep beckoned like a neglected friend. I pushed away from the table, finishing the rest of my drink before I briskly bid them goodnight.

I was anxious to leave Dalvin so we could get answers about the undercreatures, but relieved we wouldn't need to travel for several days, giving me time to work in the infirmary and practice wielding and controlling my magic.

Despite my exhaustion, I snuck down to the kitchen before returning to my room and begged Aulis for another helping of the lime-flavored sweet cakes he had served earlier. The cook had excitedly prepared a platter full of sweet cakes and sandwiches and told me to send word if I was ever hungry.

Stomach full and muscles aching, I finally crawled into bed. I didn't even bother pulling the sheets up before rolling onto my back to stare at the ceiling.

Recounting the clash with the drekavac and my list of undercreatures had been surprisingly draining, and not just because of the sheer time we had spent in that room.

The guilt lingered, gnawing at me a little more with every breath, a shadow I couldn't shake. Emil and Leif deserved to know the truth.

With each day we spent together, I felt like I was becoming more entwined in their circle. They deserved to know my story.

Everything seemed to be shifting. I felt like my very sense of self was being challenged with each passing moment. The tides of my life ebbed and flowed in a torrent of change as I struggled to keep my head above water with every passing breath. The life I'd known was slipping through my fingers, replaced by something unknown, something vast—and I wasn't sure if I was ready for what lay on the other side.

Sleep came quickly, and as I drifted into the darkness of my dreams, I kicked myself for not asking Theo what life had been like before the creatures of the Underworld had been banished to the Holvik Woods. Instead, I was left imagining what type of hell was about to be unleashed.

34

Theo and Leif had been gone for a week. Each day that passed felt like an eternity as we waited for their return.

I spent my days working with Laila in the infirmary. Slowly, the healer started to speak more freely, and I was relieved to discover her dark sense of humor and absolutely *foul* language. Our conversations could make an Akureyrian sailor blush.

Each morning, Torben knocked on my door to wake me for our morning run. Each day we ran farther down the coast of Dalvin, exploring the jagged peaks and rolling hills.

I could feel my muscles stretching to accommodate the strength I was adding with every mile. Even with Torben encouraging me to use my magic, I still preferred to rely on my strength to carry me most of the distance, but Torben's relentless encouragement usually tempted me to pull on my magic. Now, when I felt my power flood my veins I didn't fear losing control.

This morning our run felt wilder. Torben pushed us deep into the woods near the coast and we were both gasping for breath by the time we returned to the palace. The unspoken concern for Leif and Theo weighed heavily between us as we walked the cobblestone path that led to the training yard. As we approached, we noticed a guard running towards us, his pace too quick to be recreational.

"Your Highness!" the guard bellowed. Torben's ears twitched and he began running. I ran after him, feeling the pounding in my chest as panic ripped through me.

The guard was breathing heavily, his words came out between choked breaths. "Your Highness... forgive me... General Helvig... he needs you to go to your room... he said to come *now*."

We looked at each other briefly before sprinting towards the palace.

Emil was standing in the center of Torben's room, staring into the air around him, his face void of emotion. I lunged to check on him before Torben blocked me with his strong arm.

"He's fine," he snapped, his voice jagged. "It's Leif—he's transmitting with Leif."

I watched the blank stare on Emil's handsome face—his eyes pinched in blank concentration as if he wasn't actually in his body.

Seconds passed and then Emil was blinking wildly as he looked across the room. His voice caught in his throat. "It's Theo," he gasped. "There was an attack in

Nuuk... Leif is trying to get Theo to jump the portal, but he doesn't know if Theo will be able to do it."

"What kind of an attack?" Torben asked, his voice eerily quiet.

"Drekavac." Emil paused as if trapped in disbelief. "And a pack of garmr."

Bile filled my throat and I had to reach out to hold the chair in front of me to steady myself. Emil's face darkened and his shoulders rippled with tension. "The beasts destroyed an entire village."

The room seemed to spin as the words settled.

An entire village was destroyed.

A pack of garmr.

Seeing *one* in Árnes had been concerning—but to see a pack of the wolf-like creatures that guarded the gates to the Underworld was unimaginable.

"We need to get to the tunnel in case they make it through the portal... I don't know how Theo will be...."

"I will meet you there. I need to grab some supplies." The two men nodded to me before they began running down the hidden stairs that led to the tunnels. I was sprinting an instant later, my mind racing about Theo's potential injuries and my heart in shatters as I imagined the loss of an entire village.

I found Emil and Torben waiting outside the portal, anxiously pacing, their hands clenched into fists at their sides. I could feel the thrum of Torben's power as gusts of force seeped from his fists. Leif hadn't given any details about Theo's injuries, only that he was wounded enough that he wasn't sure he would be able to make the jump.

A whirling sound came from the depths of the portal and an instant later, Leif came crashing through—his arm wrapped around Theo's blood-soaked torso. Torben and Emil were there in an instant, helping to lay Theo on the ground and I lunged to get closer to them. Leif's face had lost all its golden color by the time he let go of his friend.

I pulled Theo's shirt over his head, desperately searching for the source of the bleeding, the sound of my blood pumping in my ears making it hard to focus. A gruesome gash stretched across his chest, starting just under his collarbone and extending to his naval. Blood had dripped over the contours of his muscles as I used a strip of cloth to wipe the stains away. "I need to get a compress on here before we move him." I folded a large bandage and pressed it tightly against the wound. When it was secure, I said, "Ok, now," with more confidence than I felt.

Working together, we were able to carry Theo to the bottom of the stairs that led to the library. After seeing the extent of his injuries, Emil ran ahead to find some guards who could bring a stretcher so we could carry Theo to the infirmary.

There was so much blood.

Theo had managed to clot some of the wound, but after so much initial blood loss the effort to heal his body was failing.

His head lolled to the side as the life seeped from him in crimson waves—the compress failing to control the extent of the bleeding.

"We can't wait!" I yelled. "I need to stop this bleeding *now*." Torben's eyes flashed as he looked from me to Leif. I kneeled on the dirt floor of the tunnel next to Theo's limp body and closed my eyes. Slowing my breathing in a state of panic felt like forcing myself to breath under water.

Finally, blue light began to simmer under my palms. I let it build until warmth spread through my arms and down my back. Somewhere in the distance, I heard Leif gasp, but I had reached the point where my magic made me lose touch with my surroundings.

I could feel the blood flowing through Theo's veins—a dangerous trickle that moved too slowly to sustain him. I needed it to flow *faster*. The smell of ether filled the narrow tunnel as I dug deeper into my magic, willing the flow of my light to fill Theo's empty bloodstream. I could feel the pull of my magic against his skin as the blue light flowed through the mangled wound, as if magical sutures were tying the flaps of skin back together.

It felt as if I had jumped off an endless waterfall as I pushed more and more power into Theo's body. My breath was quickening, and the walls of the tunnel seemed to spin around me in an endless vortex of light and power. I felt the refreshing kiss of an ocean breeze on my face as the vortex led me through a wooded forest. My magic pulsed with the rhythm of his heartbeat, steadily beating faster. His blood was wild and powerful, and it seemed to burn as it tangled with my magic.

A voice called to me—telling me to pull back, that he was alright—but it sounded so far away. A moment later, a strong hand was gripping my shoulder, the connection was enough to bring me back to myself as I struggled to pull the magic back under.

I was covered in dirt from the floor and Theo's blood was smeared over my arms and chest. I blinked several times, not believing what I saw. Theo was struggling to sit up, still pale, but alive. Leif was lifting under his shoulders and whispering words of encouragement.

I reached for the hands that had centered me and brought me back after I had fallen into the void of my magic. Warm hands held my face, grounding me to the present.

"Kaari," the voice called, and I blinked again as the face in front of mine came into focus.

Torben.

"Kaari… are you alright?"

My voice was still lost as if the magic had wrapped around my vocal cords and hadn't yet melted away, but I nodded as I looked into the prince's golden eyes.

It could have been minutes—or hours—later that I was finally able to speak. My voice felt raw and I desperately needed water. But I could feel the awareness as it came back to my body.

"Theo? Is—is he alright?"

"Yes, he's alright. Kaari... you saved him." Torben's eyes were filled with wonder. "Your magic... it was like it filled him. It brought him back."

Emil and Leif had already moved Theo to the infirmary where Laila was waiting, leaving me and Torben alone in the tunnel. My body felt oddly warm and as I looked down at my hands, I saw the small blisters that had formed on my fingertips.

I had never pulled on so much of my magic. It had felt wild and desperate, as if I dove into a well and the deeper I went the heavier I was with the weight of the power. That well of power had felt endless as if I had barely scraped the surface—leaving a vast ocean just waiting to be tested.

35

Torben managed to lead me back to my room. My body felt unseemly warm and I was trembling slightly as I walked. He filled the tub with cool water and stripped off my blood-soaked clothes before gently lifting me into the tub. I gasped as my naked skin dipped into the cool water, but my eyes closed, and I moaned with relief as I felt the fire going out inside of me.

Torben watched me closely as I lay in the oversized tub. Slowly, he reached out his hand and gently brushed the wild strands of hair out of my face. I purred softly at his touch, and he seemed to breathe a sigh of relief.

My head bobbed, exhaustion threatening to pull me under.

I was only vaguely aware of Torben as he slipped—fully clothed—into the tub behind me and wrapped his arms around me, using his solid form to hold me upright. He held his breath until I finally leaned into his chest, letting my head fall back onto his shoulder.

"Thank you," he whispered as he held me against his chest. I was still glowing faintly, illuminating the water in the tub like a pool of molten fire. I had never let my power go like that. In all my years as a healer, I had never poured so much magic into someone—as if I was replacing a vital function with pure power.

I shuddered as I remembered the way it had felt when my magic tangled with Theo's blood. It was an intoxicating rush that left me feeling dizzy and warm.

I would have extinguished myself completely if it meant saving him. Theo would be furious when he realized how much power I had used, and how it had left me utterly drained and on the verge of collapse. Yet, even now, as exhaustion pressed down on me, I could feel the whisper of something deeper—a vast untouched well of magic, pulsing with an indomitable strength just beneath the surface.

Gods, my skin was burning up.

Through blurry eyes, I watched Torben reach for a cloth and then drip cold water over my face and shoulders. His touch was slow and gentle as if he worried my skin would melt away from the contact. The chill soothed my flushed skin, yet beneath it all, I could still feel the lingering heat from my magic, like smoldering embers that refuse to die out.

Candlelight flickered across the stone floor of the washroom as clouds rolled in across a stirring sea.

Rage boiled inside my heart like the storm gathering on the horizon, dark and unrelenting, as I thought of the people who had been killed in the attack on the northern village. We had managed to save Theo but how many others had been lost, swept away like debris in the torrent? Was this our new normal—a life constantly bracing for the next thunderclap, the next strike, each assault leaving scars like lightning scorched across our world?

"I've got you," Torben whispered as he carefully lifted me out of the tub. He held me like he feared I would float away, his heart racing beneath the broad muscles in his chest. My mind lingered somewhere between awareness and a fever dream. Torben wrapped a thick towel around my shoulders, always keeping my intimate parts covered even though he had just held my naked form in his lap. His hands moved slowly, as though each motion was its own vow of care. His fingers lingered at the ends of my damp hair, squeezing out the last traces of water with a gentleness that made my breath catch. He brushed the towel over my arms in long, careful strokes, warmth and tenderness radiating from every touch. As he crouched to dry my legs, his gaze never left mine, steady and reassuring, like an anchor in the quiet intimacy of the moment. I felt myself soften, the tension melting away under his careful, reverent hands.

Once I was dry, I felt him lay me down—the silk sheets delightfully cool against my scorched skin. Soft lips pressed against my brow, sending me into a blissful sleep.

36

I blinked my eyes open as I reached out to feel the silk sheets. The room around me was not mine, but it was familiar.

Torben.

I was in Torben's bed.

Goddess, I was *naked* in Torben's bed.

The room was dark but whether it was the middle of the night or early the next morning, I couldn't say. Torben was sitting in a chair he had pulled next to the bed, his elbows leaning on his strong thighs as he watched me.

He jumped up when he saw my eyes fluttering open and rushed to my side, helping me sit up and pushing a large glass of water into my hands with a concerned look on his face.

"I'm fine," I rasped. My throat felt like I had swallowed gravel.

Torben rolled his eyes. "You're *fine*? You fell asleep in a freezing cold tub and then slept for five hours without moving."

I reciprocated with an eye roll of my own. I was not used to someone coddling me. But the look on Torben's face was enough to tell me that I might not *look* fine.

"Theo," I whispered, suddenly remembering how we ended up here, "is he alright?" My hands pulsed with warmth and my blistered fingers stung. The memory of my power flooding through Theo's veins tingled like hot coals under my skin.

Torben spent the next several minutes telling me what happened. He told me how it had seemed like Theo was beyond saving until I had filled him with my power, and they had watched his veins glow with my blue light.

Hearing Torben describe the resuscitation was surreal, and I realized how disconnected I had been as I used my powers on Theo. I remembered seeing his mutilated body—the torn skin that had pulled away from muscle and bone coating the floor with bright blood. But then I had willed my magic to sustain him.

After that, all I could remember was the way my skin burned like a solstice fire as my magic took over completely.

Torben watched my face intently as he asked, "Did it hurt? To use that much magic?"

It was not the question I had expected. I glanced to my blistered fingers, but then bit my lip and closed my eyes, trying to remember the feeling of the magic as it flowed through me. "No," I said finally, "it felt wonderful... and absolutely terrifying all at the same time."

Torben's brows pinched and the fine lines around his mouth curved as he gave me a concerned smile. "I need to find you some dinner."

"Torben." I paused, pulling the blanket to cover myself. "Why am I naked?"

"Your skin was burning with the heat of a thousand suns." He paused and ran his hand through his disheveled hair. "I brought you into the tub to try to cool you off. I barely peeked. I promise."

I laughed as his lips twisted into a sheepish smile. "I see. Well, it worked. So, thank you." I cleared my throat, unsure what should happen next. "Dinner sounds wonderful. But first I want to go see Theo."

Torben shot me a protective glare. "Food first. Then we will go see him."

I crossed my arms and scowled at him, but when he returned from the kitchen several minutes later with a steaming loaf of bread and a tower of lemon cakes, I decided I would let him win this battle.

The door to the infirmary swung open and Leif came storming out, spewing a foul string of curses. He stopped abruptly when he saw me and Torben reaching for the doorknob.

"Good," Leif huffed, "*you* go talk to him. The fool is insisting that he is well enough to go north with us."

Torben started to roll his eyes as if he thought Leif was exaggerating but I was already marching into the stone building.

"Where is he?" I barked as I walked through the door. I saw him before the two healers at his side had a chance to say a word. Theo was attempting to sit up in the small bed, the thick bandage that was wrapped around his chest hindering his movements.

"Don't you *dare,*" I roared. Theo's eyes widened as I stepped in front of him to assess his bandage before he could respond. "What in the name of the goddess makes you think you can get up and run around after you almost *died.*"

Theo looked at Torben as if expecting his friend to support him, but the prince just crossed his arms and let me continue my lecture.

Theo hesitated, glancing away before meeting my eyes again. "Kaari... I don't know how I'll ever thank you. But really, I'm fine."

"You are still the color of this bedsheet which just goes to show exactly how much blood you lost. If your body is *still* working to recover—"

"Your magic," Theo interrupted, his voice almost a whisper. He took my hand, engulfing it in the broad expanse of his rough palm. "Kaari, I could feel your magic as it flowed through me. I have had countless wounds in my life that required the touch of a healer, but this..." he looked around to make sure the other healers couldn't hear, "I—I think I can still feel it. It's as if it won't fade until my blood has been replenished. I swear I feel like I could run for miles."

I pulled my hand away—oddly shaken by the contact—then crossed my arms, surprised to find my hands trembling.

Theo had almost died.

I hadn't said it out loud before now and my stomach rolled with nausea at the thought of losing him. He might be ornery most of the time, but I couldn't deny the way he seemed to be a tether for the Treyst. Whether it was his personality or his ancient magic, for some reason it always felt like Theo was connecting to all of us with some undeniable pull.

The smell of honey wafted through the bandages, sickly sweet and mixed with the metallic hint of dried blood. *Good*, I thought in a moment of rationality, the healers were taking precautions to prevent infections by using the honey. My magic might be strong, but I didn't think it could combat bacteria.

"Well, that might be, but I certainly don't have the energy to put you back together if you go back out there and get torn to shreds again."

"Are you strong enough to portal jump?" My head whipped towards Torben, my eyes wild and not believing that he would suggest that Theo portal jump.

"Oh, aye... I think so. How many need to get through?"

I rubbed the bridge of my nose with my thumb and finger. "We are *not* having this conversation. He was just mauled by a garmr!"

"So, *you* make the jump," Theo said, his mouth creeping into a sly smirk. "And to be clear, I was attacked by a drekavac."

My arctic blue eyes must have been like daggers as I looked at him—he was suggesting that *I* portal jump. The first time Torben had suggested it, I had shrugged it off as something that might be *possible* but not plausible. This time, however, Theo was suggesting because he had actually seen the amount of power I held.

I lowered my voice to a whisper as I looked around to see if the healers were listening. "We all know that I don't know *how* to portal jump, which is why it's so important that *you* get better so you can get us north."

"Fine," he snapped. "But sooner or later I'm going to teach you."

"Fine," I huffed. "But right now you need to rest."

"She's right, we need you strong so we can head north." Torben's voice was firm.

A defeated look crossed Theo's face as he laid back against his pillow.

Torben clasped Theo on his shoulder, telling him to rest and that we would come back in the morning.

Torben and I walked down to the kitchen to find something to eat. The smells of simmering stews and roasting meats filled the air, and my mouth began to water. Aulis was standing in front of a large cook pot, slowly stirring a hearty stew. He turned as he heard us approach. His thin lips pressed into a welcome smile as he bowed his head to the prince. "Your Highness! What can I do for you?"

"Food, Aulis, we need food."

"Of course, Your Highness." Aulis quickly began shuffling around the space scooping a variety of delectable items onto two plates.

"These smell amazing, Aulis, thank you." My mouth stretched into my first real smile in hours.

While I barely managed to balance the tower of tarts and cakes on my plate, Torben led me to a small table in the corner of the kitchen. He offered me a chair at a small wooden table and then stepped behind me, brushing my shoulder gently as he passed. It was a simple gesture, but it sent waves of reassurance thundering through me. Together, we settled into the echoing stillness.

I was nearly bursting with thoughts of the undercreatures. It was a miracle I kept my voice level when I finally broke the silence. "If there are packs of garmr roaming outside of Árnes and attacking villages, it is only a matter of time before the entire kingdom will be at risk." The prince let out a low breath and I could see the myriad of thoughts circling through his head. "Would the library have any old texts that might describe the history of the time when Queen Maiken locked the creatures in Árnes?"

Torben rubbed his temples as if processing an inventory of the ancient texts that were housed in the royal library. "Perhaps. We could ask the Keepers," he said at last.

Memories of the library at my family estate in Vogar made my shoulders feel heavy. I remembered the expansive collection of ancient texts my parents had cherished. I knew there had been a collection of manuscripts about the magical queen—vivid stories told of the history of Akureyrian, and my family bloodline. *What happened to the collection when my parents died?*

After finishing the last of our meal, we thanked Aulis for his hospitality and headed towards the library. It was late, and I knew we should try to get some sleep if we were planning to head north in the morning, but I desperately wanted to find something that would help explain the magic that the queen had used to banish the creatures so long ago—and why after so long the wards had broken open.

"Did your mother ever tell you anything about Maiken's power?" Torben asked as we walked the expansive hallway.

It was a fair question—one I pondered a lot recently. "My mother was terrified when she realized I was born with raw magic. Queen Maiken was born knowing she would sit on the throne. Having raw magic was an asset for her. But for me, it was a liability. My mother only saw the risk of what would happen if I was discovered. She always feared that your father might see me as a threat to his crown if he knew Maiken's magic flowed through my blood." Torben's eyes danced with gold. I knew he wanted to argue the thought—to say his father would never see me as a threat—but he knew it would be a false promise. "My mother always said that raw magic was the very essence of the Fae—a power so pure that it could reshape the world." I felt my shoulders sag. "She didn't like talking about the Queen. I wish I knew more about her."

"You know… we could just ask Theo about the Queen's magic."

"Because he was actually alive when Maiken was?"

"Yes. He was."

"Holy gods, he *is* that old. Would he know about her magic?"

"I imagine he would know better than anyone. Not only was he alive back then, but Theo was the commander of the Queen's guard."

# 37

For a moment, I forgot to breathe.

Theo had known Queen Maiken.

My great-grandmother who had lived a thousand years ago.

Torben was smiling softly at me, and that was unnerving. "It's why your scent seemed familiar to him when we first met you. He knew you were her kin somehow. He just figured it was a long-diluted bloodline from your Vogarian heritage."

For a moment, my heart broke as I processed what Torben was telling me. Theo had watched his queen give her life to save her kingdom, leaving behind a child and a power-hungry king. And now he served the family that had replaced her.

"That's why Theo reacted the way that he did when he felt my power?" My voice was barely a whisper.

Torben's gaze softened as he nodded, his hand gently covering mine. "Yes. To him, your power must have felt like a memory—something beautiful and painful all at once. You're a reminder of the sacrifice he witnessed, and of the magic he thought was lost forever." He paused, exhaling slowly. "Theo's loyalty to your family goes beyond duty. It's woven with loss, grief, and respect for the kind of power that demands everything."

A chill settled over me, pressing into my skin despite the warmth in the hall. Torben's words echoed in my mind, each one stripping away the layers of certainty I thought I had.

I swallowed, but it felt like shards of glass in my throat. "How... how does he bear it?" My voice came out fractured, almost unrecognizable.

Torben's gaze softened, the faintest shadow of grief crossing his face. "Theo believes in protecting those who can't protect themselves. It's all he's known since that day."

The weight of it—the devotion, the duty, and the pain it must have carved into Theo—hung between us. I felt my own power stir beneath my skin, restless and uncertain, as though even it sensed the gravity of the past we were dredging up.

In that moment, I knew one thing: I would make sure his sacrifice, and that of the queen, would not be in vain.

"I'm going to talk to Theo," I said, stopping abruptly.

"Kaari, the moons are well across the sky. Hopefully Theo is sleeping so he will be rested by tomorrow."

"Well, then we need to go to the library," I said, immediately moving to continue down the hallway. Torben reached out to grab my wrist, the grip firm but gentle. As I spun around to meet his gaze, his chestnut eyes bore into me.

"Rest first, Kaari," he seemed to plead. "I promise to help you tear apart the library to find the answers you need, but right now we need to sleep."

Theo still looked like shit in the morning.

Upon our arrival at the infirmary, Torben asked the healers to give us some time with Theo and promised we would be out of their way soon. We found Theo standing in front of a large mirror as he slowly unwrapped the bandages that encircled his chest. Watching him in the mirror, everything I'd learned weighed heavily on me, reshaping the way I looked at him. He wasn't just Theo Axtell—Captain of the Royal Guard. He was the Queen's commander, someone who had fought beside her, who had watched her give her life for the kingdom. The realization made my chest ache. I wondered how much grief he carried, how much of his own life he had sacrificed to serve a different throne, a different family. A strange mix of awe and sadness settled in me. I wanted to say something that mattered, something that could convey the depth of what I felt, but every word felt small and hollow. I felt like I'd glimpsed a hidden part of him, something sacred, something I wasn't sure I deserved to know.

I caught a glimpse of his bare back before he turned to face us, and it shook me from my internal soliloquy. I marveled at the intricate tattoo that adorned his skin like a piece of fine art. From a quick glance, the lines looked haphazard—but up close they merged, creating a mirage of burning flames.

"Aye, he still looks like shit," Leif grumbled.

"They say I'm as good as new," Theo snapped, and I felt comforted that he was back to his curmudgeonly self.

We assessed him cautiously, and as he finished unwrapping the bandage, we all sighed with relief when Theo revealed his wound. The gash was now closed with tight scar tissue—and thankfully, no signs of infection.

I stepped closer to inspect the jagged scar, reaching out to gently touch the iridescent skin. His skin prickled under my touch, his eyes dilating enough to drown the ocean blue irises. When I had used my magic to slow his bleeding, I felt the power flowing through his veins. It had felt ancient and wild—like mine, but undoubtedly Theo's. I shuddered as I thought about all the power and wisdom that would have been lost if I hadn't been able to save him. As I watched him now, his face appearing just as youthful as my own, I never would have guessed how old he truly was.

His eyes were locked onto mine and he seemed to be searching them for answers. I blinked and pulled my hand away as Torben adjusted his stance and crossed his arms.

"We need to hear about the attack... and then we need to figure out our plan for going back." Torben's voice was somber as he looked at Theo and Leif. Emil widened his stance as if he needed the extra support for the story that was about to unfold.

Theo cleared his throat. "I'm going to need something stronger than this elderberry syrup," he said, grimacing as he pulled a shirt down over his muscled form.

Once medicated with a tall dram of whiskey, Theo dropped his gaze and recalled the moments before the attack. "Leif and I were helping a small troop of warriors deliver a cart of provisions to one of the remote villages. It was evening and we were racing against the setting sun. As we passed the Dauðadómur lake the air shifted. Smoke rose in curling wisps, the faint scent of charred wood and something darker reaching us even before the ruined structures came into view. I remember jumping from my horse and racing towards the village, hoping my eyes had deceived me. But there were no voices, no cries—only the quiet shuffle of settling ash and the excited call of the crows." A sheen of sweat had gathered across Theo's stern brow, his features hardening with the weight of the memory. "The beasts came while we were setting the bodies on the pyre—as if they had been waiting in the shadows for our weakest moment."

Theo dipped his head, and the light in his eyes burned. "Leif was attacked first… and had just landed a crushing blow to the drekavac when more beasts suddenly appeared like a swarm.

"When a beast came at me, I just had enough time to lift my sword to block its gods-damned claws from slashing my face. I didn't manage to block the second swing that brought its claws across my chest. Leif was there instantly and kicked the drekavac away. I saw Leif bringing his sword down on the creature's swollen skull just before my vision got hazy."

Leif explained how he had raced to Theo's side and held his hand against the wound as he helped Theo stand. They returned to the base and immediately went to the portal.

"The other warriors did not survive. I didn't want to risk Theo passing out before we could jump through the portal, so I didn't stay to help the other in Nuuk." Leif said with a hint of shame. "I just had to get him back here."

Torben clapped Leif on the shoulder, the turmoil he had faced in that moment's decision was a painful burden.

I rubbed at my temples, cursing under my breath. The infirmary suddenly felt very small with the four massive men surrounding me. Everything felt like it was changing. Torben and his Treyst had been through wars together—they knew what was at stake.

Although I was familiar with the brutality of the undercreatures, I had never had to worry about a mass of them attacking a village.

I needed to understand how the undercreatures broke through the wards of the Holvik Woods after a thousand years of banishment. I figured that the only way to understand how they had escaped was to learn how they had come to be there in the first place.

I turned to Theo, ready to pepper him with questions. Torben must have sensed the oncoming onslaught and interjected, "Come for a run with me," he said, as if he knew that my mind needed time to reset—and Theo needed to recover. "We can head to the library when we get back."

38

Torben led us down a new trail. Through my heaving breaths, I asked him if there were any trails in the woods and along the cliffs of Dalvin that he hadn't explored. The prince had laughed and told me that today he was bringing me somewhere new—to one of his favorite places.

Our pace was fast and rigorous. I knew the upcoming trip and unanswered questions weighed heavily on him—his worry for his kingdom was an unrelenting burden with each day that passed. The rhythmic pounding of our feet against the earth became a shared language, one that freed us from the tangled web of thoughts crowding our minds. With every breath, we purged a bit of that weight, grounding ourselves in the raw simplicity of movement. For a moment, we weren't haunted by the past or shadowed by the future; we were simply here, lungs burning, legs driving forward, as if we could outrun everything we couldn't control.

The air seemed to thin the higher we went up the hillside and as we finally reached the edge of the woods and beheld the expanse of sea, I gasped with exhaustion and awe.

From our vantage point, the ocean seemed to stretch endlessly. The morning sun was glittering across the rolling waves as if millions of diamonds swirled inside the deep blue water. I couldn't look around fast enough, desperately wanting to take in the panorama that had unfolded before us. Torben simply stood with his hands on his hips, a sly smile on his face as he watched the wonder spread across my face.

"I told you I was taking you to one of my favorite spots." He looked at me knowingly and then reached into his pack. "Here, I brought us a snack." I was still looking at him with astonishment as he unpacked a pouch containing some bread, fresh cheese, an apple, and a small blanket.

After eating, we lay down on the blanket—our shoulders pressed together—and watched the birds flying over the cliff edge. Thousands swarmed the rocky edge as they brought food back to their young. I could barely take my eyes off the coast while we ate, completely entranced by the beauty. After several long moments, I shifted my gaze to meet Torben's stare.

"Why did you bring me here?" I asked. "It is so wonderful, Torben. I… thank you for sharing this with me. Especially now."

Torben lifted himself onto one elbow so he was looking down at me. "Because you make me feel alive."

I held my breath, feeling warmth bloom across my skin. His gaze searched my face, intense and unyielding, as his thumb traced the line of my jaw in a slow, deliberate caress. A shiver coursed down my spine as his hand traveled down my arm, every touch sending sparks beneath my skin. He hesitated, his eyes meeting mine, as though waiting for permission. My pulse fluttered, and when I didn't pull away, he drew closer, the solid warmth of his chest pressing against me, stirring a tingling sensation that spread all the way to my toes."

The muscles in his shoulders shifted when he lifted his head over mine and lowered himself down so his lips rested next to the point of my ear. "I want to know everything about you, Kaari Eriksen." His whispered words dripped with wild desire. The feeling of his warm breath on my sensitive ears was enough to make my back arch, sending my chest to press harder against his. I dropped my eyes to look at his mouth. I hadn't allowed myself to acknowledge how much I wanted this. With everything happening, it didn't seem fair that I should give myself this release. But now, I could barely stand waiting to find out how his lips would taste.

His fingers traced over my shoulder, moving across my collarbone before stopping under my chin. He lifted my face and looked me over, his eyes wild and dark as I savored every touch.

And then time seemed to stop as he leaned in and pressed his lips to mine.

We fit together as if we were made from the same mold and I breathed in the sweetness of him, needing to taste more of him and feel all of him. Our lips parted and he tasted my mouth with his tongue, growling with building pleasure.

He pulled back, searching for any sign that I wanted him to stop but I reached up and ran my hands through his hair, pulling his mouth back to mine. His kiss was brutally tender as if he had all the time in the world to learn what I wanted. Slowly, he started to trail his lips down my throat until he reached the ribbing of my tunic. My magic warmed under my skin as the cool air caressed my skin.

You make me feel alive.

His hand reached under my shirt, trailing against my stomach until he gripped my back and pulled me closer. He flipped me onto my back, his mouth traveling down the length of my stomach as the stubble of his face scratched my soft skin sending blissful goosebumps across my flesh. As he reached the top of my pants I moaned softly—and we both seemed to realize there was no turning back as he undid the laces.

My legs were trembling. His face was so close to me that I could feel the warmth of his breath between my legs. *Holy gods*, I thought, *how is this happening?*

It took all my self-control to not scream out for him. I was only vaguely aware of the chill in the air or the storm clouds approaching overhead—the only thing I felt was molten desire that consumed me like fire. His breath on my skin was all I needed to stay warm.

His fingers reached the top of my thigh, circling in delightfully playful loops as he settled himself between my legs. "Gods, Kaari. You're perfect." His eyes were glassy with desire and a sinful smile stretched across his face as he rolled his thumb over my center and then dipped his head to place his lips on me. I buckled and arched my back, moving my hips closer to him. He groaned and took me into his mouth, using his tongue to explore while his fingers teased.

Just as I thought I might catch my breath, one of his fingers slid into my depth, his tongue still flicking in a songlike rhythm. I grabbed his head and ran my fingers through his hair as another finger slipped in to fill me. My heart thudded in a frantic rhythm, so loud I was sure he could hear it. I'd spent so long keeping people at arm's length, too afraid to let anyone see the parts of me I kept hidden away. But here he was, unflinching, as if he could see right through every wall I'd built. His touch burned across my skin, stirring up feelings I'd told myself I didn't need—didn't deserve. He slowly pulled out and then, with a low growl, gently dipped them back inside. Over and over, until I completely lost control.

I exploded in my climax in time with a flash of lightning just as the sky opened above us and rain poured down. A boom of thunder roared nearby. My body was trembling, and I realized I was still holding his head in my hands. Lightning cracked again and filled the sky with light. I looked down to see Torben's eyes on mine as he licked his lips. The smell of lightning filled the air and a massive thunderclap boomed through the sky.

"Don't think I'm done with you." He smirked. "But right now we need to make sure we aren't struck by lightning."

I closed my eyes as I groaned "I think I was. I can't feel my body."

"I'll take that as a compliment," he whispered as he lifted himself onto his arms and moved over me, pausing to kiss me gently—the taste of me still on his lips.

Rain poured down on us as I scrambled to pull on my pants. Torben held the blanket over my head like a shield—as if he could protect me from the world.

We tucked ourselves under a jagged rock wall while we waited for the storm clouds to pass.

I felt like I was floating. I bit my lip, shattering as I thought of the Prince of Akureyrian's face between my legs.

Goddess, what had we started? He watched me as I untwisted my braids, waves of my chestnut-colored hair shining in the light that reached through the clouds. I sucked in my breath as I moved closer to him, and he twisted a lock of hair around his finger. He used the edge of his thumb to trace my jaw, his eyes scanning my pleasantly swollen lips. "Darkness may be spreading through the world, but you are my light— my beacon of hope. I want to make sure you know that."

I didn't know how to respond. My heart was pounding in my chest like a battering ram before an invasion—his words breaching the walls I had carefully constructed around my heart. Normally, I would try to use humor or brush off such a comment, but this felt too raw—too honest. I reached up to cup his stubbled jaw, pulling his face to mine then kissed him slowly—the connection as electric as the lightning that splintered the sky behind us.

The run back to the palace was wordless. The sound of our feet as we raced across the moss-covered trail seemed to echo in the silence. It was as if we were both trying to process what would happen now that we had explored the temptation that had been building over the past several weeks.

A shiver went down my spine as I thought about the way Torben's hands had felt as they explored the contours of my body. The way his mouth had felt pressing against me.

Goddess above, I thought, *this is certainly going to complicate things.*

After walking me back to my room, he smiled and kissed my hand in a dramatic motion that made my eyes roll. Before he turned to leave, he squeezed my hand and a seriousness spread across his gaze. "I meant what I said, Kaari. I have lived for over a hundred years, and yet it was only after I met you that I started to feel alive."

Alive.

I made him feel alive.

The weight of his words settled around me like a warm blanket, but it was the intensity in his eyes that struck me the most. For all his teasing and playful charm, this was different—this was real. His grip lingered on my hand, and I could feel the pulse of his own heartbeat in his fingertips, steady and strong. He looked at me as though I was the answer to a question he didn't know he'd been asking.

I opened my mouth to respond, to say something, *anything*, but my throat tightened. The words that normally came so easily seemed trapped in the rush of emotions flooding me. But I couldn't deny it.

He made me feel alive too.

I met his stare, not quite able to speak. Without thinking, I reached up, grabbed the front of his shirt, and pulled him down to me. My eyes closed as I gently pressed my lips to his.

His mouth was salt and sea breeze and he opened to me as I pressed my tongue against his lips. It was only the sudden fear of being seen that made me let go.

A deep rumbling spread through his chest as he watched me. "And now I feel like I might die if I have to wait to taste you again."

39

I walked down the long hall to the library with only the echoes of my steps as my companion. I could still feel the lingering sensation of his lips on mine.

The Prince of Akureyrian.

Goddess above.

This morning, Milla broke the news that Princess Merja had returned to Dalvin and Torben had been summoned to meet her for lunch. The thought of Torben spending time with the princess made my blood boil. But I smiled blissfully at the thought of him sitting across from her while the taste of *me* lingered on his lips.

Petty, I know.

After lunch, Torben and Leif planned to get Theo out of bed, and we would all meet after they spoke with the king.

I decided to use the time while Torben and his Treyst were occupied to clear my head and get some answers. And as much as I wanted to return to Nuuk, thoughts of my great-grandmother had stirred a primal need for information, not only for what was happening with the undercreatures but with my power as well.

An ornate door with a carved image of the goddess Goath led into the expansive library. Ancient windows stretched from floor to ceiling, the sunlight flickering through the rippled glass across thousands of leather bindings. Stepping inside felt like entering a sacred realm. The rows of books and rolls of ancient texts seemed endless. In the silence, the quiet murmur of history was almost audible, as if each book was whispering, waiting for someone to unlock the magic hidden within their pages.

As I walked, I passed two of the robed Keepers sitting at the large desks in the center of the room, their faces unreadable as they poured over stacks of manuscripts. Torben had told me that he loved spending time in this library. I wondered if he had a favorite table or if he was more inclined to bring his books back to his room.

Further down the rows of shelves the air shifted, the faint scent of parchment and old ink hung heavy in the air, mingling with the earthy warmth of ancient wood. The titles in this section became harder to read, as the letters and ancient symbols faded with the burden of time. Reaching a shelf that was tucked into an alcove behind a window, a large manuscript with a ruddy leather spine caught my attention. I could just make out the title that was written in the Old Language in golden ink.

Skógarverur.

Creatures of the forest.

I choked out a nervous laugh. *This seems like a good place to start*, I thought to myself as I pulled the heavy book from the shelf and carefully tucked it under my arm.

After an hour, I had gathered an armful of books that seemed to cover the period and general location within Árnes I was looking for. I felt dusty and my stomach rumbled with hunger, but my heart raced with the anticipation of what I might learn.

Just as I was about to round the corner, a petite Fae in long white robes crossed my path, nearly bumping into me with her large stack of books.

"Oh! Forgive me, lady, I didn't see you," she gasped.

The slender Fae had beautifully dark skin and a slender, youthful face that was complimented by deep green eyes and full lips. Her hair was as white as the long robes she wore and bound in a braid that wrapped around the top of her head.

"It's fine," I said as I shuffled the books back into a sturdy pile, "it's my fault, I wasn't looking where I was going." The woman's eyes widened as she glanced at the array of books in my arms. "I guess I was just excited to start reading," I said awkwardly.

"I'm sure, lady," she said, a look of suspicion crossing her green eyes.

"I'm Kaari."

"Alaía," she said as she bowed her head. "Are you researching Queen Maiken?" she asked tentatively.

My stomach tightened into a knot. "Erh, yes. Something like that. Have you read any of these?"

"Of course, lady… I have read them all."

Of course she would have. Alaía was a Keeper.

I studied her in awe, trying to fathom what it must be like to carry the weight of centuries' worth of knowledge—histories, magics, secrets, forgotten languages—all bound and contained within a single person. It was like meeting a living archive, someone who was both the keeper and the embodiment of the library's wisdom.

"Did you find what you were looking for?" Alaía asked. She would know every book in the library— exactly where to find the answers. It would be so easy to ask her if she knew how the undercreatures had escaped, but something in my gut told me I had to search for the answers—that I needed to do this for myself.

"I want to learn about the undercreatures." The words felt heavy and tasted foul.

Alaía seemed to be assessing me as I spoke, judging whether I was worthy of her direction. "Well, it seems you have found the right section." Alaía moved ahead of me, her steps light and sure, leading me further down the aisle as if the shelves whispered directions just for her. She scanned each row with a practiced eye, reaching up occasionally to pull a book down with a gentle touch, like she was reacquainting herself with old friends. Her fingers trailed delicately along the leather spines, each one rich with age and use, and I wondered if she could sense the stories they held without even opening them.

"I need to gather some manuscripts for the king, but I would be happy to meet with you after you have gone through these." Alaía turned, her gaze steady and unfathomable, holding mine for just a moment longer. "Take your time, Kaari. The truth about these creatures will not be hurried."

She left me there, alone with the dark spines that held stories long forgotten, every book a doorway, each one calling softly to be opened. As the silence settled, I realized that what lay hidden here could change everything—if I was prepared to face it.

I balanced the stack of books against my hip, their musty leather scent clinging to me as I left the library. The weight of them seemed heavier than it should, and I couldn't shake the sense that I was carrying more than paper and ink—they held the kind of knowledge that could change things, maybe for the worse. My shoes clicked softly against the stone floor of the palace as I wove through its sprawling corridors, trying not to let my mind drift to the dark contents waiting to be uncovered.

Turning a corner, I nearly walked straight into her. Merja. Of course. Dressed in her usual crimson, she planted herself squarely in my path, a smirk curving her lips as she took me in. Her gaze swept over me—first the stack of books, then my plain clothes—and I could almost hear the unspoken judgment before she even opened her mouth.

"Kaari," she drawled, her tone honeyed but brittle. "Playing scholar, are we? Researching something bleak, no doubt. You do seem drawn to... unpleasantness." Her gaze lingered on the books again, her nose wrinkling ever so slightly as though she could smell the centuries-old parchment.

I tightened my hold on the books, lifting my chin to meet her gaze. "Knowledge isn't bleak. Ignorance, on the other hand..." I let the words hang there, calm and steady. I wouldn't let her get to me—not today.

She didn't flinch, but her smile sharpened. "I just came from lunch with Torben," she said casually, like she was sharing a harmless piece of gossip. "He's such a fascinating man, don't you think? Always so... discerning about the company he keeps." She tilted her head, her ruby earrings catching the warm light streaming through the high windows. It felt calculated, like everything about her.

For a split second, her words hit their mark, making my chest tighten. But I wouldn't give her the satisfaction of knowing that. Instead, I adjusted the books in my arms, feigning indifference. "How nice for you," I said lightly. "Though that's odd—he didn't mention it when we were together earlier."

That flicker in her expression was faint, but I caught it. It was enough. My chest eased as I pressed forward. "Torben's always polite," I added, my voice calm and steady. "He's kind to everyone. Though I suppose kindness can be... misunderstood."

A serpentine smile spread across her perfectly painted lips. "Has he told you about the plans for our wedding? Soon, I will be his wife, and then I will be by his side all day... and night. I will be taking a close look at the staff we employ."

I felt the heat of anger rise, but I forced my lips into a small, unreadable smile. "Funny, he hasn't mentioned the wedding at all. But I'm sure he and I will still have plenty to keep us busy, even after the ceremony. I can't wait to hear about it."

Merja's smile faltered, the briefest crack in her facade, but her arrogance held firm. "Watch your tongue, little healer," she hissed. "You're far out of your depth, playing in games you can't possibly understand."

I stepped closer, refusing to let her intimidate me. "And yet here I stand," I said softly, the weight of my words deliberate.

Her nostrils flared, but before she could fire back, I shifted the books in my arms and turned on my heel. I didn't wait for her response—I'd already won this round. The sound of my boots echoed in the corridor, each step steadier than the last, my heart pounding with triumph and defiance. Let her stew in her venom; I had far more important things to worry about.

My heart was still beating a little faster than I'd have liked, but I didn't look back. The corridor widened ahead of me, and the sunlight poured in through the arched windows, casting everything in shades of amber and gold.

Merja's words still lingered, sharp and cloying, but I let them roll off me. She didn't matter—not really. The truth was in the warmth of Torben's gaze, in the way his hand lingered on mine. That was something she couldn't touch—at least not until they were married. But right now, I had bigger things to focus on than her petty games.

40

I wasn't sure where to go with the pile of books I had gathered. As much as I wanted to go to Torben's room, I knew his desk was already covered with maps and plans for our trip to Nuuk. I also knew that being seen entering the prince's room alone would cause an uproar if Princess Merja found out.

My grip tightened as I thought of her smug smile and sharp tongue. Even now, her words clung to me like a thorn, but I refused to let her get under my skin. Torben's actions spoke louder than her lies, and I wouldn't let her poison what was growing between us.

Once in my room, I carefully spread the books out on my small desk. The musky scent of ancient leather filled the space as I slowly brushed my fingers over the worn titles. I stopped when I reached the golden letters of Skógarverur—*Creatures of the forest*.

I sat down at the desk and turned to the first page. My heart stopped as I read the script that was written in fading ink in the top corner of the page.

Liva Eriksen

It felt like the air had been sucked from the room as I brushed my finger along the flowing script of my mother's pen. I stumbled out of my chair, stepping away from the desk, the air escaping my lungs in quick gasps.

This was my mother's book.

Lunging back to the desk, I quickly began flipping through the others to check for my mother's mark.

Liva Eriksen. Again, and again.

The mark was written on the inside of almost all the books I had gathered.

I closed my eyes and let myself believe that this was the reason I had seemed to stumble on that small section of the otherwise massive library—as if my mother's mark had called to me like a golden beacon in the dark of night.

Had Alaía known?

I needed to talk to her to see if she could tell me more about the collection—and find out how my mother's books had found their way to the royal library. She had promised she would talk to me about the books I found after she finished gathering books the king had requested.

I have read them all, the Keeper had said.

By the time I looked up from the dusty book I had been reading the evening light spilled softly into the room, casting a warm, amber glow across every surface. Each beam seemed to linger, painting the space with a warmth that felt almost tangible, like a gentle hand resting on my shoulder. I guessed I had been emersed my mother's books for several hours, but my sense of time had been lost in a sea of demons and creatures that seemed to surround me as I read.

I had changed into a loose dress made of soft blue muslin and sat with my feet tucked beneath me. My eyes were burning, and my mind was racing as I read the history of the familiar creatures I had feared for so many years when I traveled through the Holvik Woods.

My mother's books. I still couldn't believe it.

The pages seemed to permeate with the warmth of her once-familiar embrace. I breathed in, desperately searching for a trace of her scent. I had been so young when she died—too young to understand how much I had missed by not having her by my side. The pain of her loss was like a brand I wore over the fibers of my heart. I held the books close to my chest so that the beat of my heart thumped against the worn leather that had once been hers.

A soft knock at the door made me jump, but as the door slowly opened the scent of vanilla and cedar crept through the crack. I quickly tucked a slip of paper into the book to mark my page before turning to see Torben enter my room.

The golden specks in his eyes seemed to blaze with a heat that stole the air from my lungs, locking me in place as he crossed the distance between us. The world around us faded, and all I could feel was the pulse of his intensity, magnetic and unyielding. I stood as he crossed the space until he was so close he towered over me.

I let out a low sigh as he placed a powerful hand on my cheek, while the other greedily reached to my lower back, pulling me against him with a fervor that sent my pulse racing. I gasped at the sheer strength of his hold and tipped my chin up slightly so I could meet his gaze. I felt as if I were standing on the edge of something I couldn't pull back from—an invitation, a promise, and a challenge all in one.

"Ég vil ekki lesa um skrímsli," I purred, the ancient words rolling off my tongue. A low growl escaped Torben's throat, and he dipped his head to brush his nose along the side of my neck.

"I told you, I need to brush up on the Old Language," he said as he nipped at my ear. "Something about monsters?"

I pushed him away just enough so I could place my hands on his broad chest. I was trembling and my heart was racing at his touch, but I knew we needed to keep working. I sucked in a breath and squared my shoulders. "Well, we will have to start practicing because most of the books I found in the library are written in the Old Language. And it is going to take me all night to sift through them if I am translating everything by myself." My voice quivered slightly as I spoke.

"Hmm, I had other ideas for how we could spend the night."

I melted at his words—at the promise of what we could share.

"*Ég myndi vilja að þú sleikir mig aftur,*" I whispered as I backed towards my bed, my blue eyes swirling as I watched his approach.

"Now *that* I understand," he growled as he followed me to the bed. "Where exactly would you like me to lick you, Lady Eriksen?"

Despite my exhaustion, I laughed out loud. "Typical man. What would your tutors think if they knew that you remembered the word for *lick* but not *read*?"

Torben laughed as he wrapped me in his arms again, gently nipping at my neck as his voice slid over my skin. "That is quite the pile of books, I take it your trip to the library was successful?"

"Yes." I paused. It was growing increasingly hard to fight the temptation to give in to his touch. But my discovery in the library was weighing on my heart. Torben's eyebrows pinched in concern as he read the hesitation in my voice. "Torben, these books were my mother's. They must have been sent here after she died."

Torben cupped my face and slowly ran his calloused thumb over the curve of my cheek. "You always have been one step ahead of me. My father told me about your parent's collection when I mentioned you were in the library. I should have known you wouldn't need my help to find it." His voice was low and gentle, and he slowly lifted my hand to his lips.

I smiled sadly as I thought of my mother—of the reason those books no longer had a home in Vogar.

"Are you going to tell your father who my parents were? Who I am?"

"Yes, when you're ready. I understand why you have kept your history a secret. So, he can wait a little longer if that's what you need. Especially with everything that is happening."

My voice caught in my throat. I squeezed his hand in silent thanks. There was still so much I hadn't told him. And now, with this growing connection, the unspoken words weighed heavier with each passing moment. "I know we need to get back to Nuuk, but it seems like there is so much to learn before we go."

"A troop of soldiers has already left for Nuuk under Emil's direction." Torben sighed, "Everything is in motion. The good news is that we have not received any new reports of attacks since Theo and Leif returned."

I nodded. I supposed no news was good news. "I met a Fae in the library who said she had read *all* the books I found. Her name is Alaía… do you know her?"

The look of surprise on Torben's face was brief, but it spoke volumes. I raised a suspicious eyebrow in response.

"Alaía is a Keeper. Yes, I know her, and I don't doubt she has read all your books. She has probably read all the books in the library at this point."

"*All* of the books," my eyes went wide, "but there must be *thousands*. How well do you know her?" Although a sense of jealousy pulled at the pit in my stomach, I couldn't blame him if they had a more personal connection. She was strikingly beautiful—and Torben had told me he spent a lot of time in the library.

"If you're asking if she has shared my bed, she has not," Torben said, his jaw feathering. "But I can't say the same for Theo."

"Theo?" I choked. "Are they—do they still?"

"No. Their time together was brief... and complicated."

I could tell there was more to the story, and I was coming to realize that I had only brushed the surface of what Torben and his Treyst must have experienced during the decades they had spent together. I wondered how many decades—or centuries—it would take to learn everything about them—and if I would get the chance.

"How did Alaía wind up working in the library? Or has she always been here?"

"Ah, now *that* is a story for another time." Torben stretched his back before leaning in to kiss my neck. "Come, show me what you have found so far. I asked Aulis to bring us some dinner."

Hours later, I watched Torben from my desk. He was folded over a large text, painstakingly translating the words to look for anything helpful. His features had darkened as we read the history of the creatures that had once ravaged his kingdom. So many years of terror and destruction. The kingdom lived in constant fear until Queen Maiken had sacrificed herself for their protection. I flipped through *Skógarverur* again and even though the text gave a detailed account of the wild things that lived in Árnes, it did not provide any history of how they got there in the first place.

At some point Torben stood, stretching his arms overhead and arching his broad back. As he walked closer to me, his earthy scent seeped from his skin. He pulled a chair up so he could sit beside me at the desk and I was grateful for his steady presence. His arm brushed mine each time he turned a page, lingering ever so slightly before he pulled back. Every so often, his hand would drift, tracing a line along the ancient text with a finger before pausing to brush an errant strand of hair from my face. Our eyes met briefly over the leather-bound pages, and I could feel the warmth of his gaze lingering long after he turned back to the book. In the quiet, surrounded by the scent of old paper and leather, his hand found mine beneath the table, our fingers twining instinctively as we both poured over the words, as if anchoring each other amidst the secrets and mysteries we uncovered together.

I had just opened a new book when he suddenly leaned closer until his lips were inches from my mouth. "I would really like to kiss you," he whispered.

I closed the book in front of me, my pulse quickening as I rose to my feet. Gently, I took his hand, guiding him up with me until were standing close, faces only a breath apart. His chest was firm under my hand as I ran it along the line of his shirt, and I could feel the contours of his muscles hidden below the soft fabric. I had to lift onto my toes to close the distance between our mouths. His gaze held me captive, and every nerve in my body felt like it was on edge, trembling with the weight of this moment. I hadn't expected him to look at me like that, as if he could see straight through my defenses, straight into the parts of myself I tried to hide. It was thrilling and terrifying all at once. I wanted to close the distance between us, to let myself fall into whatever this was— yet a small voice inside warned me that once I crossed this line, there would be no going back.

Teasing, I bit his bottom lip before pressing into him, taking his mouth completely.

Torben answered by wrapping his solid arms around me and I shuddered as he ran a hand down my back. Our kiss grew deeper and wilder, and I slid my hands up his muscular stomach and chest before I wrapped them around his neck.

I *really* wanted to kiss him too.

Torben breathed in deeply as if memorizing my scent. He watched me like I was the only thing that mattered. In that moment there was no sense of his kingdom or of the dangers we faced. His eyes grazed over me like my touch was the only sustenance he would ever need.

Torben's hands trailed down my sides and cupped my backside before lifting me so I straddled his hips. I inhaled softly as I pulled my head back to meet his stare. His eyes were flecked with gold and they raged with a longing that made my blood roar. Without a word, he carried me over to my bed. "You taste like rosemary and lavender," he breathed as he nibbled his way down my neck.

I reached up and grabbed his shirt to pull his mouth back to mine then slowly worked the buttons loose. When I reached his waistband, he set me down and helped me tug the shirt free. I pushed it off his shoulders as Torben lifted my chin with one hand, trailing his lips in open-mouthed kisses along my skin, his breath sending heat searing across my skin. I ran my fingers along his waistband—searching and exploring—growing more impatient with each touch. Responding to his growing need, I pushed him up against the wall next to my bed. I stepped away from him, leaving him plastered to the wall bare-chested and panting, as I started to pull the top of my dress down over my shoulders.

He watched my every movement. The way my chest lifted with each breath. The way I bit my bottom lip. The way my bronze skin glittered in the dim lights of the candles. His eyes drank me in as if I was the only thing that would sustain him. And then, as I pulled my dress down over the tops of my breasts and let it fall to the ground, I felt his magic hum and his heart soar.

He closed the distance in two steps. "Tell me what you want, I only want to serve you," he whispered into my delicate ear.

I smiled and closed my eyes. "All of you."

The room seemed to close in around us as Torben kissed me. His mouth was warm and soft, and he reached for me with an urgency that made me gasp with need. Grabbing the back of his neck I pulled him into me, needing to feel every inch of his chest against my bare skin. Torben growled as I ran my fingers through his hair, gently digging my nails behind his head.

"Kaari," he breathed, "I *need* you." The prince reached around me, swinging me into his arms so my legs straddled his core.

As he carried me, I leaned in to kiss his brow. "All of you," I managed to whisper again as he lay me down on my bed.

The flicker of the candles in my room made the golden flecks in his eyes dance and the longing in his stare was so strong I wondered how I had lived so long without him.

You make me feel alive.

I felt as if every part of me I've kept hidden, quiet, was waking up from his touch. I had lived for so long—without really living. Since meeting Torben and his Treyst I felt like I had found a purpose—a reason to wake up each day, even if that reason was terrifying. Torben's touch was like an anchor and his words had been the a spark to a flame I thought had extinguished a long time ago—and now it fueled me.

Torben crawled over me, his chest rippling with the strength that flowed through him.

"Tell me how you want it," he whispered, looking at me with an intensity that threatened to break me completely.

"Slowly. I… I don't want this to end."

Torben grinned before leaning down to kiss my neck. "Whatever you wish… Your Grace." The words were like lighting as they coursed through me—*Your Grace*. For a century I had forced myself to forget my nobility and now, the Prince of Akureyrian was calling me *Your Grace* as he prepared to pleasure me into oblivion.

My need for him was a burning ember, pulsing and sparking with every touch. I reached up to pull him down to me. Torben made a guttural sound in his throat as our bodies crashed together, the fierceness of his mouth growing stronger as it moved over my chest. Torben's lips were demanding—intense and insistent—as he reached the center of my breast. The warmth of his mouth made my world spin, and I arched to press into him, feeling the hardness between his legs as I moved.

"Torben," I breathed, and he moaned. "I need you," I whispered, echoing the words he had said moments ago.

He leaned back so he was kneeling between my legs as he slowly pulled off my undergarment. Torben groaned as his eyes caressed my bare skin, and I broke apart at the sound of him coming undone. Sitting up, I reached down to undo the buckle of his pants and he kicked them off with desperate force.

We sat there for a moment, devouring each other's bodies with our eyes before I slowly leaned back onto the bed, my knees dropping to the sides in invitation. Torben moaned with pleasure as he positioned himself over me. His eyes never left mine as he slowly pressed himself against me, savoring the touch with each kiss.

"Now, Torben—I need you *now*," I begged, scraping my fingers across his back.

"I have been waiting for this since the moment I saw you in the Woods. I plan to take my time."

Goosebumps rippled across my skin with my growing need. I hadn't realized how badly my body ached for him—how his touch felt like it could sustain me forever.

You make me feel alive.

My breaths were ragged, and I pressed my hips against him, desperate for contact as he grazed my sensitive skin. Just as I thought I would die from need, he reached his hand between us and started to slowly circle his fingers across my skin, as if memorizing the feel of every dip and curve. I bucked into his touch—desperate to grab any part of him.

His teeth clenched and he hissed in my ear before pressing his mouth to mine. Our kiss was wild and desperate and only intensified with each gentle caress. Torben pulled his face away and watched me as the side of his mouth pinched into a wicked smile.

And then we became one.

It was electricity and fire and power.

The feel of him, as he slid into me sent lightning bolts through my core. I didn't realize how hollow I'd felt until now, with his warmth pressed against me, filling every empty space I'd ignored for so long. It was almost unbearable, this closeness, this vulnerability. But as his hands traced down my thighs, I only wanted more. I leaned in, letting myself fall, wondering if he understood that he was unraveling me with every touch. And as I opened my legs wider, allowing him to sink even deeper, I felt like this connection might just be my ruin. My body was shaking from the feel of him. I wanted him to live inside me forever.

Torben bit his lip as he pulled back, before slowly entering me again. Over and over, he sunk into me as he moved his mouth to meet mine—kissing me as deep and slow as our movements. Magic boiled within me until I was pretty sure I was glowing. Torben's eyes grew as he saw the light that radiated from my skin—and his magic sang alongside mine sending a cool breeze across my skin.

I reached up, dragging my nails across his back, pulling him in to deepen our connection. I couldn't breathe and I knew my climax was imminent. I pressed my hips against him as he quickened his pace and I moaned into his pointed ear. He reached his arms under my legs to pull me closer, falling deeper into me with each thrust.

"You are mine," he whispered, as he pulled out of me completely and then moved again—and we both erupted. Light sparked around us as my magic responded to the pleasure that rippled through me as he filled me with his release. I stared at him breathlessly, moving my eyes over his face, memorizing the moment. I pulled his mouth to mine and kissed him deeply as I wrapped him with my legs, keeping him locked inside.

I didn't want to let go. It seemed impossible that I had lived so long without his touch, and it fueled me like gas to a flame.

The prince was panting and staring at me with a look I had never seen. "Kaari," he breathed, but I didn't dare speak. I kissed him again slowly and then rolled so I was on top of him.

Without a word, I began moving my hips over his, needing to feel more of him even though I thought I might die from the pleasure that seared through my skin like wildfire. Torben's eyes were locked onto me as I rode him, and I arched my back so my breasts lifted to the sky.

He gripped my trembling thighs as I felt his climax growing again. I moved faster and harder until he sat up to meet me and we both exploded again.

We lay there breathless and entwined in each other as the room glowed around us. As I caught my breath, I looked deeply into the prince's eyes and watched the golden storm that brewed in his gaze. I kissed him gently—long and lingering.

"And you are mine."

41

Once we finally left my bed, we moved to the washroom where we slithered into the steaming water that filled the large tub. Torben washed my hair, taking his time to massage my head with his strong hands, and I rubbed his back with oil, running my hand down the large, raised scar that adorned his back.

We didn't need words—and I wasn't sure I was ready to speak. I leaned my back against his chest and let the steaming water bring me back to reality. After what could have been minutes or hours, Torben breathed into my ear, "I want you to come to my room to spend the night."

I turned to look at him with an amused smile. "Didn't I *just* spend the night? Twice?"

Torben laughed, still slightly breathless. "I mean... I want you to *sleep* in my room tonight."

The pleading in his voice made my heart break for the hundredth time that night. "Torben... you're still *engaged*. And your future wife is in the palace."

"It doesn't matter anymore, Kaari." The prince paused and his eyes glowed with the reflection of the water. "Kaari, I will only belong to you. No one in this world, or any other, can change that."

I had known he was falling for me—I realized I had known all along. But hearing him say the words out loud filled a void that had felt empty my whole life. I knew I had fallen for him too.

Torben reached up to gently stroke the back of my head, tracing a line down my back and sending shivers down my spine.

"I have been falling for you since I first met you. No one has ever bossed me around within the first five minutes of meeting me like you did."

I scoffed, turning to flick water onto his chest and watching as the beads dripped down the hard contours.

My heart and head were soaring. My magic roared inside as if the acknowledgment of our connection was waking up a deeper source of my power.

But the heaviness I felt from my secrets was becoming unbearable. Especially now.

"Torben... there is something else I need to tell you. It's... it's about your mother." My voice broke as I spoke, I needed him to know that the weight of carrying this knowledge all these years had nearly broken me beyond repair. Torben sat with an eerie stillness that made the ripples in the tub come to a standstill.

"Your mother... she came to Vogar. She came to help me. My mother knew she could help me learn to control my magic, so she asked her to come to our home." Sorrow filled the room as the words poured out. "Your mother came to teach me, but someone learned why she was in Vogar, and they came for us... for *me*." Tears rolled freely down my cheeks, my voice felt raw and broken. "They murdered them, Torben. *All* of them—to try to get to me. *I* am the reason your mother is dead."

The muscles in Torben's jaw flinched as the words set in. "Who was it? Who killed them?"

"I don't know," I sobbed. "I was returning from the woods when I heard the screaming. There was a rush of magic around me, and I knew my parents were fighting something... until I felt their power stop. I climbed a tree so I could look through the windows of the manor and saw my father on the floor in the library. There was so much blood. It was suddenly so quiet. I could see others, bloodied and beaten, left strewn across the great room floor—their blood mixing with the colors of the rugs. I knew they were beyond saving. I had been too late. Every window I peered into only brought more images of my failure. Servants and maids... all of them... *dead*. I saw the assassins as they were leaving. One of them chased me—throwing a dagger at me as I raced through the woods."

Torben was shaking his head slowly. He had told me that his mother had been killed while traveling in Vogar—but he had never known that she had been at the Eriksen Estate—my family estate. Her body had been dumped outside the palace walls in the dead of night.

I was rubbing the scar on my hand as I said, "This scar has reminded me of that failure, of the way I ran away as my people were slaughtered."

"You were a *child*, Kaari. The burden was not yours."

I shook my head. It was my burden. It has been for a hundred years. "Torben… the assassins… they were *Birkerian*."

The air was sucked from the room and air gusted around us as Torben's power roared—fueled by the rage that consumed him.

"I'm so sorry, Torben." The water in the tub had gone cold, but all I could feel was the pain that flooded my heart as I watched his grief set in.

His eyes met mine, his voice was low and ragged. "Don't you ever apologize for this, Kaari," he said as he cupped my face. "This is not your fault, and I am not the only one who lost someone that day… you lost your entire family—your *identity*."

"I should have told you."

"We will figure this out together. We have each other now. You don't need to face this alone anymore," he said, wiping a tear from my cheek. He kissed my brow and shifted in the tub. "Let's go to bed, *elskan min*, I think my balls are frozen."

I choked out a laugh and leaned in to kiss him, feeling lighter than I had in a hundred years.

I opened my eyes just as the light started to slip through the windows. We snuck into Torben's room in the early morning hours, knowing that Milla would come to my room at first light. We hoped my maid would assume I had gone for an early morning run when she found my bed empty. But all hells would have broken loose if she had discovered Prince Torben in my bed.

I smiled as I felt the warm body next to me and turned to watch the slow rise and fall of his chest as he slept. We had made love again overnight, slowly and quietly. After, he held me in his arms and kissed my forehead until I fell asleep.

He loved me. I still couldn't believe it.

I reached out and ran a finger along his jaw and up the shaved side of his head, taking in the beauty of his shape. He purred at the feel of my touch and the corner of his mouth turned into a lazy smile.

"We're not getting out of bed today," he grumbled as he ran his hand down my back.

I shivered at his touch but looked at him with a stern face. "We have to meet with your Treyst."

Torben rolled onto his back and put his hands behind his head. I paused to marvel at his chest as I ran my hand over the contours of his muscles. "When are you going to tell them about me?"

"About you? Or about us? Because they will know about *us* the moment they see us."

"What do you mean?"

"Gods, you really haven't spent much time around Fae. Kaari, now that we have acknowledged this bond, everyone will know… even my father… and Merja." The prince's voice trailed off, but I could have sworn a wicked grin crossed his face as he undoubtedly thought of how Princess Merja would react to learning her betrothed was in love with someone else.

"Oh, gods."

There would be no more hiding. No more pretending that my only identity was as a healer from Árnes.

"*How* will they know, Torben?"

He rolled over so that he faced me. "I love you, Kaari. There is no longer a place where my soul begins and ends. It is entwined with yours, as yours is with mine. For as long as I live—or as long as you'll have me." His fingers continued to trace circles across my back and over the curve of my bottom.

A knock on the door made us jump. Torben gritted his teeth, calling out that he would be there in five minutes. I swore I heard muffled laughter on the other side of the door as we scrambled to get dressed. As Torben went to open the door I moved to sit in the chair by the window, trying to look poised and professional—as if we had spent the morning researching undercreatures. His Treyst were standing in a line in front of the door, their faces fraught with questions.

"Holy gods," Leif bellowed before Emil could whack him in the stomach.

"Get in here," Torben barked. The three men shuffled into Torben's large room, and they all stopped to stare at me.

"Holy gods," Leif said again as he signaled back and forth between us.

"Goddess above. Is it *that* easy to tell?" I asked, my mouth agape. It *had* been a long time since I had been around Fae. I had forgotten how easy it was to ascertain personal details about someone based on their scent. I swore to myself and made a mental note to start practicing this invasive practice.

"Are you kidding? Your scent is all over him... and not just because of whatever happened here last night," Leif said as he waved his hand towards the bed.

"Should we talk here? Or should we go somewhere?" Emil paused, considering. "The princess is still in the palace, Your Highness, and it seems like this conversation might be safest outside the palace walls."

Torben nodded and looked at his Treyst. "We will meet at Emil's in an hour. Theo, you will escort Kaari through the tunnel. I will go with Emil and Leif to avoid drawing attention."

I hadn't realized what it would mean for us to acknowledge our feelings for each other.

Of course, the Treyst would need to know.

Torben looked at me as he took my hand in his and said, "I trust them with my life." I nodded and prepared to share my life's secrets with Torben's most trusted. He kissed my hand and walked out the door with Leif and Emil close behind him, leaving me with Theo. I glanced at him as he scanned the room. His eyebrow lifted as he glanced over the sheets that had been tossed across the bed, as though a storm had passed through. Something like disappointment—or pain—clouded his icy blue stare.

Theo cleared his throat, eyebrow still raised.

"Not a word," I barked as I grabbed my cloak and turned to leave.

The tunnel felt endless. The walls seemed to close in on us as we walked, and the smell of damp ground and stale air filled the space.

"Did you always know that you were kin to Queen Maiken?" Theo asked quietly.

The question surprised me. In all our time together since he first barged into my cottage in Árnes, Theo had never seemed keen on open conversation. And this was a topic that was both personal and potentially dangerous.

"Yes, I always knew the queen was my great-grandmother. My mother didn't speak of her often, but I knew the history. My grandmother was only a babe when the queen died, but the hurt seemed to linger through our generations," I whispered.

"Did your mother have raw magic as well?"

"No. But she was... powerful."

There was another long pause and then Theo said, "That much I knew. I met her. I met both your parents."

I stopped walking and stared at him. "You *knew* my parents?"

"Well, I met them, I wouldn't say I *knew* them. But it was easy to see that your mother was kind and your father... he was one of the most charismatic men I had ever seen in court."

I imagined my parents in the throne room, vivacious and cheerful as they mingled with other members of the Akureyrian nobility. I couldn't help but smile. "He sure was."

"You are the spitting image of your mother. I can't believe I didn't see it before." A tender smile had spread on his face, and I felt the warm glow of my magic as I imagined Theo meeting my parents.

"Will you tell me about her sometime?"

"Your mother?"

"The queen."

"Oh. Aye. I suppose Torben would have told you. I wasn't with her when she sealed the creatures, so I don't know how she did it. I always tried to protect her, and I think that's why she went without me." I could feel Theo's power simmering, wild and ancient.

His face had darkened, making his blue eyes glow in the light from the torches.

"Theo, you can tell me another time," I said carefully.

His shoulders relaxed slightly, but his face remained gruff. He seemed to be having a hard time meeting my gaze.

We finished walking the length of the tunnel in silence—even though I desperately wanted to question him at length about his history with Queen Maiken. There would be time for that later.

"Where exactly is Emil's place? Is it not in the barracks?" I said, breaking the silence.

"No, he has a house in the city."

"In the city? I guess I figured you all lived in the barracks with the other soldiers. Do you live in the city too?"

"Aye. Leif and I have apartments as well, although we usually stay in our rooms in the palace. But Emil's place is the nicest, as you'll see. We tend to go there when we need to meet without the risk of peering eyes or overly zealous ears."

The house we approached was a decent size, with beautiful stone walls covered in ivy and sweet-smelling roses. My eyebrows rose as I took in the impeccable landscaping and decor. Theo pulled a key from one of his pockets and let us through the finely crafted mahogany door. The entryway was quaint and well-kept. Paintings hung on the walls with subjects ranging from lush hillsides to scenes of ocean waves crashing against jagged shorelines—I imagined they were images of faraway places in Akureyrian. The decor was certainly not what I expected for the General of the Akureyrian guard.

I followed Theo down a long hallway, admiring the artwork as we walked. An office was located at the end of the hall, a large wooden desk stood in the center of the room with various chairs and couches lining the walls. Torben sat at the desk, looking over a large map with Emil and Leif by his side.

The prince's head lifted as I approached, and I saw fire spark in his eyes. I smiled broadly at him and went to his side, reaching for his hand. I needed to feel the reassurance in his touch.

It was clear why the Treyst liked coming here for their important conversations. The room felt cozy and secluded, and the furniture was soft and welcoming. The walls were covered in a textured blue wallpaper that glimmered with golden accents. Floor to ceiling windows allowed light from the courtyard to flood the room, and the sweet floral scent of blooming flowers seeped through the cracked window.

I settled into one of the plush chairs that faced Torben and watched as the Treyst found their places.

"Emil, this is wonderful," I beamed.

"It's home."

"Ah Emil, have you not poured drinks for our guests?" The man that walked in looked like he had been carved from stone. Hard features and rich umber skin merged into a ruggedly handsome face that was topped with shaggy black hair. Green eyes locked onto mine as he spoke. "Forgive me, I didn't know we had someone new."

"Kaari, this is my partner Erik," Emil said with a smile. "Erik, this is Kaari, she is one of the healers and the Master of Undercreatures."

"I am the love of his life, is what he meant to say. And what a title you have, my dear. And to think you're stuck with these animals all day. I'll go grab you one of the good bottles and some of the bread I've been baking and leave you to it. It was so nice to meet you, Kaari." Erik kissed the top of my hand and paused to look at me, his green eyes beaming against his dark skin. "You just let me know if these four give you trouble. I've already decided I like you best and vow to always take your side over theirs."

I watched Erik as he seemed to float out of the room.

"Once you have had Erik's cooking, he will be the love of your life as well," Theo muttered.

"It's true. Come let's sit." Emil waved his hand, directing us to find seats.

Once everyone was settled, I carefully told the Treyst about my past. It was surreal to tell my story. Admiration beamed in their eyes as I spoke of the hardships I had overcome—about how above all, I had carried the burden of my magic.

Theo, having already heard the details of my heritage, was the only one who looked composed—until Torben told them about his mother. Leif and Emil were both shaking their heads slowly in disbelief and I could have sworn Theo looked at me with an immense sense of understanding for the first time since we met.

Erik returned with a tray holding a steaming loaf of bread and a decanter filled with amber-colored whiskey and a stack of glasses. We all accepted a heavy pour and drank deeply, the whiskey strong and smokey.

"Uh… just to clarify," Leif held his finger up to catch everyone's attention before returning his gaze to me, "are we supposed to refer to you as *Your Grace*, now?

I scoffed. "Oh gods, please don't."

Leif's face was perplexed. "But you're the Lady of Vogar? As far as titles go, that certainly supersedes your Master's title. And besides, Torben is *in love* with you." Torben placed his hand on my lower back in response, as if confirming Leif's observation.

"I don't feel like the Lady of Vogar, Leif. I haven't been there since I was a child."

"People will remember you, Kaari," Emil added gently.

I rubbed my hands along my arms as if pushing away a chill. "That's what I'm afraid of. They will realize that I didn't die that night, they will know I ran away—like a coward. Vogar has been in good hands. And I… I have found my place."

Leif crossed his arms, looking dissatisfied with my answer. "And what about your bond with Torben?"

"We cannot publicly acknowledge their bond until Torben tells his father," Emil said firmly. "His father will need to end the betrothal. Learning that the queen's assassins were Birkerians is enough to end the agreement. Regardless, the King of Birkeria will not be pleased."

King Havard had arranged Torben's marriage to the Princess of Birkeria to secure a political alliance with the neighboring kingdom. Akureyrian and Birkeria had faced a tumultuous history in the thousands of years since the kingdoms had separated and created a border along the canal. The War, fought fifty years ago, had left scars that never fully healed—villages burned to ash, families torn apart, and trade routes abandoned for decades. Even now, old grudges simmered with uneasy truces brokered only to be broken by whispered accusations and border skirmishes. The air between the two lands still carried the weight of distrust, as if the ghosts of that bloody conflict lingered, waiting for another spark. The King of Birkeria would undoubtedly see the nullification as an insult and a threat—especially if the he learned of my power.

"We will tell my father today. He will likely know when he sees us, but now that we know Birkerians were involved in the assassination that killed my mother and Kaari's parents, we have proper grounds to nullify the betrothal." As Torben spoke, his hand slid from the small of my back, his fingers trailing down my arm, leaving a warm line that tingled against my skin. Without hesitation, he reached for my hand, his grip firm yet gentle. His thumb brushed over my knuckles in a small, reassuring motion, grounding me. I squeezed his hand back, feeling the strength and quiet resolve.

Would this lead to war? I could only imagine the rage King Havard would feel when he finally learned what had happened to his wife. Were we prepared to fight against the Birkerians while also protecting ourselves against the undercreatures?

Any excitement or happiness I had felt about my connection with Torben dissipated as the discussion switched to the village that had been destroyed. The scope of the destruction had not been seen since the Birkerian War.

"It is only a matter of time before word of the attack starts to spread through the kingdom. We need to have a plan before panic sets in," Emil said. "We have resources in Nuuk, but those soldiers are not trained against creatures of the Underworld. We will need to make sure they have resources and plenty of food for the people there."

I swallowed. *Holy gods*, I thought, *they* are *preparing for war.*

"Until proven otherwise, this is war." Emil confirmed my thoughts as he tapped his fist on the center of the map. "The likes of which has not been seen in a thousand years."

"Kaari, we will need your help training the soldiers to fight these beasts. They will need to learn their weaknesses and their strengths if they are to fight against them." I knew Torben didn't want to ask me—that he didn't want me to be on the front lines of the fight against these creatures. But the fact that he knew me enough to know I would want to help made my heart swell.

"Good," I said, "I need to go back to the library before we leave. I'm still trying to figure out how the queen banished the creatures." I paused and glanced at Theo, and when I spoke my voice was barely a whisper. "Maybe, I could banish them again."

"No," Theo said before anyone else had a chance to speak, his voice dark and firm.

"But I am her kin, maybe I can—"

"No, Kaari. I have already lost one queen."

"I am not a queen, Theo."

"You might as well be."

42

The throne room unfolded before us, vast and imposing. The high, vaulted ceilings formed a breathtaking sweep of intricately carved stone, arching above like the ribcage of some long-forgotten, beast. Sunlight streamed relentlessly through the towering windows, flooding the room with a harsh brightness, while the scent of burning incense hung heavy in the air. Torben led the way toward the grand council table positioned just before the dais. The absence of the king's council made the room feel even larger, emptier, the space almost echoing with its own grandeur. I felt a flicker of smallness as King Havard gazed down at us from his imposing throne, a majestic seat carved from dark stone, its surface adorned with faintly shimmering designs that caught the sharp light.

I could feel the blood pumping through my veins as anticipation crashed through my stomach. I felt drained and so, so tired. The conversation at Emil's had left me feeling helpless and yet, there was an unfamiliar comfort in knowing that there were others who knew my secrets. Others who had sworn to protect me—and fight beside me.

"Your Majesty," Torben said as he approached, "we have asked to meet with you because—"

The king waved a hand, silencing Torben and I held my breath. "I knew I recognized your eyes... and your scent. Earthy like you mother," the king said, his voice a low rumble as he watched me curiously. I felt like I couldn't breathe. He had known my parents, of course, he would see the resemblance.

Torben stood, pressing his knuckles into the table. "Father, Kaari is the daughter of Steinar and Liva Eriksen and is the rightful Lady of Vogar... and I have pledged myself to her. I will have no other."

The king bowed his head as if it was suddenly heavy with grief. "I know who she is, Torben. It's how I knew she could be the Master of Undercreatures." The king paused, "And have you accepted this bond, Lady Eriksen?"

His eyes were pools of emotion I couldn't read, but I didn't hesitate as I said "Yes."

"Queen Gunilla spoke of you often, Lady Eriksen. You must know that your mother was the queen's dearest friend." The pain in the king's voice was palpable as he slammed his fist into the table, his cheeks reddened with emotion. "I should have known. I should have known that her death was connected to the murders at the Eriksen estate."

Everyone froze.

Torben looked at his father earnestly, but uneasiness flexed his jaw. "She was there," he said, his voice a forceful whisper. "Kaari was there when my mother—the Queen—was *murdered*." He paused and caught his breath. "She saw the assassins... they were Birkerian." The name of the kingdom of his betrothed came out like acid on his tongue.

The king's eyes were closed and I had the overwhelming feeling that this moment was too personal—too painful—for him to share with our group, perhaps with anyone. Slowly, with an eerie Fae stillness, the king lifted his head, his eyes piercing into me. "She went to help you with your power."

It was not a question. And it broke my heart.

It was my fault.

The tension in Torben's body made his powerful form seem bigger somehow.

But then the king smiled, his face filled with pride and affection for his queen. "I should have known," the king finally said. "I should have known that Liva's child would be destined to find my son." He let out an enormous sigh that was far from regal and I began to breathe again as a softness crossed his face. He chuckled then, the sound still laced with grief. "Your mothers would have been over the moons to see you standing here together."

The tension in the room started to lift as it became clear the king accepted our bond. Torben watched the shift in his father's face, and he had finally breathed as acceptance filled his father's eyes.

He was a good king—a good father.

Torben had told me that after his mother died, King Havard had become hardened to a certain extent. He had never been cruel—to Torben or his subjects—but any glimmer of joy had been extinguished when his wife died. His parents had not been mates, marrying instead for politics, but during their centuries together they had formed a deep love for each other. A bond that anyone would have been grateful for.

The king decided he would announce my identity in a formal ceremony later that evening. He insisted my identity as the Lady of Vogar would help the kingdom understand why Torben had rejected his engagement to the Princess of Birkeria. Akureyrians, after all, held no love for Birkerians and news that their prince was courting someone from within the kingdom would be well received.

By the time we were done speaking with the king, word had already been sent to Birkeria, that due to recent intelligence, the arranged marriage was over.

Emil volunteered to go find Princess Merja so the king could tell her to pack her things. Theo had sighed heavily, undoubtedly relieved that he had escaped *that* assignment.

While we waited for Emil to return with Merja, I stood by one of the large windows, watching the raindrops as they meandered down the glass. Torben approached quietly and gently placed his hand on the small of my back. "Are you alright?" he asked. I kept my gaze on the waves that were crashing against the jagged cliffs below.

"There will be those who remember my power. Whoever came for me all those years ago will likely come again." My voice caught in my throat. "I have always known that someone might eventually come after me. But it was just me... and now, what if I am putting all of you in danger?"

Guilt festered deep inside me—the guilt over the deaths of my parents, Torben's mother, and everyone who had been in my home that night—and the fear that my presence would only bring more death to those I cared about.

Torben reached up and stroked my cheek. "We will be ready. You are not alone anymore, *elskan min.*"

I melted into his touch and breathed a heavy sigh. "If we can survive Merja's rage, we can *probably* survive anything."

43

Princess Merja stormed into the throne room with two Birkerian guards in tow. She wore a flowing red gown that hugged her waist and exaggerated her heavy chest. Her long black hair was tied into a flowing wave, extenuating her defined chin. She bowed her head to King Havard and then inclined her gaze to Torben, her eyes raging with a sultry caress. I stood behind the prince with Theo and Leif at my side, my hands clutching into tight fists as I watched her approach.

"Princess Merja," the king boomed, "I appreciate you coming on short notice. The circumstances surrounding your engagement to Prince Torben have changed." He paused and silence filled the massive space. "We have received new intelligence about my wife's death, and until we have been assured that your family was not involved in the deaths of Queen Gunilla and Lord and Lady Eriksen, there will be no alliance between Akureyrian and Birkeria."

Confusion seemed to ripple through the princess, as her face contorted.

"My apologies, Your Majesty, I am not sure I follow." Her words were unmistakenly loathsome.

"I have sent word to your father that your engagement has been nullified."

I braced myself, feeling my magic stir—I wasn't sure if the king had intended to leave out the fact that his son was in love with someone else.

But it didn't matter.

She knew.

The princess' eyes shot at me like daggers. "Of course," she spewed. "I suppose your *Master of Undercreatures* is to thank for this *intelligence*. A fool you are for believing the word of a Fae who has been hiding in Árnes for the past century. A Fae whose allegiance you know *nothing* about." Her words came out like poison.

Torben adjusted his stance, his powerful form a clear threat to her tone. But the king's voice was calm and level. "I have sent for a ship that will take you back to Birkeria. And for your sake, and the sake of your people, you should pray to the gods that your father did not order the assassination."

"You know nothing about my father if you think he would be capable of coordinating such an execution. He will *not* be pleased. Your accusation alone is enough to prove we will never have an alliance between our people." The promise of retribution was clear as she turned and marched out of the throne room.

Once she was gone, the air slowly returned to the grand room. Leif seemed to be mumbling a silent prayer and Emil was shaking his head as he looked at the floor.

"We will deal with any threats they make," Torben said, his voice scratchy with rage.

The king turned his head to look out the massive window where dark clouds covered the sky, his arms crossed behind his back. "A storm is coming. I fear the undercreatures that are roaming the realm for the first time in a thousand years may prove to be the least of our worries."

Walking back to Torben's room felt like floating through a dream. The walls had appeared too high to be real and the emerald carpet snaking down the never-ending hall seemed to writhe as if it were alive.

The exhaustion I felt from the past several days penetrated through my bones. Managing the constant contrast of emotions was proving to be onerous and I was left feeling completely drained. How was it possible to feel so much fear, worry, excitement, and *bliss* at the same time?

Upon entering Torben's room, we found that Aulis had left a generous spread of food and a large bottle of wine. My eyebrows lifted as I looked at Torben. "Are we celebrating?" I asked as I lifted the bottle. Torben chuckled and pulled me into his chest. I felt myself melting against him, my worries fading into the background, if only for a little while. So much was changing around us—uncertainties, threats, the looming weight of what lay ahead—but in his arms, everything felt steady, secure. I traced the strong line of his jaw until I found the small dimple in the center of his chin. His lips parted slightly as I passed over the soft lines around his mouth—instantly imagining all the places those lips had explored.

"How is it that I want you all the time?" My voice quivered, barely a whisper.

Torben growled, leaning down until our mouths collided. He nearly stumbled as he pulled his pants off with one hand while the other traced the side of my ribs. Our hands were rabidly reaching and touching as if we only had a moment before the other would disappear forever.

My hands explored and I squirmed with need as he reacted to my touch. There was something powerful about watching the Prince of Akureyrian becoming undone because of *me*. Looking at *me* like I was the only thing that mattered.

After another breath, Torben slipped my shirt over my head and pulled the string on my pants, causing them to drop around my feet. Reaching down, he lifted my legs around his waist and carried me to his bed.

As his substantial form hovered over mine, I shifted my legs slightly, inviting him to press closer. His eyes never left mine as he slid into me. There was no need for teasing tonight. My need had erupted since I touched his jaw. The fullness of him as he dipped into me sent shockwaves down my spine and I clenched my legs to pull him deeper.

This moment.

This connection.

I felt like every part of me was stretching and expanding—welcoming this feeling of devotion. It nearly broke me. In his eyes, there was only me. Every kiss and every stroke were a song of his love for me.

I had forgotten how the unrelenting stamina of the Fae allowed for *multiple* rounds of pleasure. We had each come to climax two more times before we were too famished to continue.

We dragged ourselves to the small table, each of us wrapped in one of the white bedsheets and filled our plates with an assortment of foods.

"Aulis would be furious if he knew we didn't eat his meal while it was hot." Torben chuckled as he scooped a chunk of soft cheese onto his bread.

"Well, maybe we should ask him to only bring cold foods because I rather enjoyed that." I gave him an exaggerated wink that made his lip pinch into a crooked smile.

We spent the next hour lazily eating our dinner and talking about our pasts. We had promised to take time each day to share stories about the lives we had lived before finding each other that day in the Holvik Woods. The notion that we had spent over a hundred years living without each other seemed implausible now that we couldn't imagine being apart.

"Torben... will we be expected to *marry*?" The question had been heavy in the air since the king announced that he had nullified the engagement to Princess Merja. Of course, the prince would eventually be expected to marry, I just wasn't sure how quickly. In all my years, I had never considered that I would find someone to give my heart to for the rest of my immortal life.

"I certainly won't marry anyone else," he said as he casually shrugged his shoulders, sending my stomach off the cliff of a waterfall and into the rapids.

I jabbed him in the ribs for giving a non-answer answer and Torben cursed out a laugh.

"Yes," he said, holding my hands in his, "if you'll have me, one day we will marry."

I leaned over to kiss him softly. "Good, Your Highness. You are stuck with me."

"Let's see how you feel about me after I tell you we need to get going so we can go to your ceremony."

I squirmed in my seat. I wasn't sure how I felt about the king announcing my true identity and telling all of Akureyrian that I was the sole survivor of a brutal attack that left an entire estate murdered and the queen to rot on the stairs to the palace.

"Do we have to?" I did my best attempt of batting my eyes and puckering my lips—and I felt absolutely ridiculous for trying.

"It's time, Kaari. By the time we return to this room, everyone will know who you really are."

Torben's voice was steady, but there was no denying the gravity in his tone. My heart pounded in my chest, and I glanced at the floor, trying to control the wave of unease rising inside me. The weight of my past, the secrets I had kept buried for so long, would be exposed to the kingdom in a matter of hours. I wasn't sure I was ready to face the judgment in their eyes or to relive the horrors that haunted me every night. Would they think of me as a coward who had run away when my family needed me the most?

He reached for my hand, his touch warm and grounding, pulling me from the spiral of my thoughts. "You don't have to carry this burden alone anymore," he said softly.

I squeezed his hand, but my throat felt tight, and my voice was barely above a whisper when I responded. "I just don't know if I can face them... knowing what they'll think of me."
Torben leaned closer, his gaze unwavering. "Let them think what they will. What matters is that you survived—and you're here now, stronger than they could ever imagine."

44

We never made it to the ceremony. Word of the attack in Nuuk had reached us like an electric current, destroying any hope of reprieve.

Now, as I looked around, every corner of the infirmary reeked with the heavy stench of blood. Normally the sweet floral smells of Regn permeated the space. But today, the only thing anyone could smell was the metallic stench. My eyes scanned the inside of the infirmary as I brushed away sweat and filth from my brow.

Every cot held a writhing body.

Blood stains covered nearly every surface.

Laila was across the room, wiping her hands on her apron. The healer's dress which had been a cool sage when she arrived—was now caked with crimson. Sweat coated her skin, and her hair was slick and curling at the ends. I watched as the healer searched in vain to find a clean spot to wipe her hands.

Laila and I had not stopped working since Theo had arrived through the portal with the first soldier from Nuuk. He had made the jump seven more times to retrieve the others who had been injured and were beyond the healing capabilities of the healers in Nuuk—I knew there were many left behind who were beyond saving.

The northern healers had gone through all their supplies within the first hour of the attacks, leaving their infirmary barren and helpless.

Laila had been calm and measured as she tended to each of the soldiers, sending her magic into them as she tried to fix what had been broken. But it was hard to ignore the grief that was starting to settle in—we had lost two already.

As I wrapped another bandage around a mangled limb, I cursed myself for not spending more time here. My supplies were already dangerously low—I should have been prepared for this. I should have known better, anticipated that trouble would eventually find its way to us. Each new wound I treated, each face twisted in pain, weighed heavier on me. The desperation was a constant, gnawing ache, and my hands trembled as I reached for yet another scrap of cloth, praying it would be enough.

Exhaustion was beginning to weigh on me but the last of the soldiers was still waiting for my healing. I approached a tall redheaded warrior who had been impaled through his thigh with a drekavac's tooth. Another soldier had killed the drekavac and sliced through the tooth, not wanting to dislodge it in the field. Smart, if he had the Fae would have bled out instantly.

I settled my hands on his leg as I reached my magic out, feeling the depths of the injury. His breaths were shallow—although I suspected it was more out of fear than blood loss, even though there was an ample supply of both.

A gust of cool air entered the space, and I could have cried as the crisp freshness filled my lungs. Torben and Theo charged in. They wore fighting leathers and had longswords strapped to their backs. I had never seen them dressed in fighting gear and it just about took my breath away—and broke my heart.

The black leather stretched across their broad chests and hugged all their contours as if it had been poured onto their shape like liquid. They had pulled their hair back in tight knots with a braid running along the freshly shaved sides of their heads. Torben's eyes were dripping with concern as they met mine. *Are you alright?* They seemed to ask.

Yes. I tried to tell him with my heavy gaze.

Torben shifted and I realized he was holding Theo up. "What did he do?" I demanded as I nodded towards a cushioned chair.

"How do you think all of these soldiers got here?" Torben grumbled.

"I will be right there, give him water." I returned my focus to the leg—and tooth—in front of me. I had nearly surrounded the tooth with my magic, slowly repairing the broken blood vessels that had been mangled by the impact. Slowly, I began pulling the tooth out of the soldier's leg. My magic surged through the broken blood vessels, repairing the severed connections with threads of magic. Even with the bleeding controlled, the pain must have been excruciating because at some point he had passed out. With a final pull, the tooth was out. I quickly washed the wound with clean gauze and water that had been boiled with willow bark. After thoroughly cleaning the area, I packed fresh gauze into the wound and covered it with a tight bandage.

Once I was sure the bleeding had stopped and the soldier was resting, I rushed to Theo. He was pale and his skin was clammy. I couldn't imagine how it felt to portal jump that many consecutive times without rest.

"Are you injured?" I asked as I felt his forehead for signs of fever.

"No," he said breathlessly. "I just need to rest and maybe have something for the pain in my head. Unless the others need it more," he said as he glanced around the room.

"I have an oil you can use. It won't work as well as the opium, I'm afraid." But as I rubbed his temples with the mixture of lavender and featherfew I sent small bursts of my dwindling magic to relax the worst of his tension.

Theo sighed and then blinked an eye open as he looked at me. "You didn't have to use your magic, I would have trusted your little jars." His eyes were glassy with fatigue, but the intensity of his artic blue stare pierced through me.

"Is that the last of them?" Laila's voice was firm, her approach had been silent.

Theo nodded.

"But I take it this will not be the last time we can expect such an influx of wounded."

"No. There will be more." Torben had finished checking on all the wounded and was now standing at Theo's side.

"We are already sending more resources to Nuuk and encouraging the locals to evacuate. Dalvin will open its gates to anyone who wants to come." He was looking directly at me now. "Theo went through the portal to assess the state of Nuuk. When he arrived, he heard cries from outside and ran to help. A pack of drekavac had attacked one of the smaller camps in the dark. These soldiers were hit the worst, the others are receiving care in Nuuk. There were others... who did not make it."

"I will send word that more healers should be sent to the North," Laila said to Torben.

"Thank you, Laila. We need to start preparing our reserves and fortifying the city." The command in his voice sent a chill down my spine. He was preparing for an unimaginable war. This is what the Akureyrian people had experienced a thousand years ago. The relentless terror that led Queen Maiken to sacrifice herself to seal the creatures in the borders of the Woods.

"Emil's soldiers are well prepared and are training others as they move North. Once Theo has rested, he will help us get back to Nuuk."

"I am ready now," Theo argued.

"*Þú þarftor að hvílan þig*," I protested.

"I can rest when I'm dead," Theo fumed.

"You will do no such thing. Close your eyes or I will close them for you," I said sweetly.

Torben patted his friend on the shoulder. "You heard her."

When I was sure he was going to keep his eyes closed and sleep, I went to check on the others. I was stopped by Torben's strong hand on my arm as I walked by.

"You need rest too, *elskan min*." His voice was a low grumble, but his touch was soft as he slowly brushed his thumb across my cheek. I could have melted into that touch, let it replace the warmth that had drained from me.

"I will. I just need to check on them again. Laila has called for other healers to come here as well so we can take shifts."

"Shall I ask Milla to draw you a bath?"

"Oh, gods yes," I purred, my shoulders slouching at the thought of submerging in steaming water. He leaned in and gently kissed my head, unfazed by the filth that coated my skin.

"Your Highness," Laila called as Torben opened the door to leave, "you made a good decision when you asked her to come."

"Aye, it was the best decision of my life."

45

The steaming water was stained with rusty red swirls as the dried blood washed off my body. Milla was still standing in the corner of the room as if she was afraid to leave me alone after seeing the state I was in when I returned to my room. I was grateful for her presence, even though I found that I didn't know what to say to explain my ragged appearance.

The attack on the soldiers in Nuuk had been a brutal reminder of how dangerous this new reality would be for Akureyrian. If it was this bad in Nuuk with Fae soldiers, I could only imagine how bad it might be in Árnes. I shuddered at the thought of how the mortal villages further north were faring.

I was familiar with many of the villages throughout Árnes. I had traveled to several of them to trade goods and offer healing services and had always admired the resourcefulness of the people living in such a remote area. And now, with creatures from the Underworld roaming free, all those villages were at risk.

There had only been one other time that I had cared for so many injuries at once. I still had dreams about the bilious black smoke that signaled the tragedy. The market in Kulusuk burned with a raging flame that reached taller than the roofline of the surrounding buildings. The screams of the people who had been inside were like daggers through my heart as I raced to pull bodies from the building.

It had been by chance that I was in Kulusuk when the fire broke out. I had traveled to the quaint village in northern Árnes to trade herbs and offer healing services. I never imagined that I would end up staying for two weeks to help care for the injured.

There had been many who were beyond saving. The flames had not discriminated between young and old and by the time the smoke had settled the village had lost more than half of their own. The ones who had escaped the suffocating smoke, and lived through the deadly touch of flame, were brought out into the open streets where the healers gathered.

As I closed my eyes, I could still feel the charred hand of a young woman I found trapped beneath the rubble. Her skin had been hot and blistered beyond recognition, but I had held her hand until it went still.

It was one of the only times I used my healing magic. The burns, however, had been too severe. There was nothing to save after the flames had ravaged her body.

And yet, there was something about today that had felt different.

Exhaustion penetrated deep into my core as I recounted the injuries I had seen. Summoning my enervated magic, I held my hand out until a small orb of light grew in my palm. Despite feeling drained, my magic still managed to respond when called on.

I swallowed, remembering the control I had felt earlier as I wielded my magic to mend broken bones and reconnect torn skin. I wondered if I would have been able to save that woman if I had possessed the control over my magic that I felt today.

The training I had done during my runs with Torben and my work in the infirmary had taught me how to use my magic in measured doses, allowing me to stretch out my power and not fear burnout. And still, I knew there was a lot to learn.

"Is the water cold, Kaari? Would you like me to fetch more hot water?" Milla's voice was quiet and concerned. She too looked exhausted.

"Thank you, Milla. I'm alright." I forced a smile as I wrung the water from my hair. After splashing my face, I stood and wrapped myself in the towel she was holding.

Even though Milla had changed the water twice and my skin glistened and my hair smelled like rosemary oil, I still didn't feel clean.

Milla held out a soft muslin dress, her large eyes watching my every move. My skin looked surprisingly pale next to the sage green fabric.

I needed answers. I needed to know if there was a way we could stop more devastation—before it was too late.

"I need to go to the library, Milla." I reached out to hold her small hands. "I need you to find Prince Torben and Captain Axtell and ask them to meet me there."

The library was surprisingly tranquil this late in the evening. An eerie calm seemed to float through the winding corridors, making the sound of my footsteps seem intrusive to the silence. Keepers could be seen walking through the expansive hallways pushing carts filled with books to be returned or collected. The sweet smell of incense wafted through the endless walls of shelving, and I breathed in the serenity, letting it wash over the tension that tore across my shoulders.

"I see you came back for more." Alaía's voice was as smooth as silk, the sound echoing off the open ceiling despite her whisper. Her white hair seemed to glow in the dim lighting and her green eyes were wide and welcoming.

She really was beautiful.

"Alaía, I'm so glad you're here. I need your help. I'm not sure if you have heard about—"

"The undercreatures," she interrupted. "Yes, I heard. And I suspected you would be back after I saw the books you left with last time. I take it you didn't find what you needed?"

I let out a tired breath. "Not really. I know the basic history that led up to the time when Maiken bound the creatures to the Holvik Woods. But I haven't found anything about *how* it could be possible for them to escape."

"Hmm." Alaía put down the books she had been carrying and started walking down one of the long rows of shelves. Instinctively, I followed.

"It is curious, Kaari Eriksen, that you would be the one tasked with uncovering the story of how the undercreatures were released when it was your kin who put them there in the first place."

Hearing her use my true name sent shockwaves up my spine. "You're talking about Queen Maiken?"

Alaía's steps were quiet as she continued walking, her gaze intent on reading the titles of the books in front of her. "It is why your mother amassed such an extensive collection. She was wonderful, losing her was an unsurmountable tragedy."

"How did you know her?" I blurted.

"I have been a *Markvörður* for many years. Your mother, Lady Eriksen, was well-versed in our kingdom's history. I had the honor of helping her uncover some of the histories that were important to her—your—bloodline."

A *Markvörður*—a Keeper.

The Keepers had been responsible for maintaining the history of the kingdom for thousands of years.

Many of the Keepers were hundreds of years old, their immortality ensuring they were able to keep continuous historical records.

"Many years ago, before you were born, I went to Vogar to visit the Eriksen estate. Your mother's collection held some texts that had never been recorded. It was my job to read her collection and ensure that the histories were memorized and passed on amongst the Keepers." Alaía took a book from the shelf and then gently put it back with a shake of her head.

The Keepers had a unique type of magic—the power of infinite memorization—their minds were capable of remembering *every* detail of everything they ever heard or read. This made the network of Keepers a powerful system for keeping records. Each Keeper would share their learnings with several other Keepers who would then share with others. Eventually, the entire network would possess the shared knowledge.

I still found myself marveling at the lifespans of the Fae. To many, I would be considered *young*. My parents had been over five hundred years old when they had been murdered, and even they were not considered *old*.

Alaía didn't look a day older than me. Her skin was dark and dewy, and her green eyes were vibrant and alert. The only sign of her age was her snow-white hair which was pulled back in a tight braid.

"So, you have read them? You have read *all* of my mother's books?"

The Keeper stopped walking and turned to face me. "What question are you trying to answer, Lady Eriksen?" The weight of the question hung in the air between us, demanding an answer I wasn't sure I could give

I bit my lip. *What is the question we need answers to?* "Why is this happening? Why are the undercreatures suddenly free to roam Akureyrian?"

Alaía's thoughtful smile was mixed with something else. Sympathy, perhaps? "The answers to the problems of today are rarely found in the texts of the past. We can only learn what happened and then use that information to make informed decisions."

"That sounds like something my father would have said."

"Your father was wise. I will take that as a compliment." Alaía's smile was apprehensive, as if she didn't know if she should speak of my father.

"You knew my father?" I pressed.

"Oh aye, I traveled with your parents when I returned to Dalvin."

I leaned back against the towering shelves, closing my eyes as I thought of my parents. Despite the heaviness in my heart, I found something reassuring about the fact that Alaía had known my parents . "I have so many questions."

Alaía's full lips stretched into a smile that was as warm as a night in Värme. She reached to hold my hands in her own. "I promise I will tell you everything in time. But for now, I would imagine you would like to see your mother's collection."

"I found my mother's books the last time I was here."

"Those were books from her *public* collection. You have yet to see her private collection—the collection she left to me for safekeeping. Your mother's private collection holds the only known copy of *Skrímsli drottningarinnar.* If I remember correctly, that is where you will find some of the answers you are looking for."

A choked sound escaped my throat as I gazed into Alaía's bright eyes.

"I'm sure your parents taught you the Old Language."

Skrímsli drottningarinnar. The Queen's Monsters.

All I could do was slowly nod my head. My mother had possessed a comprehensive history of Queen Maiken and she had shared it with Alaía to ensure the history was not lost.

Just as I was about to ask Alaía about *Skrímsli Drottningarinnar,* the sound of approaching footsteps stifled my voice. Theo rounded the corner and stopped when he spotted me, his sapphire eyes locking onto mine. *Sorry it took me so long,* his gaze seemed to say. Torben followed behind, a relieved smile crossing his face when he saw me. He crossed the distance, wrapping his arm around me as he gently kissed my forehead.

Theo seemed frozen in place, and I noticed the way his jaw set, and his breaths had quickened. His gaze shifted from me to Alaía with an intensity I had never seen as he ran his hands through his sandy brown hair.

"Alaía," Theo managed to say.

"Captain Axtell," she responded, dipping her chin ever so slightly.

Torben cleared his throat.

"Aye. Milla told us to meet you here," Theo said, clearly flustered. I had never seen the captain flustered.

"What can you tell us about the undercreatures, Alaía?" Torben asked.

"We should find somewhere to sit. Head to my room and I will see if Aulis can bring us something from the cellars. We will need something stronger than tea for this conversation."

46

I should have known that the Keepers would not be housed in simple dormitories. I had envisioned Alaía's room as a barren, monastic style, room like those of the priestesses. The Keepers, however, seemed to prefer a space that was much more lavish. Torben led me and Theo through the library towards the west tower where the Keeper's residence was located.

Alaía's apartment was a mix between a private library and lush living space. Hundreds of books were housed on the shelves that stretched from floor to ceiling. A large oak desk sat near a sizable window overlooking the surrounding forest. There was also a soft green sofa that held several piles of documents and a worn blanket that looked cozy and inviting. A four-poster bed in the back of the room was draped with rich purple curtains and the entire space smelled of earthy incense.

I glanced at Torben. "I thought you gave me the nicest room."

Torben rolled his eyes. "Believe me, some of their rooms are nicer than mine."

Theo was pacing as the door opened and Alaía walked in. Aulis followed behind with a large tray filled with sweets and an ornate bottle of deep red liquid. I nudged Torben, asking him with my eyes for answers about Theo's sudden awkwardness. Torben leaned close enough that his breath tickled my ear, sending my stomach into a flurry. "Years ago, Alaía received a message from a Seer about Theo. Ever since then, he has been spooked whenever he is around her… but this is worse than normal." I opened my mouth to respond with a frenzy of follow up questions, but Alaía approached.

"I hope you don't mind, Your Highness," Alaía said to Torben, "I asked Aulis for one of the good bottles." A hint of mischief pulled at the corner of her mouth as she spoke. The Keepers, it seemed were allowed to make such bold requests. I imagined there weren't many in the palace who would ask for a bottle from the royal cellars without permission.

I had never really had female friends, but Alaía was proving to be someone that I could see as one.

Once we were all settled, Torben and I sat together on the worn couch with Alaía sitting across from us, a large ancient text draped across her lap. Theo stood in the corner as if he couldn't figure out how to be near Alaía. I wondered what type of message she had delivered that made their encounters so awkward. The Keeper glanced at Theo and then at me, her manicured eyebrow lifting slightly. Theo cleared his throat and looked away.

"I hope you recognize that the Fates brought you all together," Alaía said as an introduction. "The daughter of Liva and Steinar Eriksen, and kin to Queen Maiken, is found alive after a hundred years by the Prince of Akureyrian just as a threat from the Underworld is released—how did you all meet anyways?"

"It's a long story, and I promise to tell you everything once we know why undercreatures are suddenly breathing down our necks," I said.

"Fascinating. I would love to hear it. It will be an important record for the kingdom... for obvious reasons." My stomach flipped. It was unsettling to think that my presence was an important part of the Akureyrian record.

"The attacks by the undercreatures are growing in frequency, Alaía. We are trying to figure out why, and how they were released in the first place." Torben gripped my hand as he spoke, his strength settling me.

"My father... my father always told me that the undercreatures should not be forgotten. I think he knew that this could happen. And after finding all my mother's books, it seems like she may have been concerned as well." The group was quiet as I spoke. I never had the chance to learn more from them, and my voice was laced with resounding pain.

Alaía was tracing her fingers along the golden lettering on the book she held in her lap. "I was summoned to the Eriksen estate several years before you were born, Kaari. Your mother had discovered manuscripts at your family estate and wanted to discuss her findings with a Keeper to see if the texts had ever been recorded. They were discovered in a vault beneath your home that held a trove of relics from Queen Maiken's time. It was an incredible discovery and Lady Eriksen suspected there may be more vaults hidden within the grounds.

"Once I arrived, it was clear that the texts she discovered had never been recorded by the Keepers. The information was deemed to be sensitive enough that I only shared it with one Keeper."

"*Skrímsli Drottningarinnar,*" I added, "The Queen's Monsters."

"Yes."

"What can you tell us about this book?"

Alaía turned her back and reached for the bottle of vintage wine. After pouring a large glass and sipping deeply, she closed her eyes as she summoned her knowledge.

By the time Alaía was done telling us about *Skrímsli Drottningarinnar*, the bottle of wine was empty, and all our glasses had been drained.

"This information doesn't leave this room. We will tell Leif and Emil, but no one outside the Treyst can know of this. I will find a way to tell my father," Torben said, his voice raw. Everyone nodded in response. We all understood the implications. "Even though we were not able to hold the ceremony, my father has announced that Kaari is the rightful Lady of

Vogar. The lineage that connects her to Queen Maiken will be obvious to those who know the history of Akureyrian. But no one can know that the only way the undercreatures could escape the Holvik Woods is if Queen Maiken's blood was used to break the wards."

The queen's blood.

The same blood that flowed through my veins.

47

The sky over Akureyrian was like a vast canvas of deep indigo, stars shimmering with a golden glow that lit the worn path. Each star seemed to pulse with its own heartbeat, creating a sense of infinite possibility in the serene, velvety expanse above. I had to force myself to slow my breathing as I ran down the forest trail, my muscles already screaming from the speed I had maintained for the past several miles.

After we left the Keeper's quarters, I told the others I needed to go for a run to clear my mind. I kissed Torben's cheek before racing back to my room to change.

The air was sweetly laced with salt from the sea that surrounded the city. A cool mist had settled across the rolling waves and coated my skin with a fresh layer of dew.

I removed my shoes after the first mile and my feet were growing raw as I raced across the damp earth. I willed my magic to coat the bottoms of my feet, padding them from the sticks and rocks I passed over.

I was utterly exhausted, but it felt good to let my magic out—even if it was just a little. It felt like freedom and power, and it filled me with resolve.

The path hugged a flowing stream, and I slowed my pace as I watched the reeds sway with the current. Small white flowers glistened against the clear water like whitecaps in a raging sea. I had always been delighted to find the flowering brook weed that flourished near the ponds and streams—but those had been simpler times. As beads of sweat rolled down my cheek, I wondered what would have happened if I had stayed in Árnes when the attacks started—would I have figured out that my family's bloodlock was the only reason the undercreatures had remained within the borders of the Holvik Woods?

The queen's blood.

My blood.

The queen had used her magic to lock the creatures of the Underworld within the borders of the Holvik Woods and had sealed the portal with her blood offering. Alaía had said that this type of magic was eternal... unless the same magic was used to break the bloodlock. And since the queen was dead, the only way her magic could be used was through one of her descendants.

I was the last of the queen's descendants. The only Fae alive who not only shared the queen's bloodline, but her raw magic as well.

I couldn't stop the thought from crossing my mind—*had I somehow done this?*

The snap of a branch had me whirling around and reaching for my sword until his familiar scent embraced her.

"Would you have stabbed me with that?" Torben's voice was low and slightly winded.

I tossed the sword into my other hand before tucking it back into the sheath on my back. "I just needed to *move*. It feels like my whole world has been turned around. I don't even know who I am anymore."

Torben walked to me until he was close enough that I could feel his breath on my neck and gently cupped the side of my cheek.

"I know who you are."

I closed my eyes and felt myself melt into his touch. The feel of his hand on my skin had become the most familiar thing in my life.

"Kaari, you have only had yourself to rely on for the past hundred years, but it doesn't have to be that way anymore. What we learned today does not change who you are. You, Kaari Eriksen, are stronger and more resilient than anyone I have ever known. I know you feel obligated to figure this out on your own...but you don't have to."

"You never asked if it was me. If I opened the wards." It seemed like it should have been the first question after we discovered it would take Maiken's blood to open the wards.

His head tilted as he leaned down to gently kiss my cheek. "I didn't have to, Kaari. You spent decades protecting the people of Árnes from the undercreatures. I know your heart, and I know you would never do it."

"But what does it mean, Torben?" I reached my arms around his neck and pressed my forehead to his, closing my eyes against the weight of the world. "Do I have kin out there I don't know about who is opening the gates that Queen Maiken erected?" I paused, my voice catching in my throat, "The only other option is that it is me. That *I* am somehow doing this."

"We'll figure it out. The undercreatures have been banished before, they can be banished again. Theo doesn't usually talk about Maiken, for many reasons, but there are some things he remembers that might be helpful."

"I still can't believe he knew her."

"Theo has been a brother to me for most of my life. He doesn't like to talk about his time as the queen's commander and closest advisor because he feels like it is treasonous to me and my father. He is stubborn and hell-bent on his honor. But I know that Maiken was more than just his Queen—"

"They were *lovers*?" I interjected with surprise.

"No, no, not like that. They grew up together. They were as close as friends could be. And he certainly loved her, but not as a lover. We will ask him, *elskan min*."

I squeezed his hand, grateful for his presence. "I need to go spend a little time in the infirmary. We are dangerously low on supplies and Laila and I want to be sure we are better prepared—for next time." It was getting late, but I would still have a few hours of sunlight.

"I must meet the Treyst. I will find you after."

As Torben left, my mind raced with thoughts of the preparations Laila and I would need to make. The wind had picked up and my hair swirled around my face in a violent dance as I watched the water in the stream. The flow rushed by, steadily carrying the water that would eventually feed the stream that ran behind the infirmary. The same water that would be boiled and used to soak the bandages that Laila and I would ultimately use the next time there was an attack. *It's fitting*, I supposed, *even the most serene moments can have a morbid end.*

48

By the time I woke in Torben's bed the next morning, the sun had already crossed the horizon. The silk sheets felt like a spring breeze against my skin as I rolled over. I reached my arm out and frowned, realizing I was alone.

I sat up and looked around the room. I vaguely remembered Torben leading me back to his room and helping me undress before gently pulling the sheets around me. He had laid next to me while I fell asleep, his gaze never leaving me as he gently stroked my cheek. I worked in the infirmary with Laila past midnight and although we had replenished many of the depleted supplies, I still felt a heavy sense of unease.

My eyes paused on a folded note on the table next to the bed. Torben had attempted to write to me in the Old Language. I smirked as I deciphered what he had written.

Pack your things, elskan min. We're heading north. And don't forget to eat breakfast, we're portal jumping.

North. We were finally heading north. I only hoped we would find answers along the way that would help protect our people.

I shuddered at the thought of using the portals again but decided it was better than taking a boat or riding a horse for days. I had just finished splashing my face with cold water when the door opened and Milla walked in, a broad smile spread across her face.

"Good morning, Milla. I didn't think I would see you this morning."

"Oh Kaari, I am so happy for you. Look at you, rolling out of the prince's bed! I knew he was in love with you. The gods have surely blessed Akureyrian if they helped the prince find you *and* returned the rightful Lady of Vogar. I could just burst with joy."

My heart tensed as I saw the undiluted joy on the maid's face. Was this how the rest of the kingdom would feel as the news spread across the kingdom? I had barely allowed myself to think of Vogar since my identity had been revealed to Torben and his Treyst. I hadn't given myself a chance to think of how things might change.

The Lady of Vogar—my mother's title belonged to me.

After my parents had been murdered, and I was assumed to be dead, the highest seat of honor in Vogar had gone to my father's top advisor, Lord Haraldsen. I had fond memories of the lord who had been like an uncle to me during my childhood years. I wondered if word of my survival had spread as far as Vogar and if Lord Haraldsen felt joy or despair when he learned that the rightful heir had returned.

"It certainly has felt like a whirlwind," I said as a smile tugged on my cheek. "I'm sorry I didn't tell you about my past, Milla."

"I have been around a long time, Kaari, I knew you were special from the first moment I met you—and it has nothing to do with your nobility."

I reached out to grasp Milla's hands, looking at her with deep appreciation. Just as I was about to formulate some semblance of thanks, a loud knock on the door drew our attention.

Milla opened the door to find Theo casually leaning against the doorframe. I pulled the blankets up around myself as his eyes glazed over at me in Torben's bed. His magic seemed to pulse in heavy waves, filling the room with his presence. He wore his fighting leathers, and a large sword was strapped across his back. The sleeves of his shirt were cropped, revealing a large tattoo that snaked across his broad shoulders.

"Kaari, I'm sorry to interrupt, but I need you to meet me in the tunnel."

My heart jumped like a burning flame. "What happened? Is everyone alright? Where is To—"

"Torben is fine. Nothing has happened… that we know of." Theo glanced at Milla who had moved into the washroom. Still, he lowered his voice so she couldn't hear. "I need to try to teach you how to make the jump."

"Through the portal?" I gasped. "I have no idea how to tap into that magic on my own."

"I will be with you, Kaari. Your magic is strong, it's time to test the bounds of your power." Theo's voice was gruff. "Think of it as a practice run, then you will be ready to do it on your own. Oh, I recommend wearing pants... and bringing your little sword—just in case."

I had now been in the tunnel system several times and was convinced that experience did not help to make it more enjoyable. The air was acrid and bitterly cold as I walked with Theo to the hidden alcove that housed the entrance. I had changed into brown pants and a lavender tunic, tied my hair into a tight braid, and strapped my sword to my back. The weight of the weapon grounded me despite the tremor I felt in my knees.

Theo started his lesson as we walked through the tunnels. Portal jumping, he had explained, was simply a mastery of knowing where you want to go and having the conviction to get there. My magic, he assured me, should do the rest.

I appreciated the simplicity of the instruction but couldn't fathom how I would walk through the portal and come out where I wanted to go. The portal had felt so vast, so disorientating, that I couldn't imagine knowing when and how to get out.

Relief flooded my chest as we approached the portal entrance and found Torben waiting for us with a stash of supplies. The prince's brown eyes were watching me sharply, seeming to assess for signs of discomfort or fear—I was sure he found both in my gaze.

Torben nodded to Theo in greeting and then approached me, placing his hand on my cheek as he gently kissed my forehead. "We can't delay any longer and it seems like a good time to teach you how to use the portals. They may become a necessary means of travel if the undercreatures continue to spread across the kingdom." Each day, new messages had come in about attacks in the rural areas surrounding Nuuk. Most recently, a family from a rural farm had been killed—leaving behind a devastated village and more questions than answers.

I nodded slowly. I knew from my father's stories that the portals had been used for centuries as a means to quickly travel across the kingdom, and as a way to escape when danger approached.

"I don't even know where to start with this kind of magic," I whined, rolling my eyes.

"But you know how to access your magic. Whether it is for healing wounds, increasing your speed, or growing a flower from thin air, the wielding of the magic doesn't change. You just need to remember to control the power so that it doesn't control *you*," Theo said as a matter of fact. "The portal is simply a magical void where reality doesn't exist. This allows the magic wielder to bend the direction of space to their will."

Theo paused as if gathering his thoughts. "When I enter a portal, I summon my magic and allow it to fill me completely, and then I simply think about where I want to go."

"You make it sound easy," I grumbled.

"You have been to Nuuk, Kaari. Once you feel the portal surround you, command yourself to *be* in Nuuk. I will go with you the first time—hold my hand and you won't go astray."

My stomach felt like a bottomless pit. It seemed ironic that the thought of the portal still scared me more than the creatures I might find on the other side.

"I am going to go through with the supplies. I will come back for you, and we will make the jump together," Theo said. He lifted his gaze to Torben as if giving his friend permission to take the time to comfort me—and say goodbye.

Before I could say anything, Theo grabbed the large pack and stepped through the void, leaving me and Torben standing in the dank tunnel alone.

"This is absurd," I said, rubbing my hands over my face.

"You will be alright, *elskan min,* the magic that flows through your veins is ancient and raw, you just need to command it to take you where you want to go. It is no different than the way you have worked on summoning your magic during our runs." As he said this, he brushed his body closer to mine, resting his hands on my hips as the warmth of his breath tickled my cheek and golden specks danced in his eyes.

I tipped my head back as Torben began kissing down the side of my neck, arching my back to press into his strong embrace. "Gods, I have missed the taste of you," he growled into my ear. "I will be here waiting for you. Stay with Theo, *elskan min*, he will always keep you safe."

My hands had been sweating since Theo went through the portal and my heart was racing as bile threatened the back of my throat. I wasn't sure why portal jumping made me so uneasy, but I could feel my power trembling inside.

The portal swirled and Theo stepped over the threshold, looking completely unfazed by the travel.

"Ready?" he asked.

"No," I responded.

"Great. So, remember, just concentrate. Think about where you want to go and let your magic guide you there. I'm going to pull back on my magic so you can use yours to guide us. I will hold your hand, Lady of Vogar—just don't let go."

I stepped away from Torben and stared at the portal. Theo's warm hand was suddenly on my back, steadying me with a pulse of ancient magic. His other hand was outstretched, patiently waiting for me to take hold. When I finally reached out, his callused hand was warm and reassuring. The last thing I heard as I stepped through the void was Torben saying "I love you."

I didn't have time to respond before the endless void consumed me, sucking the air from my lungs. I was vaguely aware of Theo's hand holding mine, although the only thing I could see was a vast expanse of nothingness. For a moment I wondered if I had gone blind from the fear.

Just think about where you want to go, I told myself.

My power seemed to roar inside me, burning like a flame that had been doused in oil. It could have been seconds, minutes, or hours that passed. I felt myself screaming, although there wasn't any sound. And suddenly, my knees were crashing down on solid ground. The void around me had receded and a cool mist poured into the air. The smells were vaguely familiar—moss and trees and decay. I rubbed my hands on my face, willing my eyes to open to see my surroundings. As I did, my hands burned, and shock filled my belly.

I no longer held Theo's hand.

49

Panic flooded through me as I desperately tried to recognize my surroundings. The ground was covered with moss and ancient trees towered overhead like giants. The portal behind me had been built into a large stone wall that was covered in vines and shaded by the surrounding foliage.

I was *not* in Nuuk.

I retched as bile overwhelmed my throat. I was alone—Theo was nowhere to be found. I didn't remember letting go of his hand. I could only imagine his reaction when he reached Nuuk and realized I had been lost in the void. I should have known my power wasn't ready for this type of test. My eyes welled with tears of shame and fear. I needed to figure out where I was and how to get back.

I knew the obvious answer was to go back through the portal and hope to land in Nuuk or back in Dalvin, but the chance of being lost in the void, or going somewhere else entirely, seemed like a real possibility and I couldn't face another failure.

I wiped the corner of my mouth, cursing Theo for telling me to eat something before making the jump. I set my shoulders, steadying myself against uncooperative shaky legs.

Theo and Torben had told me that most of the portals in Akureyrian had been constructed inside tunnels. It seemed curious that this one had been built directly into the features of the land. I ran my hand over the stone that marked the edge of the portal entrance. I could feel power thrumming inside it and my magic sparked in response.

"So much for my power feeling at home in the portal," I quipped, begrudgingly.

The air was clean and smelled of the flora that surrounded me. There was a comforting familiarity to my surroundings. *Just think about where you want to go*, Theo had said. A shudder ran down my spine as I considered his words. I hadn't really *wanted* to go to Nuuk—even though that was where I was supposed to go.

Oh gods, I thought, if I was honest with myself, I knew where I had wanted to go. I wanted answers. I wanted to see what was happening in the north and learn how the undercreatures were evading their boundaries.

The only place to get those answers was the Holvik Woods.

I was suddenly hyper-aware of the sword that was strapped to my back—thank the gods Theo had suggested I bring it. I needed to get my bearings and figure out exactly where I was, especially since none of this looked familiar. I didn't even know there was a portal in Árnes, let alone within the Holvik Woods.

The mist was heavy and thick with the scent of the peat covering the ground. It was eerily quiet. The branches above seemed frozen in place—like the breeze I had always known to fill the Woods didn't blow here—as if time had paused around me. It was unsettling to say the least.

It was cold here—as it always was in the Woods—and while I was grateful that I was wearing pants instead of one of my summer dresses, I wished I had a cloak to keep the chill from my neck.

I know these woods, I told myself. Adjusting my sword, I started to venture away from the portal—heeding the advice of the voice inside that told me to move. The further I got from the portal, the more the air seemed to clear and before long, the breeze had returned.

The forest was densely packed with tall trees and the canopy above was so thick it was hard to tell where the sun was. I needed to find water. There were only so many streams within the Woods, if I could find a stream, I could find my way out.

I chuckled to myself at the irony of this situation. After everything that had happened, I was back where I started. Either the gods were playing tricks on me, or I was meant to come here for answers.

A dull ache settled into my chest as I thought of Torben. Did he know that I hadn't made it to Nuuk? And what did Theo think when he arrived in Nuuk and

I wasn't there? *"Bölva."* I should have asked Leif to teach me to transmit—it would certainly simplify things if I could just tell them where I was.

The ground clover stretched across the floor of the Woods like a jade carpet, the expanse of green occasionally interrupted by scattered leaves in various stages of decay. An apple tree in the distance caught my attention and I began to salivate at the thought of the sweet fruit that tended to grow more abundantly in the Holvik Woods. For millennia, that abundance had tempted both mortals and Fae to cross the border and risk an encounter with the undercreatures.

The apples on the tree were the color of ripe rhubarb and the juice inside helped to soothe my dry throat that still tasted of bile. I picked a few more and tucked them into my pockets for later.

Even after an hour of walking, my surroundings were still unfamiliar, which surprised me. I had spent decades venturing into these woods and felt like the paths and trees were as familiar as the lines on my hand. A sudden movement in the bramble behind me made me pause and slowly reach for my sword. I braced my feet and allowed my magic to swell in my hands—I no longer feared using my magic in the Woods.

A familiar scent of lavender and fur drifted on the faint breeze, and relief rushed through my body.

"Lyyli?" I gasped.

Another rustle of movement and then the small enfield stepped out of the bramble.

I ran towards the creature and dropped to my knees. Lyyli was whining with excitement as we embraced, her bushy tail wagging as fast as my heart beat.

"How did you find me?" I said through a sob of joy.

The enfield, of course, didn't answer. But she nuzzled her auburn head against my chest.

"I screwed up, Lyyli. I don't know how I got here, and the undercreatures have escaped the Woods and I don't know why." I was in tears as fear and despair rushed to the surface. "I'm so sorry I left you. I hope you can forgive me."

The foxlike creature nuzzled her head against my knee. I choked out a laugh. "You won't believe this, I have bonded. I think you will like him." I chuckled again under my breath. "I should probably mention that he is the Prince of Akureyrian." The enfield tilted her head as if she too was surprised.

Sitting under a tall spruce tree, I told my old friend about my travels and about the attacks by the beasts that had escaped the Woods. Lyyli sat curled up in my lap, listening intently to the story. After a while, we sat in silence as I gently stroked the soft feathers of her wings.

For two days, I walked through the woods with Lyyli by my side. We made camp in the evenings, nuzzling close to keep warm and relying on each other to listen for trouble. A few times, I pulled on my magic to let the warmth thaw out my toes. I had never used my magic to create fire, but thought it might be possible. I decided against it, not wanting to burn down the ancient forest with a wild spark—I could practically hear Theo scolding me for such recklessness. We ate a sampling of edible plants and found water in the streams.

It was *almost* peaceful.

We had stopped to snack on dandelions when Lyyli suddenly lifted her head to look at me, as if instructing me to follow. "What is it, girl?" I asked as I picked a piece of the bitter leaves from my teeth. Lyyli twitched her nose and scratched the ground, beckoning me to follow.

We traveled through the dense forest until we came across a well-worn path. My senses were on high alert as I tried to recognize the area, but Lyyli only led me deeper into the Woods. Here, the ancient branches twisted around us, the light from the sun struggling to penetrate through the dense leaves overhead.

Through a clearing ahead, I could see the outline of a worn stone archway. Without warning, Lyyli raced ahead, leaving me standing outside the entrance. Beyond the arch, scents of fire and cooked meat wafted on the mist-dense air, and I could see small buildings in the distance. I never knew there were settlements within the Woods—but someone certainly lived here.

Lyyli came bounding back down the path leading a small figure who hobbled behind. I had to stifle a gasp as the faerie approached. The Faerie of the Woods were notoriously elusive, and many believed that they had moved out of the Holvik Woods when Queen

Maiken had trapped the undercreatures within the borders. My father had theorized that the faerie had moved south to the Fulufjället Mountains in Holmarik. But as I watched the small figure approach, I had no doubt this was one of the lost faeries.

"Welcome Kaari Eriksen." The faerie's voice was high-pitched and laced with an accent I had never heard. His face was handsome with a long beard that billowed like a cloud, highlighting his eyes that were the color of sea foam. His small frame seemed to drown underneath his flowing green robes.

"Um, hello. How… how do you know my name?"

"Oh aye, of course, I am Tjikko. Come, come let us get you something to eat and a warm cloak to wear," the faerie said as he scanned me from head to toe. "Although I'm afraid, my lady, our cloaks may be a bit short on Fae."

Despite the strangeness of the encounter, I felt a wave of relief and comfort as I followed him through the arch.

"Come Skadi, let us find something warm for the Lady of Vogar." As he walked away, he patted his leg and Lyyli obediently followed behind, her bushy tail wagging and her wings folded and relaxed.

My mind raced with confusion and wonder. *Who in all hells is Skadi?*

50

Tjikko leaned heavily on a twisted rosewood staff. His voice was smooth and heavily accented, making his words sound like an ancient lullaby. "Skadi tells me you call her Lyyli."

"Her name is Skadi?" My mouth was agape. I felt a mixture of awe and guilt. I had been calling her Lyyli for as long as I had known her.

"Yes, *heilari*. She also told me that you healed her after she sustained a grave injury." He paused. "Tell me, why did you not use your magic on our Skadi? What were you afraid would happen."

It caught me off guard to hear the faerie speak the Old Language, but of course he would. *Healer*, he had called me, although I didn't know how he knew. The legends said the faeries could speak to the animals of the forest and that they treated them as equals. As a child, I had dreamed of having this power.

"I did not want to hurt her," I admitted. "My power is... unpredictable. And when I met Lyyl—Skadi, I did not know how to control it."

"Do you know now, what you are capable of? How many years have you spent locking your power away? Standing with you now I can feel the thunder that rolls through your veins."

"I *do* use my magic," I countered, instantly feeling childish.

"Oh, child. *Kraftur þúsund sóla*. Does it sometimes feel as though you might split in two?"

"What do you mean by that? 'The power of a thousand suns'." I shuffled my feet nervously as I felt my power swell in my palms.

"You, *heilari*, possess a powerful magic that has not been seen since Queen Maiken lived. Her power flows through your veins and has been building within you since the day you were born. But you also possess your father's power.

"As he took his last breath, his sacrifice allowed him to transfer his power to you. You may have a healer's heart, Kaari Eriksen, but your magic will make you a warrior of legend—once you learn how to embrace it." The faerie shrugged, sending ripples down the length of his robe.

The realization struck me like a blade, sharp and relentless, slicing through my thoughts. My father's magic... all this time, I'd carried a piece of him within me without even knowing. A legacy buried in my blood, bound to me by his final breath. I felt the weight of it settle, pressing against my soul, heavy and unyielding. It wasn't just power—it was responsibility, purpose, a silent vow I hadn't known I'd made. My chest tightened, a mixture of fear and fierce pride swirling within me. I was the keeper of his strength, the bearer of his will. Every time I had swung my blade, he had been with me—he had never stopped trying to protect me.

I continued to think about my father as Tjikko led us down a cobbled path towards several small stone homes. My curiosity eventually took over and I was able to tuck the memories of my father deep into my heart. Smoke billowed from the chimneys, carrying the smell of stews and simmering meats. Dried herbs hung in the windows and bushels of wheat lay stacked on large pallets.

I could see other faeries as they went about their daily business. Smaller than Fae, the faeries moved with ethereal elegance, seeming to blend in with the nature that surrounded the village. A faerie sat on a tree stump grinding flour while several children played a game that seemed to involve zapping each other with small bursts of magic. They giggled merrily with each contact, their smiles revealing glimpses of their pointed canine teeth.

They watched me with cautious interest but seemed to ease when they realized I was with Tjikko. How many years had I spent in proximity to these Folk and never known they were here?

Tjikko stopped to speak with a faerie with brilliant red hair. She nodded feverishly and then went into one of the homes. "We have been simmering a wonderful stew since yesterday and there is bread in the oven. Helena will ask Katla to get you some. You will feel better in no time."

"Thank you, Tjikko." Although my stomach twisted with hunger, I couldn't stop thinking about what he'd said—that my father had given me his magic when he died. "What about my mother, Tjikko? Did… did she transfer any magic to me when she died?"

The faerie scratched his chin as a sadness stretched across his face like a plague. He wouldn't meet my gaze.

"A wild power for sure. No, Kaari Eriksen, you do not have your mother's magic. And as I stand here before you and feel the thrum of power that lives in you, I think that is for the best," Tjikko said. "Come, let's get some food in your belly."

51

I woke with the overwhelming feeling that someone was speaking to me. I must have dozed off while I sat under one of the willow trees while I waited for Katla to return. The voice was muffled as if I was still hearing the voices from my dreams.

Realization forced me to sit up and concentrate on the sound that seemed to scrape against my mind.

"Leif?" I questioned, feeling rather foolish for trying to speak mind to mind.

"Where in the seven layers of hells are you?"

Relief flooded my heart at the sound of the gruff tone, unmistakable even across magical wavelengths. I choked out a sob. It was Theo.

"How? I'm in the Holvik Woods. I didn't know you could transmit!"

The silence was deafening as I waited for him to respond. I imagined he was telling the Treyst that he had reached me.

"There are many things I can do with my power and none of them are important right now. Goddess, Kaari,

we have been searching for days. We are coming for you."

"I don't even know where I am. I've never been to this part of the Woods. I met a faerie named Tjikko who brought me to his village."

"Tjikko? We'll check with Alaía. Stay there if you're safe. I will find you."

The connection, however brief, had felt like returning home after a long journey.

They found me.

A small faerie approached holding a steaming bowl of stew and a large piece of warm bread. My mouth watered as the smell of onions and garlic wafted towards me. The faerie wore a flowing dress with a neckline that dipped between her small breasts, the diaphanous fabric leaving very little to the imagination. Tjikko had worn a heavy cloak, but it seemed this faerie was not fazed by the chilly air.

"Lady Eriksen, we are honored to have you in our village."

"Eh, thank you. You must be Katla?"

"Yes, lady. We couldn't quite believe it when Skadi told us she had found you near the portal," Katla said. "There aren't many who would dare enter through that portal. Although I guess the undercreatures who roam here are not new to you." The small faerie shrugged and her silver hair bobbed like waves of moonlight.

Why did it seem like everyone here knew who I was? Had Lyyl—Skadi really told them about me?

I sat at a small table. My legs tucked close to my chest since the seat had been built for the smaller faeries. The stew was savory with a hint of brine, the strong flavors reminding me of the stews I made when I lived in Árnes. Watching the twenty or so faeries scurry around the small village, I was perplexed by the relative peace I felt here. There seemed to be no impending fear of being overrun by the creatures from the Underworld.

After finishing my stew and using my bread to soak up every drop of broth, I went to find Tjikko. The faerie was sitting by a roaring fire, still wrapped in his billowing robes despite the heat, his dark brown skin glowing with the kiss of light from the flames.

"Something troubles you, Lady of Vogar," the faerie said, lifting his chin to meet my gaze.

"Where are the undercreatures? I haven't seen any signs that the Folk here fear being attacked by the beasts."

"Ah," he sighed, "and you are wondering how this is possible, especially since the beasts have breached their ancient wards and are roaming Akureyrian."

I stared at the faerie, hoping he would fill the silence with an answer.

"We are protected here. Queen Maiken would not have banished the undercreatures to the Holvik Woods and left us unprotected."

"But I always thought the Faeries of the Wood left Akureyrian and went south."

"An interesting idea, but no. The Queen made sure we could stay in our home. Tell me, Kaari Eriksen, what have you seen beyond the Woods?"

I told him everything. I told him of the garmr in southern Árnes, and the drekavac that were attacking villages in the Grimsey Coast. My voice felt raw and breathless by the time I had finished the account, and I could feel my magic rumbling inside me as fear mixed with anger. Tjikko watched me intently, barely blinking.

"Then it is as we feared."

I didn't have time to ask Tjikko to elaborate before a horn blew from somewhere in the village—someone was sounding an alarm.

I pulled my sword from the sheath on my back while the faeries raced to grab their weapons, one of them using their magic to snuff the fire. Tjikko stood slowly, bracing himself against a tree. I instinctively stepped in front of the elder faerie as I lifted my sword.

Just as I was about to rush to the entrance to the village, I felt a familiar pulse of power.

I thrust my sword back into the sheath and ran towards the entrance, feet pounding against the moss-covered ground. I saw him the moment I passed under the stone arch that marked the entrance to the faerie village. His eyes met mine and my chest heaved with relief as a sob escaped my throat.

I blinked and Torben stepped in front of Theo. He clapped Theo on the shoulder and ran to me, relief and desperation filling his eyes. The world was a blur as his arms wrapped around me. I tucked my face into the warmth of his broad chest. Too soon Torben pulled back, but only to hold my face in his hands, his golden eyes scanning me for any signs of injury.

"Are you well?" he breathed.

"I am now."

Slowly, he dipped his head until his lips were pressed against mine, his touch soft and tender. He kissed my mouth, my cheeks, my forehead.

"How did you find me?"

"Alaía. She knows the Keeper here."

I glanced behind Torben and saw Theo slowly walking through the clearing, Alaía now at his side. I looked at Torben and brushed my hand across his cheek before running to greet the others. Alaía's smile was radiant as I hugged her.

"I hope there was never a worry in your heart, Kaari Eriksen. These two would have moved the Innnes Mountains to find you."

I squeezed the Keeper's hands and then turned my gaze to Theo. The warrior's face was unreadable. His jaw was clenched, and his blue eyes were as dark as the deep sea. I stepped towards him as he bowed his head.

"Kaari... please forgive me."

I had never heard the captain sound so defeated. "Theo, it wasn't your fault. I... I think I *wanted* to come here. I think I was hoping to find answers."

"Still, I should have known."

"Well," Alaía said, interrupting Theo from his lingering guilt, "I will go speak to Tjikko."

"How do you know Tjikko?"

"He is the Keeper here and the reason Theo was able to transmit with you once you were in the village. It's lucky you found him, Lady Eriksen."

I didn't understand why we could transmit within the village but not in the surrounding Woods and I didn't know that faeries could be Keepers, but that at least made sense. The Keepers kept the record for all of those living in Akureyrian, and the surrounding kingdoms. Although they tended to be less powerful, many faeries possessed the basic magics that were common amongst the Fae.

As Alaía walked off to find the Keeper, I turned again to look at Torben and Theo. They both looked worn and haggard as if the weight of their worry had stolen any glimmer of peace they once held.

"I'm fine," I said, sounding impatient. "Now tell me what's happened? Where are Emil and Leif?"

Torben and Theo exchanged a somber glance. Torben's brown eyes suddenly seemed much darker, the golden specks muted with anger.

"Dalvin," they said in unison.

"Why Dalvin? Have things settled in the north?"

"No," Theo said. "The attacks have spread. We started getting reports of garmr roaming west of Vogar—"

"Heading towards Dalvin," I interrupted.

"Yes."

My mind was spinning. Everything I knew about the creatures from the Underworld no longer seemed relevant. But then again, there had never been a time in my long life when the beasts had roamed free.

"Is this what it was like before Queen Maiken banished the creatures to the Holvik Woods?" I asked Theo. His face was tense, the scar that stretched across his cheek almost iridescent against his bronze skin. I still had a hard time believing he was old enough to know.

"Yes," he said after a moment. "But this feels more... coordinated." When I didn't say anything, Theo cleared his throat and started to explain. "This feels different, it's hard to describe. Back then, the undercreatures roamed mindlessly and violently. Thousands of people met their end because they encountered a beast which is why Mai—the queen— erected the border around the Woods." Theo's words came out low and firm, but the slight hitch in his breath betrayed the calm front he was trying to maintain. He shifted his weight, rubbing the back of his neck as his eyes darted momentarily to the floor. "The risk back then was ever-present. But there was also a sense of predictability. Everyone knew about the undercreatures and took measures to stay protected. Now... now there are not many of us left who lived during the time before Queen Maiken's reign."

"Gods, sometime you will have to tell me how old you are."

Fireflies danced outside the windows of the small cottage that Torben and I had been given for the night. I watched as the tiny lights moved against the suffocating darkness of night as if the stars had dropped from the sky.

Tjikko had insisted we wait until morning to return to the portal, not wanting us to travel through the Woods after dark.

Torben's body was pressed against mine, the heat that permeated from his skin was more than enough to repel the chill in the air. I turned to face him and found that he was awake, his golden eyes grazing my face. He reached up and cupped my jaw, never taking his eyes away from mine. Shifting, he pressed closer to me until his lips rested on the side of my jaw and he began kissing down my neck. His movements were slow and patient and I felt heat spread through my core.

I traced my fingers across his chest, feeling the strong threads of muscle beneath his shirt. A quiet hum of pleasure escaped my lips as his mouth wandered beneath my chin and his hand grazed the curve of my hip. Neither of us spoke, but our eyes were heavy with the longing we both felt—of the fear we had carried while we were separated.

Finally, his lips found mine. His kiss was slow, and my lips parted as his tongue pressed to sweep against me—teasing and tasting. I reached between us to feel his growing desire, and Torben let out a low growl.

He sat back and pulled my shirt over my head then he devoured me with his golden gaze. His fingertips traced my collar bone, then trailed down my sides, passing my breasts, until they splayed across my hips. His eyes ran up my body and met mine again before he dipped his head, letting his lips wander over my chest. It was as if he was relearning the taste of my skin and the curves of my body, his movements unhurried and savory.

"Torben," I moaned. I needed to feel more of him—all of him.

His lips trailed lower, the warmth of his breath gently bloomed deep in my stomach, spreading through me like a slow, simmering fire, filling every inch with a quiet, thrilling energy. He lifted my hips to pull my pants and undergarments away and seemed to melt as he took me in. I arched my back and ran my fingers through his hair as his lips explored between my legs, his tongue making small circles as if he was savoring a delectable dessert. His tongue teased me in a blissful rhythm and I shuddered as his moan sent euphoric vibrations through me.

"Torben," I whispered—pleaded.

My prince lifted his head, lips glistening, and slowly crawled up my body. "I love you," he whispered as he pressed himself inside, filling every part that ached for him.

I gasped at the feel of him and at the words he spoke. I hadn't realized how my disappearance might affect him, but I could feel it now. He had been wrecked. I reached up to touch his face and he dropped his forehead to mine, so we shared the same breath. Torben pressed his hips harder, his steady rhythm exploring deeper. His eyes were wild, gleaming gold and brown despite the darkness around us.

"I love you," he said again as he moved. "I would have searched every inch of the world to find you." His voice was a whisper, each word accentuated by the brush of his hips.

"I'm here," I said, wrapping my arms and legs around him and pulling him to my chest. I had never seen him this raw, this undone. And as my release began to reverberate through me in wave after wave of pleasure, I managed to whisper, "I love you, too."

At my words, he moved through me again and a shiver went down his body. His jaw clenched as he pulsated deep inside me. I kissed his lips, his neck, his chin while he came down from his release. I had never known this feeling—this bliss.

When he finally pulled himself from me, he gathered me up into his arms, our bodies slick from lovemaking.

"Tell me everything," he said after several silent minutes, running his fingers through my hair.

So, I did; I told him about the sensation of the portal and how I became aware that I had let go of Theo's hand. How I had felt Theo's anguish and smelled his lingering magic that reminded me of sea salt and pine. The void in the portal had felt endless, and I hadn't known if I spent seconds or hours tumbling through nothingness before I was suddenly lying on the mossy ground in the Holvik Woods.

I told him how Lyyli—Skadi—had found me and led me to the village. And how Tjikko had welcomed me without hesitation.

"*Kraftur þúsund sóla*," I whispered.

"The power of a thousand suns?"

"That's what Tjikko said when he described my power. He said it was the power of Queen Maiken's bloodline... and my father." As I explained what Tjikko had told me about my magic a heaviness filled my stomach. The words felt foreign, too vast to wrap my mind around.

Torben kissed my forehead. "I have felt that power in you since I met you."

I turned to face him and then sat up so I could straddle his waist. His fingers lazily tracing circles around the sides of my hips. I couldn't help but admire the way his features caught the dim light, and I felt an overwhelming urge to close the distance between us. Everything else faded away, leaving only the intoxicating pull of desire.

I felt myself lose control as I grabbed his length between my hands and began caressing, savoring every inch of his silky skin. A groan erupted from his chest as I leaned over, adjusting myself so I could take him into my mouth.

He tasted like salt and cedar, but I could also taste the sweetness that still lingered on his skin. I sucked harder and used my hands to match the rhythm of my mouth. I could feel his release building again and I quickly licked him from base to tip before pulling away. He looked rabid with need as I climbed on top of him and slid him into my core. I arched my back as I began grinding my hips against his. The first time was slow and tender as we worked through the pain of losing each other. But now, I felt wild with need.

Torben held my hips and pulled me closer, deeper, with every pumping motion. He sat up suddenly to meet me. Our chests slick and warm as we pressed together. I dropped my head back and he devoured my neck with his mouth, his movements becoming more desperate.

"Gods, I love you," he growled, and I lost it completely.

Release flooded through me again and I grabbed his shoulders to ground myself. He kept pumping and my magic flared as I felt my climax immediately building again. Heat flooded my skin, and I knew I was glowing. Torben lifted my hips so that he pulled out completely and I gasped at the sudden emptiness. Just as quickly, he slammed himself back inside me and we both erupted.

When I opened my eyes, the small cabin was glowing with the soft blue light of my magic.

"I never want to lose you again," I said. I pressed my hand against his chest, feeling the steady rhythm of his heartbeat beneath my fingertips, grounding me. It was more than just warmth I craved—it was the feeling of his presence, the reassurance that he was here, real, and mine. My breath hitched as his heart pulsed against my palm, a silent reminder that this connection was everything, that I couldn't bear the thought of living without it.

"I am always with you." Torben kissed me again and we laid down, our bodies still tangled together. "Sleep, my queen. I fear it may be some time before we have another night like this."

53

Torben was already gone when I woke. The small cottage felt cold without his powerful form filling the space. I pulled the quilt over my shoulders as I looked through the window. I could see Torben talking with Theo outside the cottage. Theo was shaking his head at Torben, who had his arms crossed. Alaía approached them, and I watched Theo tense as she came up beside him. Her small frame commanded their attention as wisps of her white hair swirled around her face. Theo's jaw was somehow more tense than before as he lifted his hands to hold the back of his head, his eyes scanning the canopy above, a look of disbelief stretched across his stern face. Torben nodded somberly and Alaía bowed her head and walked away towards the stream that passed through the village.

I quickly dressed in my tunic and pants and tied my hair into a tight knot. As I put on my worn shoes, the door opened and Torben walked in, his broad shoulders filling the frame. His familiar scent enveloped me like the smell of a homecooked meal as he approached.

"We need to leave."

"What's happened?"

"It's Dalvin. It's under attack."

Bile burned the back of my throat. "How did the garmr get there so quickly I thought they were in Vogar?"

"No. *Birkeria* is attacking Dalvin."

A bitter rage flooded my stomach, my magic tingling in my fingertips.

"How?" I whispered, my voice trembling with fury.

"They arrived from the sea—a mass of ships carrying a thousand soldiers. Leif and Emil have managed to hold the wall, but are outnumbered since so many of our forces were sent north. My father is powerful in his own right, but the years have not been kind to him. I fear he will not be able to hold the palace for long." Torben's eyes were wild with rage. "The undercreatures were a distraction."

"But why? And how do the undercreatures play into this," I said, feeling breathless. "Is this all because you ended your engagement to Princess Merja?"

Torben cupped my cheek and despite the rage that swirled in his eyes, his touch was tender and reassuring. "Together. We will find out together, *elskan min*. Alaía said the undercreatures attacked alongside the Birkerian soldiers, as if they were under their control." Torben paused, picking his cloak up off the floor and pulled it over his shoulders. "I doubt it has anything to do with the engagement. If anything, they agreed to the marriage so they could embed one of their own within our walls. Akureyrian has never truly allied with Birkeria, the hatred runs deep from centuries of bloodshed. My father was naive to think a marriage could heal those wounds."

I started hurrying around our small room, gathering my clothes that had been strewn across the floor the night before. "How did Alaía know about the attack? Did another Keeper send her a message?"

Torben shook his head. "No, Leif spoke to her. Transmitting is difficult when the distance is great. But it is easier for him when he speaks to someone as old as Alaía. She came to us right after the message came through."

I paused after I had pulled my dress over my head. "Are they alright? Leif and Emil? Why didn't Leif just transmit with Theo?"

"I can feel your mind racing, *elskan min*. Aye, they are alright for the moment and Theo was... unavailable."

I lifted a brow in question.

"He traveled through the Holvik Woods last night to see if he could find the portal to the Underworld. He must have been beyond reach if Leif couldn't speak to him."

"The portal to the Underworld? Why would Theo try to go to the Underworld?" I felt utterly panicked.

Torben shrugged his shoulders as if this was a casual decision. "He wanted to see if creatures were actively leaving to come above ground."

Frustration surged through me, a hot tide that made my fists clench at my sides. "Are you kidding me? Goddess above, he is a fool. He knows the dangers out there, especially now!" My voice rose with each word, a mix of anger and fear, as I struggled to comprehend how he could make such a reckless choice. "What was he thinking?" I fumbled with the clasp on my cloak, my fingers warm as my magic responded to the wave of emotions.

Torben stepped in front of me, reaching steadily to secure the clasp. "He wanted answers," he said simply.

I looked deeply into his golden eyes and saw his worry and rage churning like a storm. I could only imagine what Emil and Leif were going through back in Dalvin. The walls around the city were strong, and there were many High Fae who would lend any powers they had to protect Akureyrian. But the Birkerians undoubtedly had those with powers of their own. And if the undercreatures were somehow under the control of the Birkerian forces, the gods only knew what it would take to defeat them. I thought back to Alaía's description of *Skrímsli Drottningarinnar* as I began to pace the small room. It would take Maiken's blood to release the undercreatures in the first place—just as it would take Maiken's blood to seal gates that had been opened.

I only wondered how much I would have to spill.

e made it through the portal and reached the tunnels under the city without incident. I griped Theo's hand so hard my knuckles had turned white and only let go after he assured me we made it to Dalvin. He had not mentioned his attempt to find the gates to the Underworld, and I hadn't asked—partly because I was still angry he had gone, and partly because I was angry he hadn't brought us with him.

Our relief from landing back in Dalvin was short-lived. The chaos overhead rumbled through my marrow like a hammer.

"How will we find Emil and Leif?" I asked breathlessly.

"We will head to the palace. The Birkerian's target will be gaining access to the palace, so my father will be there. And Leif and Emil will be with him."

"I will go first," Theo declared as he patted Torben's shoulder.

Torben simply rolled his eyes. "We do this together, brother."

I could all but feel Theo's frustration and my heart pulled at the strength of their connection.

"The west tower will likely be the last place the Birkerians would target. We should head there. It will also give us the best vantage of the center of the palace and the city walls," Alaía said, stepping forward.

Theo and Torben nodded in agreement, and I felt relieved that they seemed to have some sort of plan.

"Kaari," Alaía said quietly, "can you feel any shifts in the magic that surrounds you? Perhaps you can locate Leif and Emil."

"I'm not sure. I've never tried to feel anything like that."

Alaía stepped closer and tapped her delicate fingers over my heart. "Here, this is where you focus your attention. Feel the thrum of your power and then reach out as you sink inward."

"That doesn't even make sense," Theo grumbled.

Alaía rolled her eyes. "Just because Kaari is more powerful than you, Captain doesn't mean you have to be cynical. She can do it."

I wasn't sure I could, but I closed my eyes and focused on my power as Alaía instructed. A warmth started in my chest and rippled through my veins. Sinking deeper, I felt like I had dived into a simmering well as the power around me swirled, engulfing me in a suit of embers. I had the vague sense that I was in fact warming but pushed the thought away as I tried to reach out to my surroundings. I could feel Torben's power—a whirl of relentless wind—and my heart swelled as I sensed the steady hum. Alaía's power felt much older and a bit wilder. It was the color of dusk and felt cool and refreshingly simple. The vibration that stretched from her was more powerful than Torben's.

The last orb of power that pulsed around me was undoubtedly Theo's. It was ancient and wild and simply frightening. It felt like being pulled into an archive that held the answers to the darkest questions in our world. His orb was the color of the setting sun and radiated with streaks of sunbeams that felt hot against my magic. I felt lost in the presence of his power. Theo was *much* more powerful than I had ever dared to assume.

Further, I told myself, dragging myself away from Theo's power. I had to reach out much further. I couldn't tell how much time had passed since I started Seeking. My magic spread like woven threads of fire across the palace. I could feel magic around me as if there were pockets of power that were as unique as the people by my side. The air around me began to feel heavy and I gasped as the taste of smoke and ash scraped across the back of my throat.

Molten power—burning and rancid.

I had the distant sense that someone was holding my arm, but it felt muffled and strange. Ignoring the sensation, I reached out further until the heat building in my chest made it hard to breathe. *There*, further than I had ever thought to reach, was a sense of power I had not felt since before I had fled my home in Vogar. I let the power mix with my own. It was a bone-chilling cool that matched the heat of my magic. As the powers met in a steaming dance of ice and fire, I felt myself collapse.

"Kaari!" a voice was yelling.

"She's alright," another voice replied, "just give her a minute."

As awareness returned, I knew the second voice had been Theo's—ever the level-headed one in our group. I let out an exhausted groan—overly aware of my smoldering skin. Torben must have caught me because we were both kneeling on the ground, his arms wrapped around me in a firm embrace. Opening my eyes, I saw the others staring at me nervously.

"Where did you go, Kaari?" Theo finally said.

"She's here. Merja is here in the palace."

Torben cursed and Alaía paled.

"What else?" Theo asked tentatively. "Who was the other source you felt when you were Seeking?" I couldn't understand how he knew that I had felt someone else.

"I... it's impossible." I didn't understand—*couldn't* understand—what I felt. A surge of disbelief coursed through my body, momentarily stealing my breath. Heart racing and mind reeling, I struggled to grapple with the whirlwind of emotions—the sting of past grief, a slap of confusion, and an overwhelming sense of hope—each conflicting feeling colliding like waves crashing against the shore.

"I felt it too, Kaari. I could sense when her power mixed with yours."

I shook my head as I stared at Theo's hardened features. "But she's not *here*. I don't understand. It's *impossible*."

"No, I would agree that she's not in Dalvin. But she is most certainly *alive*. I don't know how much distance you crossed to find her."

I choked out the sob I had been holding ever since I felt the familiar power as it twisted around my own. Theo's jaw was clenched, and his blue eyes were like a stormy sea.

"Will one of you tell us who else you found?" Torben asked as a befuddled expression crossed his face.

The air in the tunnel had shifted and the musky scent of the damp ground was now mixed with the metallic smell of ether and smoke. Memories flashed in my mind as I tried to catch my breath—a glimpse of running through the forest near my home, my bare feet sweeping across the mossy path as sweet laughter followed close behind. The warm embrace after I had fallen from the tree I had been climbing. The constant hum of icy power that had filled my home.

"Are you sure, Theo?" I managed to whisper.

Theo met my gaze, his expression firm but tinged with something that could only be sympathy. "As sure as you are, Kaari."

I swallowed hard, my chest tightening with disbelief. Slowly, I lifted my eyes to Torben and Alaía, feeling my jaw tremble under the weight of the truth that now threatened to break me. "My mother is alive."

55

Torben unleashed a forceful blast, sending the door at the end of the tunnel shuddering on its rusted hinges before it swung open with a groan. The stagnant air inside the library stirred, carrying with it the scent of ancient parchment and forgotten secrets. Dust speckled the dim light as we stepped through the threshold. Shelves rose like shadowy monoliths, towering in silence, their contents long abandoned. Torben moved cautiously, his gaze cutting through the darkness as if expecting danger to emerge from the stillness. The tension in his body was palpable, a coiled force ready to strike.

To our relief, the library seemed empty.

Alaía exhaled softly, visibly relieved to find that the other Keepers had already fled. "There is a passage on the other side of the library that leads to the Keeper's tower." She gathered the bottom of her skirt, using one hand to hold the fabric while the other tucked a loose strand of hair behind her ear. Theo had managed to transmit with Leif to tell him we were heading to Alaía's room. Theo's face had paled but he assured us that Leif and Emil were alright.

Theo grabbed a torch from the sconce by the door and nodded to Alaía to lead the way. Sounds in the distance made us pause and Theo narrowed his eyes towards the darkness ahead. I watched as he gathered a small orb of white light in his palm and sent it down the aisle, illuminating the way as it floated. My eyebrows knitted together as I watched him.

"There is something at the end of the last row of shelves, but I can't tell what it is."

"Fancy little trick, Captain," Alaía whispered.

We walked down the aisle until the smell of rotten meat wafted towards us. Theo cursed and adjusted his hold on his sword as he stepped in front of me and Alaía. The sound of scratching on the stone floors made my teeth hurt. "Sounds and smells like a drekavac."

"I'll go ahead." Theo hadn't given an option for anyone to join him, but Torben pulled a second dagger out of its sheath and followed behind.

I was straining to see in the dark space, each shadow that danced across the walls of books seemed to take the shape of some foul beast. Alaía was standing at my side and rested her hand on my arm—looking for reassurance or offering comfort I couldn't tell.

Theo's voice boomed through the space in a foul curse before the sound of crashing swords reverberated down the stone.

"Stay behind me," I commanded Alaía through gritted teeth. I wasn't sure if the Keepers practiced any swordplay or had power outside their memory magic.

My heart was thundering inside my chest as I crept to the edge of the shelf. The sound of swords clashing against claws and bone echoed down the expansive aisles as Torben and Theo confronted the creatures.

A pack of drekavak stood on their spindly hind legs, awkwardly balancing the weight of their oblong heads. Yellow foam dripped from their mouths, frothing as they screeched like hawks from hell.

Torben lunged, alternating between slashing his sword and sending gusts of power to push the beasts back against the wall. Theo came from behind him, stabbing with graceful power. Pools of black blood coated the floor like globs of oil. Two more drekavak charged at them and I could only marvel at the way they fought together. It was a perfect harmony of brutal strength and skill, the culmination of their years—decades—of fighting together.

It was foolish of me to stare. I didn't notice the last creature until it was dropping to all fours and charging towards us. The drekavac's face was covered in blood that dripped across its already yellow teeth. I whirled my sword, connecting with its swollen head in a resounding *clank* of metal against bone. The beast stumbled and then let out a blood-chilling scream, lunging again with its final breath. I braced for the impact, but the beast was suddenly tossed against a wall of books with a blast of wind. When it landed,

Torben slashed through its neck with his sword, sending the bulbous head rolling.

I gasped and locked eyes with him. His face was splattered with blood as black as his fighting leathers.

Theo cursed again as the last two drekavac circled him. I heard a crack as he slashed out with his sword and a summoned a blast of magic, using the power and his strength to slice through the clawed arm that reached for him. Alaía gasped as blood splatted across a collection of manuscripts, covering her eyes to block out the destruction.

Torben and Theo adjusted their positions and then advanced again. Torben sent another blast of power and Theo swung his sword with unnatural speed—connecting with the beast's chest and shattering its ribs. The armless one made a final lunge at us, but I jumped forward and brought my sword down on the back of its neck, severing the spinal column.

When all the beasts had fallen, the rancid smell of blood and lingering magic permeated through the air. "Is everyone alright?" Torben asked as he mindlessly wiped his sword on his pants.

"Never better," Theo mumbled. "I *hate* those things."

I hugged Alaía and helped her step over the bodies that covered the floor, her white robes dragging through the inky pools of blood.

Theo twirled his wrist, gathering a ball of light that he spread over the tip of the torch, igniting a magical flame.

"How did you do that?" I asked, my eyes wide.

"Later." The dismissal was as sharp as daggers.

The walls of the Keeper's tower shook with a thundering force. Dust scattered off the ornately carved stone with each distant explosion and a fine layer of powder coated the hallway. Alaía was relentless as she raced through the tower. The adrenaline that surged after the encounter with the drekavac and the anticipation of what would happen next was becoming unbearable. I could feel my power as it stretched and simmered under my skin. Seeing the undercreatures within the palace walls had felt surreal—like something out of a nightmare.

I swallowed, attempting to catch my breath as we began climbing a set of narrow stairs. I still couldn't believe that I had felt my mother's magic. When I first felt the familiar embrace, I had assumed my mother's spirit was coming to me in this time of need. *Perhaps I am about to die,* I had wondered—but it had felt so real, so close. I trusted that Theo knew the difference.

Images flashed of my father, the queen, and all our family's servants bloodied and discarded throughout the estate. Bile filled my throat, and I lurched forward, heaving out my guilt in wave after wave of bitter regret. I had never actually seen my mother's body. The others stopped and watched me, their stares filled with sympathy. Torben placed his hand on the small of my back, gently guiding me to keep moving.

"We're with you, *elskan min.*"

My eyes were blurry with the tears that threatened to undo me. Torben's touch was the only thing grounding me as the guilt ravaged my soul. Where had my mother been all these years? What had she endured? And how was she connected to what was happening now?

Up ahead, Theo and Alaía reached the door to the Keeper's room. Alaía held her hand against the door as if she was feeling for what was inside. She nodded and then Theo pushed his way through.

"It's about time," Leif said from within the chamber. He rushed forward, clapping Theo and Torben on their shoulders. "Alaía and Kaari, you are both looking as radiant as ever."

"What happened here?" Torben asked and Leif's face became somber.

"The Birkerians. They descended on us like a plague. We held them at the wall for a time, but they have powerful magic wielders among them and there are undercreatures across the city—-the princess is stronger than we could have imagined. She seeks something. We can feel her foul magic snaking through the halls."

"Me. She's looking for me."

"I doubt she's *that* jealous that you got the prince and she didn't," Leif said.

"It's her magic." Theo rolled his eyes. His powerful arms were crossed, and his jaw was clenched. I could all but feel the tangle of thoughts going through his head. "What of the king?"

Emil turned to face Torben, his voice was strained, barely more than a whisper. "Your father... he ordered us to fall back, to save ourselves. He said the kingdom needed us alive, needed us to protect it. We tried to stay, Torben, we tried to fight with him, but he commanded us to leave." Emil's gaze dropped, his hands clenched into fists as if he still felt the weight of the moment.

"He held his ground against the Birkerians alone." Emil swallowed hard, lifting his eyes to meet Torben's. "His last words were for you. He told me... he said, 'Tell my son he is king.'"

The words hung in the air, heavy and irreversible.

Torben's jaw ticked with tension, his hands clenching into fists as he slowly nodded. "He was a good king." I could see the glimmer of hurt and anger in Torben's eyes. I knew his relationship with his father had been tense ever since his mother died, but there had still been love between them. Another wave of guilt flowed through me, sparking my magic into a fiery hum—Torben had just lost a parent and I had rediscovered mine.

"We need to find Merja and make a stand," Emil interjected, "with all of us we may have enough power to end this. But we need to keep Torben safe—if he is lost, Akureyrian cannot stand."

"No." My voice was filled with rage and raw emotion. "I will not see the people I care about put themselves at risk because she wants *me*. If they want my power, I will gladly show them my power. This ends now."

The room grew eerily silent though the explosions in the distance rumbled on like a thunderstorm in

Regn. Torben was shaking his head slowly as he scratched at the stubble that had grown on his jaw.

It was Theo who broke the silence. "Fine. You can draw them out. But we are coming." I opened my mouth to argue, but he continued, "I don't doubt your power, Kaari. None of us do. But your mother being alive changes *everything*. She will use that against you. Merja will threaten to destroy her if you don't give her what she wants."

I could feel my power burning under my skin. The heat was electric as it spread through my belly and siphoned to the tips of my fingers. I had spent the past one hundred years believing my mother was dead and had hidden my existence to protect the power for which my family sacrificed their lives. I clenched my fists, trying to steady the surge of emotions Theo's words brought to the surface. "And what do you expect me to do? Stand by while someone else risks their life?" My voice was low, but I could feel the sharp edge of desperation creeping in.

Theo met my gaze, unyielding. "No, Kaari. I expect you to fight, as you always have. But not alone."

"I can't let her harm anyone else," I pleaded. "She killed my father. She killed Torben's mother and my entire household. She sentenced my mother to a fate that has likely been worse than death. And in her pursuit of power, the goddess only knows how many others she has harmed, and how many more she will destroy if she is allowed to live."

Grim faces stared at me. They all knew I would give my life to end this if it meant protecting Akureyrian and avenging those who had been lost. Torben approached, grasping my arms and leaning his forehead to touch mine. His grip was firm, and it grounded me to the moment, his scent reminding me what I had to live for.

"You are mine, and all of Akureyrian is yours. I will be with you with every step and every breath. That day in the woods was the best day of my life because it brought you into my world." Torben's kiss was gentle and slow as if he was memorizing the softness of my mouth and the taste of my lips. His eyes raged with Akureyrian gold as his power began to build. "When this is over, I'm going to marry you." He kissed my hand, sealing the promise to my skin.

"Well let's get this over with so we can make that happen."

"I love a royal wedding," Leif quipped.

"I doubt you will be invited," Emil said, rolling his eyes. "Here we are in the throes of war, and all Leif can think about is the chance of wedding sex."

Leif grabbed his chest. "You insult me, General. I am excited about Kaari being our queen... *and* at the chance of wedding sex."

"Let's go." Theo was pacing, his hand was white as it gripped his sword. "We head for the courtyard. If Merja isn't already there, Kaari will extend her magic enough that Merja knows where to find her. We know she's waiting to sense her magic."

I looked around and slowly reached out to hold Torben and Theo's hands. Alaía stepped forward, reaching for Emil and Leif until we created a consecutive circle. Static snapped through the air around us as our connection flared with the power that radiated through our bond. It didn't matter that our power ranged from ordinary to extraordinary, in that moment, with that connection, we were one.

The explosions had stopped, leaving an eerie quiet that sounded like the deepest layer of all the hells. I walked cautiously through the courtyard, holding my sword against my side. The palace, which once stood tall with four great towers, was now peppered with holes and two of the towers had completely collapsed. If I strained my ears, I could still make out the echoes of clashing swords and the harrowing screams of battle in the distance.

I closed my eyes and let images of my family flood my mind. Memories of running through the woods in Vogar with my mother, the laughter that filled our throats making it hard to catch a breath. The feel of my father's broad hand on my back as we sat in the library while he told me stories of the past and his dreams for the future. Darkness gathered in my mind as the images altered to those of blood-stained floors and the feeling of my ragged breath as I ran through the woods from my home, my hand dripping with blood.

"Have you finally started to remember, Master of Undercreatures?" The princess' voice was sickly sweet, her tone ruthless and vile.

I whirled around to find Merja standing in the middle of the courtyard as if she had appeared from thin air. She wore black leather pants and a tight red tunic that matched the charm she still wore at her neck. Her green eyes were serpentine and seemed to glow as she assessed her prey.

I was her pray.

But she was my mother's captor, and I would rip her to pieces—healer's vow be damned.

"Where is my mother?" My voice trembled as it echoed off the shattered walls around us, cutting through the unnatural stillness.

"Ah yes." Merja clicked her tongue as she looked absently at her nails as if she were already bored with the conversation. "Quite stubborn that one. A hundred years in my possession and she has only recently started to earn her keep. I should thank you. It was only after she learned you were still alive that she became helpful."

The ground under my feet had started to vibrate as my magic surged. I hadn't let myself think about what my mother had endured in the years since I last saw her, and as I did undiluted rage raced through me.

"The undercreatures. You used her to release the undercreatures." My breath was heavy as realization flooded my heart. "You used her blood—Maiken's blood. But why?"

"Stupid girl. You are much too young to understand what this vile kingdom has put my people through. For so long, I have watched this kingdom grow and prosper. It was Birkerian blood that enriched your weak Fae bloodlines. It was only a matter of time before we came to claim what was ours.

"The gods smiled upon us when your laughable king took the throne—so soft he couldn't even dispose of the biggest threat to his line. But when the king sired a measly prince who only wielded the power of force, I knew it was time—it was all so pathetic. Although I'll be honest, I wouldn't have minded taking his body for a ride. Tell me, Master of Undercreatures, is his cock as pretty as his face?"

I threw my power in a blast of blue embers that collided with the wall of magic that Merja erected.

"Ah yes. But then there's you... and your mother. Descendants of a power worthy of ruling all. She was beautiful, Queen Maiken—a nearly perfect queen. I would be lying if I said I didn't envy her during her reign—until she showed us all how weak she was by sacrificing herself to save a kingdom of ungrateful Fae and mortals. Your mother was not blessed with the queen's raw magic. But she has shown promise. I owe her a great deal of thanks for helping me release those poor undercreatures from their prison."

Her vile power thrummed around me like a poisonous hive. As much as I wanted answers, I could feel her using the time to draw upon her magic. I didn't know what she was capable of, but what I had felt in the tunnels had been wild and dreadful. I remembered what Torben and Theo had taught me about controlling and directing my magic, and it filled me with resolve. My sword was heavy in my hand as I sent my power into the blade until it glowed a brilliant blue.

"Incredible," Merja whispered, her eyes glowing like emeralds.

I flung myself towards her, the sword slicing through the air with the force of my rage. My vision tunneled as magic pulsed through my veins. The familiar warmth was the only thing that seemed real. Merja lifted another wall of power to block the blow, but the strike of my sword caused Merja to stumble. There was a brief pause in her shield of power, and I twisted so I could lift my sword again. A blade appeared suddenly in the Princess' hand—summoned from some dark hidden place. The clank of metal echoed off the crumbling stone walls as our blades collided, sharp and deafening.

Power shifted around us in a cloud that mixed the colors of our magic—my icy blue colliding with her darkest black.

Sparks flew as our blades met, and I tightened my grip on the hilt of my sword. A white light suddenly burned down the blade, etching runes into the steel— old magic I thought was long forgotten. I didn't have time to ponder how they had appeared or what they meant, but I felt a surge in my power. Across from me, something like shock flashed across Merja's face as she watched the runes appear. Her eyes blazed an unnatural green, her magic coiling around her fingers and creeping along the edge of her blade like a serpent ready to strike.

The ground beneath my boots trembled, responding to the heavy weight of our power.

Merja flicked her wrist, and a bolt of black magic surged toward me.

I raised my blade just in time, deflecting the blast with a force that sent a shockwave up my arm. The magic hissed and crackled in the air, sizzling against the enchanted steel. I grit my teeth and lunged, my sword slicing through the air in a deadly arc. Merja's blade met mine with a screech, and the impact reverberated through my bones, driving me back.

Merja twisted, impossibly fast, avoiding my strike as she sent another wave of darkness toward me. It slammed into my chest, the force of it like a hammer blow, knocking the breath from my lungs. I hit the ground hard, the cold stone scraping against my skin as I scrambled to my feet, gasping for air.

Merja was already there, her blade raised high, crackling with magic. I barely had time to raise my sword before hers came crashing down. Our blades locked, and the pressure of her attack nearly buckled my knees. The heat of her magic seared the air between us, and my muscles strained to hold her off.

"You took *everything* from me," I growled through clenched teeth, letting my pain fuel my movements.

Merja's lips curled into a cold, mocking smile. "Not everything. Not yet."

She flicked her fingers again, and this time, tendrils of shadows shot toward me, writhing through the air like living things. They wrapped around my arms and legs, tight as iron chains. I gasped, struggling against them, but the magic burned into my skin, sending searing pain through every nerve.

With a vicious yank, Merja pulled me forward, her face inches from mine. Her breath was hot on my skin, her eyes gleaming with triumph.

With a guttural scream, I drew on every ounce of strength I had left, forcing my will through the blade. The runes along the sword's edge flared bright, blazing with a fierce, blue light. I slashed at the tendrils holding me, severing them with one powerful stroke. Merja's eyes widened in shock as I twisted my body and drove my blade upward, aiming for her heart.

But she vanished in a burst of shadows, her form dissolving just as my sword cut through the space she had occupied.

"*Bölva!*" I cursed.

I spun on my heel, scanning the courtyard, my breath coming in sharp, ragged bursts. Chaos surrounded me as the Treyst fought against the mass of Birkerian warriors that had joined the melee. I could hear the sharp sound of swords and feel the rush of power from the others, and it whispered to me to keep fighting.

The air crackled behind me, and I whipped around, just as Merja reappeared, a blade of pure energy in her hand. She lunged, striking with deadly precision, but my magic had reached its crescendo and I was ready. I brought my sword up to meet hers, our blades clashing in a storm of sparks and light. She unleashed another blast of darkness, stronger this time. I barely managed to raise my sword, the force of it slamming into me like a wave. My legs trembled under the pressure, but I stood firm. I wasn't going to let her break me. Not now.

Not ever.

I pushed back against the magic, forcing it away with everything I had. My sword burned in my hand, its light growing brighter until it cut through Merja's magic like a knife through water.

I charged her, my heart pounding in my ears, my blade flashing with lethal intent. Merja's eyes widened as I closed the distance between us, her defenses faltering for the briefest of moments.

That was all I needed.

With a roar, I slashed through her shield of shadows, my sword connecting with her shoulder. Blood sprayed across the courtyard, staining the stones beneath us as Merja staggered back, clutching her arm. Her eyes blazed with fury, her lips curling into a snarl.

"You'll pay for that," she spat, her voice trembling with rage.

I stepped forward, my sword still raised, my chest heaving.

A blast of wind sucked the remaining air from my lungs. I felt Torben's power before I saw him. He was behind me, his arms outstretched as he sent a wave of force towards us—pushing relentlessly against Merja's darkness. She lunged, sword heavy with ire, and I willed more power into my blade as I spun again.

Another magic started to mix with my own, wrapping around my arm in a supportive embrace. The power was strong—stronger than Torben's—and it felt as wild as mine. The runes on my sword seemed to react to the foreign power, glowing fiercely as if feeding off the energy in the air. The power was an embrace of reassurance and a promise of devotion.

It fueled me and I landed a blow across Merja's arm that prompted a guttural scream from the princess.

"Aren't you curious?" Merja yelled over the rush of power. "Don't you want to know what I have done with your mother? What I will do with *you* when your power burns out?"

The power we emitted pulsated off to the surrounding stone walls, some crumbling and falling behind me. But I kept fighting as Merja blocked my strikes and the magic that we sent towards her. The heat radiating from my blade intensified, sending a pulse through my hand, up my arm, and straight into my chest. It was as though the sword itself was urging me forward, amplifying my strength, matching Merja's magic with a force of its own. The air hummed with tension, the runes flickering in tandem with each surge of deadly shadows, waiting for the moment to strike.

But I didn't get the chance.

"You should have told your friends to stay behind." Merja's lips twisted into a mocking smile as she raised her arm. A surge of fiery magic shot skyward, exploding into an inferno above us. I barely had time to throw up a shield before the flames descended—but the searing heat wasn't aimed at me. My blood surged as I realized her true target. She wasn't trying to defeat me head-on; she was going after the others.

A scream behind me made me turn, my eyes wild with fear. Dust swirled, settling like a curtain being pulled back on a nightmare. There, on the shattered stones of the courtyard, lay Torben—his massive frame crumpled, broken. Theo's hands gripped his chest, desperation etched into every line of his face.

Emil and Leif were desperately trying to wake him, but his once-powerful body was limp and lifeless.

I couldn't breathe.

Theo grabbed his sword and ran towards me, rage and fury burning in his sapphire eyes. But he stopped as dozens of garmr prowled into the courtyard and surrounded us. Their eyes glowed with possessed hatred, their claws scraping on the tile as they stalked us.

I would be dead in an instant if I tried to run to Torben.

"A distraction," Merja purred, as if she had released me of a burden. I turned back to her, a smile on her face as she opened her arms, welcoming the garmr to come closer. "The crown should have been yours, you know? You didn't need the prince to step into that line of power."

I reached inside myself, deeper than I had ever reached. There in the well of my power, memories of Torben surged up, raw and vivid, like a lifeline in the darkness. I could feel the rough texture of his skin under my fingers, the steady beat of his heart, the way he had smiled at me, as if I were his whole world. I could feel the warmth of his hand on my cheek, that gentle, grounding touch he always gave when words weren't enough—when he *knew* I needed someone to believe in me. The Princess of Birkeria had already taken everything from me—my home, my family, and now my future. I couldn't face the thought that she had also taken the one who had reminded my heart I was allowed to *live*.

Torben had been the anchor to my storm, the one who reminded me that I was capable of more than just survival.

The ground began to tremble, and I felt Theo stop behind me as I lifted my arms to the sky. *Kraftur þúsund sóla*. Let it be the power of a thousand suns.

I let the words fill me as power rushed through my blood, my heart shattering with every drop of pain. I used it to fuel me. When I brought my gaze to the princess, my eyes glowed with the force of sunbeams.

The blast of power was an inferno of blue flame that descended over the courtyard. I watched through a haze as Merja screamed, her body contorting into a cloud of ash and smoke. The garmr that had surrounded her yelped as my power ripped their bodies apart.

I was the sun—a flaming orb of power that only knew rage for those who had caused me harm—for those who had taken Torben and my parents away from me.

Someone in the distance was yelling my name, but it seemed too far away to be real. I felt like I was sinking into space as if my body was shrinking into the nothingness that consumed my soul.

Hands gripped my shoulders and then pulled away reacting to the searing heat of my skin. My knees buckled and I collapsed onto the ground—stones and glass scraping into my skin with the impact.

"Kaari." The name was like a prayer on the wind that drifted away, keeping me from the here and now. The hand gripped me again, stronger this time, until awareness pulsed through me.

Theo was crouched in front of me, gripping my face in his hands as he searched my stare for anything to tell him I was alright. I was gasping for air as if I had forgotten how to breathe. *"Come back,"* he pleaded. But I didn't know how.

The princess must be dead if I was no longer under attack. I needed to find a way back to my body—I needed to get to Torben so I could heal him.

There must be a way to heal him.

Theo's voice thundered through me again, raw and wild with desperation.

I followed the sound of his voice and my eyes connected with his, as if I was seeing him for the first time.

His face was covered with blood and ash and I felt myself sinking into the depth of his ocean-blue eyes.

"Torben," I breathed, and I was crawling across the ground towards his body. Everything around me was charred and my knees scuffed with soot. My hands were desperate as I grabbed his tattered body. The ground beneath me trembled as I willed my magic to heal him, to bring him back—but I had nothing left. I pushed an orb of power into his chest, willing it to heal his heart, but the light that gathered in my hands was faint and his heart was unbearably still. I ran my hand along his jaw—trembling as I remembered how his face had looked when he smiled.

I felt Theo pull back, giving me space as I settled into unbearable grief. Emil and Leif were standing over me, their shoulders heaving. *Why aren't they fighting?* I wondered, screaming internally.

"It's over, Kaari."

I tilted to see Theo. My face felt like it had been coated in plaster from the tears that had crusted with grime. *How can it be over when we have only just begun?*

"I need to save him," I pleaded.

"He's gone, Kaari." Theo's voice was breaking like the stone walls that surrounded us.

As I laid my head on my prince's chest, the silence that rang from his heart echoed like the emptiness I felt.

It could have been minutes or hours that I lay there next to him. I had lost all sense of time and space the moment Merja's magic had stopped his heart. My mouth was parched, and my eyes burned from the lingering smoke. I was vaguely aware of the Treyst's movement around me. I could hear their hushed voices and my heart cried out when I thought of their pain.

I hadn't been able to save their friend.

I hadn't been able to save the Prince of Akureyrian.

I hadn't been able to save the one who had taught me how to love again.

Theo sat next to me, his head resting on his knees. He stirred as I lifted my head.

"Kaari?"

"Is she dead?" My voice was cracked and raw.

"She's gone. They are all gone."

My eyes fluttered as I tried to focus. "All of them?"

"Your magic, Kaari. It was as if the sun came down and swallowed all the Birkerians and all the undercreatures that were in the palace—they are *all* gone."

57

The cup of coffee that sat on Torben's desk had gone cold. Papers lay in crumpled piles around me as I rubbed my swollen eyes. As the silence surrounded me and the flames from the candles flickered on my cheeks, I could almost forget everything that had happened hours ago. A knock on the door startled me and I lifted my chin. I knew it was Theo on the other side—he had been trying to see me ever since we had moved from the courtyard.

I could only imagine his grief—he and Torben had been like brothers. And yet he was here trying to check on me.

The lock clicked and I opened the door. He had wiped some of the blood and dust from his face, but his eyes were as swollen as my own.

"Kaari, I—"

"I'm so sorry," I gasped, as I wrapped my arms around his waist. Silently, he pulled me closer, holding me tightly as if to absorb my grief. His head shook slightly, but he swallowed any words he might have offered, letting the quiet comfort speak for him instead.

We sat in Torben's room in silence for a while, watching the waves as they crashed relentlessly against the seawall. The room smelled like cedar and vanilla and if I closed my eyes, I could imagine Torben was sitting at his desk as if nothing had changed.

"Theo," I whispered through the quiet, "do you think Torben was my mate?" I don't know what made me ask him. Perhaps it was the way my heart felt like it had been ripped to pieces. Torben had been my light—the one who had shown me the way back to myself and my purpose. He had believed in me and seen me beyond the scope of my magic.

Theo leaned back as he rubbed his hands over his haggard face. "I know that he was in love with you. I know you made him happier than he had ever been. You don't need to be mates to feel a love like that."

It wasn't exactly an answer. It didn't matter if he was my mate—not everyone was destined to have a mate in this life.

"Why? Why did she have to take him? Why didn't she take me instead?"

Theo reached out, gently tilting my chin so I was looking into his sorrowed eyes.

"Kaari, Merja wants you alive... and she wants you to burn with the rage of your pain."

"She is dead. How can she want me to be anything?"

"Her magic, Kaari. I still feel it, but it's not *here*."

Waves crashed in the distance. The view from Torben's room that had once filled me with awe was now just a reminder of the vast emptiness I felt. I closed my eyes, not believing Theo until I felt it for myself. I pulled at my magic, it felt distant and exhausted. I tried to remember the way Alaía had taught me to reach out to feel for the powers that surrounded me—but all I felt was emptiness.

"Take my hand," Theo said, willing me to pull from his power.

His hands were rough and warm, and I felt his ancient power crashing into mine. I slipped into the void where only magic dared to roam. New magic and ancient magic churning through an endless expanse of power. I could feel Theo's thrum of energy and reached further beyond until I felt the singe of smoke and darkness that filled my throat with bile.

I gasped, releasing Theo's hand. The world around me blurred as the weight of the revelation crashed down on me.

Merja was alive.

My blood roared in my ears, drowning out every sound but the violent thrum of my heartbeat. My hands curled into fists so tight my nails dug into my palms, but the pain was nothing compared to the searing rage in my chest. How could she still breathe after what she'd done? After she took him from us—from me? My vision sharpened, every edge in the room stark and jagged, as if the world itself mirrored the fury twisting inside me. I wanted to scream, to tear apart anything in my path until I found her. She didn't deserve to breathe, not after she'd stolen the only person who ever made me feel whole. Revenge surged through me like a living thing, demanding justice, demanding blood.

"I'm going to find her." I started to stand, ready to leave for Birkeria.

"Kaari, I need to tell—"

A knock at the door interrupted his desperate words.

"Lady Eriksen? May I come in?" Alaía's voice was as soft as a feather on the wind. I met Theo's gaze before reaching to open the door. Alaía's white robes were tattered and covered in dust, but her features were as pure and strong as they were the first day I met her. Her eyes shined like emeralds and as she reached to hold my hands tears filled her eyes.

"Kaari, I'm so sorry."

I shook my head, not wanting to acknowledge our loss. My jaw set as I cleared my throat. "Are you alright, Alaía? The other Keepers?"

"We lost one of our own, she fought valiantly but the creatures overwhelmed her before we got to her."

I could feel my heart shredding. In my grief for Torben, I hadn't considered how many others had been lost. At that moment, he had been the only one in the world who mattered.

"Alaía, I'm so sorry—for everything."

"You saved us, Kaari. You must know that."

I shook my head. It didn't feel like I had saved anyone when Torben and the king and countless others were gone—and the princess lived.

"We should get going. Everything is prepared."

"What do you mean? Where are we going?" I looked from Alaía to Theo, my heart racing.

Alaía glanced at Theo, any awkwardness that had once raged between them was gone—all that remained was their shared silence.

"I was just about to tell her—"

"Tell me what?" My voice was barely a whisper as uncertainty surged.

"About the coronation," Theo said gently.

"Whose coronation? Torben didn't have an heir."

"Yours, Kaari."

Visions of my past swirled in my mind. I felt the rush of wind as I ran through the halls of my home in Vogar, the summer breeze spilling into the hall from the open windows. *Someday I will be queen*, I sang to my mother as I spun in a golden gown. My mother's smile filled my heart as I twirled alongside her. *You are the light of the sun, my child*—my mother had said, *the world would be blessed to have you as queen*. I squeezed my eyes shut, forcing the memory away.

"But why?" I paused, my heart twisting. "Torben and I were not *married*? We had only started to—"

"With King Havard and Prince Torben both gone without another heir to their name, the crown goes to the last royal bloodline—to Queen Maiken's heir. And

478

since we don't know where your mother is... you are the rightful heir of Akureyrian."

To be continued...

Acknowledgements

When I was young, I used to play with an old typewriter and pretend that I was an author. In these moments of play, I imagined myself sitting in a cozy cabin while a fire crackled in an antique hearth and a cup of tea warmed my hands. In reality, when I decided to write A Healer's Heart, most of the words were written in my car while sitting in a school pickup line or outside my daughters' dance studio—certainly not as glamorous as I had once imagined—but I wrote them nonetheless.

First and foremost, I want to thank my two girls. Whenever they saw me writing they would enthusiastically ask "Is that your book?" Or "Did you write *all* those words?" While I don't necessarily want them reading this book for many, many years, their support was always close to my heart.

Thank you to my family and friends who agreed to read this before it was published. You listened to me whine about my uncertainties and your support was unrelenting.

To my editor, Kelly, you are the real MVP, and I am so grateful I found you. Thank you for your humor and incredible attention to detail. I promise to never kill off Lyyli—I make no other promises.

I would like to thank Nirvana Coffee Company in Barnstable, Massachusetts. On those rare days when I actually had time to write while somewhere other than my car, this was my favorite place. Settling into the cozy chairs as the morning sun beamed across my laptop always filled me with inspiration—and my favorite coffee. Writing in a coffee shop is so much cuter than writing in the parent pick-up line.

To my parents who let the girls run to their house in the morning so I can have a few minutes to unwind—thank you (they live next door). You both have supported me in every darn venture I have ever been on, and I am forever grateful. I also hope you are just reading these acknowledgments and didn't read the book—that would be embarrassing.

To my brother, thank you for always talking about magical things with me and for always challenging my perception of reality.

I can't forget my fur babies who snuggle next to me on my day off while I write. Thank you for keeping my seat warm whenever I get up to make more coffee.

And to my husband, thank you for being able to fall asleep to the sweet sounds of my MacBook keyboard. Thank you for pushing me to keep writing, even though it meant I spent a lot of time ignoring you.

Thank you for designing the incredible cover and map for this book—it is everything I could have dreamed of (at the time I am writing this, you haven't done it yet, but you promised you would, and I know it will be amazing). You are my rock through it all.

And if you aren't mentioned above and you have made it this far, thank you.

I love you too.

About the Author

Molly Parker is not a best-selling author (yet). A nurse by trade, she has spent the past 13 years working in healthcare with specialties in complex wound care (hence the gory wound descriptions) and data analytics (hence her type A personality). As a child, Molly dreamt of one day being an author. It took a global pandemic to finally convince her to start writing. A Healer's Heart is her first novel.

Molly lives in Massachusetts with her incredible husband, two fierce daughters, two rather insane cats, and one dopey dog.

Find her on social media @mollyparkerwrites

MOLLY PARKER

FOLLOW FOR UPDATES
@mollyparkerwrites